In *Big Horn Legacy*, award-winning archaeologist and accomplished storyteller W. Michael Gear has created a rich historical novel set against the background of an unspoiled American West. Gear, who holds a Master's Degree in Anthropology, has worked as a professional archaeologist since 1978. He is coauthor with his wife, Kathleen O'Neal Gear, of the bestselling People books of pre-Columbian North America, which have sold over three million copies. His next novel, *The Morning River*, which Norman Zollinger, author of *Chapultepec*, has called "a towering achievement, rich in imagery, energy, and excitement," and Mike Blakely, author of *Shortgrass Song*, has described as "an adventure of epic proportions," will be published by Forge.

# Big Horn Legacy

## W. Michael Gear

A TOM DOHERTY ASSOCIATES BOOK
NEW YORK

This is a work of fiction. All the characters and events portrayed in this book are fictitious, and any resemblance to real people or events is purely coincidental.

BIG HORN LEGACY

Copyright © 1988 by W. Michael Gear

All rights reserved, including the right to reproduce this book, or portions thereof, in any form.

Cover art by Brad Schmehl

A Forge Book
Published by Tom Doherty Associates, Inc.
175 Fifth Avenue
New York, NY 10010

Forge® is a registered trademark of Tom Doherty Associates, Inc.

ISBN: 0-812-56724-2

First Forge edition: June 1996

Printed in the United States of America

0  9  8  7  6  5  4  3  2  1

*This book is dedicated to*
*Harold and Wanda O'Neal*
*for their constant support,*
*their love of the craft of writing,*
*and their unceasing optimism.*

## ACKNOWLEDGMENTS

My wife, Kathy, spent long hours reading the manuscript and goading me to complete revisions. Katherine Cook and Katherine Perry of Mission, Texas, both exercised editorial court. Last, but not least, my thanks go to Richard S. Wheeler, author, friend, and teacher, for taking the time from his own busy schedule to savage the manuscript. Thank you all.

# *Prologue*

The narrow trail slashed whitely along the mountainside. A faint thread of a track, it stood out in the dying light—contrasting to the black rock and the stygian abyss below.

Snow whirled out of darkened sides, blowing down from the black-timbered reaches of the Sangre de Cristo Mountains. Angular black shadows of rock began to fade under the clinging mantle of white.

Where he crouched, waiting, Branton Bragg shivered as cold began to pierce the warmth of his buffalo coat. He raised numb hands to his mouth and puffed steamy breath onto frost-stiff fingers, flexing them before lacing his index finger into the trigger guard of the heavy rifle.

"Oughta brought mittens," he grumbled, squinting into the wreaths of snow that whirled down from the heights to disappear into the black gash of the canyon. Weberly Catton *had* to come this way; no other trail snaked out of the high meadows where Web ran his trap-lines. *It would be settled, here, in the snow, after all these long angry years.*

Sudden doubt caused Bragg to spit a brown streak of tobacco juice into the soft flakes around him. Catton wouldn't have thrown up a camp somewhere, would he?

Darkness—almost complete—drew its curtain over the snow-bound mountain. Another ten minutes and Branton wouldn't be able to see the front blade of his sights. Grunting a curse, he stood to go, brushing out traces of his long wait. He squinted a deadly eye at the empty trail, turning to leave.

Muffled in the swirling snow, he barely heard it: the click of a shod hoof on rock. Branton crouched and raised his rifle, earing back the big hammer of the heavy Lyman gun.

The wind blasted at his face, flakes of snow stinging his cheeks and sticking in his beard. As the fury of wind gusted, a horseman rounded the bend of the trail, the rider crouched low in the saddle, huddled under a worn buffalo coat, his shoulder to the storm. Behind, on a lead, followed a pack animal, bundles of furs slung over the sawbucks with a tight diamond hitch.

Branton sucked in his breath as the horse picked its surefooted way along the edge of the precipice, head back, ears pricked, nostrils flared uneasily. Totally absorbed, the rider centered his attention on the difficult section of trail.

Bragg's heart started to pound in his chest and a curious lightness filled his body. He swallowed hard and rested his cheek against the stock. Through his squinted eye, he settled the sights on the dark form and felt the slack go out of the trigger.

The boom roared, deafening, in the purple-dark silence—muzzle flash an orange glow on his vision. Getting to his feet, Bragg pulled his heavy Dragoon Colts and stepped forward as the rider slumped in the saddle. Frightened, the horse sidestepped onto the flats before the rider slid out of the saddle. His body thumped as it landed on the rocks, the unfired rifle clattering loudly.

Bragg's cold face curled in a wicked smile. Feeling curiously warm, he centered the pistol on the man's back and triggered the gun.

"All them years, Catton," Bragg gritted, hoarse with emotion. "Everything you took from me gets paid back here. Now, all I got to do is find them vermin kids of yours and Laura will be laid to rest."

Pistol ready, Bragg toed the man over so he could see Web Catton's face. He barked a laugh at the spreading stain of frothy red trickling down the bearded face to pool in the snow.

"You killed my father, Web. Your brats will die for my Laura. My sister was too good for you. She should have had better than a drifting fur hunter. Should have had better than six kids who took her strength and left her frail and dying." Bragg's voice caught suddenly at the memory. Feeling his rising rage, he kicked the corpse off the trail, watching it roll down the steepening slope before it disappeared into the blackness. It would pop like a ripe pumpkin when it hit the black rocks below. The horse stood still as Bragg picked up Web Catton's rifle and turned to the animal. Smiling, he took up the reins and led the big grulla closer to the edge. The gelding snorted at the odor of blood, and shied.

"Quit that, damn you!" he snarled. With quick fingers, Bragg undid the saddlebags and packs. Almost as an afterthought, he raised the rifle and shot the gelding behind the ear.

The horse dropped, legs kicking once as it slid over the edge and thumped down in a snapping of brush and branches. Bragg then swung Web's rifle like a bat and sent it sailing out into the blackness. A clatter far below signaled its impact.

He eyed the furs on the pack animal—all winter prime—sighed, and blew a hole in the animal's brain with his heavy Colt. He had to lift a leg to tumble it over the edge. Then he went to the saddlebags.

Bragg found a letter marked with a fleur-de-lis, a square of tanned leather folded neatly, and changes of clothing, bedding, and personal effects. The letter he crammed into an inside pocket. Squinting, he had to hold the square piece of buckskin up to the light to see it: a map. Only one word stood out on the hide.

Feeling his excitement grow, Branton Bragg threw the looted saddlebags into the dark chasm, stuffed the map into his buffalo coat, and hurried down the trail to where his horse waited, picketed. That one word held Bragg's attention. That word—*Gold!*

# Chapter 1

*R*obert Campbell caught his reflection in a darkened window. Through all the years, he'd come to dread this day—knowing it lay inevitably just over the horizon. The butterflies in his stomach wouldn't leave him in peace. Fortunately, they didn't show in his face. He studied the reflection in the dark glass. He'd grayed since the old days. His face seemed longer, lined, nose becoming more bulbous, and pads of flesh lay under his hard brown eyes.

"It's harder than you thought, isn't it?"

Filling his lungs in the cool damp air, he walked on, turned the corner, and found the little white sign indicating the AC Freight Company.

Abriel Catton Campbell wouldn't expect him to come strolling in out of the Saint Louis night this 21st of March 1850. Abriel had just "purchased" the AC Freight Company from old Andy Crank, who owed Ab a little more money than his poker habit could stand. Turning the company over to Ab had settled the accounts, which beat having to call him a deadbeat in public. Saint Louis still lived too close to the frontier and its unforgiving ways.

Campbell reached for the doorknob, seeing the yellow glow of lamplight through the smoke-stained window. He hesitated, fighting the urge to simply walk on—forget this hanging debt from the past. The brass knob lay chill under his fingertips. Heart in throat, Campbell entered, booted heels sounding hollowly on the hardwood flooring.

Ab peered up from a set of ledgers. All the years on the river toting Campbell's freight from hither to yon and back again had built beef on his shoulders. The hard plains sun had darkened and lined his face. He stood, the sudden familiar smile lighting his lips. "Good to see you, sir! Just trying to figure out what Crank did with all his money."

Campbell nodded, words stuck in his throat. "You look . . . fit. Being a man of property seems to agree with you."

Ab laughed heartily, pouring a tin cup of thick black coffee from the battered pot gurgling on the heat stove in the corner. "When a kid goes up the trail, be it to Fort William or Taos or if you chunk wood into the steamboat boilers bound for the Upper Missouri and the Montana lands, you stay fit. It's not the business, sir."

Campbell nodded as he stared absently into the coffee in his cup. "You're a man, Abriel. You can take care of yourself—in more ways than one."

Ab's eyes narrowed. "I've had some go-arounds, and with some big and mean men too. I wouldn't swear I could clean up a full-grown grizz with my bare hands but he'd know I'd been earnest!" Then the lines in his forehead tightened. "You look like the army just welched on a twenty-thousand-dollar deal."

Campbell chuckled. "You know me pretty well, Ab."

"Ought to. You raised me. What's wrong?"

Robert Campbell took a deep breath and looked around. A shy sort of office, it beat the rented corner of rat-infested warehouse he'd started with back in the prime beaver days. One little window looked out on Olive Street, a desk, a safe that might have withstood the curious efforts of a five-year-old, a stove, and back door that led to the stable and the jakes made Abriel's empire. A couple turn-legged chairs lined a wall.

"You've done well, Ab." Campbell remembered his own scrambling existence. He'd come from Ireland and gone west with Jed Smith in 1822 as a lunger, a man dying of consumption. In the Rockies he mended, tussled with the Blackfeet and Crow and helped build the American fur empire in the Far West. He unbuttoned his gray broadcloth coat and hung his tan beaver hat on one of the nails serving for coat hangers.

"You didn't come all the way down here to tell me that." Abriel leaned back against his battered desk, patient, waiting.

Campbell hitched up his trousers and sat, crossing his legs and sipping at his coffee, trying to find a place to begin.

"No, Ab, I didn't." Campbell frowned, staring at the grain in the floorboards. "You had . . . I mean, you were raised knowing some pretty interesting characters. Tom Fitzpatrick, Gabe, uh, Jim Bridger, Os Russel, Kit Carson, Clyman, Liver-Eating Johnston. Men who had the bark on."

"If you're in trouble," Ab said, face darkening, "you just tell me and I'll—"

"Now, Ab, you've always been that way. Impetuous.

Too ..." His face tightened. *Say it. Go on, get it out.* "Too much like your father."

There, he'd said it. Abriel's frown deepened.

"I never thought you were impetuous. You've always been a keen trader. But impetuous?"

The boy still didn't understand. Campbell felt the beginnings of a headache as he looked up into those honest amber eyes.

Campbell's voice stumbled, hesitant. "For years you have been ... been like my son. I've loved you like you were my own boy. Tried to give you the best, like I did my own."

"But I don't ... What are you saying?" Ab shook his head, confused.

"I've talked about Web Catton." Campbell sipped his coffee, meeting Abriel's serious look.

"Yes. Sometimes until I couldn't stand to hear it. Said he'd always been one of your special friends. Named me after him." Abriel gestured with a hand. "So? You'd better go on, I'm having trouble reading this trail you're laying."

For a brief instant Campbell itched to simply stand up, apologize, cover his tracks with some cock-and-bull story, and walk out. "Abriel, what do you remember when you were very small?"

Ab Catton chewed his lip for a few moments, eyes lost in old memories. "Well, there's a lady with golden-blond hair," he said. "I remember other kids, littler than me. Somebody was always crying in the background. I can remember the lady with golden hair picking me up and making me feel better. She kept me from being afraid."

Campbell snorted amusement, the image drifting into memories of Abriel scrapping with every kid in Saint Louis. "I doubt anyone ever needed to keep you from being afraid!" Then his voice turned soft. "That was your

mother, Ab. A very beautiful lady. Her name was Laura.
Laura Catton. I married Virginia just before you came to
live with us. You are so much older than my own children. Still you've become very special to me. I'm so
proud of you. But Web Catton is your real father."
Campbell cleared his throat. "Ab, you'd better read this.
This is the last will and testament of your father, Web
Catton. Kit Carson wrote and told me he was long overdue from a trapping expedition."

From an inside pocket, he handed Abriel the oil-paper
envelope.

Abriel swallowed as he looked at the creased, stained
papers. With cautious movements, he lifted a letter out
and unfolded it. Nervous fingers clutched the foolscap as
he studied the strange scrawling writing in the lamplight.

My dear Abriel:
By the time you read this, two things have happened.
First, you have reached your majority, and second, I
am dead. I have left you in the care of my best friend,
Robert Campbell, for reasons he will explain to you.
Upon the death of your mother, it was no longer possible to raise you or your brothers safely. I'm afraid
your uncle, Branton Bragg, blames all of you for your
mother's death. I can't kill him. I promised your
mother. At the same time, I'm not the father you boys
need. I can't stay in one place and farm or run a business the way men like Campbell and Sublette can. I'm
called to the wild lands, Ab. I'm doing the best thing
for all of you. I hope to God you'll understand. You
have four brothers and Arabella. I placed each of you
where I thought you would do the best and where
Branton wouldn't think to look for you. I guess I tried
to make up for what I didn't give you. Each of you has
a section of map to what I hope will be a satisfactory

inheritance of fifty thousand dollars in gold. I don't suggest that you take any of it to Santa Fe as Governor Armijo's heirs might want to argue ownership. To find it, you must reunite the family. Robert will tell you how. Ab, don't hold what I did against me. I've done the best I could.

With All Love,

Weberly Catton

Ab looked up, a haunted expression on his face, seeking an explanation in his foster father's eyes.

"Abriel, don't hold it against Web. Branton would have killed you. All of you. The Braggs were a very wealthy family in Kentucky once. Web killed Laura's father—your grandfather—here in Saint Louis. They fought a duel one morning down on Bloody Island. Used sabers. No one would have thought Web knew anything about sabers."

Campbell's lips curled with a smile. "I won't say what I thought of old Bragg's manners. Branton went berserk over his father's body. Needless to say, Web offered to take him next. Branton backpedaled most adroitly and Laura went ahead and married your father anyway. Branton disapproved, but he couldn't stand up to his sister—let alone Web—who would have killed him outright.

"Dear Laura, she was quite a woman. Her death left us all . . . Well, never mind. It happened, is all. Died in childbirth . . . Tom's. Web wasn't the man to raise five young boys—let alone Arabella. He left you with me. Jeremiel he left with a family recommended by the missionary Marcus Whitman. Jake went to Colonel Oord and his wife. Bram ended up with One-Eyed Mike." Campbell's face twisted with contempt. "I'll never understand that!"

"And the last brother?" he asked, looking shaken.

"Tom." Campbell nodded, running slow fingers through his gray-shot brown hair. "Tom was left with the Cheyenne. I think you'd better look up Tom Fitzpatrick to find him. Fitz usually knows where White Wolf's band can be—"

Abriel stuttered, "O-One of my brothers is an *Injun*?"

Campbell felt his gut tighten. With the blood-chilling tone of command he'd used to organize his fur caravans, Campbell said, "White Wolf was your father's blood brother. Since you weren't there, I suggest that you keep your own counsel."

Robert Campbell narrowed his eyes, noting that old familiar flush of shame climbing Abriel's cheeks. Just like when he'd been a little boy—he looked the same now. Chastened, disciplined, until the next time.

"I'll think on that," Ab muttered, dropping his eyes.

"See that you do."

Silence.

Ab lifted his chin. "What are they like? My brothers, I mean. And this . . . Arabella?"

"I've met Jeremiel and Jake." Campbell drained most of his coffee. "I'd best leave you to your own impressions when you meet them. Suffice it to say Jake and Jeremiel have done very well in their respective fields. Bram will be the most . . . um, interesting, I suppose. I don't think Web figured One-Eyed Mike was going to become the sort of—"

"One-Eyed Mike?" Abriel straightened. "You mean from down south? The . . . the . . ."

"Horse thief," Campbell supplied. "That's him. Used to be a trapper until the beaver played out." Campbell smiled. "Learned his present, shall we say, trade, from the Crow. No one can steal a horse like a Crow—and

One-Eyed Mike became as good as the best of them."
Campbell winced.

"And this Injun?"

"Tom? They call him Wasatch now, after the Ute word. Well, he's a strange one—powerful among the Cheyenne. And at his age too."

"And Arabella?"

Robert shrugged. "I can't tell you. She's spent her life in the East. I know virtually nothing about her except that Carson wrote her the same time he wrote me. Evidently he kept track of the family that took her in."

Ab's lips pinched and he rubbed the back of his neck. "Well, she won't be involved anyway. If Web was the man I remember you forever telling me he was, no woman is going where he'd have hidden gold."

Campbell grunted his assent and stood, walking across the room. He reached around Abriel and picked up the Damascus blade that rested in its leather scabbard beyond the heavy ledger books.

"Remember this?"

Abriel nodded. "You gave me that for Christmas one year. It's my one prize possession. Never seen another like it."

"This knife," Campbell told him, the words coming slow and sure, "was from Web, your father. Every year, the Christmas gifts came from him. Had to spoil my boys so Ginny and I could give you gifts of our own." He smiled. "There are only five knives like this in the world. Your brothers have the mates to this one. That's how you'll know them. Somehow, they hold the secret to Web's fortune."

Ab considered, head shaking. "The frontier's a big place to find five young fellas with knives. Gold? At the end of the rainbow, sir? A legacy from a man I never knew?" He shook his head, eyes dancing. "There's always more gold in hard work."

Campbell nodded. "Generally. But not this time. If Web says he set you kids up . . . he set you up." He allowed himself a smile of reminiscence. "Web never stretched anyone's leg over his kids. No, I know for a fact that Armijo lost a fortune when Santa Fe fell to Kearny's troops in '46. Too many Taoseños and traders had fingers in that pie—and I knew them all. Kit Carson and Broken Hand Fitzpatrick were there. They heard it too. Now, Web had a hand in all that. If he says he got it—he got it!"

Abriel grunted, head down as he fingered his chin. "West is a big place," he repeated.

"Not that big a place."

Abriel reread the letter in the long silence that followed. Outside, beyond the window, someone yelled a greeting in a heavy Irish brogue. The answer came faintly, beyond Campbell's hearing. From the stove, the fire snapped and crackled. A wagon lumbered down the spring-muddy streets, hissing and squishing.

"I guess I always knew," Abriel said at last, looking up from the letter, meeting Campbell's eyes.

"Yes, you did." Campbell sighed heavily. "You worked real hard to forget . . . once . . . just after your mother's death. That hurt so bad I think you made yourself forget."

"Why didn't he ever come back?" Abriel asked.

"Afraid Bragg would find you . . . somehow, someway."

"But the letter says Bragg's my uncle! An uncle wouldn't hurt his nephew!"

"Oh, come on!" Campbell sniffed his disgust. "This is Saint Louis, Ab! You know what old family honor means here! The Old French poisoned this place. Laura spurned her own people! Married the man who gutted her father! To Branton you're like a . . . a living shame!"

"Old blood," Abriel whispered, reaching up to push his thick hair away. "Old blood, bad blood. Isn't that the statement?"

"Tainted with black honor," Campbell added. "That's why Web never came back. Branton has friends in Saint Louis."

Abriel looked up, a subtle vulnerability in his eyes. "Why did you do it? All those years ago, I mean. Why take on a kid?"

Campbell felt time slip away, seeing the bandy-legged boy Abriel Catton had been. "Because I just plain liked you. You had grit, Ab. Even then. And I, like most people who ever had anything to do with him, owed your father. Saved my life once. Blackfeet would have taken me alive. In those days, it would have been worse than a death sentence."

Silence stretched again.

"How do I thank you?" Abriel began. "I'll make it up to you somehow. I . . ."

"That will be enough of that, Abriel," Campbell said, a warmth filling him. "You owe us nothing. No debt is implied. Web sent us more than requirements needed anyway. No matter, even if he hadn't, you were . . . my son." It hurt, that admission.

"I just don't—"

Campbell waved him down. "Maybe blood mattered in the old country. Here, who knows? To be a father is more than a matter of birth. It's a matter of raising." He reached and took Abriel's hand. "You always have a home with us."

The young man stood, engulfing him in a fierce bear hug that threatened to crack Campbell's ribs. Pushing back, Abriel gazed into Campbell's eyes. "And you think I ought to find my other family?"

Campbell raised an eyebrow. "Ab, aren't you just a little curious?" He could see a faint scar on Ab's cheek. Another ran through an eyebrow where a boatman's fist had cut it. Indeed, no dandy, this one. He'd raised a boy worthy of the western lands—worthy of Web Catton.

A slow smile spread on the lips. "Yes," Abriel admitted, warming to it. "I suppose I am."

Campbell clapped him on the shoulder. "Good. Go." He frowned. "You know, there was always something else Web never told me. Something about the inheritance. Some secret he never let slip. Laura knew. Every time the subject of Bragg and his disgust with your father came up, she'd smile, knowing." Campbell dropped his hands from Ab's shoulders. "Web had a secret. He was somebody . . . important. More than a fur hunter, you understand."

"Criminal?"

"No, that's not what I mean." Campbell gestured. "Take the time up at Chouteau's. Laura was in a family way with Jake at the time. Bragg, like usual, had just made some brutal comment about her bastard child and stomped out. Laura, your mother, instead of blushing with shame, got this incredibly angelic look on her face and whispered, 'If he only knew.' "

"Cryptic," Abriel admitted. "Well, perhaps if I find out I'm George Washington's illegitimate heir, I'll let you know." Slowly his wry grin grew.

"You do that."

"All right, the letter says you know how I can find my family." Abriel turned to the stove, refilling Campbell's coffee cup.

Campbell turned it to balance on his knee, feeling the blistering heat through the tin. "Your brother Jeremiel is only as far away as Independence. I believe if you hurry you can make it by Sunday." Campbell waited, seeing the sudden concern on Abriel's face. No slouch this one.

"Sunday?" Abriel ventured hesitantly, reserve in the tilt of his lips.

"Absolutely," Campbell chimed, voice clipped. "You see, Jeremiel is a preacher."

"Aw, now, *Paw!*" he cried out, obviously trying to figure how to go packing some preacher along after Web Catton's gold.

Campbell jumped lightly to his feet. "First, Ab, I am *not* your father. Second, I taught you long ago that you address your elders as 'sir.' Simply because we have a change in relationships is no excuse for bad manners." Campbell reached for his hat and settled it jauntily on his head before tossing down the hot strong coffee and placing the cup on the desk.

Abriel began to grin evilly.

In a muted voice, Robert Campbell continued, "And third, Abriel, there are preachers and *there are preachers!*"

With that he raised his finger and touched the brim of his hat. At the door he hesitated. "Don't worry about the business. I'll handle the freighting during your absence." He opened the door, turning back one last time. "And Ab, Branton Bragg probably killed your father. He'll be after the rest of you now. Be very, very careful!"

# Chapter 2

Bram Catton shot a quick look over his shoulder as he walked the blowing roan through the tall grass. Pretty dicey, this. One grimy hand on the roan's nose, he waited, hearing the horsemen talking to themselves, the creak of saddle leather, the thudding of hooves as they rustled through the grass.

Bram couldn't help but grin at the grass-thick patch of prairie. No one in that posse would think he'd doubled back this close to his backtrail.

He felt the roan take a breath to snuffle and he gripped the soft nose tighter, chucking softly as the animal tried to jerk its head away. The roan danced in irritation as Bram soothed it.

Not long now, another couple of minutes and they'd be in the trees. Coming out the other side, they'd find a long limestone outcrop—figuring he'd taken that trackless route. Yep, oughta be hours afore they come to know they'd been foxed. Why, old One-Eyed Mike would flip-flop in his grave over this one!

Bram grinned success and led the horse forward. He sniffed the warm air, feeling spring coming with the gliding puffs of cloud that slid out of the west. Sure nuff, spring was coming. Time to fetch up a batch of good stock and trail them down Texas way for sale. Not only that, but pickings had improved out here in Kansas territory. All these squatters coming—sometimes with good stock—and plopping themselves down on the Injun reserves.

Business looked to be plumb good this summer, Bram decided.

Glancing back, he judged he'd made enough distance and legged up into the saddle. Clucking to the roan, he trotted off across the greening prairie, headed for a far copse of trees—lime green with new leaves sprouting. Yep, he'd made a clean getaway this time.

"So much water?" Arabella mused, looking back at the sudsy foam the big paddles slapped out of the Ohio River.

"Makes you wonder how much water is in the world, doesn't it?" James smiled at her, the splaying lines of his face going deep under his gray peppercorn hair. "We've crossed our share."

She hated the dullness that had grown in his brown eyes in the last month. The last years—and concern for her—had taken a wretched toll.

"I hate dragging you along, James. I don't know anything about all this. I really don't care either. My father? You're my father. You raised me."

"Shhhh!" he cautioned, placing a black finger to his thick lips. His eyes darted uneasily to the side. "Remember, little bird, this is America. They'd swing me from the nearest tree—and throw you off the boat." Amusement glittered briefly behind his ancient eyes.

Arabella straightened, chin thrust boldly out, amber eyes playing over the swirling wake behind them. "Odd, isn't it? How the roles have changed?" she mused. "All those years in Africa and India, we pretended I was *your* slave to keep my throat from being slit—or worse, stolen away for some Somali's *real* slave. Now, here, we play that you are my slave?" She shook her head. "Like you always said, ain't no one dumber than people!"

Carefully, as if his side had gone tender, he bent over the taffrail, absently watching the huge drivers working the wheel crank. He sighed wistfully. "Americans are no more despicable than Arabs or Somalis, or Mandarins or Moros or any of the rest we've dealt with."

He cocked his head curiously, the breeze tugging at his long swallowtail coat. "No, humans are just mean, Arabella. What the French did to my people on Santo Domingo—and what we did in return . . . it's all just human baseness. A fear of difference."

She placed her tanned hand on his, marveling again at the difference in color, his so deep black, hers so creamy. He took his hand away, looking quickly over his shoulder to see if anyone had seen. "I told you, you mustn't. Someone—"

"*Shaitan!*" she hissed in Arabic, hunching her broad shoulders in anger.

"Arabella, it is uncomely for a young woman like yourself to curse so." He smacked his lips in chastisement and couldn't hide the smile dancing behind those dark eyes.

She ground her teeth, knotting her ivory muslin dress between angry fingers. "But it irritates me! They make you sleep with those . . . those . . ."

"Slaves," he supplied easily, throwing his head back,

laughing. "Oh, I don't mind. You didn't care in Mombasa when Sab Had had his Kikuyu slaves waiting at your beck and call . . . All right for Kikuyu? But not for me? Hum?"

"It's different!" she protested hotly, cheeks flushing pink to contrast with her thick, tumbling honey-brown hair. She flashed fiery eyes at him, pert mouth prim.

His eyes softened with his voice. "We're all humans," he reminded. "All men together in the sight of God."

His mood sobered her.

"You learn that, Arabella. For all the hate and hurt we cause mankind because others are different. When I look back, men died because of me. Well . . ." He lifted a shoulder in a solemn shrug.

She whispered fiercely, "They died *freeing* themselves. With dignity. Able to protect . . ." She cut it off as a man strolled past, touching his hat to her. She smiled innocently.

They stood, side by side, watching the water foam behind the big stern wheel, lost in thoughts.

"America," she growled. "Why did we come here? Why did you leave me in Brussels that last trip?" She tilted her chin to study him.

"East India Company was getting too close. A dhow is no match for a fifty-gun frigate. I think if they could have caught us, they'd have blown us out of the water. I couldn't take that chance with you, favorite girl." He reached to pat her in the old familiar manner . . . only to draw back, biting his lip.

She clamped a hard throttle on her frustration.

"And . . ." he continued. "You needed more time at Madame Saëns. You had lost the polish expected of a mannerly young—"

"So you left me there to become a lady again?" She burst into giggles, a hand over her mouth. "Oh, James.

I can be a lady whenever necessity requires. Well, the Royal Navy didn't catch you. The Malays got their . . . cargo. And I'm all ladylike again." She crossed her arms, turning away from the railing. "Why did you bring me back to America? Here, you have to act like a slave when you've had more education and—"

"For your father," James added honestly, facing her. "I owed him for my life—and my brother's. How many men would have taken a running Negro at his word? Why, the French would have paid him enough to . . ." He snorted. "Suffice it to say, my girl, that he kept me from an ungodly fate."

"And now we hear he's dead?" She rubbed her arms nervously. "So let's go back. Pick up another shipment at Liege and sail for . . ."

Through half-lidded eyes, he asked, "And don't you want to meet the rest of your family? You have brothers, Arabella. And I know Web. You have an inheritance."

"This isn't my country," she added, motioning to the wooded shores passing on either side. Here and there farms had been hacked out of the hardwoods. Men already followed in the earth-black wake of plows, earnest in spring planting.

The expression on James's face reflected grief. He closed his eyes and shook his head. "My fault. I kept you far away so Branton couldn't . . . But we've been through all that so many times . . . Uh!" He staggered suddenly, grabbing the rail, bending slightly at the waist.

*"James?"* She grabbed his elbow, steadying him despite the reproving glances.

He took a deep breath and swallowed hard, straightening. "I'm . . . all right. Ate something, I suppose." He didn't restrain himself from patting her this time.

"Go lie down," she ordered. "Get some rest. I'm going to go take a nap myself." She took him, steering him toward the area restricted to slaves. "Barbarians!" she hissed. "Can't even get a decent cabin for you!"

He stopped her at the companionway. "Promise me, Arabella . . . promise that you'll see to your kin? If anything happens, you'll find your people . . . learn about this country of yours."

"Barbarians who won't let a man like you have his own—"

*"Arabella!"* he barked before the stitch in his side paled his deep-black features, pain lines running out from his broad nose.

"I promise!" she cried desperately. Worried now. "Go lie down! I'm going to find a doctor!"

"I'll be fine." He smiled, love reflected in his eyes.

Carefully, the tall man eased out to watch them walk forward. He smiled at the bend in the old black man's posture—at the way he held his side. Leander O. B. Sentor brought the vial from his pocket, glancing around quickly to ensure no one saw him. Furtively, he dropped the corked glass tube over the taffrail. It hadn't proved so hard to get the poison into the old man's food after all.

"And there goes another of your enemies, *mon général,*" he whispered. "Now let's see if luck is truly on my side. Let's see if Arabella leads me to the Cattons . . . and this ridiculous claim!"

Leander stepped back into a shadowy archway to watch, and wait.

Independence, as always, bustled with activity fit to burst it open at the seams. Especially now, coming up on the first of April, the commerce of the West camped around the town, awaiting warm weather and new grass for the stock. Gold and California lay beyond the far horizon. Wagons, freighters, immigrants, herds of bawling cattle, rivermen, sharps, thieves and cutthroats, drummers, wagonwrights, soldiers, and every sort in between crowded into those packed streets.

The westbound throngs waited, getting last-minute repairs completed while merchants exhausted their stores. The streets rattled and banged with jockeying wagons while horses screamed and snorted and oxen lowed in bass bellows. Men cursed and blustered while women hurried, skirts held high above the slime and manure.

The mud had slowed Abriel some. By the time he pushed his sweaty sorrel down the clogged streets, dusk gathered itself on the eastern horizon. He'd made it by Sunday—barely. His pack mule, Molly, trotted along behind on a long lead. A big-boned dapple gray animal, she shied at the crowds, ears back. Ab loved her despite her unlovable disposition—even if her tail kept growing shorter and shorter by the year.

"Well, we're here," Ab muttered to the back of his sorrel's pricked ears.

As darkness dropped over rollicking Independence, Ab found the little white church where his brother supposedly preached. He climbed the wobbly stairs out front and could see a tall man at the pulpit. The speaker wore a black frock coat as he gestured vigorously. He looked to be a strapping man with brown hair and a neatly trimmed beard. His face glowed with the fervor of his words, and behind amber eyes a fire of righteousness burned.

Abriel winced, screwing his face up. *A blood-and-thunder, fire-and-brimstone preacher?* He looked back to where Molly stood shifting under her pack. She lowered an eyelid over one deep brown doe eye in disgust.

"Ain't we lucky, girl?" Ab whispered dryly. "My brother's a cussed preacher."

Jeremiel's voice carried loud over the congregation,

ringing with truth. "For truly, the Kingdom of Heaven is for the faithful. Yea, the sinner falls into the pits of despair. He turns on the spit of Satan and roasts in his wickedness!"

A shout of "Amen!" went up and Abriel swallowed, slowly backing down the steps.

His breath fogged in front of his nose as he wondered about this Jeremiel. He worked his mouth dryly, shaking his head.

"Confound it, Web Catton," Ab grunted under his breath. "Why in the name of he . . . er, heck, did you leave him to become a da . . . er, darn, sky pilot?"

The thought of all those long miles of open grass and wind stretched before Ab's mind. The distances beckoned, calling him on as they always did. He ached for the freedom and the companionship of a buffalo chip campfire . . . The dream popped like a bubble in the Missouri. Camp? With a fire-and-brimstone preacher? Lordy, it was fixing to be a long trip already!

"Preachers!" Ab grunted to Molly. She ground her teeth in agreement, jerking her head to indicate displeasure at not having her load removed so she could roll. Seeing no improvement, she swung her head, butting him hard.

Staggered, Ab turned around, glaring. "Damn you, Molly! That cuts it. You can damn well ride with *him*!" He shot a knobby thumb over his shoulder at the church door. "Put some respect for man and God in your cranky bones, I say!" To accent it, he swatted her with his hat. Molly glared at him—plotting.

In answer, her ratty tail lifted, followed by the soft splat of green road apples on the muddy ground.

"Preachers and mules," Ab hissed. "Born for each other."

"Lo, the sword of Michael will level *drunkards and sots*

*and brawlers*, harrowing them into the pits of hell!" Jeremiel's voice blasted from the open doors.

Abriel screwed up his lips like he did when his maw . . . er, Virginia, used to make him eat lemon peels for a chest cold. "Drunkards, sots, and brawlers?" he wondered, ticking each one off on his fingers. "Oh great! There's all my fun!"

The thought began circulating through his mind how much sin it would be to kill a man who was both your brother . . . and a preacher?

Then he noticed the three toughs sauntering up the street. They pulled up alongside of the little door that led out back of the church. One rolled a cigarette while another pulled a whetstone from his pocket and began honing down a long blade. The third just stood there, arms crossed over his chest, waiting.

They stayed right there while the sermon ended and people began filing out of the church, faces all aglow with the sin they'd conquered and the Word in their lives.

Ab's gut tightened. Suddenly real sin hung heavy in the air.

"Miss," Captain Morrison repeated, "there was nothing we could do. Sometimes the heart just . . . stops. Your slave was—"

"You could have let me be near him," she insisted icily, a throb in her voice.

"For a young lady to . . . It would have been unseemly." He looked duly horrified.

"Damn you!" she hissed under her breath.

"What was that, miss?"

"Nothing," she amended, struggling to keep her face straight. *Think, Arabella! Sure it hurts, but he taught you to use your wits! For the moment, you need this silly ass.*

Morrison cleared his throat and swallowed. "He was an old man, miss."

"He was my . . . yes, a man, a good man," she agreed. Desperate, she bit her tears back.

Cowed by her expression, he asked, "You were with him a long time?"

She nodded. "All my life. He . . . he raised me."

Morrison held himself at his full height. "We'll see to your passage back to Pittsburgh, ma'am. From there, we'll contact your people. Arrange for you—"

She bit her lip to keep from growling. "I'm sorry, Captain. I *must* go to Saint Louis to see about my father's estate."

One eye narrowed skeptically. "I assume you have people there? Someone to—"

She raised her chin. "I am to contact a Mr. Robert Campbell. He is the executor of my father's—"

"Ah!" Morrison bowed smartly, a sudden light shining in his eye. "I see, ma'am. On behalf of the line, I offer my condolences again, and let me assure you, we will handle every detail." At that, he strolled off, back straight as his heels clicked on the polished deck.

Arabella closed the stateroom door, latching it. She crossed to the bed and sagged onto it. "Oh, James," she whispered, "what am I ever going to do without you?"

For the moment, she let grief take her.


Jeremiel walked down the aisle, smiling, shaking hands.

He'd given a good sermon, one to touch the very lives of these people. The Reverend Mr. Blair, who had invited him, nodded and smiled from the rear.

Indeed a good sermon! Jeremiel traded compliments with a little white-haired lady. He shook hands with merchants and farmers as they dwindled away into the night.

"Most well done, Jeremiel," Blair added, a huge smile on his ruddy face. He shook Jeremiel's hand and sighed. "You have touched their very hearts—given them a feeling for the spirit of the Lord!"

"I do my best, Reverend Blair." Jeremiel smiled back. "I simply follow the calling of our Lord Jesus Christ. I speak through my heart, and the children of God hear . . . or they don't."

Blair nodded, a nervous smile twitching at his lips. "Ah, I fear I shall be hard-pressed to follow your lead, Jeremiel."

"Let the Holy Spirit take you and your light shall shine from under its basket, brother," Jeremiel assured.

"Um, you've made plans for supper?" Blair asked, scuffing his shoe nervously.

"None, brother."

"Would you perhaps break bread with Mary and me?" Blair's face puffed rosy. "We'd love to have you."

"Why, I'd be delighted, brother." Jeremiel clapped his hands together, well aware of the grinding emptiness in his belly. "I must check my animals, however. The man at the livery is . . . well, I fear him to be less than a worthy soul for salvation. Given to dissipation of the flesh."

Blair chuckled heartily. "Very well, I'll close up here. Pick up the hymnals and sweep up—"

"Oh, let me help. Your offer of supper withstanding, it is my pleasure to see to the keep of the Lord's house."

"No, Jeremiel, run along. Go. You've already blessed us with the light of the faith. Check your animals and meet me at home. Mary left a bit early to stoke up the stove and prepare a humble meal for—"

"Humble?" Jeremiel lifted a black eyebrow. "Beware of falsehoods, Reverend Blair. I've sat at Mary's table before. Humble?" And, laughing, he made for the small side entrance as Blair shut the double doors out front.

As he stepped out, the three closed on him. "Good evening, gentlemen, you're a little late for the sermon." Jeremiel straightened, studying their faces. Hard men these, thugs and brigands. The flashing blade of a honed knife caught the faint light. Satan spawn in need of God's wrath!

"Reckon that was yer last sermon, Rev'rend," the one with the knife grunted, and lunged. Jeremiel shifted, a sudden surge of adrenaline and anger filling him. He went high on his heel, blasting an elbow into the knife wielder's kidney, rebounding and cracking his hard knuckles into the second's face, the satisfying snap of bone loud in the night.

Jeremiel danced out, lungs heaving as he bounced on his toes, facing the third. "The spirit of the Lord is upon you, sinners!" he gasped, feeling that light exhilaration that came with knuckle and skull.

"Get him!" the third ordered as he circled, trying to turn Jeremiel's back to the other toughs, pushing him back into an ell of the church.

"By God," the knife artist gasped, slightly bent, I'll . . ."

"Dost thou take the Lord's name in vain?" Jeremiel thundered, pivoting and ducking as the man cut. Too many! No way out of this one. He bit his lip, knowing he ought to shout for help. Yet a fourth figure rushed forward through the darkness.

A single thought stuck in Jeremiel's mind as he bellowed and charged: *Why?*

He caught the third, swung him around, and planted a solid right into his stomach just under the ribs. Jeremiel jerked back as the man vomited . . . and kicked his kneecap out. On the way down he clipped his chin for good measure.

The other two bulled into him. *What happened to the*

*knife?* Jeremiel roared and swung his blocklike fists, gasping breath, feeling blows on his ribs and face.

Then they fell back, the fourth man wading through them, flinging them away, like rags. The knife man hit the church wall with a thud, tumbling senseless, blade clattering, as Reverend Blair opened the door, silhouetted, mouth hanging in an open O.

Jeremiel danced, turning, looking for an enemy as the last of them fled into the black of night, stumbling, cursing as he ran.

"Damned soul!" Jeremiel hurled after him. "Taste the wrath of the Lord God thy Father! Thou art vermin in the sight of the Lord! Repent, sinner, for thou shalt burn in the fiery pit!"

"Brother Jeremiel?" Blair asked weakly, eyes ghastly where he studied the two motionless toughs. The knife blade gleamed wickedly in the grass.

Jeremiel turned, studying the newcomer. "You're quick with your fists."

"Learned from Charles Autobees, and he said he'd learned it from Mike Fink . . . but I reckon he was a little young for that," the big man added, looking curiously at Jeremiel and taking a step toward him, hand out.

Jeremiel noted the big knife at the man's waist. The faint light flickered eerily off the familiar fleur-de-lis.

Jeremiel grabbed him by the collar and shoved him up against the church wall. Finding himself staring into amber eyes so remarkably like his own—and no give there either. With the other hand, he ripped the knife from its scabbard, dancing the point below the man's nose.

"All right, brother," he grunted, voice backed by steel. "You'd better start talking . . . or Gabriel's horn will call you from your wicked ways and the Lord will rend you asunder! Why have you brigands set upon me and what Satan's wrath do you bring to a servant of the Lord?

*Speak wretch!*" He tightened his fist, closing the collar tight. "*How did you get my knife?*"

Reverend Blair swallowed so loud, he gulped.

The big man's amused easy tone caught him by surprise. "Reckon I'd ease up, Jeremiel. I hate to have to start our relationship by licking you—*little brother*—but seeing as to the circumstances, you'd better think back on who just dusted that bunch out of your way. That jasper with the toad-sticker was plumb onto skewering your guts but good!"

"You did lay them about like the harrow of the Lord," Jeremiel relented, frowning, head cocked. "Just what did you mean by 'little brother'? What do you, sinner, with my knife?"

The man smiled, amusement in his eyes. "Let's go get a drink. This'll take some explaining. That's not your knife, it's one of five . . ." He hesitated. ". . . brother."

"Go!" Blair agreed hysterically, wringing his hands. "I . . . I think we should perhaps . . . perhaps delay our dinner, Jeremiel." Blair shook his head nervously, making his double chins wiggle.

*Sheep!* Jeremiel thought suddenly. Though the Lord Himself was often likened unto the lamb. He released the big man, stepping back warily.

He squinted ominously. "By drink, I hope you mean perchance a glass of milk . . . or at most a cup of coffee. Your story interests me . . . but I'm afraid I have no brothers outside of the children of the Lord."

"My name's Abriel. Abriel Catton. It's a long story," Catton grunted with a sigh. "Don't reckon you'd know why these here fellers wanted your scalp?" At that, he bent down, picking one up with one hand, muscles knotting.

Jeremiel looked into the eyes of the knife artist—the

one Abriel had tried to plant in the church wall. "Had you a reason to assail me, brigand?"

"No ... no," the fellow groaned, staring at the knobby fist Jeremiel shoved in his face. "Paid off. Down at the docks. Twenty dollars apiece to slit yer ... gullet and dump you ... dump you in the river. Didn't know the man. Big ... big fella, blond beard, scar on his chin." His voice stumbled, thick, half-conscious.

"Satan spawn," Jeremiel said sharply, as Abriel dropped the man. "Abriel Catton, you say?"

"And you are Jeremiel Catton," the big man added with assurance. "Find your outfit ... and you'll see those two knives match. I also have our father's will here."

Jeremiel continued to squint, puzzled. "My parents were simple folk. Missionaries. I had no brothers."

"Oh, but you do." Abriel smiled. "That knife is mine—a present from our father."

Father? Jeremiel's heart bumped his breastbone. So many times his parents had told him they had adopted him to raise in the way of the Lord. Adopted? He'd never wanted to believe that. Now, out of the night and a brawl, comes a man, obviously a sinner—no pious man bore those scars of brawling—with a knife like his own? And perhaps a legacy?

Finally, he shrugged. "The Lord works in many ways, Abriel Catton. Come. I will share a glass of milk with you. Tell me your tale ... and let me see this will you claim is my father's."

Abriel's face contorted. Under his breath he whispered, "Milk? The stuff makes my stomach ache."

What he wanted was a stiff belt of amber rye. Reckoned he could do without the sermon, though. On the way past, one of the toughs grunted and sat up. The smack as the preacher hit him could be likened to an axle snapping under an overloaded wagon. Like Robert Campbell said, there's preachers and then there's *preachers*!

Arabella leaned against the railing as the steamboat *Anderson* chuffed and squeaked its way toward the rocky piers under the gray bluffs of Saint Louis. Murky brown water swirled as the paddles slap-slapped the water into foam. Smoke and cinders curled through the misty rain to sting her eyes.

Saint Louis. Her birthplace. Arabella's heart—leaden since the funeral in Cairo—warmed slightly. Here, for the first time, she would meet her family.

Black men raced along the rocky pier, deftly catching the thick ropes as they sailed out from the bow. The pilot skillfully cut the wheel, bringing them parallel to the rocks as willing hands tugged the boat into a slip where wooden fenders kept it from the jagged limestone. Above her, the whistle gave one final shriek.

The city—what she could see of it—looked squat and sullen in the darn drizzle. The men appeared rough, crude, unkempt. Hardly the image of the frontiersman she'd garnered from James Fenimore Cooper's writings.

She watched men, women, and children crowd the deck while the plank lowered. Like Somali porters, they filed over to shore. Some were met with hugs and cries; others stumbled up the rock-studded roadway toward the buildings above.

"Miss Catton?" Captain Morrison called from below. "If you will permit me, I'll call a phaeton."

"Yes," she called, oddly excited. "Thank you, Captain." She waved her handkerchief at him and rushed to her cabin in a rustle of taffeta petticoats. Her trunk—packed that morning—lay ready. She grabbed up her parasol and made one last check as two of the deckhands knocked discreetly and inquired for her baggage.

She followed them into the drizzle.

True to Morrison's word, a light carriage clattered down to the dock, oilcloth cover rain-sleek. Morrison saw to strapping the trunk on behind as she climbed in.

To her surprise, Morrison himself settled in across from her.

"Captain! You needn't—"

"Tut tut. Hush, miss. Anything the line can do for you is most generously offered." He smiled, friendly, chattering as they bounced up the rocky lane and meandered down nefarious Olive Street and turned into town.

Campbell's house at Lucas Place loomed large, two-storied with French windows in white casements. Morrison stepped out, offering his hand.

As Arabella straightened her blue velvet and looked up, the doors opened, a colored man stepping out primly, one eye cocked to the soggy heavens. He bowed to Arabella and Morrison. "May I be of service, sir . . . madam?"

Arabella's heart tightened. Something about him reminded her of James—the voice, the lined dignity in his face.

"I am Arabella Catton," she introduced, opening her parasol against the drizzle. "I have come about my father's death. Colonel Kit Carson wrote. He mentioned I should contact Colonel Campbell about my brothers."

The dark man bowed again. "Mr. Campbell is in the city, ma'am. If you will follow me, I'll see to your comfort. My name is Tepper, at your service."

On Morrison's arm, she followed.

"My good man," Morrison added airily. "As master of the *Anderson*, it has been my most definite pleasure to escort Miss Catton through some difficult times." He smiled anxiously. "Please, may I leave word with Mr. Campbell at how delighted we are to have been of service?"

The dark servant's lips wiggled slightly and he nodded, poker-faced. "Yes, sir. I shall inform the master. I'm sure he will be most grateful."

As he closed the door behind Morrison, Tepper's mahogany face crinkled with amusement. "Been after those shipping contracts for years!" He laughed and sobered as he looked at Arabella. "Pardon me, ma'am. Miss Catton, you say? Any relation to Abriel?"

Arabella closed her parasol, frowning at the water spots on her dress. "Well, I'm not sure. I . . . I feel most uncomfortable just appearing on your doorstep. I'm afraid Colonel Carson didn't send a real letter of introduction."

His eyelids lowered, giving him a sleepy catlike appearance. "Your father's name, ma'am?"

She flushed, looking at him nervously. "Weberly," she told him. "Weberly Catton."

He nodded. "You do have the same eyes." He pursed his lips, chin slightly forward. "Ma'am, if you don't mind my asking. Arabella Catton had a man of color in her . . . shall we say, employ. Could you tell me who?"

Startled, she cocked her head. "James," she whispered, aware of the sting. "You remind me of him," she added, looking up into his kind eyes.

"Is he coming?" Tepper asked. "Delayed perhaps?"

She closed her eyes, fighting for calm. "No. He's not. I . . . I buried him at Cairo." She smiled wistfully, remembering better days, other places—aware of the warm tingle back of her eyes. She sniffed, afraid she couldn't blink back the tears. "Excuse me. It's so recent. James practically raised me, you see. I . . . miss him." The loneliness closed about her.

"He came from the Bahamas, you know," Tepper added, watching her intently.

She frowned, suddenly wary. "He always told me he came from Santo Domingo. Napoleon's soldiers made him a prisoner when he was fighting with his father, Toussaint L'Ouverture. The French were taking him to Europe as a hostage when he escaped the ship in New Orleans with several others of his family."

Tepper gave her a wistful smile. "Yes, that was James. And you *are* Arabella."

"Who else would I be?" she asked, uncertain, suddenly uncomfortable at the implication of his words. *Why should I be anyone else? What is involved here?*

"Branton," she correctly surmised. "Yes, James told me."

"How did he die?" Tepper asked softly.

"In his sleep. They think it was his heart."

Tepper closed his eyes, taking a deep breath. "He was my brother. I jumped off that ship with him that night."

Bram kept moving. Had he lost them? Cussed luck! He maintained his trotting lope, the big bay hobbling along behind him—led by the reins. Talk about a fella's bad luck! He'd *had* to take that trail along the shale outcrop knowing the stuff cut hell out of hooves.

Bram looked over his shoulder, staring at the split hoof that lamed the horse. Hell! He'd stole one damn fine horse, too! The bay moved well, thick muscles bulging under a glossy hide.

"Cheap gawddam immigrants!" Bram spat into the breeze. "Could afford to head to Santa Fe—but couldn't afford a farrier's fee for good shoes! Kee-*rist*! I done ya a favor stealing ya away from that clod-footed sod-buster, pal." He reached back and affectionately slapped the bay on the shoulder.

Bram squinted at the dark clump on the horizon. "Council Grove, pal." He pulled his hat off and wiped at the trickling perspiration that had built under the sweatband. "Water there. Hell, maybe somebody to fix that hoof too, huh?"

Always cautious, he saw them first. Three riders cutting down his backtrail.

"Aw hell!" Bram studied his options. The grass grew thick and tall here. Might just work. He slapped the bay on the butt and dropped to his belly, worming his way through the dry grass, seeing the green stuff growing under his nose. Like a snake he wiggled along, counting seconds, knowing the riders closed the distance.

His heart battered against his ribs. His mouth had gone dry again. Cuss it, of all the drawbacks to hoss thieving, fear ranked right up there.

That and ropes.

He could feel the hooves thudding into the ground. Bram froze, heart sounding like a smith's hammer on an anvil.

"Got the hoss!" someone called. "Lamed up. Split hoof."

"Where'd he go?"

"Backtrack him. In this grass, there'll be a trail."

Bram winced. Maybe they'd just take the bay and ride off? He waited, scarcely breathing. A horse blew—close!

"All right, amigo!" a gruff voice called out. "I see you. Come off the ground slow or I'll blow you right in two like the snake you are."

Bram lifted his head far enough to see the man had him. Another rode close, already shaking out the rope. Bram's heart stopped dead in his chest, leaving his impish grin paralyzed. He could see no forgiveness in those hard faces peering down at him.

# *Chapter 3*

*J*eremiel pulled his black slicker tight around his frock coat as he stared down the mud-shiny track. From the looks of things, the road south out of Independence would be long, wet, and cold. As his black slipped and splashed, it left him time to think—and he had plenty of that to do. The ways of the Lord had always left him awestruck—the revelations made by Abriel Catton staggered him no less than his Lord's.

Catton? A name he'd heard somewhere, whispered by his parents in the night? Catton, it fit, falling into some slot in his head long empty. Jeremiel Catton.

William and Mary Sunts had taken him by the hand, always forgiving of his unusual verve and energy. Forever patient, they'd excused his brash youth and pointed the way toward the Lord.

"Foolishness is bound in the heart of a child," Jeremiel

quoted from Proverbs. And William Sunts had made no sparing of the rod of correction to drive it from him.

Jeremiel tucked a corner of oilcloth over the special pouch hanging from the saddle horn like a scabbard. The boxy gutta-percha-covered leather held his Bible, making sure no trickle of drizzle got past to wet the pages.

Jeremiel Catton? Indeed, no wonder he'd been such a wild boy. Oh, for the anguish he'd caused dear Mary. For the pain he'd laid at their doorstep; but as the Good Book stated so clearly, Ecclesiastes, "This is an evil among all things that are done under the sun, that there is one event unto all: yea, also the heart of the sons of men is full of evil, and madness is in their heart while they live."

He hawked and spat into the mud along the trace. The son of a heathen mountain man? There lay the root of the evil—traced through the blood: bad blood.

Oh, to be sure, he'd seen them. Dirty men who spoke vulgarly, they thrashed the Lord's name in the dirt with every other breath. They prayed to heathen Indian gods. Whiskey sots dissipated from drinking skullpop by the gallon, mountain men lived enslaved to the wanton appetites of the flesh, carousing carnally with every doxy Cyprian they could find! The vilest of Satan's blood, their damnation would raise no cries of anguish from the Holy Host!

. . . And his father? A man like that?

Jeremiel winced, rubbing his fingers over the wet waterproofing of his worn leather-bound Bible. He raised his eyes to the lead-gray clouds masking the Lord's skies.

"Tell me, my Lord. Doest Thou truly vest the sins of the father against the son? Know me, my Lord. Your bidding is my command." He squinted, "Yea, though my own brother Abriel I fear to be a hearty sinner."

What a shock to have encountered a stranger and come away with a brother. Jeremiel tipped his head, a stream of water trickling off the brim of his black hat to spatter on his slicker.

"Best to split up," Abriel had said. "Do you want to go to Fort Kearny to look for Jake . . . or head south and see if you can rustle up Bram?"

He'd chosen the route south, having ridden his Bible circuit through the straggling frontier of western Missouri, northern Arkansas, and the fringes of wild Kansas. Perhaps someone would know this Bram—point a finger in the right direction. Jeremiel had connections, people he knew living in the isolated farms.

One-Eyed Mike? Jeremiel winced. A common vulgar thief! His reputation bandied about the hill country on every lip. Good Christian people sought him high and low, hoping to string a rope around his neck and leave him twisting from a high branch.

Jeremiel winced. *And this other brother I ride to find is a horse thief?* A restriction tightened under his heart, as if his very soul would wail. "You have saved others, my Lord! You blessed the thief, raised the woman Magdelene. I pray You now, make me Your hand to raise this flesh of my flesh from the fires of perdition."

*But a . . . a horse thief?*

"Confound it! Fitz needs goods." A stentorian voice brought Arabella bolt upright. "We've got the wagons! The Indians are waiting, Tom's got his personal word of honor on the line . . . and we're virtually strangled by a federal contracting officer! Heaven help this country if we ever have to fight a war! English soldiers will be lunching in Washington before the damned contract officers get the procurement on their desk!"

Arabella opened her door, having refreshed and talked

most of the afternoon with Tepper. She'd met Virginia—a woman no more than ten years her senior—now pregnant with yet another child. In a rustle of pulled-up skirts, Arabella hurried down the hall to the head of the stairs.

She looked down at an older man, dressed as a gentleman in a gray coat with frilly shirt and neat tapered pants. He stopped in the act of pulling a beaver hat from his head and smiled up. "You must be Arabella. Welcome to Lucas Place."

"Mr. Campbell?" she asked.

"Morrison ran me down." Campbell grinned. "Told me in great detail about your trip and how he bent over backward to help." A wicked light filled his brown eyes. ". . . After he heard you were coming to see me, I'd wager."

She laughed. "I suppose so."

Campbell climbed the steps to take her hand, smiling into her eyes. "So much like your mother."

Arabella stalled. "I . . . I wouldn't know, sir."

"Come, talk to me." He turned and hollered. "Virginia? Have Tepper bring Miss Catton and me two cups of coffee." He escorted her down the stairs and into the parlor, after shooing his boys, James and Hugh, out of the way.

"I'm sorry you missed Abriel," Campbell told her, taking the cup Tepper handed him. "He left only two weeks ago for the West."

"I told Miss Catton most of the story, sir," Tepper added as he handed Arabella her cup. "Made sure she was gold instead of lead first too."

Campbell nodded, fingering the nob at the end of his long nose. "So, you know about Branton Bragg and his . . . insanity?"

She nodded. "Yes, sir. James told me about him years ago. In our travels, he—"

"Travels?" Campbell raised an eyebrow.

She smiled. "All over. France, England, Greece, and Italy. We spent some time in Palestine and Persia as well as Mombasa, Bombay, and the Cantonese ports."

Campbell looked at her quizzically. "All those places? I had no idea. I knew James to be a remarkable man . . . but to take a young lady such as yourself to such . . . such barbaric places as China?" He looked skeptically at Tepper.

"My brother began life as a king's son, sir. We both traveled until the French came." Tepper smiled warmly at Arabella. "I envy you."

She nodded, that tight knot of grief in her chest. "He gave me more than I could ever tell you." She studied Campbell. "It came as a shock to land in Charleston. The man who raised me as a father became less than human. Treated like some . . . animal."

Campbell winced. "Yes, well, tell me. How did you support yourselves out and about like that?"

*What do I tell him? He knows about the state of the Catton finances, no doubt. Can I be honest? No, Arabella. He'd never believe it to begin with. And it might be worse if he did!*

Smoothly she added, "James followed several financial ventures, trading spices from Africa to India to China. In return we carried European manufactured goods to the Orient." She sipped her coffee. "At the same time, the expenses of travel can be ameliorated by trade—as you no doubt understand, being a merchant yourself."

Campbell nodded, studying her like a hawk. "A typical Catton," he muttered. "Always glib of tongue. No doubt you were a constant terror to poor James."

*Glib? Could he see she only told a half-truth? She*

smiled easily, keeping her best European manners. "Indeed, sir. I exasperated James to the limits. But enough of my past. Tell me about my brothers and how I can find them."

Campbell straightened, seeing the earnest look in her amber eyes. "Find them? But Miss Catton, they're beyond the frontier! Out in the plains. The West is a big place—and certainly *not* the sort of place for a lady of your breeding and social grace!" He swallowed, looking to Tepper for reassurance.

Arabella leaned forward over the fine china cup and saucer, tilting her head coquettishly. "Mr. Campbell? I *will* go."

Branton Bragg let the dead man sag to the deck. "A preacher and a freighter beat you all? Three of you let them get away? Three of you?" He growled under his breath as he kicked the body hard in the side, watching a loose arm flop. "Incompetent imbeciles. And stupid to boot! Coming back here to whine to me!"

Bragg grunted as he lifted the limp man in his arms. "Fail me, will you?" His boots thumped hollowly on the deck as he walked to the rail. "Let them kids get away? Took my money and let *me* down?"

Bragg sneered down at the slack man in his arms. "Feed the catfish!" He dropped the flopping body, stepping back to avoid the splash.

Bragg leaned over to watch the dark form bob up, swirl around, and sink, a black trail of blood whirling away in the river's suck.

"Now I find the other two who let me down." He filled his huge chest, rippling bearlike bands of muscle across his chest and back. "Then I go after Jeremiel and Abriel myself!"

He looked down, disgusted by the splotches of blood on the deck.

A group of fine folks, Bram thought to himself. Most rested in the shade of yellow-green spring leaves, sprawled or hunched, hard eyes showing no give as they studied him. The cool breeze rustled through the new leaves, plucking at clothing, whispering soothingly through Council Grove.

Bram bit his lip, feeling the scratch of hemp against the tender skin of his neck as the big blond man settled the noose around his neck. He'd never known just how rough and scratchy a rope could really be—or how damn scary!

"Cigar?" the blond man asked, frowning as he studied his knot.

The ugly bay horse under Bram stamped nervously before shifting to stand hip-shot.

"You betcha," Bram croaked, nodding like a crazy man. He froze, feeling the grating scratch of hemp on his neck.

A lucifer flared and his nostrils caught the odor of sulfur. Bram clamped the cigar in his teeth, enjoying the sensations of taste and smell, puffing if alive. Now, how long could he keep it going?

The length of that cigar represented the remaining span of his life. He stared down at it cross-eyed, heart galloping on his sternum.

Time passed. Bram played the white knob of ash for all it was worth. He made it halfway through his last cigar when he saw the stranger coming, his vantage being a little higher.

He couldn't make out the man through the haze as the spring sun shimmered across the plains. Bram looked up at the thick branch over his head, calculated the age of the rope around his neck by how scratchy it felt—and knew he was a goner. The limb wasn't about to break and the hemp felt too new and stiff to part when his weight hit the bottom.

"Will you hurry it up, hoss thief!" one of the burly freighters growled. "Never took *me* so long to smoke a damn cigar!"

"You wasn't about to be hung neither!" the big blond man told him. "The kid's young. Reckon a little longer ain't gonna hurt him. 'Sides, we'd a never caught him ifn his hoss hadn't split a hoof. Reckon ya can't hate a kid who wouldn't ride a lame animal inta the ground t' save his hide."

"What name do we put on your slab, mister?" a gruff slope-shouldered man asked, exposing missing teeth in his lopsided grin. A thick mop of greasy black hair hung down over his ears; little pig eyes squinted nervously.

"Bram. Just Bram will do."

"Huh! you got it." The man picked up a section of board and began carving.

"Shoulda had him dig his grave afore we hung him," another groused.

"Be happy to see to that little chore for you," Bram agreed eagerly, thinking about how far he'd get before they shot him down.

"Shut up!" Slope Shoulder grunted, tongue out the side of his mouth, brows pinched in frown as he carved studiously.

Bram watched that black-frocked figure ride into the Grove and realized he could feel the heat from that cigar warming the end of his nose. Just about done. His time trickled away. Ah, hell, it had been fun. A fella couldn't ask for more than that.

The circle of faces around him turned to stare at the rider.

The stranger sat tall, long limbs at ease on the black horse. Broad of shoulder, his black frock coat showed travel dust, as did the white boiled shirt with tight collar. His dark hair ruffled in the wind as he doffed his hat. A square leather case hung on the side of the saddle, the black prancing nervously.

Those amber eyes—so very much like his own—drew Bram's attention. They burned into him, searching, scathing, practically glowing in the thin neatly bearded face. A strange light kindled in the rider's eyes as they looked at each other.

Bram couldn't resist one last impish grin.

"Good day, gentlemen," the stranger's voice rang through the afternoon air. "What deeds are you about?"

"Hangin' a hoss thief! You a preacher?" The big blond looked uncomfortably at the black-frocked stranger.

"I am Jeremiel Catton, minister of the Gospel, at your service, sirs." He bowed deeply, eyes pinning Bram, hot with disgust.

Well, a fella couldn't expect salvation from a Bible thumper. He'd probably bore the hell out of him, praying and singing, then praise the Lord as he slapped that bay right out from under another sinner.

"Has this man made his peace with the Lord?" The ringing voice rose in the air. "Has he made peace with his Maker for his wicked ways?"

Bram let himself groan. The amber eyes burned into his and he squirmed, uncomfortable.

"What is your word, sinner?" A pointing finger shot out.

What the hell. A chance is a chance. He swallowed, acutely aware of the tight noose around his neck. The horse on which he sat shifted, tightening the rope. The fools had tied it too short, he'd strangle rather than have his neck broke!

"I done sinned, preacher." He couldn't help but grin, keeping his cigar clamped in his teeth. It had only been bad luck that brought him here. If that horse had stayed around, he'd have made it to Arkansas by now.

"Would you seek redemption?" The preacher's words thundered over the heads of the teamsters.

"Reckon I would," Bram agreed, feeling a searing pain as the cigar burned under his nose. Damn, the thing couldn't be more than a nubbin.

"Would you dedicate your soul to the service of the Lord your God?" The preacher's voice boomed loud, causing the teamsters to back up, wincing at the power it conveyed.

"Reckon so," Bram agreed, a sudden hope beginning to wiggle in his chest. "Reckon I done seen the error of my ways, preacher. I see Satan all around me!" He couldn't help but glance at the suddenly confused faces surrounding him. The horse shifted again for emphasis, pulling the noose a little tighter. Bram's tongue crowded the back of his mouth and he gulped.

The preacher rode forward, even with Bram's mount. He could see the preacher closely now. Cigar smoke curled into his eyes, making them water, and he just knew his nose was starting to sizzle.

"Will you swear to serve me? Will you make the Lord's work your own, sinner?" That voice boomed louder than a double-barreled shotgun.

*"Hell, yes!"* Bram agreed fervently, feeling a quickening pulse.

Whoops. Wrong words. He winced as the preacher's face went thunder-black.

Relief washed through him in an ecstasy as his bowie knife appeared in the preacher's hand and the noose went loose around his neck.

"Now, just a confounded minute," the big blond protested. "We was havin' a hangin here!"

The preacher turned, eyes boring into the big blond immigrant's. "Vengeance belongs to the Lord thy God, sinner! Yea, that ye should raise thy hand to take the Lord's will from His servant! He who seeks the wrath of the Lord is damned unto perdition! Does your soul yearn for hell, sinner?" That long finger hovered at the end of the blond man's nose like a spear ready to pin his soul. The big man wilted before the power in those amber eyes.

"Reckon not," he mumbled reluctantly, dropping his eyes.

"Will any man here take the place of the Lord in his wrath?" the preacher bellowed, face tight with anger. "Will any of you men, born of woman, claim that vengeance is not the Lord's? Will any of you deny the salvation of Barabbas? Let him speak who would mock the will of the Lord God and set himself upon that golden throne?" The very air seemed alive. The teamsters backed up, a step at a time.

"Hand me this man's possessions, for he is bound unto me." The voice changed to a command. Like Moses on Sinai, they walked carefully over to hand up a bundle of clothing, pistol, and a leather-bound bowie knife. Bram spit out the acorn-sized cigar that blistered his lip.

His eyes never leaving their faces, the preacher picked up the reins of the horse Bram sat on and led it slowly out of camp. The last thing he heard from behind was, "Hell, that preacher done stole our hoss!"

The blond man's report was, "Uh-huh, *you* go git it back!"

* * *

Jeremiel studied his young charge. "Your name is Bram?"

Their eyes locked, but through the scruffy wisps of beard, the bent nose, and dirt, Jeremiel could see the likeness. A tingle rose under his heart. This . . . this *brigand* was his brother!

"Yep." The youth grinned, and a twinkle found light behind his eyes—a twinkle mindful of the devil himself. Jeremiel's gut tightened. "Bram Catton, at your service. I . . . What'd you say your name was?"

Throat tight, he admitted, "Jeremiel. Jeremiel C-Catton."

Young Bram hooted with glee, insatiable grin widening. "How 'bout that! Why, we might be kin somehow." Enjoyment flickered across his face, turning it into a heathen impish thing. "Uh, Mr. Catton, if you could do me the favor and cut my hands loose, I'd be mighty grateful."

Jeremiel kneed his snorting black over and severed the bonds with his bowie.

Bram sighed relief, throwing a quick look over his shoulder at the trees behind them. "Thought I was a goner for sure, back there." He plucked the bits of rope from his wrists before lifting the hangman's noose from his neck and inspecting it with a critical eye.

"Your life is mine. I have bound you to the Lord God—sinner."

Jeremiel watched Bram's grin widen, thoughts racing behind his amber eyes. "Why, of course, Mr. Preacher. Um, no use you totin' my outfit like that. Reckon ifn you'll hand it over, I'll take the burden from yer hoss."

Jeremiel slitted his eyes, handing the grubby bundle over. "You have given your word, brother."

"Hell, yes, I . . . Uh, I mean I done give my word," Bram hedged, reaching for the belongings. That's when he noticed the knife on Jeremiel's belt. Slivers of frown deepened his forehead as he looked to his own bowie where it lay atop his blanket and coat.

"You are planning on leaving," Jeremiel decided, closing his eyes. A deep sadness filled him. "There is no salvation. Your soul is blacker than the pits of hell. You are cursed among men and—"

"Now, kin Catton, you gotta understand them folks back there was a fixing t' see ifn this hyar rope"—he waved the short section—"was tougher than my neck. A fella will do—"

"Lie? Cheat?" Jeremiel thundered, glaring hotly. "Oh, no. Not you, Bram Catton!" He reached like lightning, horny hand grabbing the boy's muscular arm, half dragging him from the shying horse until they stared nose-to-nose. "You promised yourself to me . . . to *your* God!"

"Now, preacher . . ." Bram began.

"Jeremiel! You call me Jeremiel."

"Now, Jeremiel, even if we might be kin, I ain't agonna go Bible spoutin' with you all over hob's creation—"

"You are sorely tainted with the touch of Satan . . . *little brother*!" There, he'd gotten it over with. Bram's mouth fell open so Jeremiel let him loose.

"Little brother?" Bram muttered dubiously, looking Jeremiel up and down from booted foot to black broad-brimmed hat, face screwed up skeptically. "*Naw,* I just can't believe old Web Catton's kid could turn out like . . . so . . . different."

"Mutually agreed," Jeremiel added fervently. "Then you know One-Eyed Mike wasn't your father?"

Bram's lips twitched and he spit into the dust at the side of the road. "Yep. He told me story after story about my pap. Quite a man, old Web." His eyes narrowed. "Mike never said nuthin' 'bout no preacher brother."

"Nor did I hear about a *horse thief* from William

Sunts," Jeremiel added acidly. "Nevertheless, the knives seem to indicate—"

"Yep, Web give me that." Bram nodded, pulling his hat down tight on his head. "Or so Mike told me. Now, if you'll hand that outfit of mine over, brother Jeremiel, I'll thank ya fer lending a hand back there and be on my—"

"You'll do nothing of the kind," Jeremiel gritted, stomach knotted, upset. "Your brother Abriel and I both need you to—"

"Whoa up," Bram warned, lifting a hand. "Now, I ain't about to go foolin' round with no kin dealings. Reckon I got me a nice little operation right here. I don't need no weepy sisters or stiff shirts nor none of that stuff. We'll just smile right nice, tip our hats, and be gone, brother Jeremiel." Bram pulled his horse up.

*And that would be a blessing!* Nevertheless, Jeremiel leaned over his saddle horn, fingers tracing the outline of the Bible on his saddle. "Web Catton is dead."

Bram cocked his head, sandy wisps of hair batted by the wind where they straggled out from under his hat. "So?"

"We have to go after the inheritance together. All of us. You, me, Abriel, Jake, and Tom," Jeremiel added reasonably. "The gold is hidden somewhere—"

"Inheritance." Bram's lips traced the word. A sudden interest sparked back of his eyes, grin exposing straight white teeth and a couple of holes. "Uh, you mean *real* gold?"

Jeremiel straightened in the saddle. *Forgive me, my Lord. Sometimes, a carrot must be used to lead a mule to the trough. As thirty pieces of silver were used by Satan to betray You in Gethsemane, so shall I use them to bring this young man—this brother—into the fold of my love and Your salvation.*

"The treasure of Governor Armijo of New Mexico. Our . . . father"—Jeremiel winced, a pang in his heart— "appears to have . . . stolen it."

He raised his head, seeing Bram's mouth hang open wider, a gleam in his eyes. Jeremiel whispered, "O dear Lord, is there no end to my travails with the wicked?"

"Hot damn!" Bram crowed, slapping his thighs with callused hands. His stolen bay pranced sideways, nervous at his explosion. "Now, that's just plumb dandy!"

"Forgive them, Father. They know not what they do. Lead them into green pastures. Show them the light of your . . ." Jeremiel jerked around. "What do you, sinner?"

Bram turned his bay off the road. "C'mon!"

"Where do you go? Bram? Get *back* here!"

Bram pulled up the bay, sighing and throwing his arms wide. Exasperated, he explained in a pained voice, "Brother Jeremiel, I got fifteen hosses hid about six miles from here. Ifn I'm agonna ride plumb t' Santy Fee, I sure as hell ain't agonna do it on this crow bait!"

Jeremiel gasped, trying to form the words. "Y-You w-would ride a stolen horse in . . . in *my* presence?"

Bram's vigorous nod mocked. "To go find stole gold? You gawddam bet! You comin'?"

Jeremiel turned his black, a growing anger possessing him. He galloped down on the boy, raising his blocklike fist to blast Bram out of the saddle, to thrash the very blasphemy from his sassy grin.

Bram saw, kicked his horse to the side out of the way, impudent grin on his face.

"Hey, Jeremiel, ain't there sumpthing in that Bible you tote about getting all het up?" He laughed, amusement writ large in his eyes as he skillfully kept backing the bay out of harm's way.

Jeremiel pulled the black up, face falling as he reddened. Crestfallen, he replied, "Ecclesiastes. 'Be not hasty in thy spirit to be angry: for anger resteth in the bosom of fools.' "

"Couldn't o' said it better myself!" Bram chortled. "Now, come on, brother Jeremiel. Let's go get them hosses. Reckon it's long ways to New Mexico. Reckon I got a lotta sinnin' I done that you can tell me about. Besides, how come God ain't struck me down dead yet ifn I'm such a sinner?"

"Then hear the word of the Lord thy God, sinner," Jeremiel retorted, seeing Bram's impudent grin spread. "Ecclesiastes 8:12 states, 'Though a sinner do evil an hundred times, and his days be prolonged, yet surely I know that it shall be well with them that fear God!' "

"Huh!" Bram frowned, spurring his horse out across the tall-grass prairie. "Reckon I'll just have to sin a little harder, brother Jeremiel. Maybe all these years I done it wrong. With you hangin' round, I kin be sure I don't make no mistakes in my sinnin'. I'd hate to be doing it half-assed."

# Chapter 4

*M*olly brought him wide awake. Worth fifteen watchdogs, Abriel's mule had saved his life more than once. The first rule of survival in wild country is to keep your wits; Ab didn't move. His fingers crept to wrap around the use-polished, sweat-stained wood of his old Hawken. Head unmoving, his eyes searched the darkness. The fire had burned down to coals. Frost glistened thick on the packs.

Molly's ears pricked and Ab's riding mount, Sorrel, had his head turned out to the darkness. Ab moved easily as he slid out of the blankets and pulled chilly air deeply into his lungs. The frost melting through his socks gave him an unpleasant shiver.

A clink sounded out in the dark—like a lanyard ring going suddenly slack. Ab crouched down low and waited. Sorrel let out a low whicker and shifted.

The first came in silence—a faint shadow moving in

night. He didn't ear the hammer back until he crouched over Ab's bedroll. He stopped, perhaps thinking the blankets looked a mite flat. Ab watched his head come up, grim eyes searching frantically.

A second form came rushing up from the other side and hissed, "Shoot him. Git his stuff . . . and let's get outa here!"

White men? Bent on murder? Robbery? Heart hardening, Abriel bit his lip, knowing he couldn't cover both of them from where he lay. So, they'd come at him out of the dark with the express intent of killing him, had they? Such doings seemed plumb uncalled-for . . . and lacking in social grace besides. Fear forged itself into a blazing anger.

The steps of a third man rustled through the grass. Typically, Molly wasn't liking the situation at all. Her ears had gone back and down, black eyes smoldering with hot mule thoughts.

True, she hated strangers; but worse, she hated to have guns out and being waved around. Abriel rolled his tongue over his lip, studying her, remembering the time, years back, he made the mistake of shooting a whitetail from the saddle. She'd been a good mule to shoot from—*once!*

That third man couldn't read sign or he would have noticed Molly's eyes going wide as he walked up. She took one long look, eyes locked onto his rifle. When she kicked—spot on target—she knocked him and his rifle clean over in a perfect flip.

Ab leapt as they turned to see what made the smashed-pumpkin sound as the rifleman thudded into the frozen dirt. The butt of Ab's Hawken clunked number one's skull—the impact sounding like punky wood—before he whirled, dropping to a crouch, Hawken centered on number two's chest as he stumbled to a wide-armed halt.

"Ev'ning," Ab drawled out pleasantly. "Care to let that rifle of yourn settle softlike to the ground? Reckon it'd be right pert of you to let that pistol and knife take a little rest too."

Some men get that tightness around their eyes when they're upset. Ab noted number two's face pinching just like that; he did what he'd been told. About Abriel's size, the man needed a shave and smelled like he'd been rolling in bear bait. Ab's lip rose. Bear bait generally consisted of horse guts left in the sun for a couple of weeks.

"That's real good," Ab decided, tight with the fear-flush. The man straightened from laying out his weapons, arms spread, wary, as he looked for an opening.

Ab cocked his head, listening to the night before he softly added, "Reckon you can throw a couple of them sticks on the fire. But be real careful, the hair trigger's set and the adjusting screw fell out during a rough trip down the Missouri. Still, reckon I wouldn't want you making no wrong assumptions. This here rifle had a lot of Sam Hawken's tender lovin' care. She shoots plumb center."

Hands up, Bear Bait listened real good. Like a man walking around rattlesnakes, he reached for the wood. As the flames leapt up, Ab looked him over and pulled the bowie. Bear Bait's eyes fastened on the bright blade, a sudden flicker of excitement in his expression.

Ab narrowed his eyes. Why the glitter? Why the sudden leap of interest? He ran his thumb over the wire-bound leather of the handle. Surely, the man didn't think the knife less a danger than the Hawken?

"I suppose I better explain," Ab told him, noting the way the man eyed the knife so intently. "I'm going to give you a once-over and make sure there's no more hardware on yer body. Now, if I kept the rifle on you, all you'd have to do is get past the muzzle—but nobody with sense messes with a knife. Even a thumb-fingered fool will cut you, and I assure you, I outgrew that when I was ten."

Smart man, Bear Bait didn't move.

Ab backed away with the man's weapons and picked up his Hawken. The fellow Molly had kicked gave a low moan. The dapple gray mule stood braced, head down, at the end of her picket, ears pricked forward, hot black eyes watching the crumpled form.

"What about Hank?" the man asked, tossing his head toward the groaning lump.

"What about him?" Ab cocked his head, studying on the situation. Were there any more out there? Circling even now to get a shot?

"Oughta do something, ain't right to leave a man hurt like that." His black eyes bored into Abriel's, making a judgment, trying to see how far he could push.

"Wasn't it you said something about shooting me when you wandered into this shebang?" Ab gave him a suspicious squint, face hard. The man kept mum. "Seems to me that changes any of my . . . uh, humanitarian impulses."

The kicked man crawled slowly toward the fire, grip tight on his rifle. The weapon bent in the middle where Molly's hoof had landed. Ab winced, seeing the damage Molly had done. Jaw dislocated, one side of his face stuck out. Blood dripped in a stringy mess from the ruin of nose and mouth.

Lip jutting, Molly continued to stamp uneasily as she pulled at her rope.

"Good thing I always pound that picket pin in good and solid," Ab grunted.

The wounded man looked up at her and whimpered as he cowered in the beat-down grass. Ab toed the one he'd clunked with the Hawken: out cold. Within seconds, he had bound him up with pigging strings and settled back, easing his coffeepot onto the fire.

"Seems to me," he began, looking up at the strapping man who faced him, "this is a real good time to tell me who you are and why you took such an interest in my camp. A week ago, three fellas tried to take my brother. Tonight, you come in out of the dark and start talking about shooting me in my bedroll. What's yer name?"

"Cal Backman," the man's voice growled, black eyes still hot and hostile. His fingers knotted and unknotted themselves into fists.

"Well, Cal, let me guess. You was hired, huh?" Ab made a distasteful sound with his mouth, snaking a tin cup from his pack. The Hawken never wavered from its hold on Backman's chest. Backman's eyes followed the black bore of the .54, swallowing on occasion.

"Nope." Backman's face twisted up, lip caught in his teeth as if he might say too much.

"By who?"

"No one."

"Cal, I'm growing a little short on patience. Yer a liar!"

Backman stiffened. Men got shot for that kind of talk.

"If you ain't, prove it." Ab's voice went tight. "You come to kill me. If Molly hadn't been so blessedly cantankerous, I'd be lying there with my blood soaking through the blankets. Such doings change your perspectives of right and wrong in a big hurry." He added softly, "I could blow a hole through your knee. Wouldn't kill you—but you'd never walk again."

Cal's throat worked spastically—like he tried to swallow a knotted rag.

Ab grinned wickedly, knowing how the firelight had to be flickering on his face. He must have put the right tone in his voice because a little bead of sweat trickled down the side of Backman's nose. Given the temperature, the second trickle from under Backman's hatband had to be worry. Ab chuckled softly.

It came like a flood. "He didn't tell us no name. Just said we'd get paid plenty if we brought him yer knife and yer . . . yer ears. Didn't make too much sense . . . but for the money he offered . . . we took it." Cal lowered his eyes uncertainly.

"What's he look like?" Ab asked, rubbing his chin, thinking.

"Big man," Cal grunted, heaving a sigh as Ab relaxed a little. "Has a blond beard with a white streak running down the side. I guess it's kinda like there's a scar under it. His eyes is blue and kinda funny. I don't know, you look a little like him." Cal shrugged.

"Uncle Branton." Ab didn't know he spoke aloud. "Branton Bragg!"

"Some kin you got, mister," Cal Backman muttered. "He looked dog-killer mean to me. Me and Hank and Jeff thought it was plumb funny he didn't come after ya hisself but money's money." A long pause. "What ya gonna do with us?" His eyes narrowed again.

"Lie down!" Ab pulled himself to his feet, disgusted at the cold frost leaching ice-wet through his socks. One thing freighters know like no one else is knots. Afterward, he warmed and dried his feet at the fire and pulled on his boots.

Pulling a blanket over his knees, Ab settled back, Hawken ready, coffee cup in one hand. Backman shivered and coughed periodically. The kicked man groaned. Ab sipped his coffee, frowning up at the stars.

The feller he'd belted with the Hawken butt didn't look any too good when morning came. His color had gone gray and his eyes had a funny hollow look, the pupils two different sizes. His breathing jerked erratically. The one Molly'd kicked made a sight fit to scare strong men. Only Cal looked human. He squinted up from where he lay on his belly shivering in the morning chill. "You can't ride off and leave us!"

After repacking Molly, and tying their weapons behind his cantle, Ab swung into the saddle, staring out at the Kansas prairies. The land had begun to green up, buds burst full on the trees where they lined the watercourses. The sky beckoned, a bright blue splotched with white fully clouds. Somewhere a meadowlark trilled.

"Now, Cal, is my memory gittin' bad . . . or don't I remember you boys coming to kill me last night?" He cocked his head and raised an eyebrow.

"But you can't let us die out here!" he protested, rolling around in sudden anger.

"Son of a gun, I tied them knots plumb good in the dark! . . . Rather I shot you now?" Ab asked reasonably, pulling out the Hawken.

Backman glared redly up at him, jaw muscles bulging as Ab lined Molly's lead rope out and booted Sorrel in the slats. Under his breath he added, "You'd think a feller like that would learn."

Arabella entered the barn outside of Independence, eyeing the animals. A fine place, the stout new structure gleamed under a fresh coating of red paint. She nodded approval, seeing the stalls freshly shoveled out. The animals looked prime, healthy, their coats glistening. Her information had been correct. Brown sold good horses.

A firm-boned steeldust caught her eye. She walked to the stall, looking at the big horse, head cocked.

He snuffled and tossed his head, ears pricked as he looked at her over his shoulder.

"He'p ya, ma'am?" The voice sounded wheezy.

She fingered her chin, eyes tracing the lines of the steeldust's legs. The owner's arrival barely dented her concentration. "Yes. How much are you asking for this gelding, Mr. . . ."

"Brown, ma'am. Seth Brown. Why, ma'am, that horse isn't the thing for a little lady like you. No, indeed. Now, over here I've got a couple of ponies that will—"

"Take him out, please, Mr. Brown. I'd like to see him move," she decided, stepping back to meet his eyes. A big man in grimy overalls, he swallowed nervously as he looked her up and down. He cataloged her yellow bombazine dress with ruffles. A stricken expression crossed his watery-blue eyes, the coarse features of his face reddening.

"Why . . . why, ma'am, if you really want to see that horse. Sure, yep. I reckon I'd be happy to show him."

She smiled graciously, seeing the impact her charm had on the suddenly stumbling Mr. Brown.

He practically fell over himself backing the big animal from the stall. All of seventeen hands, the horse moved well. The steeldust eyed her nervously, still snuffling, but evidently enjoying the attention.

"Could I see his teeth, please?" Arabella asked easily.

"Now, ma'am," the owner hedged. "Uh, a lady like yourself don't go round looking in a horse's—"

"Please?" She cocked her head, letting her eyes harden.

The big man scratched the back of his thick neck, wincing as he tried to avoid her gaze. "Yes'm."

He pried the steeldust's lips apart, allowing Arabella to see the teeth. "I'd say seven years old. Wouldn't you agree, Mr. Brown?"

He looked at her, grudging respect in his faded-blue eyes. "You know horses, ma'am."

Arabella smiled. "Why, thank you for the compliment, Mr. Brown. Lift his feet, please. I'd like to inspect his hooves." She bent forward, holding her skirts out of the way so she could check the white line and frog, looking for thrush or sand cracks.

"Oh, he's sound, ma'am," Brown assured. "I might let a gentleman take his chances ... but not a lady." He grinned shyly. "I might be a horse trader, ma'am. But shucks, this one ... why, he's all the horse he looks to be." A red flush crept up his face.

"Excellent! I take it, then, that you would have no objection to saddling him and allowing me the chance to check his wind?"

"Why, I ..." Seth Brown shook his head, and a catching sound came from deep in his chest. "Ma'am, I don't think you understand. That horse is a *man's* horse, ma'am. Sure, he's good. The best I got here. But for manners you need a horse what's broke for a woman—"

"Saddle him, please." She smiled up at him. "I shall be happy to leave whatever collateral you need to ensure I shall return with the animal."

"Now, ma'am, you didn't hear a word I ..." Brown swallowed hard, nodding slowly at the narrowing of her eyes. "Yes'm," he declared in glum defeat, "I've got a sidesaddle here somewhere."

A week later Ab rode into New Fort Kearny. He'd camped there when it consisted of nothing more than a flat spot overlooking the Platte at the foot of Grand Island. Still, to his eyes, when the army dickered two thousand dollars in trade goods to the Pawnee for a military reservation, they got took. The grass grew plentiful, but the cottonwoods had already been depleted all along the river. The Pawnee thought the Mounted Riflemen would keep the Sioux and Cheyenne off their backs. The immigrants and freighters thought the trail would be made safe. Somehow, the Sioux never quite got the hint they were supposed to be afraid. They didn't molest overland travelers—but they sure loved to come kick hob out of the Pawnee.

Second Lieutenant Charles Ogle happened to be in command pending Captain Chilton's replacement. When Ab asked for Colonel Oord, Ogle nervously pointed to a squat structure of irregular cottonwood thickly chinked with sandy mud.

Colonel Jason Oord's office still smelled of green wood, and the plank flooring looked a little rough, splinters sticking up here and there. Briefly, Ab tried to figure out what an unattached colonel of artillery actually did in Lieutenant Ogle's Fort Kearny. They only had a couple of mountain howitzers on their rattly caissons. Somehow, Oord never seemed to be listed on the duty rosters. He didn't even have an assignment—but most people attached to the frontier military always knew where he could be found.

Ab looked around and noted the fold-up portable desk—ink-stained and battered—a rusting portable stove, and in the corner, tipped up, a Ringgold saddle with accoutrement, packed and ready to go. The door opened behind him. Ab turned to stare into two of the deadliest green eyes he'd ever seen.

He knew Colonel Oord by sight only, having seen him around Kearny and Fort Laramie. Then Oord had passed him once on the way to Santa Fe, sitting bolt upright in that saddle, not a whisker out of place. Face like chiseled walnut, the ends of his graying mustache flicked slightly as he looked Ab up one side and down the other.

*Feel like a side of beef!* Ab decided to himself.

"At your service, sir." Oord's gruff voice came clipped and he nodded his head, bowing slightly. "How may I help you?"

*Where do I start?* "Well, sir, I'm looking for your son."

Those green eyes bored into Abriel's like Oord could pick through his mind.

"And your interest in Jake?" Oord barked: an order.

Ab swallowed, pulled himself up, and glared back. "He's my brother."

They stared eye-to-eye for what seemed like an hour. When Oord finally nodded, Ab almost missed it. Then the iron man seemed to lose some of his stature. A flicker of pain passed behind those cold green eyes. "I see, come."

Ab followed him through a little door in the back and into a small spare room with a bunk. Books, neatly stacked, crowded the floor in one corner. He could see Plato, Euripides, Descartes, as well as the usual field manuals. A painted portrait of a brown-haired woman with big eyes stared out from the wall. The colonel pulled up the oiled canvas covering the window and poured something into two tin cups before handing one to Ab.

"You must be Abriel," Oord said as he studied him.

"Yes, sir." Abriel lifted the cup and drank. He tasted real live cognac!

Oord smiled, an ironic glint in his eyes. "And your father? Did someone finally hang him . . . or did his scalp end up dangling from some Indian pony's bridle?"

"I'm not sure, sir." *Hanging?* Just who *was* Web Catton? "My father, er . . . I mean Robert Campbell, received word from Kit Carson that Web Catton was overdue from a trapping expedition."

Oord's eyes cooled thoughtfully, and a sour smile bent the corner of his lip. "Only when I had thrown the last shovel of dirt on Catton's grave would I believe that rapscallion dead."

He paused before he shook himself. "No matter. The truth will come out eventually. I suppose this is as good a time for Jake to learn as any." A pause. "You will find him at Fort Laramie. He is on special duty there." The green eyes warmed. "He graduated from West Point last year, you know." The mustache twitched with a smile, and pride flooded in those terrible green eyes. "Fifth in his class."

So, somebody in the family had brains.

"Web left us an inheritance," Ab said. "I have already found Jeremiel and he's on the trail looking for Bram. I'm to meet him at Laramie. After that, I guess the hardest one to find will be Tom."

Oord's eyes narrowed, black pupils shrinking in the green. "You won't know who Tom is when you find him. The Cheyenne call him Wasatch now. Has quite a reputation among them. They say he talks to animals, and his medicine is reputed to be as good as the old men's. At his age, that's some accomplishment. The other young men don't like him. He's obviously white. His eyes are like yours and Jake's. His hair is sandy, lighter than yours—although considerably longer."

"You've seen him recently?" Shocked, Ab managed to pull his mouth closed.

"Last year," Oord said. "On the upper Arkansas with Left Hand's Arapaho. Agent Fitzpatrick would know where to find him. In fact, you might run into Wasatch on the trail. He might . . . find you. Like I say, a strange boy. He sees things."

Abriel nodded, irritated by a strange fluttering of his heart. He opted to change the subject.

"According to my instructions and the will, Jake gets one-sixth of what Web left us." Ab winced. "That is . . . if we can find it. For some reason, the knives are important."

He hedged over mentioning Armijo's gold, stopped by

some inner reservation. That statement about Web hanging bothered him.

"And your sister . . ." He frowned. "Anabelle . . . no . . ."

"Arabella," Ab supplied. "We don't know. She's somewhere back in the eastern states. My fath . . . Mr. Campbell wrote her. Naturally, we'll be forwarding her share." Ab chuckled. "I doubt a lady—like she is reported to be—would have anything to do with us hard cases."

Oord seemed to pause, weather-beaten face lined with hard thought. Then, "I'll write out a pass. I doubt that his commander at Laramie will buck." He smiled knowingly. "I receive certain . . . latitude in my requests."

Ab didn't ask why. Oord wasn't a man anyone pushed.

Oord stood there, arms crossed, cup cradled in one tanned hand. His gaze never wavered from Abriel's.

Shifting uncomfortably, Ab asked, "If you don't mind, sir, why you? I'm having problems understanding how Web Catton divvied his children up."

The green eyes smoldered. The mustache quivered. When he spoke, the voice came soft. "Web saved my life. At the time I was carrying a dispatch from Captain Bonneville to the United States. I was considerably greener then . . . young. The Gros Ventres caught me by surprise. It was only luck that Web heard me screaming—followed the tracks. I won't go into the details, but he rode right through the middle of their camp, cut me loose, and carried me away. He nursed me back to health. Somewhere in that long journey, I told him once how my wife and I had never had children.

"We talked a lot on that trip. He practically wet-nursed me to the settlements. I suppose he taught me everything he knew. I never got lost, never hungered, and rarely thirsted in all the years after that. Jake was a blessing when he came to live with us. I tried to give him as much in return as I once got from Web."

"I think I can understand that, sir." Ab finished the last of the cognac.

Colonel Oord's voice turned hoarse, eyes dropping for the first time. "Tell Jake that so far as I'm concerned, he's still my . . . my boy. If he ever needs anything, I'll . . . I'll come running. To me this doesn't change any . . . Well, he'll know."

Ab bit his lip. Was he crazy? Or were those green eyes pleading? "I'll tell him, sir. To me, Robert Campbell will remain my father. I only wish I could have known Web Catton; he sounds like quite a man."

Oord smacked Ab on the shoulder. "He'd be proud of you too, son. Come, I'll write out a leave for Jake. Lord knows where Catton might have squirreled away that inheritance. I have no doubts but it will be in the tall timber back where the wolves wear their hair long."

Anson McGillicuddy stood, arms crossed over his tightly fitted black silk vest, disapproval lining his dark face. One toe tapped at the bottom of his striped pants. The whole thing was totally unthinkable! Why, look at her! A mere slip of a girl, and every inch a lady to boot! Absurd! Some vagrant thug would . . .

"Again, Miss Catton, let me implore you to forget this incredible idea of yours. Among my connections are many fine young fellows who would act as your agents. The West is a man's—"

Arabella looked up from her trunk, a sullen anger smoldering behind her amber eyes. With all her self-control she replied reasonably, "Mr. McGillicuddy, you are being paid handsomely for keeping my personal possessions safe. Beyond that, I thank you for your advice. Nevertheless, I have five brothers out there, somewhere."

She waved a hand in the general direction of the Rocky Mountains. "And I sincerely intend—"

"You don't *understand*!" McGillicuddy wrung his hands, deep brown eyes pleading as he looked up at the ceiling. "That 'somewhere' you go on about is full of savage men, wild un-Christian Indians who will murder you *at the very least*! Fierce beasts are out there. Creatures of such horrors as wolves, grizzly bears, and catamounts. There are snakes and . . . and . . . poisonous insects that . . . What is *that*?"

He bent forward to peer. No matter that she acted "touched" in the head. Her trunk had proved a marvel of incredible oddities the likes of which his Pennsylvania-bred eyes had never seen.

"Tiger skin," she told him, laying the gleaming yellow-and-black-striped hide on the trunk. Her perfect brow lined and she bit her lip. "Let's see. I killed him in Jopalphur. Hum, four years ago? No, must have been five. Good shot, don't you think? I put a four-hundred-grain bullet right here between his eyes. Would have kept the skull too—but the bullet made rather a mess of it."

"I . . . I . . . Yes, I suppose so." McGillicuddy straightened, walrus mustache twitching as he inspected the long claws dangling at the flat ends of the feet. "My, rather large, aren't they?"

"This fellow went almost eight feet," she mumbled absently, pulling a pile of muslin skirts from the bottom of the trunk and placed them on the tiger skin. "Another five feet and he would have had me. James missed his shot so I had to follow up. They're remarkably quick when they charge. Wretched express rifle left a bruise on my shoulder like you wouldn't . . ."

"Ah! Here!" She settled back, bringing a long silk-wrapped bundle from the bottom.

McGillicuddy tore his eyes from the fabulous tiger

skin to the billet of silk—a wealth of material. Surely this genteel lady had no use for a couple hundred dollars of silk in the western lands. Why, if he could put that on his shelves, he could demand the most outrageous . . . He craned his neck to see.

With competent fingers, Arabella began unraveling yards of silk. Something gleamed, catching the light through the thin material. McGillicuddy mumbled under his breath, as the last of the fine fabric fell away from . . . *a rifle?*

"Oh, my." He hung there, staring, disbelieving.

"You like it?" Arabella asked innocently. "It's a Benjamin Bigelow seven-shot revolving rifle. The cylinder turns on the lower barrel which is a shotgun barrel. Most ingenious, don't you think? The upper hammer fires the rifle balls, the lower hammer ignites the shotgun charge. The ivory inlay and gold and silver filigree work were done by Omar Ammon in Bombay. The engraving by Iji Keet'hil in Bangkok."

Her practiced fingers broke the rifle down. Arabella studied the loads—yes, it was lethal—and snapped the pieces back together before removing a corroded percussion cap. From a jeweled tin, she extracted another and fitted it tightly over the cone.

"Ready for action," Arabella sighed, laying the rifle to one side and diving back into the magical trunk.

McGillicuddy's heart seemed tight. "My dear lady, surely you don't know how to use that . . . that . . ."

Her amber eyes took him by surprise, slightly flustered. "Oh, but surely I do," she informed him seriously. "With this rifle I can put seven forty-caliber holes in a foot square at one hundred long paces."

When she pulled the Belgian copies of Colt pistols— gleaming a wealth of gold and silver as well as several sparkling jewels that played beams of color over the ceiling—McGillicuddy felt faint. Of course, that was before she lifted the vicious-looking knife from the bottom of the trunk.

"And . . . and that?" McGillicuddy gasped.

"A creese," she told him. "An eastern form of dagger. The wavy form of the blade makes a larger hole when it slips past the ribs."

Hand knotted at the bottom of his throat, he barely heard her say, "Very well, that should be it. I shall leave tomorrow."

# Chapter 5

Cal Backman hawked and spat. Pulling off his brown felt, he dragged a hand over his forehead to soak up the sweat and jammed his hat low over his eyes. Hank moaned again where he lay to one side, the wreck of his face enough to turn a man's stomach.

Hank had finally come to his senses enough to undo Catton's knots. Then Cal had walked the half mile back to get their horses and outfits. The sight of Jeff's horse and belongings was enough to stir the ache.

Damn, the sun burned hot—and this still so early in the year. Summer would sizzle like a cast-iron fry pan on a Chinaman's stove.

Cal bent to his hole, the stubby handle of the shovel gripped tight in his calloused fingers as he pitched thick Kansas dirt from the hole. Oh, he'd pay Catton back for every second of this. He'd make him pay . . . real good.

"Deep enough." He chucked the shovel into the back dirt pile blade-first like a spear so it stood there. He shot a nervous look to Hank where he lay, jaw an inch off to one side like he had a fistful of hard candy stuck under his cheek.

"I'll kill that damned mule too," he promised.

Climbing out of the hole, he looked out over the tree-thick bottoms of the Big Blue River, the Oregon Trail a broad swath of thin narrow ruts and trampled grass. A thousand horses crossing the bottoms had left the ground wounded and stippled.

Growling, Cal Backman grabbed one of Jeff's limp ankles, dragging him roughly over the mashed grass. Without ceremony, he rolled him to flop into the shallow hole.

Hank Tent's eyes—pain-glazed—followed his movements as he began shoveling the loamy black dirt back into the hole. Refilling a grave never took as long as digging it. Funny thing, Cal thought. Maybe like God wanted a man to be able to get it over with faster once he'd chucked out the ground—knowing someday, somebody'd have to do that same thing for him.

*"Waaaa waaa."* Tent's mumble brought him upright. Hank pointed back down the trail along the shoulders of the green-fuzzed hills—emerald in the morning sun.

Several men rode there, dust roiling out from under the feet of a couple dozen horses they herded. Rough-looking men—they moved fast.

Panting with effort, Cal bent to shoveling. When the riders circled them, they caught him in the process of stomping the mounded dirt down.

"Backman!"

Cal looked up, eyes narrowing. "Branton Bragg."

The big man swung off his horse, eerie blue eyes narrowed to thin glowing slits. The white streak in his beard blazed in the brilliant sunlight. He moved easily, dressed in leathers, fringes waving as he walked.

Devil eyes, Backman thought as he looked into Bragg's face.

"What happened?" Bragg's voice reminded him of a growl. Big himself, Branton Bragg made him feel small—like he stood before a grizzly bear of a man.

"Thought you said this Abriel was an office boy . . . a businessman?" Cal let his anger buck him up, feeling his face go torrid.

Bragg's lip twitched, jiggling one corner of his white-shot golden beard. "Thought he was," he grunted surly. "I didn't have no time to keep track of them bastard kids. Campbell raised him. I just heard he owned a freight company."

"Campbell spent his time on the hard side," Backman reminded. "You forget he led brigades. Ordered them old trappers around."

"You want out?" One grizzled eyebrow went up, a glint behind Bragg's eyes.

Backman shook his head slowly, measuring. "Jeff's dead. Catton brained him with a rifle barrel. Hank's jaw's broke so bad he can't eat nuthin' but soup. No, Bragg. We're in. We want Abriel Catton. We're gonna kill him."

"Git yer hosses. Catton's headed fer Laramie, sure. We got extra mounts, we kin take some shortcuts and beat him there."

"Now, ifn the Lord woulda wanted a man t' sit on his ass through a Sunday, he'd put them thar church benches all over the world!" Bram insisted stubbornly, kicking the dirt with a round-toed boot that had seen better days.

Jeremiel shook his head stubbornly. How did he reach this bright-eyed brother? How did he get the message across that his everlasting soul already tilted over the line toward the Beast and the Pit?

Filling his lungs, Jeremiel began, " 'Thus the heavens and the earth were finished, and all the host of them.

" 'And on the seventh day God ended His work which He had made; and He rested on the seventh day from all His work which He had made.

" 'And God blessed the seventh day, and sanctified it: because that in it He had rested from all His work which God created and made.' This day, accordingly, is sanctified. A day for rest and——"

"Long-winded old bastard," Bram began, kicking dirt over the fire pit before grabbing for his saddle.

Jeremiel chewed the inside of his lip, desperately working his fingers. "I'm not a long-winded old——"

"Not you!" Bram looked disgusted, lips screwed up. "I's referring to God. All them mades an' therefores in that speech o' his. As if a fella'd be allowed t' fergit—specially with the likes of preacher folk around spoutin' the words every chance they git!"

"Blaspheming spawn of Satan!" Jeremiel exploded, seeing the twinkle of enjoyment in Bram's eye. He grabbed Bram's arm, spinning him around, waggling a finger under his nose. "You better start thinking, little brother. You've got to make some decisions about your life. Stealing——"

Bram yanked his arm loose, shoving Jeremiel away with callused hands. "Reckon when I want you piddlin round in my life, I'll ask ya! Till then, ya blowhard——"

Rage burst loose.

Unthinking, Jeremiel loosed a roundhouse, catching grinning Bram full on the point of the chin.

He bent down, grabbing the boy up by the collar, fist back for another punch when a little voice echoed in the back of his mind. *And Cain rose up against Abel his brother . . .*

He hesitated, dropping his blocky fist to stare into Bram's wobbly eyes. "I . . . I . . ." He patted Bram's cheek, reaching to lift him to his feet. "Forgive me, my brother, to have—"

Bram's right started low, building strength as he put all his might behind it. Lights in streaks blasted through Jeremiel's brain. He hit the ground full on his shoulders, feet slapping down in a puff of dust.

"I fergive ya," Bram mumbled. "Well . . . maybe after the next punch."

Jeremiel rolled away as Bram reached for him, kicking out to trip the younger man in a heap. Fists flying, biting, gouging, twisting, and wrestling, they went at each other. Bram wailed like a caterwaul. Jeremiel bellowed on his own, unleashing his frustrations as they belted each other back and forth over the torn ground.

Lungs heaving, Jeremiel broke loose and struggled to his feet, blinking against the gray fuzz in his eyes. Bram rolled to one side, clawing his way up, deep chest falling, shirt in ribbons.

Jeremiel danced in, planted himself, and swung. Bram blocked it and countered with a jab that caught Jeremiel under the ribs. Driven by anger, Jeremiel backheeled him and punched to the kidneys as Bram tumbled.

Not undone, Bram rolled hard against him, flinging him flat into the dust. Roaring anger, Jeremiel twisted, looking back in time to catch a full fist on the cheek. The world spun as he hammered back, feeling a hard right connect with a smacking of flesh and bone.

"Holy . . ." Bram groaned, winded, as he rolled away.

Lungs on fire, all of his body throbbing, Jeremiel propped himself up on his arms, hardly aware of the blood dripping down on the tattered remains of his frock coat. Blinking, he looked at Bram, satisfied with the bloody nose, the angry red of incipient bruises.

"That missionary, Sunts, teach you knuckle and skull like that?" Bram rasped, mouth hanging slack.

Jeremiel tested his teeth with his tongue. "No. I fear I ... have no ... little sin ... of my own ... to atone for."

"Wasn't eggzactly a model preacher's kid, huh?" Bram managed, tenderly probing his jaw with scraped fingers.

"My temper," Jeremiel agreed. Then, as if by magic, his stinging lips bent into a sheepish smile.

"Reckon as I could set a spell ... for one Sunday outa my life," Bram admitted, gasping as he poked at the cut over his eye.

"Perhaps ... if we prayed ... the Lord would understand ... a Sunday's travel," Jeremiel amended. "Brother Abriel ... is ahead of us."

A strange new voice came from behind them, jerking both up straight. "Then perhaps you *are* the men I'm looking for?"

Abriel had a lot of time to think about Colonel Oord and who his real father had been. Oord had a reputation for riding longer, harder, and rougher than anyone in the frontier army. That didn't amount to much of a brag from the army's standpoint. They had a habit of stationing infantry in places like Fort Mann. Ever see a foot soldier run down a mounted Comanche war party? Neither had anyone else—but men like William Bent nodded with respect when Oord's name came up.

Ab pulled a carrot of tobacco from a use-creased saddlebag and cut himself a chew with his Damascus-bladed bowie. When he got it juicing, he spit a streak into the white dust of the trail and squinted at the blue-gray rain clouds building beyond that flat horizon of spring-greening grass.

Having it in his hand, he looked at the big knife. Fourteen inches of blade long, the weapon weighed just over one pound. The cast brass hand guard bore little etched stars in the sides of the quillions. The laminated metal in the blade waved where the hammer strokes had forged each of the thin sheets of metal together. The handle of leather had been tightly bound with some sort of silver wire woven into a fleur-de-lis design. The pommel consisted of a heavy brass butt cap. Jeremiel's had looked exactly the same.

And his brother Jake's? Would his knife be the same? What sort of man would he be? Given the stiff-backed approach Oord showed the world, what sort of character was this next brother of his? Would he, too, have that spark of quality Jeremiel had shown? Abriel worked his chew, thinking, guts feeling funny and nervous.

He squinted, the first puffs of wind batting at his face. His eyes lifted to the torn-looking black clouds on the horizon. A damp odor of storm pushed ahead of the cloud bank, intermingling with the dust.

Ab pulled his poncho from behind the Mexican saddle. It began as an icy-cold rain; but being early spring out on the high plains, snow fell in twirls and wraiths by the time night darkened around him.

With two horses, it didn't take long to make Fort Laramie. Ab grinned to himself, considering the times he'd made the journey looking at the dirty end of a couple yoke of oxen; this trip proved a plain pleasure. On the long ride from Fort Kearny, he only passed a squad of Mounted Riflemen headed east and five trappers loaded to the gills with buffalo hides making tracks for Independence. The Mormon mail express, on the other hand, passed him like clockwork.

Laramie had changed, the officers' quarters—all two stories of it—were up. Two rows of stables stood complete and the company barracks had a permanent look. Ab could smell bread from the bakery. The old adobe American Fur Company structure where he'd had Mr. Husband sign manifests still loomed massive and square, looking somewhat better than the rest of the fort but only used for storage now.

Nestled under the bluffs where the Laramie River empties into the North Platte, the location enjoyed modest protection from the weather. Ab rode down from the swale that cut through the sandhills and looked over the growing cantonment. Here he would meet Jake.

"Or has he been ambushed too?" Ab bent over the saddle horn, keen eyes noting the details of the fort. "You here, brother? You here, Jake Catton?"

Black smoke curled out of the smithy as he rode across the trampled parade ground. A couple of drab gray-wood trading posts had located within a few miles of the fort. Several semicircular camps of Sioux and Arapaho had erected smoke-tanned tipis down on the floodplain. From his vantage Ab could see the children and dogs running around. On the hills, two large horse herds grazed. As Sorrel and Molly plodded past, men in yellow-trimmed blue dragoon uniforms waved and watched speculatively.

He shook his head, preoccupied with the changes that had come since Lieutenant Woodbury paid Mr. Husband four thousand dollars for the post. He missed him at first. Ab's gaze flicked across him, then stopped. He turned and studied the man who stared at him so intently.

A big man, he stood maybe six feet seven, shoulders square and packed with muscle. His waist looked thin, a tightly belted buffalo coat hiding most of his body. Nevertheless, he appeared traveled, trail-grimed, like he'd ridden hard and long. Two Colt Dragoon pistols hung at his belt along with a walnut-handled bowie. He sported leggins, beaded and fringed, and a broad-brimmed felt hat covered his head.

Ab met the intent stare, curious at the threatening posture and squinted eyes. But most of all, the bushy blond beard set the man apart. The whiskers glittered in the morning sun. An off-centered white streak of hair marked his right cheek—as if there were a scar hidden beneath.

*Branton? Is this man my uncle?*

They eyed each other, measuring, like two dogs with their hair rising, walking stiff-legged. Ab turned the sorrel and started to ride over. Too many questions needed asking. What could Bragg have against him? Or his brothers? Why was he hiring men to kill them? What secret lay hidden in the knives?

As he reined Sorrel, Bragg turned, rounded the corner of a building, and disappeared. Laramie wasn't that large a place. Ab chewed the inside of his cheek and rubbed the back of his neck. He'd find him. Only then did the sudden chill run down his spine. What if Bragg had already found Jake?

Worried, he headed for the headquarters and reined in Sorrel and Molly. Stepping down, he entered Major Sanderson's office and had to wait five minutes before they granted him an audience.

Behind Sanderson's battered and stained mahogany desk stood a guidon for Company E of the Mounted Riflemen. Sanderson rose and shook Ab's hand, brown eyes searching. He wore his light-colored hair clipped short. His face bore that distinctive look of a field officer now bound to a desk.

"Abriel Catton, sir," he introduced, finding the name

wasn't so strange anymore. "I've come to find my brother."

Sanderson frowned. "We've no Catton here, sir. Could you be mistaken?"

"This will explain." Ab handed him the letter of introduction and the request for leave Colonel Oord had penned for his son.

Sanderson's eyes scanned the page, stopping at the signature. His face furrowed before he looked up. A burning curiosity showed in his eyes; but he was too good a soldier to say anything.

"Lieutenant Oord . . . or should I say Catton . . . is due back this evening, sir. He went north with a couple of Sioux scouts to locate and map some water holes on the Dry Fork of the Cheyenne River. I'll send him to you as soon as he arrives. Given the colonel's request"—he motioned to the letter—"there will be no difficulty in granting him leave until such time as his personal affairs are in order."

And that's all? Ab stood, mystified. "Um, does he have to be back by any certain time?"

Sanderson smiled, a slight wry twist to his lips. "As long as it takes will be fine with me. Jake is a man of considerable honor and worthy of all my trust. If his affairs indicate a long leave is in order . . . so be it."

Ab traded some pleasantries, bandying information on the trails and talk of Indians and contracting, sharing scuttlebutt about who was doing what, but everything seemed finished. Stepping out by the hitching rail, he couldn't believe it. The army just didn't work like that, even in peaceful 1850. He frowned, puzzling over Jason Oord's peculiar authority.

Ab took up the horses, leading them by the reins, and found a place to camp in the immigrant grounds below the fort.

Ab built his camp, laying his packs out in an orderly manner and went looking for that bearded man. Odd, he never did find him. Only the drunken roaring of the notorious local guide, Mister Skye, broke the night as his Crow squaw wife, Victoria, chased him home with shouts of "Sonofabitch! What you do this time, Chief Skye?"

Silence continued, pickets calling out as evening fell.

With Jake coming in, Abriel became all the more nervous. As night thickened he wandered down to jawbone and chew tobacco with the men who ran the ferry. To ease his nerves, he grabbed up a section of broken cottonwood, whittling with that Damascus-blade bowie. Darkness fell and still no Jake.

On edge, some hidden part of his mind got its nose up, uneasy. Like the shivering of hair before a lightning bolt strikes, Ab chafed. Heeding that deep unease, he knew not to walk across scuffed parade ground. Instead, he circled, keeping to the shadows, moving with the night wind.

"Can't prove anything would have happened to me," he grumbled under his breath. "Then again, can't prove that I wouldn't have been lying out there with a hole in my tender body either."

The thought he might have the heebie-jeebies irritated him. Glaring into the darkness, he turned his collar up against the chill wind slipping down from the Rockies and grunted his annoyance. "Fool! Yer a hobble-footed boobolink."

So he went the long way back to camp and found Jake first.

Jake hadn't crossed by the ferry. Instead—spooky as a longhaired pilgrim in Comanche country—Jake crossed upstream.

Ab heard his horse coming out of the night, scrambling up the embankment from the Laramie River.

"Who goes there?" Abriel called out softly, still feeling that eerie sense of warning tweaking his bones.

"Lieutenant Jake Oord," a baritone answered as the horse—a big rangy dun that blended with the night—heaved itself over the lip of the cutbank. The animal blew its exertion. Ab could barely make out his brother's form as he dropped lightly to the ground.

"I've been worried about you," Ab said by way of greeting, hearing the funny sound in his voice. "Guess I sound like a . . ." Ab slapped his hands to his sides in frustration.

He sniffed at his bafflement. With Jeremiel, he'd been spared this awkwardness. Now he faced someone he should have grown up with. They shared a mother and a father neither one had ever known. What secrets and memories should have been theirs? Ab's heart began to beat fluttery and something big grew at the back of his throat.

"And worry you might. What's happened here?" Jake's voice came controlled, obviously on edge. "Who are you?"

*As if I wouldn't be on edge too—confronted in the dark by a hesitant stranger!* Abriel shifted on his feet, nodding, already liking this strange brother's calm way. In the faint light, he could make out the fist closed on the holstered pistol butt.

"Nothing's happened that I know of. Jake, I've just come from Colonel Oord. Is there someplace where we can talk alone. I have a letter for you . . . and there are some things which will be difficult to understand. Seems there's fellers trying to kill us too."

"Does this have anything to do with me being attacked?" he asked quickly. "Is this another of Dad's plots?"

"Huh?" Ab demanded, startled. "Was it a big man? White streak in his beard?"

"No." His voice came soft, deadly. "My Sioux scouts turned on me. Tried to kill me. They weren't fast enough ... and I know too much about the Sioux. They tipped their hand before they moved." He paused. "When I searched their bodies, I found something very interesting—gold coins. Too much for an Indian to carry. Before he died, one told me they'd been paid to kill me ... that the traders would give them ten gallons of whiskey for the yellow metal coins."

"Branton," Ab whispered. "Even here. Wonder what he'll do to get at Tom? Wonder how Jeremiel's doing with Bram?"

"You want to explain that?" Jake asked, reserved, hand still on the pistol butt.

Abriel filled his lungs to capacity, sighing his confusion. "It's a long story. One you won't believe until you read Colonel Oord's letter." Ab grinned. "And if he's been playing tricks to keep you on your feet, you might not even then." His throat constricted. "My name is Abriel Catton. Believe it or not, I'm your brother."

A long silence.

"You're right," the cultured voice added. "I think we'd better go someplace where I can read this letter of yours."

"Not across the parade ground," Ab warned. "I got me a feeling about that."

"You too?" Jake wondered. "We might be more closely related than I suspect." He hesitated. "Um, having just discovered a plot to kill me ... and having been shot at recently, would you mind walking ahead?"

Under Jake's direction, Abriel led the way to a stable

and lit a lantern after they cleared the corporal of the guard.

In the light, Ab turned, studying this new brother. Taller than Abriel by about four inches, Jake wore his uniform like he'd been born to it. A weariness lay in his face, as if he'd covered too many miles too quickly. They shared those eyes, the sensation similar to looking into his mirror in Saint Louis. Only Jake's face appeared more burnished by weather—even if he was younger. The resemblance affected Jake too.

"I think this letter from Colonel Oord will explain, Jake." Ab handed it over and Jake read it quickly. His reaction came as a surprise. No evidence of fluster in his manner, he didn't meet Ab's eyes as he turned to his horse, swiftly stripping the Ringgold saddle and brushing the animal down, seeing to the water, grain, and hay. He did it silently, face pinched, eyes somewhat grim.

Ab told him firmly. "I'm your older brother."

Jake stopped, bracing himself on a stall pole with one arm. Then, eyes level, he asked, "And how did my father, the colonel, take it?"

"He said that this changes nothing so far as he is concerned. Anytime you need him, call and he'll come running." Ab kept his voice neutral. "We have an inheritance coming. Compare these knives." He handed over the bowie. "There's some sort of secret. Some way the knives fit together to get us there. First, though, we've got to get all of us together."

Jake pulled his knife and looked at the two specimens before handing Abriel's back. "I don't understand."

"There are only five of them. You have three other brothers besides me; each one of us owns a knife. There are no others like them in the world. Somehow, they're the key to this inheritance Web Catton left us and we're supposed to have part of some map. I don't. Do you?"

The soft voice from the shadows took them by surprise. "Very good, Abriel. I must say, however, that the presence of both of you here is shocking to say the least. I thought I'd hired good men. It was with great difficulty I kept Cal Backman from coming in to kill you."

Ab turned, catlike, to face the big man. He stepped out, holding his two Dragoon Colts. Ab could feel Jake tensing beside him. The deadly barrels of the two .44 pistols glared blackly.

"Don't move, boys. If you do, I'll kill you just like that. I can take the knives from your dead bodies as well as not. Perhaps, however, that won't be necessary . . . not quite yet."

That golden beard with the white streak held Ab's eyes. He looked behind it to see Bragg's blue eyes, partly shaded from the lantern by the big hat. Satisfaction—backed by death—glittered there. This man could really hate.

"Are you my uncle? Are you Branton Bragg?" Ab managed, voice strangled. "Why are you doing this to us? What have we done to you? If Web killed your father . . . it was long ago!"

Branton nodded slowly, eyes still glittering deadly, as if he dearly wished to shoot. "That he did. Killed my father on Bloody Island in the Mississippi River . . . and made a mockery of honor by marrying my sister. To me, Abriel, you're all bastard rape spawn that he sired off her. You're also money." The voice gloated oily, then turned deadly serious. "Where's the ring, Ab? You're the oldest. It would have gone to you."

Ab shook his head slowly, frowning. "Ring?" *He's out of his mind! Look in his eyes, he's crazy. Insane!*

His voice cracked like thunder. "Yes, damn you, the ring! Give me the damn ring! *Now!* Or I'll find it on your dead body!"

The knuckles whitened on the hand centering the big horse pistol on Ab's heart. Here, he would die . . .

"Wait," Jake said quickly as Ab's chest quivered, waiting for the bullet. "I don't understand any of this! Why should I even believe either of you? My father is Colonel Jason Oord."

Death—looking through Branton Bragg's eyes—shifted away. Abriel tried to still the hollow quivering in his muscles. His body felt frozen—terror-locked. His tongue lay dry in his mouth.

"Believe what you will, Jake Catton," Bragg snarled. "It won't matter in the end. Like Abriel, you'll leave these stables on an ambulance stretcher. I killed your father, Web Catton, with pleasure. Now, here, you've both come to me at once."

The eyes shifted to Ab. "I missed you on the parade ground tonight. I had to hunt you—but you made it easier."

"I still don't understand. Why kill us?" Ab had recovered enough to get his wits together.

Bragg looked disgusted. "Each one of you bastard children took a part of my Laura's life. Each of you helped kill her. The money you're worth makes it that much better. Where's the ring? Tell me and you'll die quickly . . . like Web." His voice sounded persuasive, a coo.

"What money?" Ab heard the disbelief in Jake's voice. When Branton looked, Abriel jumped, knocking the pistol aside. The Colt cracked loudly, burning powder singed Ab's beard. His ear went numb with a squealing ring.

From the corner of his eye, Ab could see Jake fall to one side as the other Colt banged. Then he grunted, pounding brawl-hardened fists into Branton Bragg, trying to floor him with a boatman's uppercut, stamping at his feet, seeking to crush an arch or bark a shin.

With momentum, Ab bowled Bragg backward, one pistol flying into the hay. The horses began stamping, whinnying fear. Ab let out a bellowing roar backed with anger and fright.

A big hand grabbed his chest, twisting in the buckskin of his jacket. With no more effort than a terrier tossed a rat, Bragg lifted and threw Abriel off.

Rolling, he rose to his feet as the second pistol came to bear. The clicking as the hammer went back crackled the very air. Ab dove for a stall, heedless of the milling hooves battering dirt and manure about his head and shoulders.

Jake kicked Bragg's hand as the gun exploded in crashing smoke and fire—the bullet smashing the hock that planted itself before Ab's eyes. The horse screamed. Ab rolled away from those frantic metal-shod hooves and jumped to his feet in time to see Bragg smash Jake with a wicked left, kick him viciously, and reach for Jake's neck.

Ab took a flying leap, crushing Bragg backward into saddletrees and tack.

For all the good it did, Ab entertained the illusion of beating a tornado with a straw flail. Lights exploded in his brain. He shook his head, blinked to clear his eyes, and wondered how he got to the floor. Something smashed behind him, making him stagger to unsteady feet, fists up, ready to kill.

A funny light glowed in Bragg's eyes as he lifted Jake off the ground and threw him across the room to crash into the wall. Jake bounced to his feet and they both charged at once, howling rage.

Jake hit him. Ab hit him. Branton Bragg battered them both into the wall and turned as the corporal of the guard ran in, shouting, musketoon rising. Bragg spun quickly, beating the weapon up, discharging it, and pushing the man over headfirst. Then he disappeared—gone into the night, dirt sifting down from the roof where the musket ball had blown a hole through it.

Ab gasped, feeling his aching ribs where he lay piled against a stall. Blood ran in a steady stream from his nose. His ear sounded like someone held a tuner's fork next to it. Groaning, he flopped upright, lifting his hands, peeled and bleeding.

He blinked owlishly at the damaged knuckles. "Never let me down before. I think my leg's been pulled out of joint." He poked his tongue around in his blood-soaked mouth. "Two teeth is loose."

Ab looked at Jake where he'd been piled in a mess of harness. One eye had begun the process of swelling closed. Blood trickled down in a zigzag from a cut in his cheek, and his uniform had been shredded as thoroughly as if a mowing machine had been at it—but damned if he wasn't smiling!

"So, that's *really* my uncle?" Jake started to laugh, face stitching up in pain. "Then this whole crazy thing's true?"

The guard moaned, legs flopped, holding his head with two hands as he rolled upright. "What the hell . . ."

Ab pulled himself up the stall hand over hand until he got to his feet. Woozy, he weaved back and forth, willing the world to slow down and quit whirling.

Outside, beyond the stables, men shouted, booted feet pounding across the compound.

"We got to get out of here," Ab decided, trying to think despite the jackhammers that had broken loose in his head.

"Why?" Jake wondered, crawling over to pick up something gleaming in the lantern light. Branton Bragg's pistol!

"Army'll have more damn questions. They don't take

kindly to folks ruckusin' in their stables." Ab reached a hand to pull Jake to his feet.

"You say you had a letter of introduction from my father?"

"Colonel Oord, yep." He patted the bulge in his coat, satisfied to hear paper crackle. Blue uniforms poured in the doorway. Abriel groaned at the slit-eyed stare of the corporal. Didn't look good.

"You got a letter from Oord." Jake grinned. "There won't be any questions."

# Chapter 6

Traveling alone proved exceedingly difficult from several standpoints. Unsure, Arabella stared toward the west. For the first time, James didn't loom large at her elbow to protect her as he had through the years. Riding along, she kept fighting the urge to turn and talk to him, to share her thoughts and feelings as she had her entire life.

Now, behind her, where he should have ridden, clopped a strawberry roan packhorse. James existed only as a hollow memory, a pain in her soul. A vague phantom, he hovered at the edge of her thoughts, almost there while so achingly absent.

And of course, her fellow travelers made her miserable. The immigrants—their rocking dust-billowing wagons creaking along—stared openly, pinch-faced women eyeing her hostilely from under bonnets. Men, gawking worry mixed with astonishment, muttered under their breath.

She'd learned long ago that people meant trouble—be they Malay, Berber, Persian, or English. She could expect Americans to be no better—or worse. Someone would want to either protect, rob, marry, convert, or possess her—any of which would interfere with her liberties. Chalking it up to human nature, she accepted the reality and promptly altered her plans, leaving the trail.

For days, Arabella had navigated with her Saint Louis–bought map and her compass. At the same time, all those years at sea paid off. The familiar face of the heavens—learned by endless hours of listening at the elbows of Arabian helmsmen—showed her the way as clearly as her compass did in the light of day.

If only it weren't for the awkward and uncomfortable sidesaddle. Propriety! She spit into the evening shadow. A sidesaddle's only redeeming feature would be as a centerpiece for a bonfire!

"We live a brigand's existence," she giggled into a back-turned blue-gray ear as her sprite-footed steeldust wound down an upland ridge to the Platte. She called him Efende, Arabic for "friend." To the west, an orange-pink sunset flamed the sky, the horizon a dark purple silhouette.

She watered the animals at night, attending to ablutions. Through the day, she traveled back from the south side of the river, cautiously scouting her way, leading her packhorse around drainage heads and skirting thick patches of brush and ever-dwindling groves of scrubby trees, rifle butt resting easily under her fingers.

Her horse snuffled, ears pricked in the half-light as he followed the sandy ridge. Below her, the broad Platte shimmered silver among the cottonwoods, and braided through sandbars. Far behind, she could see the twinkle of fires around an immigrant train.

She had crossed from the Little Blue to the Platte, still hanging back from the rutted trail, keeping to the dissected uplands. Wondering at the changing environment, she enjoyed the solitudes of this wild country. No stranger to arid lands, she found a wild freedom here—a freshness of unspoiled wilderness. She'd never experienced the like—with the possible exception of the east African plains.

Happy, she filled her lungs to bursting, slowly exhaling the weariness of her long day's travel. The river lay just over there. She could wash the dust from her face, enjoy the cool—

"Well, well." The man's voice caught her off guard. The steeldust snorted, hopping sideways, leaving her scrambling for a hold on the clumsy sidesaddle. Fright paralyzed her for a split instant, heart hammering.

Arabella turned Efende sideways, squinting into the faint light. "Where are you?" Horse blocking her action, she slid the Benjamin Bigelow from the scabbard.

He stood up in the brush, a tall man wearing a well-tailored but travel-stained gray jacket. His pants fit tightly to his hips and thighs, and the rifle held low in his hands seemed well made and polished. Broad of shoulder, he looked to be in his midthirties, a broad-brimmed felt hat cocked back at a jaunty angle to expose his face.

Reserved brown eyes met hers. Over full lips, his nose fit his face, straight, patrician. A slight dusting of whiskers shaded his firm jaw in contrast to his pale high forehead.

"What in hell?" The man lowered the long Kentucky rifle to the ground, fingers lacing over the muzzle as he cocked his head and leaned on the weapon leisurely. "*A woman?* Riding alone? Now, indeed I have seen most everything in these western lands. You will allow me to escort you back to your wagon? Your people must be worried about you." His eyes narrowed. "What are you doing out here?"

A curious accent. French?

Arabella soothed her steeldust, moving Efende to keep the roan from cramping her with his lead rope. "I have no wagon. Now, you might answer the same question. What are *you* doing out here?"

He chuckled, shaking his head with amusement. "Uh, deer hunting, my lady. Which . . . I might add . . . is eminently more reasonable than anything you can come up with." He turned, indicating the brush-choked ravine below. "You see, whitetail deer frequent this little draw. A run goes down it. I had hoped to drop one for dinner—a prospect now most dismally dashed, I'm afraid."

Arabella straightened. "And how's that, sir?"

"By your movement and this conversation, any deer would be long gone, alerted to our presence. Second, a gentleman of breeding and honor would find it unthinkable to allow a vulnerable young woman to proceed alone. I have been told of savages, Pawnee, loose in the area. And"—he smiled—"there are other forms of rabble—frontier riffraff, the ones who have cast off the raiment of civilized behavior."

"Hardly a serious threat to my—"

He fingered his chin, lowering an eyebrow as he evaluated her. "Where is law out here, lady? Do you see the institutions of justice surrounding you? What brooding society watches to protect the rights of a lady here in the grass and wind? Eh? To where would you run?"

"And which sort are you, Mr. . . ." She lifted an eyebrow, keeping her combination gun hidden in her skirts. How would the steeldust be to shoot from?

"Leander O. B. Sentor, my lady. At your service." He bowed low, raking his broad hat off his head and sweeping it in a wide gesture that swatted it into the grassy soil. Straightening, his powerful eyes bored into hers. "And you, my lady?"

Something about him ... what? ... prickled her distrust. A hardness lay behind his eyes; a tightness etched by suffering or misery lay in the set of his mouth.

"Arabella Catton," she responded coolly. "And now, if you'll excuse me, I'll ..."

He held up a hand, shaking his head. "Impossible! What sort of a gentleman would I be if I allowed you to—"

"*Thank you*, Mr. Sentor," Arabella interrupted firmly, scowling. "You have failed to answer my question. Are you a ruffian or not?"

He laughed suddenly. Left hand easy on the rifle, he tucked his right into his belt and thrust out his jaw. "I only seek to accompany you ... to see to your safety and well-being, Miss Catton." A dangerous glint animated his eyes. "The word 'ruffian' carries many ..." A quick hand snagged Efende's bridle, causing him to shift.

She slid the barrel of her Benjamin Bigelow across her knee, pulling the shotgun hammer back in a loud click. "Release my animal! Quickly, Mr. Sentor. I don't have all night and my horses need to be watered."

In the gray dark, he squinted at the heavy barrel centering in his direction and chuckled. "So, you are a worthy one, aren't you, Arabella?"

She shivered when she saw what lay behind his eyes. Swallowing, her finger caressed the trigger.

"*Mister* Sentor. You will move aside ... *now!* If not, I will shoot you as a brigand." She kicked prancing Efende forward. Sentor promptly stepped aside, hoarse chuckling coming from deep in his chest. Arabella followed him with her rifle barrel as she rode past, the image of his laughing eyes threatening . . . no, promising he'd see her again.

"Have a nice evenin', ma'am." He laughed from behind as her horses scrambled down the slope. He shouted, "Do be *careful* of the dark!"

Desperate, Arabella clung to the sidesaddle, cursing the Christian propriety that made women endure such contrivances—and men in general—glad of the darkness so Sentor couldn't see how she had to cling madly to the saddle as the steeldust pounded down the dark slope.

She didn't camp that night, preferring to push her horses and herself—damning the sidesaddle and the stitches of pain that lanced through her legs, bottom, and back. Late that night, she led her horses into a brushy draw and dropped, aching and weary, to the ground.

Black patches of cloud obscured portions of the sky as she rolled out her blanket and ground cloth. Her legs cramped and howled from the perch of the sidesaddle. The thing *had* to go. If it took every penny that remained in her purse, she would have a man's saddle. And Allah could pour scalding water into the nostrils of anyone who disapproved!

As tension eased, she drew a deep sigh. She'd met her first threat in the form of Leander O. B. Sentor—and escaped. The memory of his words brought a sudden shiver to her.

And these mysterious brothers of hers? Would they be the same sort of men? Did they share that same predatory nature? Or were they longhaired and bearded? The kind bred by this wild land. Illiterate, uncouth, and unwashed?

Exhausted, she slipped off to sleep.

Her saddle proved easier to replace than she suspected. The thickset trader at Fort Kearny didn't bat an eye as she traded her sidesaddle and five dollars for a used Ringgold. She saddled, reslung her gear, and rode south into the bluffs before anyone proved the wiser.

As the day progressed, she made good time toward the confluence of the South and North Platte.

She thought of avoiding the tethered knot of horses at first. Then someone screamed in pain, the sound carrying horribly to where she sat partially screened by a swale. Another voice shouted something incomprehensible. Sentor's warnings returned to haunt her. And if bandits had captured some poor innocent. James would never have . . .

She bit her lip, remembering his warm humanity. Could she do less?

Cautious, Arabella let Efende walk up, her Benjamin Bigelow ready at hand. From the sounds, a man—or men—was being hurt, possibly even tortured. Her mouth went dry, heart thudding soddenly in her breast.

*Oh, James, where are you?* He'd know what to do. Like the time he stopped the Portuguese captain from beating that slave to death at the fort in Mombasa.

Loud in the morning air, the sounds of flesh being abused came to her ears. Wincing, Arabella pulled back the hammer on both barrels. If she didn't miss, she could dispatch eight with the rifle. Her .31-caliber Liege pistol she loosened in its scabbard. Heart in throat, she reined the big horse closer to the infernal wailing and bellowing.

She rounded the horses, and saw no torture, no captive being abused at the stake, instead she witnessed two men savagely beating the sap out of each other. The knot of horses looked on, amused, casting periodic glances her way and whinnying—the men oblivious as they mauled each other like enraged pit bulls.

Arabella looked around, seeing no more. She counted packs and two bedrolls as the men clawed their way apart and got to their feet, weaving. No more than a second passed before one lambasted the other and the brawl roared on again.

First Sentor, and now this? A loathing rose in her chest.

When the bearded man smashed the younger, she cringed, her very bones aching. Efende snorted at the flying mass of fists and feet and she pushed him close, thinking to put an end to it before murder occurred—only she appeared too late. They flopped apart one last time, panting, gasping, glaring at each other through blood and bruises.

Such *disgusting* barbarians, these Americans. The very thought of their bestiality left a nasty taste in her mouth. How many times had she witnessed knifings, Moslem executions, or whirling clinking scimitars ending in gushing blood and offal? The range and scope of human cruelty never ceased to turn her stomach. Nevertheless, fights in the rest of the world didn't seem so animalistically, physically . . . *American!*

Arabella shook her head slowly, praying her brothers were unlike these vermin.

"Reckon I could set a spell . . . for one Sunday out of my life," the young one panted.

The elder looked like a Christian preacher. The younger like a common thief. The thought seeped into her brain that one of her brothers allegedly preached. Could it . . . She narrowed her eyes, seeing how dirty and mangled the man appeared. *Impossible!* Surely no brother of hers could stoop to such behavior.

"Perhaps . . . if we prayed . . . the Lord would understand . . . a Sunday's travel."

Arabella decided she had enough. While they were down, she could simply ride away. By the time they got to their feet and saddled up, she'd be long gone. Leander O. B. Sentor—snide manner and all—proved a better lot than the like of this rabble.

The words caught her by surprise. "Brother Abriel . . . is ahead of us."

*No! Not these barbaric . . .*

Arabella bit back a solid Arabic curse and called out. "Then perhaps you *are* the men I'm looking for?" *Make it be that these . . . rabble are simply vagrant vermin!* She added, *"Allahu akbar!"*

They jerked up straight, turning to look. To Arabella's slight relief, neither jumped to his feet. They simply stared stupidly, disbelief writ large in their battered smeared expressions.

"Your names, please . . . *gentlemen?*" Arabella kept her rifle ready at hand.

The young one recovered first, an insolent grin begging to spread over his swelling face. "Bram, lady, Bram Catton."

*Oh, no!*

Arabella's heart stopped. Her gut seemed to sink—the sensation that of standing in the bow of a baggala as it dropped into a deep ocean swell. She fought the sudden urge to scream. "And you"—she looked at the blackfrocked man—"you must be . . . Jeremiel? Jeremiel Catton?"

"As the Lord is my witness," he nodded, mouth slackly open, chest heaving as he tried to catch his breath, still sprawled and propped—eyes slightly glazed.

Arabella closed her eyes tight, shaking her head as if to

break the spell of a mirage. "And this Abriel you speak of? He is Abriel Catton?"

"Why, shucks," Bram hooted, "y'all know 'bout us." He hopped lithely to his feet, walked impudently over to grab Efende's reins, grinning up at her. "What's a purty thing like you doing out hyar . . ."

His eyes grew round as a tsava melon as she slid the shotgun barrel into his face and added coolly, "You will release my horse and back away this very instant."

Bram's swallow reminded her of a dry bilge pump. He scrambled backward, to Efende's relief.

Jeremiel stood slowly, eyes on her combination gun. "There is no need for fear or hesitation on your part, ma'am. I am a man of God, a preacher of the faith, and—"

"Ya mean yer a man with a right solid left hook!" Bram sputtered, dabbing at his bloody nose.

"Just a taste of the thunder of the Lord, little brother." Jeremiel's smile went shy. "Like Samuel's thunder was delivered unto the Philistines out of Mizpah!"

Arabella jerked up as a familiar voice called, "I see there's no need of my rendering assistance. Once again, Miss Catton, you have handled yourself superbly!"

She turned to look, seeing Leander O.B. Sentor standing up from the grass, his long Kentucky rifle easy in his hands. Bram and Jeremiel spun on their heels. Bram immediately began to inch toward the horses.

Arabella heaved a sigh as she looked from one man to another. "How did *you* get here, Mr. Sentor?"

He shrugged, rifle ready as he walked forward, form-fitting pants legs rustling on the grass. "Let's say I was concerned, Miss Catton. How could I live with myself should you come to grief with the likes of these . . . uh, cutthroats?" He had his head cocked in that familiar manner, studying Jeremiel and Bram with a hard squint.

Arabella sagged in the saddle, easing the hammer down on the Benjamin Bigelow and sliding stiffly off her new Ringgold. "They may be cutthroats, Mr. Sentor. But they are also my brothers." Never in her entire life had she uttered such difficult words. She looked at Sentor and fought the subconscious urge to shiver.

His brown eyes shifted to her, knowing, satisfied. A curious look.

Bram grinned again and whooped something that sounded like an Indian war cry. Jeremiel looked confused.

These were kin? Looking back and forth from each blood-streaked face, Arabella felt ill.

Branton Bragg had vanished into the night like the Dakota Territory wind. Major Sanderson sent a detail out to bring him in; they found nothing. Curiously, no one really seemed to question what happened in the stable—although eyes spoke volumes. Ab began to speculate on just what sort of special assignment Jake enjoyed. Jake didn't say anything about it, and Ab didn't ask.

The next day, Ab sat propped in Jake's bunk, sore scabbed fingers laced over his belly as he looked at Jake. His brother sat on the facing bunk cleaning one of the pistols Branton had lost. "We need to find Indian agent Fitzpatrick," Ab decided. He would have grinned at the size of Jake's eye—but it hurt his swollen mouth too much.

"Fitzpatrick left here on the fourteenth of February. Seems he's trying to put together some big council with all the plains tribes. He and my father, uh . . . Colonel Oord, cooked it up. As usual, the colonel's name stays out of it."

"Where'd he go?" Ab wondered, seeing the trail stretching out across the wilds in his mind. He hoped

Jeremiel would show up with Bram and there would only be one more brother to find.

"Big Timber down on the Arkansas," Jake supplied, holding the cylinder up to the light where he swabbed out chambers. "He was supposed to meet with the Cheyenne, Arapaho, Comanche, Kiowa, and some Apache down there."

Jake slipped the cylinder on the spindle and glanced thoughtfully at Abriel.

Ab sighed. "I guess it's tough when a perfect stranger turns your world upside down, almost gets killed with you in the stables, and wants you to ride halfway across the territories."

Jake chuckled hollowly. "Doesn't happen every day."

Ab winced at the thought of the distance. Then he gasped at the pain in his face.

"What was that business about a ring?" Jake asked suddenly, somber. "Was that human grizzly bear really my . . . uh, our uncle?"

Ab ran a wet tongue over the stinging split in his lip and shrugged. That hurt too. "Don't know anything about any ring. All I know is that Branton Bragg supposedly hated Web Catton for killing his father. Laura, our mother, made Web promise not to kill Branton. From what was said last night Branton killed Web. Somehow, these five knives solve the puzzle of where Armijo's gold is buried. This ring is all new to me. I never had it."

"He said there was money involved. Do you suppose he inherits something with the heirs dead?" Jake's face remained still as moonlight on the pond, but a whirlwind twisted behind his eyes.

"You look like you enjoy this," Abriel grumped.

Jake's eyes flashed. "Mr. Cat . . . Abriel. *Brother Abriel*," he corrected. "You will learn that I am very good at intrigue. Between the colonel and West Point, I've learned a lot about ... well, let's call it intelligence work."

"Spying." Ab grinned—and regretted it as his battered face lanced pain. Jake's mind appeared to have that devious bent to it. Fifth in his class at West Point?

Jake's expression looked smug—proud. He said nothing, but drove the barrel key in place.

"You read the will and letters," Ab grunted, feeling a sudden frustration. "That's all I know." What was he doing out here? How could Web Catton have him all stirred up with mad uncles, hidden gold, some unknown ring, and who knew what else? In Saint Louis, he could concentrate on building his freight company, enjoy good food and drink, read what he wanted for entertainment, and relax until the next big contract.

"Perhaps the answer will become apparent when we are all together," Jake mused.

Ab's thoughts went to Bragg, remembering how he'd whipped them both. And if that guard hadn't showed up when he did? Bragg would have killed him and Jake with his bare hands. Not only that, but Bragg had to be forty if he was a day!

Abriel ran a hand over the hard-packed muscle in his shoulders. He didn't know many men stronger than he. He could hold up the back of an oak freight wagon while they changed the wheels and never break a sweat. Yet Branton Bragg had flung him around like a cloth doll!

Jake carefully loaded the pistol and slipped it into a new holster. Scowling, he slid his knife out of the scabbard—Oord having given it to him the same Christmas Abriel and Jeremiel had received theirs. He had his lips pursed as he studied the knife, running his fingers over the fleur-de-lis pattern on the handle.

Ab could see the question in Jake's eyes before he

asked, and handed his blade over for Jake's careful scrutiny.

Some minutes later, Jake leaned back and took a deep breath, the knives in his strong hands. "Bragg knew where to find both Jeremiel and me. We will assume that you were on the trail before his men could get to Saint Louis. We must also assume that he knew where Bram and Wasatch would be too. One of our brothers may be dead. If that is the case, we can assume Uncle Branton would have at least one knife."

"How would he have known?" It didn't make sense; none of them knew about the others. Ab couldn't even convince himself Jake believed any of it yet.

Jake looked up, giving Abriel one of those stares people give mules, dogs, and—he guessed—brothers when they weren't being smart. "He claims to have killed Web Catton. Of anyone, Cat—our father—would have known where we were. Who we'd been left with. Assume that he had something written down. Bragg would have obtained it."

"Or else Bragg tortured it out of him." Ab's voice went husky as he remembered those odd blue eyes. He didn't want to think what it would take to get a man like Web Catton to talk. As scared as Uncle Branton left Abriel, the thought proved sobering.

"That," Jake whispered, his voice almost hoarse, "is always a possibility."

Bram bent over to look at his reflection in the pooled muddy water of the Platte. Damn! His nose looked like a puffball stuck on a cow flop. Some wallop old Jeremiel had in them big bony fists of his.

"Better that you let us take you back to Independence at least," Jeremiel insisted. "Really, the preference would be to escort you to Saint Louis. There you could stay with Mr. Campbell until—"

"Absolutely not."

Bram grinned at his reflection. She sure didn't like any of them. Why, he'd seen kinder looks in the eyes of folks digging screw worms out of a cow's side!

"Indeed, Miss Catton," Sentor insisted, "I would find it a singular honor to see you back there. The least I could—"

"No."

Bram winked at himself, straightening and walking back to the fire. He swatted at an early mosquito and hunkered down, enjoying the stubborn look on Arabella's face. Jeremiel brooded, looking like one of them thar patriarchs he insisted on spoutin' about.

Sentor, now, he didn't set right on Bram's stomach. Why? The way he looks? Some contrariness in his eyes? Nope, Leander Sentor has him a secret—and it ain't whar the old hen hid the egg neither. But the man seemed fascinated by Arabella, a calculating look in his eyes when he studied her in the firelight.

Reckon he's plumb gone on her, Bram decided. He studied his sister. Yep, she's a looker. Too bad she's my sister!

Jeremiel pleaded, "The *only* thing you can do is return to—"

"No!"

So Arabella had Jeremiel stonewalled? That tickled Bram plumb to the bottom of his little pitter-pattering heart! "Reckon y'all kin head back t' Independence without me." He looked mildly at the storm building in Jeremiel's bruised countenance. Placatingly, he raised his hands. "Now, brother Jeremiel, nuthin' in yer Bible 'bout it bein' a sin to find a feller's kin, is thar?"

"You got enough sin," Jeremiel grunted, "to do for one lifetime."

Arabella's lips twitched. "I, too, shall proceed on my own."

Jeremiel's preacher voice boomed, "It is unseemly for a lady to travel these—"

"And if I refuse?" she asked, glowering. "What will you do then, Mr. Catton? Beat me like you did . . . him?" Her voice dripped disgust as she shot a finger Bram's way. Bram smiled impishly at her, enjoying the scowl he got in return.

Jeremiel wilted, dropping his eyes. "We all have our moments with the weaknesses of the flesh. The lot of man—"

"Is not my concern," Arabella finished, voice clipped. "The fact remains, you and the rest have engaged in a quest. I shall not remain behind, stuck in Saint Louis, while you seek my father's estate."

Sentor straightened suddenly, mouth going hard, head cocked to look keenly at Arabella.

Bram squinted. Sentor looked like a bull snake sighting on a bird. He could see thoughts racing in the man's mind. Aw, he couldn't know nuthin' about all Armijo's gold. Naw, thar's sumpthin' else making that fire burn in Sentor's eyes.

As quickly, Sentor resettled himself, facing them calmly. "Then you must go. I extend my condolences to you and your brothers." He seemed to soften then. "I, too, lost my father." He lifted his fingers to study his nails, frown lines deepening in his forehead.

Bram watched Arabella's face go tight. She turned on Sentor next. "And I certainly have no use for your services, Mr. Sentor. I appreciate your concern. At the same time, I remind you that my business is none of yours. You are quite at liberty to return to your deer hunting."

"One of the great truths of this country lies in the fact that no man may dictate to another, correct?"

"Nor shall you dictate to me, Mr. Sentor."

Sentor's eyes narrowed a hair. "Nor would I attempt to. Indeed"—he waved at Jeremial and Bram— "you have found your brothers. Nevertheless, I, too, am headed west." He looked at Jeremiel. "If you wouldn't mind another man in your party, I—"

"No!" Arabella snapped.

Jeremiel waved a bony hand. "Mr. Sentor, in view of my . . . sister's objections, I think not, though we offer our Christian gratitude for your fine offer."

Sentor nodded, a perfect gentleman. "Very well, I shall leave in the morning."

Arabella closed her eyes, hands clenched tightly in her lap. Bram sucked his tongue, waiting as she fought for control. He appreciated the way she sat so prim, back straight, just like the ladies he'd seen in fancy carriages in Little Rock or on the big plantations around Shreveport or Galveston.

He noted the way Sentor seemed to have relaxed, his expression that of a cat in the sun. Confound it, Sentor *was* hiding something. Bram pulled at his ear. Heck, here he'd just found a sister and this jasper shows up to pay court to her and she don't like him. And neither do I, Bram grunted to himself.

At the same time, he had started to like Arabella. She had a certain spunk he respected—even if she looked at him like a tick in a cow's udder. She might look like a china doll—all dressed in fancy silks and rustly things that caught in the brush—but, hang it, she had gumption.

"Y'all can come with me, Arabella," Bram grinned—shooting a sly baiting glance at Jeremiel. "Shucks, we kin talk about how much fun sinnin' is ... or sumpthin' Jeremiel, here, might lose his soul over ifn he heard."

His brother's eyes glowed with sparking ball lightning. A warm satisfaction lit in Bram's chest as he smiled smugly. Jeremiel's eyes narrowed to slits. Got him again!

The look Arabella gave him mighta froze a rattlesnake in the sun. She forestalled Jeremiel's hot remark. "Thank you, Bram." The muscles slid under her tanned skin. "However, I'm not sure we'd have much ... sinning ... in common."

Bram smacked his knees and laughed. "Nope, reckon not, but I could sure teach you a thing or two about hoss thievin'!"

Jeremiel dropped his head into his hands. "This is all *impossible*." Groaning like a man trying to lift a mule, he looked up, eyes pained as they searched the heavens. "Lord, what sin hath I committed that I be saddled with the burden of Job? In Your light I find my—"

"Does he preach to you all the time?" Arabella asked.

Bram started to answer, only to have Jeremiel cut him off.

"When I found him, a group of men were in the process of hanging him for his sins," Jeremiel said coldly, although Bram thought he could detect a slight thread of humor hidden in there. "You see, he'd stolen one of their horses, and in this part of the country—"

"Horse thief?" Sentor wondered, looking Bram up and down with a scowl. "From the way he looks, he's certainly not much good at it."

Bram caught Jeremiel struggling to keep his dour composure.

"Now, just a confounded minute hyar!" Bram howled, feeling his face go hot. "I done stole more hosses than—"

"As poorly as he steals horses, you can imagine the

state of his salvation. Slipshod as well, I'm sure."
Jeremiel's finger lanced at Bram, his voice dropping.
"And I *will* show you the error of your ways."

"But if that hoof hadn't—"

"And they were going to hang him?" Sentor asked, secret humor in his eyes.

Resigned, Bram sighed heavily. "Had the rope round
my neck. No 'gonna' about it. They's in the process
when ole Jeremiel, here, rode up."

Arabella's eyes were on him, disbelieving. "And he
talked them out of it?"

Bram screwed up his face, despite the bruises and cuts.
"Wall, now that ya brung it up, he didn't eggzactly talk
'em out of it."

"Now just you hold it, little brother," Jeremiel sputtered. "I don't know what you're about to . . ."

"Ya see," Bram continued, enjoying the effect he had
on Jeremiel, "they was all so plumb set to stretch hemp,
and Jeremiel started apreachin'. Preachin' like you
wouldn't b'lieve."

Even Jeremiel watched him now, leery.

"Why, the word of God filled the air!" Bram added,
letting a feeling of excitement grow in his voice. "And
sumpthin' happened then and thar." He balled his fist,
enjoying the sudden gleam of anticipation in his brother's eyes. "Jeremiel here, he asked me, 'Do you see the error of yer ways, sinner?' Yep, I says, I shure do!" Bram let
his eyes go wide, hand to his heart, seeing he had
Arabella's attention and Sentor's as well.

"Go on," Jeremiel whispered uneasily.

Bram licked his lips. "So I stared around at them pil-
grims and told that I see'd Satan all round me." He nodded seriously. "An' shore nuff, I plumb did."

"And then Jeremiel started apreachin' and preachin',

his voice athundering as he held up that Bible o' his!" Bram asserted, hesitating. "Like I said, it filled the air!"

"And then what happened?" Arabella asked.

Bram looked nervously down at his patched homespun jeans. "Most amazing thing I ever see'd," he whispered, fingering a hole in his knee. "Most amazing thing."

"Yes, go on," Jeremiel added quickly. "I am witnessing for you, brother."

"Reckon that's good," Bram nodded soberly. "'Cause otherwise, folks might never b'lieve a word of the miracle what happened next." He pinched his split lip, looking up, seeing the animation in Jeremiel's eyes.

"Yes . . . yes," Jeremiel prodded.

Bram swallowed hard and added, "Why, brother Jeremiel put all his heart into that preaching an' his voice rang in the air like I done told you. And he plumb . . . bored them sinners so bad he put 'em right to sleep and I rode off 'thout 'em knowin' I's gone!"

Shocked silence, then Arabella giggled. Sentor laughed under his breath. Jeremiel made a strangling sound, his fingers reaching like snags for Bram. But he was too late. Bram—fired with adrenaline—hopped to his feet and bolted into the darkness.

# Chapter 7

*J*eremiel blinked awake, the cool dewy air refreshing as he drew it into his lungs. Carefully, he unknotted himself from the huddle of blankets and stood stretching in the gray light of predawn.

Bram, ears like a rabbit's, cocked one blackened eye open and gave him a satiric grin before flopping over on his back and snuffling off to sleep again. Jeremiel turned his boots upside down and shook them vigorously, grimly remembering the time he shoved his foot in on top of a scorpion.

He pulled his coat over his shoulders and walked out past the horses. He cast a glance back at the camp. A raucous snore erupted from Bram's uptilted mouth and Jeremiel entertained a devilish prodding to drop something wiggly into that yawning maw.

He bit off a slight chuckle, remembering Bram's story of the hanging. Little imp, he'd proved to be a handful.

He frowned at the sight of Arabella's blankets, wincing as he thought about her first impressions. A preacher engaging in fisticuffs with a horse thief. Worse, he cringed under his tarnished self-image. What could he do with this Arabella?"

The horses watched him, heads up with interest, nickering and snuffling, awaiting attention. He passed them, walking to a gray rise to the east. There, he lowered himself to a sandy bare spot, deflated by wind, and clasped his hands.

Lost in prayer, he watched the eastern horizon glow purple, red, and finally orange. The plains breeze was tugging lightly on the wisps of hair hanging over his ears. Birds added their melodies to the morning and far off a coyote made one last complaint to the dawn.

"Lord?" he pleaded, reaching with his heart as well as his words. "Lord? I am Your servant—yet I feel I am losing my way. Take me, I give myself over into Your hands. Show me the path of Your righteousness. Forgive me my sin of passion when I raised my hand in violence to smite my brother." A hollow emptied under his heart.

"Forgive me, my Lord. Hold not the sins of my father, Weberly Catton, against me." His eyes beseeched the red disk of the rising sun. "As Your apostle Matthew wrote, You, too, were led into the wilderness to be tempted by the devil. As You dealt with and vanquished the devil, share Your strength for my coming trial—for I know not the tempter's guise . . ."

How long he knelt there, he couldn't say, but the sun rose a hand's-breadth above the slightly irregular horizon when he heard voices. Swallowing hard, he stood, brushing sand grains from his knees as he turned toward the camp. Arabella stood, feet braced before Leander O. B. Sentor's horse. The dapper gentleman sat easily in the saddle, elbows braced on the horn, his long rifle over the bows.

As Jeremiel walked closer, he heard, "You're sure you want me to leave, Arabella?"

" 'Miss Catton' to you, sir."

Jeremiel could see a red flush to her cheeks. Did she spend all her life angry and disapproving? Of course, if she didn't want the protection of a man, it shouldn't be forced on her. He hesitated. Or should it? He glanced half-expectantly at the sky. "This family business is too new . . . too strange."

That smooth deep voice replied, "Indeed, Miss Catton, I shall proceed west . . . and perhaps our paths may cross again."

"I sincerely hope not." She crossed her arms, sandy-blond hair flicking in the morning breeze, expression uncompromising.

A most striking woman, Jeremiel thought. No wonder Sentor is attracted to her. But who is he? Jeremiel studied him, oddly reminded of Psalms, "For strangers are risen up against me, and oppressors seek after my soul." . . . Or my sister.

Sentor worked his lips. He shot a quick evaluative glance at Jeremiel, where he stood looking on. "No doubt God will keep an eye on Jeremiel. And if chance should fail, Bram has the ability to steal enough horses to get you away."

Jeremiel eased the sudden bristling, remembering the trouble his temper had led him to with Bram. He studied the man. Sentor had a certain military bearing about him. The look of command—of unforgiving dedication to duty—wrapped about his shoulders like a mantle. One could almost think of Napoleon on his . . . But how silly.

Arabella gasped an irritated breath and added hotly, "Mr. Sentor, if you don't mind . . . leave!"

Bram stood up, fists knotted at his side, jaw sticking out as he took a step forward.

Sentor chuckled lightly, tipped his hat off curly brown locks, and bowed in the saddle. "Pleasant journey." He turned his horse and left at a gallant gallop, riding smoothly.

Jeremiel turned, shading his eyes to watch Leander's horse pound into the sunrise. He sighed wistfully. "There is something about him . . . something wrong."

"Reckon snakes is better kept in a barrel whar ya know ya won't git bit unawares-like," Bram added from where he packed.

Ignoring Bram, Arabella looked distrustfully at Jeremiel. In a cultured voice brooking no dissent, she added, "Best that he be gone. I shall have my hands full enough with you and Bram now. Provided the two of you can keep your tempers from flaring, we'll get along quite nicely until we meet Abriel." She stopped, finger to her chin as she thought. "Tell me. Is he as rough as you and Bram?"

Jeremiel shrugged, exasperated, hands wide. "What you observed yesterday . . . I mean . . . Oh, never mind. And as to Abriel, I'm not sure how you would judge him, Miss . . . uh, Arabella. Unlike Bram and myself, he has the look of a . . . a . . ."

"Ruffian?" she supplied, head cocked, measuring. "I'm sure I can't wait." At that she turned in a swirl of skirts, stepping away, back straight.

"Wait. I . . ." But he stopped, mouth working emptily as Bram snickered behind him.

"Got yer size real good, Jeremiel," Bram goaded.

Flustered, Jeremiel swung to glare at him, seeing the cunning narrowing of Bram's eyes. Bram lifted his chin, shrugging slightly as he looked quickly away. "Course, I heard her saying she wisht she had someone ta read Bible with of a night." And he walked away, a curious swing to his shoulders.

Jeremiel hurried to where Arabella checked the cinch on her big steeldust.

He laid a hand on her shoulder. "Ab's not a ruffian. It must be difficult with your raising, but out here, things are not as simple. Grace and style do not make the measure of a man here. Instead—"

She carefully plucked his hand from her shoulder, before inspecting her fingers for smudges and wiping them on her skirt. "Brother Jeremiel, grace and style do not make a man anywhere in the world. Either he is a man . . . or he isn't."

She spurned his offer to help her mount, swinging lithely onto the big horse.

The way she set the horse didn't—oh, no. He gasped. "You know, it is highly improper to ride a saddle astride. A most unladylike—"

"I got rid of that abomination in Fort Kearny," she told him crossly. "I am well aware of what is and is not considered seemly and proper for a lady. Currently, I am more interested in survival than propriety."

Well, how could even a preacher argue against that? "Seriously, Arabella, why don't you allow us to find you a way back to Saint Louis, where—"

"No."

He looked into her frosty eyes and shrugged. "Very well," he capitulated, leaving to go about his own packing. How did he reach her? Bram's attention he could always get with a good uppercut. His ears reddened.

Bram? Bram suggested Bible readings.

As Jeremiel mounted, he reined his black over to where Arabella waited under her pink parasol.

"Forgive me. I seem to be getting off on the wrong foot with everyone. This sudden family business ... well, it must be very difficult for you—as it is for me. Perhaps you would tell me about your, um, foster parents? You must come from a good Christian home which—"

"A good Christian home?" Amazement gave way to giggles, causing her to place a hand to her mouth. Wryly she added, "Well, I'll admit I've been to Canterbury, Notre Dame, the Vatican ... and even the cathedral at Wittenburg where Martin Luther tacked up his theses." She fingered her chin, studying him sideways. "On the other hand, I don't suppose Mecca, Polannaruwa, the Temple of the Emerald Buddha, or the Ganges would meet those requirements. Let alone—"

Jeremiel's heart caught. "My God, *a papist*? Surely the hand of Rome isn't upon your soul?"

Her mouth twitched amusement before she sputtered a laugh through her fingers as she walked Efende away. Within several paces she burst out, "Hardly a Catholic at all! *Allahu akbar!*"

Jeremiel sat, rooted to the saddle, as Bram walked his loaded roan over. "Y'all have a nice chat with God out yonder?"

Jeremiel shook his head, muttering listlessly, "The tempter in the wilderness." To Bram, he added, "Lord forbid. Let us hope she is not Roman. Or worse, tainted by Babylon."

"Huh?" Bram asked, face screwed up. "She been to all *them* places?"

"I fear so," Jeremiel agreed.

Bram looked back to where Arabella walked her horses down the trail. "Golly. Why, if she's been that far, why, I reckon she's even made it so far as New York and Baltimore and Boston!"

\* \* \*

Spring on the high plains proved to be no joy. Arabella squinted into the cold blowing wind, wincing as fine grains of sand and dust pelted her. A storm front loomed ominously in the west, tendrils of cloud twisting out from the puffy thunderheads.

She pulled her steeldust up and stepped down, going back to her pack. From under the manty she pulled a burnoose and *kafia*. Quickly slipping into them, she noted Bram's amazement and Jeremiel's baffled curiosity.

She glared into the preacher's face as she caught up her stirrup and practically vaulted into the saddle. Her *kafia* she pulled tightly about her face, enjoying the relative protection of the heavy cloth.

"Now, that's sumpthing!" Bram laughed. "Why, I reckon that's the latest style in them eastern cities."

"It is, Bram," Arabella shouted over the wind. "Only the cities they wear these in are more eastern than you can appreciate."

Rain pattered and spit at them as they passed the trading posts at Scotts Bluff, and watched the Mormon mail go rattling past in a flurry of flying manes and quick waves.

As the cloud-masked sun slid lower into the west, Jeremiel pushed his black next to Efende. Bundled in his damp blanket, hat pulled low, he licked his lips.

"Yes, Jeremiel?" Arabella asked, trying to keep the acid from her voice. The question had been eating at him all day.

"I . . . You . . ." He blinked, mouth a thin line under his neatly clipped beard. "Arabella, you are my sister. At the same time, I know nothing about you. You and I must talk about your soul, I mean. I'm not just concerned as a man of God, but if I'm your brother. Well, have you thought . . . thought . . ."

"To save my soul?" she finished, studying him through her *kafia*. "Are you so sure it isn't saved?"

The muscles jumped in his cheeks and he had a pained look in his eyes. "Arabella, are you a Christian? I ask you point-blank. You use words I do not understand. This allyou ackbar—"

"*Allahu akbar*," she corrected. "It's Arabic for 'God is great.'"

His mouth opened slightly. "Arabic?" His fingers knotted tightly around the reins, knuckles standing out whitely. "Arabella, are you a Christian?"

She bit her lip, a quickness in her heart. Slowly, she shook her head. "To you, brother Jeremiel, I am an infidel."

He seemed to wilt in the saddle, eyes going closed as his mouth worked. "My own sister," he whispered miserably under his breath. He raised his confused eyes. "*Why?*"

"My soul is fine, Jeremiel," she told him, the gentleness in her tone coming from the heart. "You see, I've been many places, seen many religious men. I've seen blood running in the streets over God. Protestants and Catholics, Sunnas and Shi'ites, Mahayana Buddhists against Taoists, and the Hindus and Sikhs hack each other to pieces. No matter where—"

"But are you familiar with the message of Christ? That God gave His only begotten son to die—"

"Quite familiar," she asserted.

"Then you accept that Jesus is the son of God?"

"Of course. The Koran states that emphatically."

"Then how can you believe this Mohammed?"

"Because there are many ways to Allah."

He scowled at her. "I know little about the other religions you mentioned, but I've read of Allah. We barely discussed Islam in seminary. The Crusades were fought against Islam . . . to bring Jerusalem back to the fold of Christianity." His fist pounded the saddle horn, anguish in his eyes. "I don't . . . Very well, Islam claims to spring from the flesh of Abraham, but you have already stated you believe Jesus is the son of God. How can his Holy Word be usurped? How can you tempt your soul away from God? The influences of Satan—"

Arabella gritted her teeth. "Allah is *not* Satan! That's what I was trying to point out earlier when you interrupted. Everyone kills in God's name—condemning themselves to perdition in the process, I might add." She shook her head furiously, thundering, "Allah, Christ, Yahweh . . . *it's all the same damn God!*"

Color drained from Jeremiel's face, a dazed look filling his eyes. "Thou doest *damn the name of God*?" Jeremiel's mouth worked soundlessly, face stricken.

Arabella swallowed, seeing Bram chewing his lip, looking nervously at the back of his horse's head. "My beliefs, Jeremiel, do not include Satan. They do not include churches."

"Figgered she'd make a fine hoss thief," Bram mumbled.

"But the Bible . . ." he began, rubbing fingers over the gutta-percha cover.

"There are many books," Arabella replied, seeing the fire born in his eyes. "The Koran, the Dhammapada, the—"

He opened his hand in supplication, voice dropping. "I . . . I can help you. Please, let me show you the way to avoid the fiery pit before—"

"I will avoid it on my own, Jeremiel." Her voice went wry, a curious deadness in her heart. "I . . . Thank you. I know what you're trying to do. I can hear the earnestness in your voice—but no, my soul is fine, thank you."

"But the Lord of Hosts is waiting!" Jeremiel licked his

lips. "The sin of Eve lies heavy on womankind. You've only got one soul, can you afford mistakes? The hand of Satan may lie upon you without—"

"Where?" Bram demanded, standing in the stirrups, gawking. "Musta washed his hands first 'cause he didn't leave no smudges!"

Jeremiel scowled at Bram, turning back to Arabella. "In the book of John, we read—"

"Enough!" Arabella hissed, anger electrifying her as she glared at Jeremiel. "Stop it! My soul is my concern, *brother*, and none of yours."

Jeremiel bit back his anger, face contorting. "I am no more than a minister of the gospel." He rapped his knuckles on the heavy Bible.

"I *will not* be preached to," Arabella insisted. "Now, leave me in peace." She kicked Efende forward, cantering out in front, thankful to have escaped, feeling the sodden emptiness in her heart.

Bram whooped out behind her. "Why, brother Jeremiel, reckon she's got more gumption than yer right hook!"

So she had found a brother—and driven a wedge between them. Would it have hurt to have listened . . . just a little?

"Oh, James," she whispered, "why did you leave me like this? Who can I talk to? Who can understand?"

They camped that night, a silent trio. Overhead, the weather closed in on them, oppressive, threatening, thunder rolling out of the high-piled clouds, lightning flickering in the distance.

Jeremiel, face pinched, took his Bible and walked out into the dusk.

"Reckon he's plumb upset," Bram offered. He flashed his gaze from the fire to Arabella. "He ain't really a bad sort. He's just got God ridin' him purty hard is all."

Arabella nodded. "I know."

They sat silent, the fire crackling up, gusting this way and that with the wind. "Reckon, for a man of God, Jeremiel's got more than his share of devils to wrassle with."

Arabella chuckled softly. "Yes, I suppose. They all do."

"All?" Bram cocked his head, thinking.

"All that I've ever met. Men of God, I mean." She leaned back trying to keep the wind from invading her burnoose. "All over the world, Bram, people try and find truth in their concept of God—and it always remains elusive for all but a lucky handful."

Bram seemed to roll that around in his mind some before adding a cryptic "S'pose so."

Arabella added softly, "Not every American minister ever comes face-to-face with a practicing Moslem either. It must be quite a shock."

Bram looked back to the little knoll Jeremiel had climbed. In the dusk they could barely make him out, a lonely figure, head bent. He faced into the coming storm with the thick book cradled in his arms. A sudden flash of lightning outlined his silhouette on the little knoll.

"Reckon," Bram added huskily, "that this hyar trip's agonna be hardest on him of us all."

They rode into Fort Laramie in a pelting spring rainstorm—the high plains kind with temperatures in the high thirties. From where he sat under an awning whittling Ab spotted Jeremiel. Sure enough, two others followed. Bram? And perhaps Tom?

Jeremiel didn't look any different as he stepped down and shed his slicker. That black frock coat might have been a little grayer from dust and had been torn here and there. His eyes were duller, less fiery. He still carried a heavy leather-bound Bible over his saddle.

The other man—well, boy—drew his attention next. He was long and lanky, beard still spotty with youth on hollow cheeks. At nineteen Bram hadn't filled out yet but he'd be a strapping man. Amber Catton eyes stared out from under a greasy worn-looking hat. Those eyes, in contrast to Jeremiel's, laughed at the world—a twinkling dancing behind them. The nose between them wasn't the straight specimen Ab had come to associate with the Catton family. Bram's looked like it had stopped more than one hard object.

Ab fingered his own nose, broken here and there along the way between Saint Louis, Fort Lewis, Santa Fe, and Salt Lake City. He decided maybe he shouldn't pass judgment.

He looked hopefully up at the third rider, head wrapped in a rain-glistening slicker. He looked young— very young. Tom? Wasatch? Had Jeremiel found him? Ab stood nervously, letting the stick he'd shaved down drop as he slipped the bowie into its scabbard.

"You found Bram . . . and Wasatch?" Ab asked, shaking Jeremiel's callused hand.

His deep baritone voice rang out with authority. "The paths of the faithful are beset by tempters, brother. My trip has been a trial of the wilderness." He tried to keep his face straight but a sour smile twitched at the corner of his mouth.

"You must be Bram," Ab greeted the grinning youth who slouched down out of the saddle, muddy worn boots plopping onto the puddled sod of the parade ground with a splash.

The grin widened. "Howdy, big brother!" Bram's voice sounded higher, almost shrill compared to what Ab expected. Bram stuck a paw his direction and shook, the grip firm. "Thank Gawd y'all ain't like this hyar Jeremiel!

'Nuther day of the Lord this an' that an' the other thang, an' I'd be plumb set t' slit my own throat!"

"Any trouble?" Ab asked mildly, seeing Jeremiel's jaws clenching.

"The salvation of the weak and evil is a constant trouble to the servant of the Lord!" Jeremiel pointed out, fierce eyes on Bram. The youth simply grinned, showing straight white teeth before he mocked a bow. Then a deep reservation filled his eyes as he looked up at the third rider.

"You must be Tom," Ab greeted, stepping out into the rain and offering his hand up to the slicker-hidden youth.

"No, Abriel. I'm not." The words left him stunned.

"You . . . you're a woman. Uh, sorry ma'am. I thought you were . . . were . . ."

"Your brother Tom," she added positively. "No, I'm afraid not." She slid off the saddle, and Ab realized he'd been fooled by her riding astride too. "Indeed," she added, taking his hand in her long slim fingers, "I'm your sister, Arabella Catton."

Ab's mouth dropped open. He stared into her tawny eyes and gaped, undone.

"Well, for God's sake, don't just stand around in the rain," Jake called from under the porch.

"This here's Jake." Ab motioned to the lieutenant, eyes locked on Arabella. "How . . . I mean . . ."

She looked at him, hard eyes meeting his. "It's a long story, Abriel. Perhaps a cup of coffee or tea would be in order and I'll try and explain."

Jake moved forward, subdued, and took each of their hands in turn, mumbling greetings under his breath.

"And this sinner, in the name of God, is your responsibility, brother Abriel." Jeremiel shook his head sorrowfully and pointed a long finger at Bram. "Yea, that I should find him about to dangle from a hangman's noose. The word of the Lord God should fall upon his deaf ears." Jeremiel raised his voice to a roar at that. "Such are the trials of Abraham and the Prophets. Take him, brother. Keep him from harm, for this servant is sorely tried!" He paused. "Oh, and keep one hand on your money when your back's turned."

"Now, just a cussed minute!" Bram cried. "I wouldn't never—"

"All yours, brother," Jeremiel reminded, winking.

After that, Jake's voice seemed comparatively quiet. "I think sister Arabella's suggestion of coffee might be most appropriate." His glance shifted from Jeremiel to Arabella. "I think we've all got a lot of catching up to do." He turned, shouting, "Private! See to these horses. Bring their gear to my quarters."

A miserable-looking private nodded, saluted, and collected the reins of the horses—a considerable herd, Ab noticed.

"Servant of the Lord, my royal butt!" Bram groused. "Shoulda seed him talk that bunch outa stretching my neck. Didn't have no other trouble agittin' hyar. Wall, maybe that left hook of his rattled my box a little. My teeth is still loose!" Bram's face screwed up. "And then thar's all that cussed noise 'bout that Brabbas feller. Reckon ifn I heared his name agin, I'd puke!" He stabbed a stubby thumb Arabella's way. "And keep me from being atween them two. Lord o' God, they can go on some!"

Jeremiel's eyes lowered under his water-dripping black hat. He avoided Arabella completely, the strain heavy in the air.

"What's this hanging business? Didn't One-Eyed Mike take care of you?" Ab couldn't help but ask, remembering Campbell's hesitation.

Bram's eyes clouded. "Posse ketched Mike 'bout a year ago. Put a bullet through his right lung. We outrun 'em but I couldn't do nuthin' fer Mike. They fetched him good. Things was kinda hellacious fer a while 'til I found me a market for my hosses."

"You raise animals?" Jake asked, interest perked.

"Naw," Bram grinned. "Reckon I stole 'em for a living!" He stuck his thumbs in his pockets, and dogged if he didn't actually blush while Ab's mouth fell open. Jake's expression pained.

"Give me strength, he's bragging!" Jeremiel's voice rolled stentoriously. At the same time, Ab caught a faint glimmer of affection hidden away in the tone.

"You gonna yarn me 'bout that Brabbas feller agin?" Bram looked annoyed.

"Barabbas!" Jeremiel thundered in correction.

Ab could see Jake looking back and forth, face mirroring his own. Whatever else, life on the trail with these two wasn't going to be easy. To soothe the situation he added, "Reckon all that leaves is Wasatch. Sooner we make tracks, the sooner we catch him."

"And lose Mr. Sentor," Arabella added fervently.

"Who?"

"Aw"—Bram scuffed his toe—"she's got some dandy eastern jasper flush in love with her. He's been adoggin' the trail like a coon hound after a skunk. Why, he'd be abringin' posies in—"

"That's *sufficient*, Bram," Arabella said coolly. To Abriel, she added, "He was hardly welcome."

Bram's voice had a note of amusement as he changed the subject. "Ain't gonna make many tracks with this coon in yer party." He stuck a knobby thumb in Jeremiel's direction. "He sits on his ass . . . uh, assets of a Sunday. Cain't git him t' break camp t' save yer soul."

Jeremiel's response came just as quick. "It's to save

your soul, sinner, that we rest upon the Sabbath! The commandments of the Lord—"

"Hell!" Bram spat. "He's started again! I'm gonna sell these hyar extry hosses, find me a jug and some o' them wimmen, and tie one on in a road ranch that'd rot ole Jeremiel's soul ta git close to!" And at that he left, hobbling purposely on his bowed legs.

"Whiskey? Cypriate women?" Jeremiel gasped, apoplectic. "The work of the Lord is never done!" He sprinted after Bram, bellowing vigorously, arm upraised and finger pointing.

Ab must have looked worried when he faced Jake, because the lieutenant burst out in a laughing fit and slapped Ab's back. "How are we gonna live with that?"

Arabella shook her head. "It isn't easy. Come, gentle—uh, brothers. Lead me to something warm to drink. After those two, I need *sane* companionship."

"The Ottoman Empire is in dire straits, isn't it?" Jake asked, awed at the revelations Arabella continued to startle him with.

Abriel snored softly, feet sprawled out from his chair, long since bored with the topics of conversation.

Arabella lifted a shoulder, lost in thought as she cradled her teacup in long fingers. "They can't hold on much longer—at least not to their far-flung possessions. The Balkans are falling apart and the Russians are pushing to expand their base in the Black Sea. England is pressuring the Turks for influence." She smiled wistfully. "A man with intelligence and money can make a fortune there now."

"But you spent your time in the Indian Ocean?" Jake pressed, seeing how lines of fatigue lay in her face, unwilling to give up the fascinating conversation.

She looked up at him, a knowing smile tracing the corners of her lips. "You're very good, you know."

Jake caught himself, a sensation of delight filling his breast. He *liked* this sister of his. She had an exceptional head on her shoulders. "How's that?"

She chuckled softly, walking to the dented blackened coffeepot and pouring another cupful. "Dreadful stuff this. In the Arabic states, they make coffee as thick as honey and flavored with spices."

She turned. "But to answer your question, I've been questioned by the best on three continents." She made a motion with her hands. "It's the way the questions are asked which give an agent away. Everything is leading—to allow the subject to freely give away more than they intend."

Jake nodded, respect growing. "Then, point-blank, what did you and your James do for a living? Just carry spices and fabrics?"

Arabella nodded easily, but Jake noticed the teasing misdirection in her eyes. "That's right. In exchange for European manufactured goods."

Misdirection? Why? What trade item would have left her . . . "Guns," he whispered, a sudden tension in his gut. "Of course." He watched the corner of her lip tighten. Her eyes seemed a little harder. She gave him no more clues.

"You have a very romantic imagination," she added lightly. "I assure you, that would have been too dangerous. The Royal Navy—at the request of the East India Company—would have taken a very dim—"

Jake nodded to himself, putting the pieces together. "And that's why you can be so conversant on the tribal wars. Who else but a gunrunner would know where—"

The door opened and Bram slipped in, grinning like a fool. "Whew! Thought Jeremiel was agonna gab my ear off! Shoulda seed his expression when I bought that jug o' whiskey!" Bram stuck out his lip, staring at Abriel. "Huh! So that's what a big brother looks like? Somebody pulped him not too long ago."

"Branton Bragg," Jake supplied, knowing his own eye didn't look all that healed. "And he's still out there somewhere . . . waiting."

"Then we had best leave in the morning," Arabella added. "We have four of the knives. It remains now to find Tom and the last knife before we move to recover Armijo's gold."

"We?" Jake asked.

She smiled at him, eyes narrowing. "If the British, Portuguese, Turks, Malays, Siamese, Cantonese, French, and Russians couldn't stop me, Jake, do you really think you can?" She sipped her coffee, challenge in her eyes.

"Shucks," Bram offered, swaggering across the room to settle himself in a creaking chair. "Let her come. She takes some of Jeremiel's attention off me."

"Impossible!" Jeremiel entered, closing the door behind him. He studiously ignored Arabella where she stiffened in her chair, a predatory glare in her eyes. "Granted, Arabella is a most accomplished traveler, the wilderness is no place for a woman. We do have a responsibility to see to her safety."

"He has a point," Jake conceded, keeping his voice even. "This is not the sort of land you're used to, Arabella. There are no cities——"

"Nor are there in Africa," she retorted.

"A lady doesn't belong in the wilderness," Jeremiel declared absolutely.

Jake felt the tension between them, hostile, heavy in the air like an incipient lightning strike.

"You didn't exactly think I was a lady a couple of days

ago, brother Jeremiel. Surely, if my soul is already damned, I have nothing to lose."

Stunned silence continued.

Jake swallowed. Jeremiel had told her she was damned?

Jeremiel turned toward the wall, dropping his head, voice lowering. "I didn't say that."

Arabella stared at him, cup resting lightly between her long fingers.

"They're right," Abriel added, stretching and yawning where he sprawled in the chair. He met Arabella's eyes, unflinching. "You'd have no privacy on the trail. The food's bad. Most of the streams got what we call gyp water in them. Uh, causes stomach upset. Cleans you right out—if you know what I mean. For a woman, well, it'd be an unnecessary hardship."

Jake smiled at her, reassuring as he knelt by her chair and told her earnestly, "Don't worry. We'll see to it. I promise. We'll bring you your share in Saint Louis."

"I'm coming along."

Abriel took a deep breath and blew it out slowly. "No, Arabella, it's impossible . . . like Jeremiel says." He got to his feet, boots scraping on the wooden planks. He walked to the little window and stared out over the sloppy parade ground. "Branton's out there. We can't take the chance of you getting hurt. He's not right in the head. Crazy. He could do anything. Ambush us. I'm not sure he'd stop if he knew a woman was with us. And if he caught you . . ." His thick shoulders rose and fell. "He's got a lot of rough men with him."

"I've faced rough men before," Arabella replied reasonably. "Some of whom would appall you."

Jake hated to say it. "He's right, Arabella, I'll make arrangements here for you to ride back to the States with a military detachment. It's for your own good."

She closed her eyes, muscles sliding under her smooth cheeks. "For my own good," she repeated under her breath. She opened her eyes, nodding slowly at Jake. "Very well, you may make your arrangements, brother."

# Chapter 8

Arabella watched them loading up, Jeremiel haranguing Bram about the tin of whiskey he'd roped to a packhorse. Jake effortlessly flipped his Ringgold over his dun's back and caught up the cinches, pulling them tight. He saw her, smiling, buckling the breast strap and crupper before walking over.

Such a handsome man, she thought. Too bad he's my brother.

"Don't worry about us," he began, then saw her eyes. "Look, I'm sorry. Seriously, Arabella. It's for the best. You don't have any idea what it's like out there."

She crossed her arms, extending a toe to draw an arc in the hoof-scuffed dirt. "I did come up the trail."

"That's civilized. Out there"—he waved toward the distant Laramie Range—"is another world. There you'll find no roads, no people except Indians and occasional trappers—and danger is everywhere."

She sighed, smiling up at him. "All right! I told you to make the arrangements with Major Sanderson."

Jake sniffed in the cool air and looked over to where his bay mouthed his bit, slapping his tail at nonexistent flies. "He'll put you on a supply detachment headed for Leavenworth."

She looked down at the arc she'd dug in the dirt. Tapping the ground with her toe she asked, "And you think you'll find Tom Fitzpatrick on the Arkansas?"

"Yep, place called Big Timber." He hooked his thumb in his belt. "That's just downriver from Bent's Fort. Someone is always going up or down the Sante Fe Trail. I'll write from there and give you a progress report about what we've learned."

She smiled gracefully and took his hand. "Thank you, Jake."

He nodded, slightly off balance, and went to his horse.

"Take care, Arabella," Bram told her sincerely when he led his stolen roan over. He lifted a shoulder nervously as he kicked the toe of one boot with the heel of the other. "Reckon I'd as soon have ya come 'long. Keep me from eatin' all Jeremiel's fire."

She lifted an eyebrow. "I'm sure you would."

He grinned, a lock of sandy hair falling into his devilish eyes. "Yeah." Then he sobered. "Uh, look, I know Jeremiel ain't been doing all that well fer hisseff, but don't hold it agin him, Arabella. I think he's a good man inside. He's just got that hang-fire temper is all. Reckon he didn't mean what he said out thar on the trail."

"I'll keep it in mind, Bram."

His impish grin widened. "Aw, I only agreed with Jeremiel and the rest so's that Leander Sentor an' you could have a bit o' privacy fer yer courtin'."

Arabella started forward, seeing the devilment twinkling in his eyes. She ended up laughing. "Bram Catton, you are the most reprehensible young rascal in all ..."

Bram vaulted onto the roan, guffawing as he kicked the big horse away. "See ya, sis!"

Arabella glared at his retreating back.

"Take care." Ab waved as he trotted past. "We'll see you in Saint Louis. Tell my fath ... uh, Robert Campbell, we'll be back in a couple of months."

She waved. "I'll tell him as soon as I see him."

Jeremiel trotted past, eyes forward, refusing to look her way. Arabella lifted her chin, breathing deeply. The pack animals lined out at a trot, flipping up bits of sod as they hurried along.

"Miss Catton?"

She turned to find Major Sanderson at her elbow.

"I hope we can make your stay here comfortable for the remaining time you're with us."

She smiled warmly at him, curtsying. "I'm sure you will, Major. I'm only sorry my time will be so short."

"Looks like they're leaving," Cal reported, sliding off his lathered horse. "They headed up the trail. Probably goin' t' Reeshaw's bridge ifn I's a guessing man."

Branton Bragg sniffed, rubbing his hands back and forth over his knees where he hunkered by the fire, fringes swinging. He pulled a creased envelope from his pocket, squinting at the words.

"Four of them?" he asked.

"Yeah," Cal added. "Abriel was with 'em. He's the one I want."

Branton Bragg looked up from the letter, ice in his glittering eyes. "You wait, Cal. You ride with me, you do things the way I say."

Cal's face tightened. Jaw set, he nodded.

Branton grunted satisfaction and studied the letter

again. "Says here that the youngest boy is with the Cheyenne. White Wolf's bunch." He leaned back, thinking, scratching his beard as the other men watched. "White Wolf runs to the south of here. So, why they going west? They only got four of the knives."

"False trail?" Cal wondered.

"Uh-huh." Bragg looked up. "That's my guess."

Jake kept one of the Dragoon Colts Branton lost that night in the stables. He gave his old Walker to Jeremiel the day they left Fort Laramie. Ab kept the other Colt and Bram ended up with all the single-shot horse pistols hanging on his saddle. Thinking about it, Ab decided that Bram liked the way it made him look.

During the days they had let the stock rest up at Laramie, Ab came to the conclusion the only benefit accrued to their horses. No sooner did Jeremiel pull Bram away from a whiskey jug than the kid ran down to the "ladies" who worked one of the nearby road ranches, Jeremiel exhorting and preaching as he dragged Bram out of the house and back to the fort and safety. There Bram immediately started a game of three-card monte with a group of soldiers. Using Jeremiel's frantic sermon as a distraction, he cleaned the soldiers out of all their pay and most of their personal possessions. There at the end, Bram listened to Jeremiel long enough to give the privates back the things they'd need to survive.

In the meantime, Arabella and Jake spent considerable time in conversation about people and places Ab had never heard of. Must come of a West Point education, he decided. And then he had time to muse on the strain between Jeremiel and his pert young sister.

Summer seemed to be around the corner as they rode west out of Fort Laramie. Ab looked back at the string of pack animals, Molly doing her best to run the lead rope under Sorrel's tail. Ab yanked hard on the heavy rope, causing Molly to lower her eyelids thoughtfully, ears back. Jake led the way, turning off after dark along a trail left by a herd of buffalo, the tracks mixing in the damp chopped soil. They wound over cobble-covered ridges as they climbed the drainage divide, Jake taking them down the Laramie River. The next day, they made it to the mouth of the Chugwater. That night, he gave his old Walker to Jeremiel.

Frowning, the preacher stared at the heavy pistol, a curiously confused expression on his face.

When they had camp lined out, Ab walked out with Jeremiel. "This is how you load a Colt pistol. Cap the flask with your finger, turn it like so, and press the lever. Now pour the powder into the cylinder. Drop the ball on like so and drive it home with the loading lever. Pinch the cap on the nipple back here and that one's ready."

Jeremiel followed the steps until he had loaded five of the cylinders.

"Wait, now," Ab warned. "If you know you're in a fight, load all six. Otherwise leave that one empty for the hammer to rest on. Safer that way. Less chance you'll shoot yourself."

Jeremiel nodded, raising the pistol and aiming. When the prairie dog—watching thirty yards away—stood up, Jeremiel shot the top of his head off.

"Not bad for a first shot," Ab muttered.

"Perhaps the Lord steadied my hand, Abriel." Jeremiel smiled, a twinkle gleaming in his eye.

"Maybe," Ab agreed, slapping him lightly on the back.

Jeremiel put the next five shots into a four-inch circle on the prairie dog hill. He reloaded and proceeded to do the same thing again. Abriel pulled his hat off and scratched his head, looking quizzically at his brother.

"You sure you never shot before?" Ab shifted uneasily. No pistol could put every bullet in the same place—but Jeremiel had just come close. "That ain't bad fer a preacher."

Jeremiel's hard eyes masked his true feelings. "My parents were devout, Ab. I never even touched a gun until Jake handed me this one." He stared thoughtfully at the cold steel in his hand.

"Go ahead," Ab prompted, "Talk to me. You look worried. What's on your mind?"

Jeremiel sighed wistfully. "The tempter in the wilderness, brother Abriel. In Independence, they tried to murder me. I am reminded by Psalms 45:3 in the Holy Book to 'Gird thy sword upon thy thigh . . . and in thy majesty ride prosperously because of truth and meekness and righteousness,' "—he looked at the pistol filling his hand—" 'and thy right hand shall teach thee terrible things.' "

He smiled, amber eyes like a tiger's. "No, Abriel, it is that the concept is so very simple. Align the sights on the target and pull the trigger so the hammer falls on the cap without the gun moving."

"Uh-huh, and I can practice for a year without coming close to shooting like you just did." Abriel squinted at him skeptically.

The memory of the hatred in Branton Bragg's eyes stirred his mind. "If we run into our uncle, Jeremiel, he'll kill you first thing. Jake and I got lucky. Don't try and talk to him. You'll have to shoot him on the spot. For some reason, we're worth a lot of money to him. Jake thinks it's over the inheritance . . . but there's more. The man's crazed like a hydrophobia skunk."

"The Lord is my shepherd; I shall not want."

Jeremiel's eyes kept dropping to the pistol, fingers running over the polished steel like a caress. "And if the agents of Satan come upon me, 'The spoilers are come upon all high places through the wilderness: for the sword of the Lord shall devour from the one end of the land even to the other end of the land; no flesh shall have peace.' "

Ab stooped and squatted, looking up at his brother. "I got another thing to lay out. I know you feel right strong about Sundays and all, but out here"—he waved a hand at the open rolling grasslands—"travel is time and time is often the difference between alive and dead."

Jeremiel looked at him, that trace of amusement behind his eyes. "I know, Ab. I have made my peace with the Lord—and Bram. It will be a sin I may perhaps yet redeem." He shrugged. "Mostly, we rested on Sundays to teach my young brother propriety. I greatly fear the wrath of the Lord shall deny him the experience of manna."

"Uh-huh," Ab agreed, wondering what manna was. "Well, didn't want you riled any when we made tracks between Saturday and Monday. Not only that, but days sort of get mixed up out here. Sometimes you can't tell what day is what."

"Moses could tell as he led Israel through the wilderness," Jeremiel reminded.

"Yep, I suppose. I guess it's up to you now . . . lessen he happens along, brother." Ab smiled weakly and got to his feet. "Take some more practice shots with that thing. You might need it to 'convert' some heathens out here."

Jeremiel laughed and shrugged as Ab walked off—then proceeded to put the next five shots into that same circle on the prairie dog mound.

"How's he shoot?" Bram asked from where he tended antelope steaks over the fire.

"Like he was born with a gun in his hand," Ab grunted. Jake glanced up from stitching his bridle back together. Leather always needed fixing on the trail.

"Huh!" Bram looked up. "Reckon I'd better pay more 'tenshion to what he's a saying 'bout God. Ifn belief gits you to shoot straighter, I reckon I kin be as Christian as the next feller."

"Did you really steal horses for a living?" Ab couldn't help but ask the question that had been eating at him. "How did you come to that? Hell, boy, that'll get you killed out here!"

Bram grinned, eyes going soft. "One-Eyed Mike was a trapper with Weberly. In fact Mike told me Web Catton stories all my life. When the fur business got bad in the late thirties, Mike turned to coarse fur. Shootin' buffalo was too much work so he drifted down Arkansas way. I don't know, one thing led to another and pretty soon he was runnin' horses from Missouri to Texas, sellin' 'em, collectin' 'nuther batch down there an' runnin' 'em back to Missouri. Peg Leg Smith and Kirker done the same over to Sante Fe. Paid on both ends and we had us a permanent camp up in the limestone country in the Ozarks.

"When Mike took that bullet, I reckon I had to do sumpthin' so I took up the trade. Mike teached me real good. Hell, ain't no better hoss thief in all the country than me!" Bram looked so proud Ab thought he'd bust.

"Yeah," Ab said, licking his lower lip, "and you was so good Jeremiel woulda found a corpse aswinging if he'd been a minute later. He told me 'bout that cigar."

Bram rubbed his nose, a pained expression on his face. "Ain't never smoked me another neither. That rope took all the enjoyment outa ceegars."

"Yep, well, little brother, you gotta make me a promise right here and now." Jake's voice came firmly. "You don't steal any more horses from anybody, you hear? I can

track you into the very dirt if I have to, and when I do
. . . you'll think hanging is a sight better than the thrashing I'll give you!" He pointed his bowie at Bram, staring
down the edge.

"You got a left hook like that Jeremiel?" Bram hedged.

"Worse," Ab grunted. "I'll tie you up so you can't get
away and have Jeremiel preach to you until yer ears fall
off or the angels come home."

Bram's face washed pale and big-eyed. He said, "Now,
I wasn't feared o' Jake thar. Reckon I can skin him when
it comes to hidin' tracks. But you, brother Ab, you jist
scairt unholy hell outa this child!"

Jake rolled his eyes.

Everyone had been so taken with Bram's antics, they
didn't notice the look on Jeremiel's face when he came
walking into camp. "We've got company," he said softly.

"Where?" Jake sprang to his feet, his Mississippi rifle
cradled in his arms, eyes on the horizon.

"I saw a man on the ridge over there. I couldn't tell if
he was an Indian or not. He was dressed in skin clothing. He'd been watching me practice shooting. I looked
up and saw him, waved a Christian greeting, and he
seemed to disappear, just like that."

"Reckon I'll go take a look-see," Jake decided, padding
silently in the moccasins he'd adopted for the trail.

"Need cover?" Ab asked. Jake just looked at him, a
knowing smile on his lips. Then he started back the way
Jeremiel had come, traveling silent as a puma in the
caprock.

Ab grunted, "What if it's Bragg out there with a rifle,
just waiting for you to be a target? You fergit what that
loco snake is like?"

"Ab," Jake's eyes chided. "I learned from the best.
Don't act like my big brother. I'll be fine."

Bram started pulling his pistols, checking to see which

of the packs offered cover. Jeremiel glared at the fouling on his dirty pistol. As he turned the cylinder, Ab could see the smoke had gummed it up a little.

Ab sneaked up to keep an eye on Jake, even going so far as to check the load in the Hawken and make sure no caps had fallen off the Colt. Then he saddled Sorrel in case he had to ride out quick.

Jake ended up making a complete circle of the camp. He returned with a puzzled expression on his face.

"Jeremiel, you sure you saw someone up there?"

The preacher looked at him straight. "A man dressed in skins, with Indian beadwork on the chest, stood there. He was carrying a long rifle." Jeremiel hesitated. "I can't swear to it, but I think he had a beard. The design on his chest looked like a blue flower on a white background. There was a skin sack at his side that looked like it was full of something. When I waved, he just seemed to disappear. Like smoke."

Jake frowned, chewing his lip. "I should have found a track out there. He didn't walk on air, did he?"

"Hoodoos," Bram muttered, eyes going big and swallowing hard.

Ab spit a stream of tobacco and threw the quid in the fire. "Did he do anything?"

Jeremiel shrugged. "He just seemed to be watching. I thought it was funny that he didn't change his expression or wave."

"This beard," Jake asked, "was it blond? Was there a white streak in it on the right cheek?"

Jeremiel shook his head. "I didn't really see. From the angle of the light, his face looked silvery in the sun."

Bram's mouth tightened as he muttered under his breath, reaching over to pat Jeremiel's Bible, eyes flickering around nervously.

"So," Ab mused, fingering his chin, elbow propped on knee, "whoever it was, it wasn't Branton Bragg."

Jake's voice sounded a little tense. "He didn't leave any tracks. That ain't right."

"Hoodoo," Bram mumbled, making signs in the air with his fingers.

Jeremiel threw him a disgusted look and bent down to pull one of the antelope steaks from the fire.

They scouted as they moved south, all eyes peeled for the Hoodoo man.

Ab delighted in the country as they rode up the Chugwater bottoms, sandstone headlands rising to either side like mystical red-brown fortifications. The cloud cover drifted slowly off to the east, displaying a dazzling view to the west. Sentinel mountains rose jagged and rocky against the sky, the remaining patches of winter snow gleaming white and in air so crystal-clear he felt he could reach over and touch them.

Bram pulled his roan to a stop, propping himself straight-armed on the swell of the saddle to look. He vaguely knew Jake had stopped beside him.

"Some doin's, them thar hills. Why, reckon that tall bugger oughta snag the bottom out of the clouds." He smacked his lips. "Never seed the like!"

"Those are the Laramie Mountains. Some still call them the Black Hills ... others the Medicine Bows. That big peak up there is Laramie Peak. Supposedly, it's named after old Jacques La Ramée, old French trapper. First in the country."

Bram sighed. "Feller oughta be able t' see the elk up thar. Why, you could almost ride over there in a couple of hours."

Jake laughed. "Now, don't let this western air fool you. You'd have a hard day's ride. You're a good forty miles from Laramie Peak."

A herd of antelope no more than two hundred yards away got to their feet, the lead doe staring uneasily at them. *Khooowww*, she barked, the white patch of hair on her rear flashing like a beacon. Instantly, they were all running, buck to the rear, darting this way and that in the manner of a school of fish, seeming to float magically over the bristly sagebrush.

"Be time for them to drop their fawns soon," Jake supplied, motioning. "Even so, it's late in the year to see a herd like that. Normally, they begin to scatter, dispersing to make the most out of the spring grass."

"Good day, Sergeant," Arabella greeted, cocking her head, lips slightly parted as she met his startled eyes.

"Uh, ma'am. Uh, what are you doing in the stables? Surely, this ain't no place fer a lady."

She smiled, knowing it dimpled her chin as she spun the parasol on her shoulder. "Oh, I just came to check on Efende and take a short ride." She turned to gesture at the outside. "Why, look, Sergeant! It's such a beautiful day! The sun is shining for the first time in a week. The flowers are beginning to open and the grass looks so lush. The trees seem to be positively afire with green. And what is that remarkable bird singing?"

"Meadowlark, ma'am," the sergeant told her, looking uneasy at her presence. "Uh, I really oughta be getting 'bout my business, ma'am. Wouldn't do if folks found you here. With me, I mean. They'd ... they'd talk, you see."

"I suppose they would," Arabella agreed. "But that's all right. You know my brother Jake. I'm sure he'd see to any indiscretions." She batted her eyes coquettishly.

The sergeant reddened, nodding too quickly. "Yeah, hell of a pistol shot, Jake is. Hell of a ... whoops. I mean heck of a . . ." Chin wiggling, he nodded hesitantly and left, practically running from the stable.

Arabella walked down to where two privates shoveled manure from a stall. "Excuse me?" she asked lightly.

They stood transfixed, mouths slightly agape, at the sight of her.

"Would you two gentlemen mind seeing to the saddling of my horse, Efende?" She gave them her most ravishing smile. "I would like to exercise my packhorse too, if you don't mind."

One craned his neck, seeing the sergeant had disappeared. "Sh-Shure, ma'am."

She rode from the stable sitting sideways in her saddle to keep from drawing too many stares. She had successfully conned one of the corporals to have her packs delivered to the trader's store outside the post. At Gratiot's American Fur Company post, she quickly packed her things, hanging the sheathed Bigelow rifle on Efende. She waved when the rotund trader's Sioux wives walked to the door.

She climbed onto Efende and reined him around, leading the packhorse south at a trot. She didn't hesitate as she cut through a cluster of Brulé Sioux lodges, smiling and waving as Efende kicked at the snapping dogs. The Sioux watched, wide-eyed, curious, and even waved back.

How like the Masai they were!

Leaving the village behind, she climbed up the long finger ridges and onto the rolling grasslands. In the near distance, she could see a large horse herd, Indian boys circling the edges of it. Beyond that the land folded in emerald swells to the distant blue mountains jagged against the sky. Not since the Hindu Kush had she seen such stark granite teeth.

A pile of rocks at the head of the ridge braced a thin

pole, at the top of which waved an Indian fetish, a couple of deer tails and some feathers with leather thongs.

"So like the Himalayas," she whispered to herself. "I wonder if there's a connection?"

Near the shrine, she pulled Efende up, looking about, filling her lungs with the fresh free air. Sanderson wouldn't know she had gone for hours at least. She pulled out her compass, studied the direction, and unfolded her map. So that way was south? Very well. She spotted Bent's Fort and the Big Timber on the map. Versed now, she made a quick plot of the distance she would have to cross and looked up the tree-thick valley of the Laramie River.

"First, my friends," she told her horses, "we get water from the river. Then we strike cross-country for the Chugwater."

Efende whickered lightly, stamping his left front hoof impatiently. The strawberry packhorse swiveled its ears, looking wistfully at the Indian horse herd.

"Come, Efende!" Arabella cried, kicking him in the ribs, checking to be sure her gaudy engraved and bejeweled Benjamin Bigelow rode easy in the scabbard. "Let us be off for the Arkansas!"

She spurred forward at a canter.

The man pulled his spirited horse up, leaning forward on the saddle horn and stretching his long legs. Then, shading his eyes, he studied the two horses, just dots now as they moved out into the Laramie River bottoms.

He laughed softly before letting his mount carry him down the slope, following Arabella's tracks.

They picked up Crow Creek and followed it to the South Platte. From there, Jake led them unerringly to

Fort Saint Vrain, where Ceran Saint Vrain met them with warm hospitality.

Jake quickly took over the job of seeing to the travel, picking the route, finding the places to camp. Ab considered that, figuring he always thought he knew his way around. Jake, on the other hand, had ridden this land with Colonel Oord. He knew the water holes, where to find the buffalo, antelope, elk, and deer. He knew how to avoid Indian camps, where shelter from the spring rains could be found, and how to pick a trail through rough terrain which was easy on the animals.

Jeremiel slowly broke through the aloof barrier of preacher to flock, the trouble with Arabella left behind at Fort Laramie. Ab thought he'd fall off his horse the day he saw him laugh at one of Bram's retorts. It took a while to get through the surface but Bram and Jeremiel actually liked each other. Bram would smile at the preacher's back when he wasn't looking. More than once Ab or Jake noted Jeremiel's concern over his sinning little brother.

Jeremiel proved a wonder at telling stories around the fire at night. He knew every Bible story by heart and could recite passages from Xenophon, Homer, Euripides, and Shakespeare.

As for Bram, not only could he bring a laugh in any kind of weather or catastrophe, but his relationship with horses proved to be a genuine miracle. He even made friends with Molly. But he really had a bright shine when it came to camp chores. He knew instantly where to put everything and in what order. Under his direction, they could break camp in five minutes. He taught them tricks with the pack saddles so they could be thrown on with a quick cinching. All those years on the outlaw trail made it second nature to him—he had a natural-born ability as a camp cook.

"Making good time," Jake observed the day after they left Saint Vrain's tumbledown trading post.

"Not bad," Ab agreed, stretching in the saddle before he led the way down a buffalo crossing. They splashed across the spring-full Cherry Creek, Molly—as usual—trying to throw a fit in the water.

Ab trotted out ahead, looking beyond the South Platte terraces to the west across to the wall of the Rockies. The confluence with the bigger river lay several miles to the north. Ab turned Sorrel toward the pine-speckled uplands to the south and headed for the Castle Rock. Jake dropped behind to add his two cents' worth in Jeremiel's behalf. Sounding like hens on the roost, they were trying to convince Bram he needed to learn to read. As usual, Bram was finding lots of reasons not to.

"Why, them papers would scare me to death!" Bram cried. "I'd get back to the settlements and read about all the crimes I done committed and git to feelin' so bad I'd hang myself!"

"The Lord God would never pardon the sin of suicide!" Jeremiel thundered.

"Yep, and bein' beat over the haid with yer religion's gonna mush my brains too!" Bram protested. "What sorta sin is killin' yer brother? I heard you read that Cain an' Abel part from that Bible o' yourn. Kill me by beatin' my brain out with religion an' you'll walk this hyar land forever!"

"Yea, and the sin of Korah be yours, sinner! Along with your total incompetence at checkers! Why, I've played five-year-olds with more sense than you!" Jeremiel blasted back.

"I think ya cheated!" Bram told him sullenly.

"Cheat? Me? A man of the Lord? You little sinning imp," Jeremiel lit into him again.

Knowing they'd be at it for hours, Ab spurred Sorrel

ahead, enjoying this open country where the mighty ramparts of the Rockies rose to the west, still snow-capped where they raked the bottoms of the clouds. To the east, the land stretched toward the rising sun in successive brown waves until the undulating horizon lost itself in forever. The wind shifted warm with spring. Spring. To Ab it seemed he'd raced it west, knowing that even now, Saint Louis was blossoming in green and color, the air already muggy and hot. Here, so high, spring lay fresh on the land, beckoning, a dream of the summer to come.

Ab let his lead lengthen until he topped a rise and saw them. Six men on horseback, they rode heads down, studying the ground. Ab could see another up on the low butte overlooking the Platte. Sunlight glinted off the brass spyglass he held to his eye to study the terrain. The observer might have been a long way off, but the spring sun lit that beard like a blaze. Abriel bailed off Sorrel and led him back down the hill, ground-reined him, and pulled the Hawken from the saddle.

Jake had seen. Ab motioned, and Jake, true to his senses, ran the rest into a drainage. On his elbows, Ab crawled up behind a large rabbitbrush and looked out. Bragg had mounted, heading down toward the searching riders.

They met, too far away for him to hear what they said, but not so far he didn't recognize Cal Backman and Hank Tent. Bragg pointed west toward the mountains, gesturing in broad sweeps of his arms. Ab chewed his lip and scratched his stubbly beard, feeling the sun beat on his back. He watched as they trotted their horses over a rise and out of sight.

How had they known? Abriel turned, draping the Hawken over his knees, hands hanging limply as he frowned.

When Jake and the rest rode up, he was still sitting there on the ground working a chew back and forth from one side to the other, lost in thought.

"What did you find?" Jake asked, reading his expression.

Ab looked up, studying the faces of each of these new brothers of his. They were hard men, each and every one of them. Men of the caliber you'd want to ride the trail with.

"I just saw Branton Bragg and six other men. They looked like they were scouting . . . cutting for sign. I recognized two of them. Cal Backman and his partner Tent. They were the two who tried to jump me down on the Big Blue."

"We might be able to end this right now." Jake's voice sounded absent, reflecting far-off thoughts. "We could face them, get it all out in the open."

"Jeff wasn't with them!" It hit him then. A hollow feeling crept through his gut. That gray tone to Jeff's features, those eyes with the oddly fixed pupils, he knew what he'd done. Killed him when he smacked his skull with the rifle butt. "I'll bet Cal's huntin' scalps. He'll blame me for Jeff."

Ab took a deep breath, bowing his head. With one hand, he traced his fingers through the gray silty soil under him, feeling the light tacky texture of the soil, aware of the thin grasses and prickly pear around him. But Jeff would never feel again.

"What?" Bram demanded, face showing confusion and—uncharacteristically—a bit of worry too.

"I think I may have killed one of Cal's men when they jumped me that night." It was hard to swallow all of a sudden. He'd never killed anyone before. Cold fingers tightened around his soul.

"Which way did they go?" Jake asked.

Ab pointed numbly to the west. Jake left as Jeremiel sat down next to him.

"Brother Abriel,"—his voice was strangely soft—"they set upon you. You aren't to blame. Not in the Holy Book and not in the law of our land. When a man raises the sword and lives by it, he must accept the consequences. Would you rather that it was you lying dead back there? Would you rather this Jeff still be loose upon the land!"

"Huh, I . . . I don't know." He looked up as Jake crested the ridge.

"Looks like their making time." Jake squatted down, the fringes of his jacket hanging up on the rabbitbrush. "Reckon the safest place for us is to take their backtrail to the east, then cut straight across country to the Big Timber. It'll be dry, but I don't reckon Bragg'll figger that's the route we took."

As they turned east, following Bragg's sign, Ab couldn't help but look back over his shoulder, thoughts on Jeff and the sound his rifle made when it hit his head. An odd sensation began to smolder in his stomach.

# Chapter 9

The trilling warble of the meadowlark brought Arabella awake. Blinking, she tried to clear the rheum from her eyes, yawning and stretching in her canvas ground cloth.

The sun had barely begun to crest the horizon as she flipped the heavy canvas back and sat up, looking around and enjoying one last yawn. She stopped, frozen, arms half extended to stretch.

Efende and the packhorse were gone.

Breath stopped in her chest, Arabella slipped her rifle from the scabbard, standing, slowly turning to search the narrow drainage she'd camped in. Nothing, the dry arroyo wound down away from her, buff sides exposed to erosion, the grassy bottom still. Above her, a lone scraggly cottonwood extended half-rolled spring leaves to the morning sun. The meadowlark warbled again.

"*Shaitan!*" she hissed under her breath, beating out her

boots and pulling them on. With a nervous hand, she pulled her sleep-snarled hair back from her face and chewed her lip. Roll up the bed? No, minutes might be the difference between survival and exposure in this wilderness.

"*Sheol* take you, brothers," she whispered as she studied the ground, found where Efende had pulled up the picket pin, and followed the drag marks it left in the soil. She climbed the arroyo sides, scrambling up by the cottonwood. Turning, she looked around, finding nothing but empty rolling short-grass plains while the Rockies to the west lit in brilliant red-orange splashes of sunrise.

Arabella sighed, checked the caps of her rifle, snugged her pistol in her holster, and took out on the trail of her wayward horses, catching a sight every now and then of the trace left by the picket rope where it dragged through anthills or pulled up a small bush. She could also find most of the tracks, the horses having been shod. The sandy silt took a good impression.

"I'm gonna put a bullet right through your twisted horse brain when I find you," she threatened. When she looked back, the wispy cottonwood had become a tiny thing, almost obscured by the roll of the land.

"Forgot the compass," she hissed to herself. "You'll get what you deserve for stupidity!"

Arabella hesitated. Go back? Get the compass? What about water? Her Tuareg water bag hung from a pack, half-full, back in camp.

"You can't have gone that far, Efende," she grunted, taking a sighting on the mountains and continuing her distance-eating stride, long skirt swishing around her legs. The cottonwood slowly sank into the swell of the land.

"Horses! People have spent more time fooling around

with them with less benefit! Constant trouble! Worse than men! Efende, I ought to—"

The rattler scared her half-witless. She yipped, danced sideways, and brought the rifle to bear. She stared. The snake stared. Arabella thumped her chest with a fear-knotted fist to restart her heart. The rattler remained coiled.

Fear-flushed, Arabella continued her trek, enjoying the sensation of walking, feeling different muscles pumping, working, living in her legs and shoulders.

"Efende, I swear," she panted, pulling another unruly strand of hair back from her face. "Where are you?"

She paused, looking around at the high spots. Nervous, she hesitated. Perhaps, if she just climbed up there, from the vantage point, she could find the horses. It might save hours of walking.

Don't do it, Arabella. Keep to the tracks.

Her fingers, sweat-damp, worked on the rifle stock. The sun stood a full quarter way up the sky. Her feet had begun to complain. What do I do? Climb or track? Minutes passed as she stood in the sun. The back of her throat had gone dry.

Climb the hill, she decided, rubbing the back of her hand across her dry lips.

She looked around at the rabbitbrush and prickly pear now hazed green by the new grass. It all looked the same. Unhesitant, she started toward the rise, counting steps so she could backtrack. The rise seemed to fade forever into the distance.

A jackrabbit exploded from under her feet, scaring her frantic and almost making her lose count. Six thousand two hundred and forty-three paces later, she crested a hump, finding more land rising ahead of her. With care she studied the gentle folds of land, knowing how much was hidden by the broken fingers of drainages and irregular rises.

Several scattered antelope watched her, stepping uneasily. She could see the black dots of buffalo on the horizon.

No horses.

Her heart sank in her chest.

The wind teased her, increasing with the heat of day as she had come to expect on the long ride south from Fort Laramie. Blinking her eyes, she expanded her lungs and settled onto the deflated gravelly ridgetop, looking around, wiggling her toes, thankful for the rest.

"Come on, girl, you won't find the horses this way," she groaned, a faint sensation of fright tickling at the bottom of her heart. "Sure," she whispered, "but which way?" Up there? Up to that high point? Or back six thousand two hundred and forty-three paces to the trail Efende left?

"If a horse made the tracks, a horse will be standing in them when you get to the end," she told herself, trudging back down the hill. She'd made no more than a hundred paces before she stopped, realizing she couldn't find her own tracks. She cut back and forth, searching the baked dirt and grass for a half hour before she found a heel print. Turning down hill, she continued, aware of how high the sun had risen in the sky. Her count was off from the zigzagging search.

Creeping fingers of desperation stroked the bottom of her guts.

As the slope leveled out, she lost her tracks. Looking back over her shoulder, she backshot to the rise and looked straight ahead, counting as she walked. At six thousand two hundred and forty-three paces she stopped, looking for the familiar rabbitbrush. The only ones around her looked exactly the same—and totally different. The angle of the sun had changed.

"Don't lose your head, girl," she repeated James's eternal warning, hearing the soft strains of his deep voice in the depths of her memory. "Oh, Efende, where are you?"

She started crisscrossing, looking for the drag marks or prints from the shod feet of her horses. Time passed, thirst goaded her dry mouth. A worried sickness began to eat desperately into her thoughts and hopes. The sun slanted over the distant mountains.

The blood in his body rushed to the rhythm of the drums. They possessed him. A Spirit heart, they beat and his body responded. Wasatch floated, feeling the impact of his heels on the hard-pounded clay of the dancing ground. His hoarse chant rose and fell with the words of the old men, the Singers, as they called the Spirit Power through their lilting tones.

They made the power and core of the Elkhorn Soldiers, the *Himoweyuhkis*, one of the *Tsis-tsis-tas* Soldier Societies. In his hand, Wasatch scratched his elk antler noisemaker in time to the songs. He'd killed a spike bull for the antler tine. Then he grooved one side with forty-five notches over which he rhythmically stroked a baton carved from an antelope's tibia. The elk rattler he had painted yellow on the bottom and blue on the top with a snake's head and tail carefully carved on each end—the gift of the sun snake.

Beside him, he could hear the *mowishkun* finger rattles made from clattering antelope hooves dangling on the long sticks. From the sky, from the ground, from the Cheyenne people, the song came, lifting his body, hiding the fatigue, washing his spirit cleaner than the four passes he had made through the cleansing sweet grass smoke.

Like Eagle, Wasatch soared, feeling the pull of *Mahuts*, the Sacred Arrows, and *Issiwun*, the Buffalo Hat. Together, they made the soul and body of the Cheyenne people. They watched—their Spirit Power thrumming in the very air—and approved. Above, *Heammawihio*, the Great Creator of All, smiled down from his home beyond the sun.

Eyes closed, Wasatch danced, feeling the turning of the land around him, knowing Wolf watched from the place where he panted in the shade, resting in the combined shadow of Lame Coyote's shield standard and the tall cairn which held the family buffalo skull medicine shrine before their lodge. To Lame Coyote, the Elk Soldiers paid respect this day through their dance.

A vision tugged at the corners of his spiritual bliss.

In the haze of power, he dreamed her face. First her eyes formed, amber like his, while locks of hair the color of autumn grasses tumbled around her face. A *wihio*, a white person, a spider person, she called to him, her voice a subtle beckoning in his mind. Wasatch could feel her need, pulling him, drawing him to a future event.

Of a sudden, Wasatch stopped in his tracks, bursting out in song to fix the image in his mind, eyes closed as he called to his Spirit Helper. Ceasing his rattling, he raised his face to feel the warm rays of the sun, lifting his arms.

He could hear the dance slowing around him, hear the falling tones of the singers as they noticed his strange behavior. Wasatch presented his antelope tibia rattle to the four directions, eyes still tightly closed. He presented it to the sky and the Great Creator and to the Earth Mother. Then he raised it four times, letting it fly on the fourth as he threw it up with all his strength.

Breath gasping in his dance-fatigued body, Wasatch opened his eyes, looking around. People watched him, the old men chanting softly, unwilling to let his strange behavior kill the dance. Other Elk Soldiers danced, eyes uneasy, watching him and the bone he'd thrown to the sky.

Wasatch followed their eyes to where it had landed, seeing where the slender tip of bone pointed: north.

"I am called," he panted, shaking the sweat from his face so as not to smear his intricate face painting. Breathing deeply, he saw Wolf stretch, and read the understanding in those fierce yellow eyes.

"Come, Father, we go." And Wasatch turned, feeling his father's, White Wolf's, spirit in the wolf. Together, they trotted for Wasatch's lodge and his personal things.

Jeremiel whispered, knees complaining where he knelt on the rocky ground, fingers laced together, eyes lowered.

". . . lead us not into temptation but deliver us from evil. For Thine is the Kingdom and the Power and the Glory forever. Amen."

Again he recited the Lord's Prayer, hearing the hollow tinny sound from behind as Bram settled the cooking pot and a skillet on the buffalo chip fire. He blocked the noises from the waking camp.

Jeremiel looked up to see the rim of the sun burn a red sliver over the irregular horizon to the east.

"Bless me this day, my Lord. Keep me from the sins of the flesh and the tempter in this wilderness. As You, Lord, were harrowed and shaped by the desert, so let it be with me. Take me as your servant, Lord. Keep me in health and in strength. Pardon me for the excesses of my passions and bear me on Your strength to keep Your will and charity." He took a deep breath, feeling the rapture of the morning. "I am clay in Your fingers, O Lord, my God. Take me, mold me in Your fashion that I might do Your work. Amen."

Jeremiel ignored the pain in his lower back, forgot the dull ache of his feet and calves where they had gone to sleep, disdained the chill that had seeped from the cold ground into his knees. Tendrils of peace drifted through his soul as he watched the sun imperceptibly lift over the purple-streaked horizon.

"A beautiful prayer, brother." Abriel's soft voice caught him by surprise.

Jeremiel bowed his head, silent, contemplating how complex Abriel had turned out to be.

"I, uh, hope you don't mind, but I shared it. Let you pray for me."

"No, I am honored, brother Abriel." Jeremiel swallowed, sucking the cool air of this new day into his lungs. Then he tried to stand up. Abriel caught his arm as he mumbled, "Feet went to sleep."

"Better stand there for a bit," Abriel cautioned. "You move and it'll make you feel like fifty thousand old ladies are sticking pins in you."

Jeremiel nodded, glad of his supporting arm. "A friend loveth at all times, and a brother is born for adversity," he quoted from Proverbs. "Don't let go, I might fall over."

Ab nodded, his bent nose sending a crooked shadow over his bearded cheeks. "Um, I was just wondering. You get up every morning to pray. Just thought . . . thought I'd join you this morning."

Jeremiel shifted his weight and felt tingling shoot up his leg. Ab had hedged. Why? He winced and gritted his teeth, freezing in place again. "You are always welcome to join me in prayer. I . . . welcome it." *What do you want, brother?*

Ab's lips twisted in a smile that reminded Jeremiel so much of Bram's. "Figger you got my sinning on the run?"

Jeremiel chuckled. "Perhaps."

"You're not the man I met in Independence." Ab let loose of his arm, noting how easily he stood as his feet recovered. Ab squatted in that comfortable plainsman's crouch that left an ordinary man gimped up in minutes.

Jeremiel reached up and pulled his lapels straight, looking out over the endless rolling grasslands, studying the lay of the morning shadows, noting a coyote slinking away in the distance. A black blotch of buffalo clustered on a juniper-covered slope that broke up in a rocky sand-stone outcrop at the top, the rocks blood-red in the morning sun.

"No," he whispered, ordering his thoughts. "I guess I'm not." *So you have come over concern about my soul, brother Abriel—not your own.*

Abriel had propped an elbow on his knee so he could finger his new beard. "Well, I'm a little worried about you. The old cocky spark is gone."

Jeremiel bent and picked up his hat where he'd laid it on a clump of wheat grass and slapped the dust away. *What now? Do I just talk? Trust this man?*

As if he heard, Abriel reminded, "Brothers are made for adversity."

Jeremiel pinned his lower lip with his upper incisors, nodding slowly. "Some of my own back?"

"No," Ab replied easily. "Just figured I'd let you know I was here." He looked up, a warmth in his eyes. "And let you know even a sinner like me is willing to listen if you want to talk." Ab pushed off his knees to stand up, nodding curtly, and started back to camp.

He hadn't taken more than two steps when Jeremiel heard himself say, "I guess that it wasn't easy anymore."

Abriel turned, slipping his fingers into his belt, head cocked. "Life changed on you, huh?"

*Oh, the sad truth in that, brother Abriel!* "Yes," he admitted. "Changed that night outside poor Reverend Blair's church." Jeremiel slapped a limp hand to his side. "That wasn't the first time I was ever violent." Jeremiel let his eyes play across the sun-yellowed plains. Birds, his morning choir, trilled in the brush. "As a boy, I was always in trouble."

"Normal for kids," Ab offered.

Jeremiel's laugh came harshly. "Not for William and Mary Sunts' kid. No, I was a missionary's boy. A model. An example." He frowned, recalling. "They did everything for me, Abriel. I . . . I tried so hard. Tried to fit the teachings into my life. I can remember spending night after night on my knees, head bowed over my bed as I recited the Sermon on the Mount over and over again, trying to carve it in my mind . . . make myself live it. Only I never quite figured I measured up. William was so . . . so pious."

He swallowed at the lump in his throat. "So kind and understanding. And me, why I couldn't ever keep my mind on lessons. I was always saying something undeserved about others. I fidgeted in class . . . had too much energy to control."

He popped a fist into his callused palm. "And then I couldn't keep out of trouble. You know, fistfights in the school yard, prodding the other boys." He hung his head. "And Will Sunts always forgave me . . . his words so kind." Jeremiel ran his hand over his face, rubbing his jaw. "And the worst part was his eyes. I could look into his eyes, Ab, and see how much pain my misbehaving caused him."

"Aw, you were just a kid," Ab grunted.

Jeremiel shook his head. "But I knew better. I'd swear to myself that I'd never let Will down again. Never see that look in his eyes or hear the hope in Mary's voice. You know . . . hope that I'd change. Then, later someone would say something, and I'd lay into him." His voice dropped. "Fight first, think later."

"You outgrew it," Ab reminded. "Became a preacher."

"Never outgrew it," Jeremiel countered. "Became a preacher? Yes, that I did." He cocked his head. "I did that to save myself—and prove myself to William Sunts." He hesitated, seeing the question in Abriel's eyes. "We were on a Choctaw Mission. Young buck, maybe fifteen, came in drunk. Called me a name and I went wild. William pulled me off before I killed him.

"My sin, Ab . . . my real sin, is that I have always preached the book of Matthew while I lived Isaiah."

Jeremiel turned in the silence, wishing he could send his soul out with the birds. "It was murder, Abriel. That boy lived because William Sunts happened to be there. But the murder was in my heart. The sin lay here, within." He hooked a thumb at his breast.

"So you became a preacher?" Ab wondered, rocking back on his heels, squinting in the morning light. "That's penance?"

Jeremiel wiggled his lips. "No, that, too, was a sin—Matthew in the mouth—Isaiah in the heart. I was young. That time—after I beat that Choctaw—I couldn't face the look in William Sunts's eyes. Couldn't go home to Mary's patient forgiving love. I . . . I ran out on them. Ran off to seminary and forced myself to study even though I chafed to be out in the open, moving. I graduated, became a preacher."

"The Suntses were happy?"

Jeremiel winced. "Never saw them again."

"Don't sound like sin to me," Ab told him evenly, letting his eyes wander over the country.

"It's the motive in the heart," Jeremiel explained, pain edging through his confession. Maybe the Papists had something in confession after all. It soothed his soul to share his burden. "I didn't become a preacher because I loved my Lord Jesus. I did it to make *myself* feel better. Lied to myself, thinking William Sunts would hear ... would be proud that his hellion kid turned out all right."

"You could go back. Tell them in person."

Jeremiel shook his head, a firm negative.

"So what changed the night at the church?" Ab pulled his tobacco out and cut a sliver with his bowie.

"The rage broke loose too quickly," Jeremiel replied. "That was the first crack in the porcelain vase. It cracked again when I heard who I was. Then another crack formed when I rode to find Bram. The vase fractured all the way around when I hit my brother because he mocked me."

"And Arabella?"

Jeremiel shrugged. "The cracks are all through the vessel, the water is leaking out, I am a sieve of lies." He took several nervous steps, studying the sandy ground at his feet. "Before the night at the church, it was so easy! All I had to do was let what I thought was the Spirit of the Lord fill me, and it poured out so strong and powerful."

"You did sound pretty good." Abriel grinned. "I told Molly all about it."

"You don't understand," Jeremiel pleaded. "I didn't preach to reach them. I was just preaching to hear myself preach. See? I did it so I could preach to myself, make myself think *I* had the power!"

Jeremiel kicked at the soft dirt. "Then I met Bram. I ended up brawling with him. That's when Arabella showed up—of all the rotten timing." He rubbed the back of his neck. "A lady, Ab. My sister, a true lady. And then I find she's a ... a heathen infidel."

"A what?" Ab scowled.

Jeremiel flipped his head. "She's a Mohammedan—a

person who worships Allah. They only accept Jesus as a Prophet. They aren't Christian. But that doesn't matter.

"What matters is that for the first time, I cared. I really sincerely cared to reach someone . . . show her the way to let my Lord Jesus into her heart . . . and she didn't listen." He tilted his head to look at the sky. "And all of a sudden, the lie became clear in my mind. I know myself for the selfish man that I am. A powermonger . . . a Pharisee."

Ab placed his hand on Jeremiel's shoulder. "At least you know what's wrong."

In a low voice he mumbled, "Her faith . . . false in my eyes . . . is stronger than my own. That's my problem. But . . . but what if I can't solve it? What if I find out I can't really believe anymore? The more I read the Bible, the more confused I become."

"Swim that river when you reach that bank, Jeremiel. You'll make it."

He nodded as Abriel turned and walked back toward camp. *Perhaps, brother Abriel, but why do I feel so confused?*

Cold and desperate with thirst, Arabella awoke as shivers racked her body. Her tongue stuck in the back of her mouth as she tried to swallow. Her eyes felt gummy, hot, as if the lids slid over gravel.

Cramped, she uncurled from the ball she'd wound herself into and stared glumly around in the gray-black of false dawn. A sliver of blackness shifted in the pre-dawn shadow, gravel pattered under stealthy feet.

Fingers stiff, she found her rifle and pulled back the underhammer for the shotgun, fear goading her as she backed against the arroyo wall.

As she settled, the blackness darted to the side and bounded away. Against the faint horizon, she recognized the shape of a coyote as it disappeared into the dusky grayness.

*"Allahu akbar,"* she whispered, wilting as the fear surge left her drained. Her teeth clattered again as she shivered, almost shaking out of control. Oh, for the blankets and packs back in her camp!

Camp? Where? Images of her frightened flight the night before haunted her. She'd panicked. The first time in years, and she'd let herself down, failed. Bone-weary, she closed her eyes in shame.

Move, Arabella. Warm up. There aren't that many drainages around here.

Stiffly, she pushed herself to her feet, using the rifle as a brace. Pain lanced up from her blistered feet. The gnawing craving for water burned like a madness at the base of her brain.

"All right, Arabella," she slurred through thick lips. "Let's at least find camp."

Walking like an old woman, she started down the arroyo, studying the fading stars to find the direction that was west.

Leander O. B. Sentor squinted into the morning light, his horse plodding calmly to the crest of the ridge. He stood tall in the stirrups and carefully studied each of the drainages, his eyes tracing out the patterns of the land.

Nowhere did he see Arabella. He swiveled in the saddle to look back at the ratty cottonwood that marked her camp. Efende and the strawberry packhorse stood heads down, tails swishing, right where he'd tied them.

All right, which way?

He'd tried tracking her out the evening before, only to lose her delicate prints in the hardpan where clays had washed off the slopes. He lifted his cap and scratched his long brown hair, greasy now after so long on the trail.

"*Sacre,*" he muttered to a back-turned horse ear. "Where could she be? Worse, how does a civilized man find her in this waste?" He squinted, grateful at least for the fact the climate here proved less severe than that he'd experienced in Algeria.

Leander lifted his chin to stretch his neck, scratched his growing beard with a thumbnail, and studied the long broad ridges again.

Speckles of white flickered, flashing in the sun. Antelope. He made out the direction they ran, how they shifted in a broad circle, avoiding one of the drainages a couple of miles above Arabella's camp. Then they were hidden by a swell of ridge.

He stroked his beard, thinking. Quite a woman, this Arabella Catton. In the year and a half he had been shadowing James L'Ouverture, he'd never paid that much attention to the young lady. If Leander O. B. Sentor could conclude that the antelope had been groused out of their gully by Arabella, then she was tracing out the dry arroyos in the area, hoping to find her camp. A wide smile spread under his shading of beard. Why, she proved to be clever indeed. No drawing room dandy this, here was a woman worthy of his skill and attention.

Of course, duty would bring them head-to-head eventually. He sighed heavily. Perhaps she could be persuaded? He had more to offer than her barbarian brothers.

Slipping out of the saddle, he settled himself comfortably, elbows resting on his knees as he enjoyed the sunshine. The antelope drifted back into view after a half hour or so, feeding, walking, heads down and unconcerned. An eagle sailed on the thermals rising with the increase in morning heat. Flocks of little brown birds dipped and slipped around him, frittering their time in the search for bugs while flies came to pester him, drawn to the odors in his blood and grease-stained leathers.

Leander noted a tick climbing surely up his leg. Nice country this, might have ticks and buzzworms, but he'd left the triple God-cursed chiggers long behind. A land without chiggers—in spite of the lack of trees, the strong winds, the freezing snows, and late spring—couldn't be counted as less than Eden. Well, at least not by a sane man.

He flicked the tick off and ground it into the deflated gravel with a pebble. "Rest in peace," he grunted sourly.

A flock of sage grouse exploded from the drainage a couple of minutes later. Whatever moved down there had its nose pointed right for Arabella's camp—unless it turned up one of the tributary channels.

He chuckled to himself, pleased with his observations about the land and Arabella. As the hour passed, he charted the course of the traveler in the gully. Of course, he could always ride down and rescue her; in fact he'd do that, since she seemed headed in the right direction. After all, she ought to be tired and thirsty; and sore enough that his arrival wouldn't raise too much of her ire.

"In the matters of intrigue, however, less is often more," he told his horse solicitously. "Indeed, let's allow her to suffer to the last minute." He flipped a pebble off his thumbnail, watching it bounce across the scrubby grass. He stood, pulling the reins to lead his horse around. Leander learned another thing about the land—a lesson he'd never come by while hugging the streets of Paris. He who sits in the highest spot can see lots of places below him. At the same time, anyone below sees him, too. Too late, he remembered the definition of the word "skylined."

They had worked around him, coming up the drainages radiating out from his bluff. Leander swallowed grimly. Checking the cap on his rifle, he swung into the saddle.

He looked behind him, seeing heads bobbing as riders emerged from a cut.

Surrounded.

"Just like the triple God-cursed Tuareg," he grunted, pulling his big horse pistol out so he could check the load. His bowie he loosened in its scabbard. "Only they're quiet." He swallowed. "And maybe don't have a gut hate for a Frenchman yet."

They stopped, no more than fifty yards off. The wind tugged at long black hair. Feathers flipped and danced, the horses stamping in anticipation. Colorful, bright trade cloth contrasted to stained buckskins. Gay ribbons had been woven into their hair. He didn't see any face paint.

Leander's horse snuffled and whickered an equine greeting.

The wind patted his face. The sun burned warm on his broad shoulders. A meadowlark trilled happily into the noonday. Leander tried to swallow—and couldn't. Images of the Algerian campaigns returned to his mind: memories of dead men and suffering.

They watched him, faces blank, eyes hard and unforgiving. The eerie part about it came from the fact that they didn't move. Like predatory statues, they waited, silent, terrible. Only the wind whipped cloth or hair or feathers.

How many? Twenty? Twenty-five? Looking around, Leander noted the trade guns. Short stubby nor'west items, they were smoothbores for the most part.

"C'est bon," he admitted to his horse. "I get two at least. Maybe I can club one or two more with the rifle. After that, the arrows will make me look like a cursed American cactus, non?"

His horse shook its head, ears pricked.

"Hello!" Leander called out.

The reply—issued by a straight-sitting man who seemed to be armed with only a stick—came loud and challenging. And totally unintelligible. At the same time, the Indian waved his hands in eloquent sign language.

"Ah, *mon général*"—Leander gritted to himself—"I have let you down." He pressured the animal forward with his heels. "You should have left me to die in Algeria."

Two warriors easily crossed, placing their horses in front of him. Leander's face tickled where fear-sweat meandered down from under his brows, sneaking into his stubble-coated cheeks. He pulled up, no more than five feet from the two stony-eyed warriors. Young men, they didn't look more than twenty, their sun-blackened faces like burnished bronze. They didn't move a finger. Only their eyes pinned him, burning, waiting.

"We will kill each other?" Leander asked reasonably, noting the nocked arrows. Trade cloth shirts flapped around muscular chests. The fringe on their leggins swayed. He could see the scar along the right-hand warrior's cheekbone.

*Like Tuaregs, they have no fear of me.*

The leader called out in a singing string of words. He motioned with his hands again, despite the long curve-tipped stick in his hands. Animal tails, bright cloth, bits of mirrors, and small locks of hair waved from the decorated wood. The man wore a blue shirt with large white spots sewed over each breast. The feathers woven into his greased hair looked odd, cut into different shapes. They stuck out at angles—lots of them.

*"No sabe!"* Leander called, looking past the two hard-faced guards.

The leader—war chief?—trotted his horse up, head

cocked. *"No sabe?"* he echoed, a smile bending his lips. *"Hablas español? Eres de Taos?"*

"Uh, I'm French," Leander stumbled. "But I speak American."

The other Indians were drifting closer, tightening the ring.

"Caballos? You hoss?" the chief asked, pointing with his long stick to Arabella's horses where they watched from down below.

"I was afraid you'd seen them."

"You come." The chief gestured as he spoke. "Make hoss mine. Yes?"

Leander studied the ever-closing ring. Each of the warriors watched him through expressionless dark eyes. The ones with trade muskets held them ready. So close Leander could see the hammers had been cocked. Others held bows, half-bent, the arrows pulled back against taut strings—not at full pull, but close.

"Maybe," Leander sighed, wondering.

"Maybe yes," the chief added sharply, turning his horse and starting downhill toward Arabella's camp.

Like magic, the two hostile-eyed guards moved aside. Leander could have believed they thought the orders to their horses; he saw no cue to the mounts. The one on the right jerked his head, rapping out a staccato order.

"You haven't taken my rifle yet, boys," Leander reminded, nudging his horse forward, instantly aware of the target his back made as they closed in behind him. From that close, they couldn't miss. He'd be dead before he could pull the trigger. A prickle of fear burned from the bottom of his boots to tingle all around his nervous scalp.

# Chapter 16

*J*ake pointed with one hand, rubbing the small of his back with the other. "There she is. That's Sand Creek. Call it a shortcut to the Big Timber."

Abriel nodded, letting his eyes play across the drainage-cut bottoms. He looked back over his shoulder. "And that big peak? That's Pike's?"

"You've seen it before," Jake told him. "Had to from the Arkansas River."

"Yep. But not from this angle."

Bram pulled up next to them, Jeremiel stopping on the other side as the pack animals lined out behind them. Sorrel sidestepped suddenly as he felt Molly's teeth graze his flank.

"Cut that out! Molly? You hear me? Cuss you, I swear you'll end up greasing a buzzard's gizzard if you don't start behaving!" She lowered her ears, pulling her gray head up, dropping the lids halfway over big brown eyes.

"What's all them?" Bram asked, pointing at the grass. "Looks like a trail."

Jake nodded. "It is. Those are travois marks." He gestured in a sweeping motion. "We're at the water divide. Behind us, everything runs into Cherry Creek and the Platte. Down there, that's all Sand Creek. Runs into the Arkansas just below Big Timber. Indians been using this as a high road for centuries. It's the only route with reliable water unless you stick to the Front Range—and the water isn't *that* reliable between August and September some years."

"Travois," Bram grunted, frowning as he chewed on his lips. "That means lotsa Injuns."

"Does come with the country," Jake grunted.

"We gonna git scalped?" Bram wondered. "Hell, think I'd rather be hung. Least they give a fella a ceegar first."

"Thought you gave up smoking ceegars?" Jake gave him a skeptical look.

Bram screwed up his lips and pulled his shabby hat off, plucking at his hair, yanking at it as if to check its tightness. "Reckon given the choice," he decided, "I could plumb git a tarnal hankering for a good smoke. The sight of a scalpin' knife jest gets my terbaccy tendency to percolatin'."

She heard the voices first, stopping, suddenly glad for the weight of the rifle in her hands. No more than a hundred yards ahead, she could see the cottonwood tree. So, someone had found her camp? She winced at the thought of her personal items being ransacked.

Sighing, she trudged along, following the edge of the arroyo. Two men on horseback rode up out of the bottom, one with his eyes bent to the ground; together, they trotted out following the route she'd taken in pursuit of Efende.

"Indians!" She turned to run, thinking to drop into the bottom of the arroyo and hide.

She hitched up her dirty skirt, weaving on her feet and hating it. One of the riders turned, saw her, and called to his companion. They wheeled their horses, coming at a trot.

Half-crazed with thirst, feet like bleeding stumps, she stopped, the Benjamin Bigelow hanging heavy in her arms. She studied them as they pulled up no more than ten yards away, chattering excitedly to each other.

Got to bluff. Got to . . . and my mind's hazy. So tired.

"Good day," she rasped. "I am going to my camp. First I will drink, then either we will kill each other or . . ."

One noticed her rifle, the gold and silver work gleaming in the sun. He pointed, mouth open before bending into a grin. His exclamation came as a whisper.

The second, a bandy man wearing a red shirt with two large feathers stuck through his coiled hair, immediately bailed off his horse, talking earnestly, gesturing at her to give him the rifle. Unaffected, he closed on her, insistence in his voice.

"No!" she growled, squinting with her thirst-hot eyes. She swung the barrel his direction, stopping him in his tracks. "I'm going to my camp," she insisted tiredly. "I haven't had a drink in a day and a half." She pointed a finger into her dry mouth. "Drink!"

Never letting the muzzle leave his midsection, she walked around them, pinning them with a wary eye. At the same time, her mind raced. They didn't seem to have any of her things—except maybe they'd managed to get Efende!

Red Shirt jumped spritely on his horse, talking and

gesturing to his companion. They separated, walking their horses to either side, slowly closing on Arabella as she staggered along, legs leaden. The first warrior, a young boy in a buckskin shirt lined with tassels, yipped out in a shrilling yell.

Arabella whirled, bringing her rifle up. Horse hooves thumped behind her. As she began to turn back, Red Shirt bore down on her, leaning from the saddle. He caught the barrel as she swung—too slow—jerking it violently from her grip, practically tumbling her under the horse's hooves.

Gasping, she lay facedown on the dirt, feeling cactus in her left leg. Bitterly angry, she stood and looked at her hand, the skin torn where the trigger guard had been ripped through her grip.

Red Shirt held the rifle over his head, yelling ululations to the fluffy clouds drifting down from the mountains.

Her restraint broke. She went berserk, flinging herself at him.

Laughing like a maniac, he artfully whirled his war-trained horse to keep her at bay. She tripped on her skirts, falling. Red Shirt laughed again, riding his dancing horse like a Berber, easy in the saddle, the shining rifle held high.

In anguish, Arabella pushed to her feet to scramble after him again, Arabic curses lacing the air fit to bring Allah's lightning down about them.

She forgot Hair Shirt, but only until he nudged his horse forward, and cleanly plucked her—kicking and screaming—from the ground. Arms like iron bands encircled her as Hair Shirt whooped his triumph to the skies. She whipped around, pounding him with her fists, wild with fear. Only then did she really notice the fine lattice of scars on his mahogany-brown features.

Her pistol! She grabbed it from her belt, trying to turn and shoot him. He caught her hand, laughing as his superior strength bent her hand away and pried the discharging weapon loose.

The man grinned at her, slapped her hard enough to daze her, and rode past the cottonwood and into the arroyo.

Arabella, mind spinning, found her camp full of men. They had strewn her dresses and underthings gaily about in wild abandon. Efende stood picketed with a line of other horses—the only thing positive she noticed during a kaleidoscopic first glance.

Men whooped and shouted as her captors rode among them, grasping hands pulled at her, leaving her panicked and screaming again. She managed to connect with one wild kick, feeling the gratifying snap of bone under her heel as she caught one man in the face.

She lost the rest as Scar Face dropped her, other men easily tumbled her to the ground, where she lay, dazed, disbelieving. Fear shot through her as she panted there. With all her power, she jumped to her feet and made three paces before a large man grabbed her, spun her in the air, and smashed her flat on the ground. Scar Face sauntered over, a calm look on his face. She blinked up at him just before he cuffed her, blasting lights through her vision.

Arabella cursed him in Arabic. To emphasize it, she spit at him. He kicked her, moccasined foot catching her under the chin. The ground thumped into her, grayness whirling around her shrieking senses.

In misery, she closed her eyes. *You fool, you learned nothing from James in all those years, did you?*

She felt at her waist, sliding her fingers into the pocket in the side of her skirt. Underneath, the hardness of the slim sinuous-bladed creese met her fingers.

Blood dripped from her nose, over her lips and chin. Blood? Given her possession by thirst, the thought she could bleed so freely came as a surprise. Defeated, she straightened and glared up at Scar Face.

She turned at the sound of horses. A whole herd, they plunged over the edge of the arroyo, filling the bottom below her camp. Two young boys rode at the edges, pushing the animals through and up over the other side.

Orders were shouted and men scrambled, grabbing up her scattered clothing, her saddle and packs being left along with her copy of the Koran and scattered personal effects.

Scar Face muttered at her, motioning for her to get up and mount her horse. She lifted her lip at him, getting to her wobbly feet. The Tuareg waterskin lay empty to one side. She staggered over and lifted it to her lips, enjoying only a drop on her tongue.

Scar Face motioned with his hand, threatening to strike her again. she cursed him roundly in Arabic and quickly gathered up her things, wrapping the precious map, compass, and Koran in the hem of her skirt. She knotted it to keep her possessions safe and pointed at Efende. "My horse!" she insisted.

Scar Face shook his head, jumping into the saddle and reaching for her.

"No!" Arabella crossed her arms, wondering if it would be worth it in the end. One of the herd boys slapped Efende across the rear with a quirt, sending him up the embankment.

"Arabella! Come on!" The call in English made her spin, looking to see Leander O. B. Sentor, where he rode, hands bound.

Biting her thirst-swollen lip, she let Scar Face lift her up. His muscular brown pony pounded up the slope, onto the floodplain, and they were off, cantering in the dusty wake of the horse herd.

Leander? Here? She closed her eyes, thoughts reeling and whirling in her head.

How had this happened? Carelessness. She'd been lax about the picket pin. Then what? Stupid about tracking Efende, and forgetting her water, and not immediately pulling her pistol to shoot the man who took her rifle. She'd been thirst-stupid. She had let events control her.

Of course, at the time she didn't know how many men there were. Still, she could have bought her death with a handful of theirs. Her heart lay like lead in her breast. What now? Rape? By all of them? A shiver started at the bottom of her spine and worked its way up.

Maybe, praise be to the name of Allah, they would give her something to drink first.

Wasatch shifted, timing his jump as the Appaloosa cantered close to his bay. In midstride, he hopped lightly to the Appaloosa, letting the bay lag on the bridle rope. He slowed, allowing the horses to walk up the long ridge he climbed. Ahead, juniper and occasional piñons spattered the north slope. He crested the worn sandstone caprock, the horses picking their way between spring-flush yuccas, stalks already rising from the pointed leaves in the promise of blossoms.

A long-abandoned Apache dwelling—like a fortification—stood to one side. Heavy sandstone slabs had been stood on edge like jagged teeth. A few moldering timbers remained, rotting into dust. Thick-walled gray pottery lay scattered about—mute evidence of the vanished peoples.

Wasatch let his eyes rove the distant horizon as the Appaloosa picked its way down the slope, weaving between the widely scattered trees, crunching the springy ground oak. No movement.

Wolf had vanished hours earlier, as was his way. He had coursed ahead in his easy ground-eating lope, leaving the man and the slower horses behind. To save time, Wasatch switched from horse to horse, reading their movements, feeling their fatigue, keeping the pace matched to each animal's ability. Already the bay had begun to fade, the long ride having eaten the animal's reserves.

How much time? Which way? Wasatch sang his wolf song, calling on the Spirit Power to show him the way. North, the bone had pointed. North he had ridden. Now he wondered at the direction he needed to take.

An hour later, the song still on his lips, he splashed across runoff-full Rush Creek and began climbing the divide toward the Platte River. As the sun slanted into the distant west, he slowed, dismounted, and walked the horses down to cool them out. In a sheltered pocket, he let the horses drink where a restricted spring issued from under the brush-choked overlaying sandstone. Head down, the bay closed its eyes, grateful for the rest.

Wasatch climbed the rock, looking out to the west where the high Rockies lay capped in cloud. The waning sunlight shot silver from the storm mass, bars of light dancing blue-white through the sky. Rain came, rushing toward him from the mountains.

Who was this woman who formed in his thoughts? He squatted on the sandy soil, plucking at the fresh leaves of a rabbitbrush, crushing them between his incisors and puckering at the bitter taste. Her eyes had been amber—like his. Her hair—a little lighter than his own—bordered what the *wihio* called blond.

"My sister," he whispered, feeling the familiar sense of rightness in his mind, like so many of his hunches. That feeling of rightness set him apart from other men—made him different.

He reached for a stalk of grass, feeling it resist as he pulled it from the clump, chewing the soft part of the stem, letting the sweet taste overcome the bitter rabbit-brush.

"So, she has come. The rumors of Web's death must be true." He raised his head, seeing a hawk whirling in the thermals. "Then Branton Bragg must know of us. He will have learned of my brothers. Perhaps he has already caught Arabella. That may have been her message. A warning—not a call."

Power flowed through him, leaving its warm after-touch in his mind and body.

"An odd boy," White Wolf, his Cheyenne father, had ad mitted to Man With Four Fingers, the old tribal medicine man.

"He hears the Spirit World," Four Fingers had grunted, beady brown eyes taking Wasatch's measure. "I can see it in him. I have watched him with the horses ... with the dogs."

"He hears things in his head," White Wolf murmured. "The Flower Man, Web Catton, brought him to my lodge many years ago. How was I to know he left a medicine child? I watch him, he tilts his head. When I ask him, he tells me he hears voices—although there is no one around. Once a big owl landed on a tree and talked to him." White Wolf touched the bowl of his pipe to the ground to affirm the truth to his words. "The boy and the owl talked for a handspan of the sun's travel across the sky."

Four Fingers nodded, stroking his wrinkled chin, eyes glinting under half-lowered lids, never leaving Wasatch's face. "He hears the *Mis'tai*, the bad ghosts."

White Wolf touched his carved pipe bowl to the

ground again. "I do not know. But my wife heard and saw a *Mis'tai*. She covered her head and ran to my lodge. There she cowered in the corner under the buffalo robes and pulled the boy down with her. When she told him, he looked up and stood, telling the *Mis'tai* to go away. Four times he did this. My wife watched, and the *Mis'tai* left."

Four Fingers stood then, politely walking behind White Wolf and bending down. Wasatch had waited, biting his lip, heart pounding as the old medicine man reached out with age-gnarled fingers to touch his forehead. That feeling of warmth had filled him then.

"Spirit Power is in you, boy," Four Fingers whispered. "When you get old enough, you come to me. I will teach you, share the secrets of the *Tasoom*, the soul, and of the *Ahk tun o' wihio*, the spirits of the earth."

Wasatch had nodded then, knowing fear.

That had been so long ago—back before his father, White Wolf, had died. Now, his other father, the Flower Man, Web Catton, must have died.

Wasatch listened to the voice in the wind. He turned his head at the scratching sound, seeing Badger climb up over the sandstone, heavy claws grating on the rock as he proceeded in his bow-legged stride. Badger stopped, rocking back and forth on his feet as he sniffed with his button-pointed nose.

"Greetings, *Ma'ah ku*," he called.

Badger lowered his head skeptically.

"I look for my sister," Wasatch explained. "She came to me in a spirit dream. I don't know which way to go."

Badger lifted his pointed nose, exposing long teeth, and scratched with his claw before waddling in a wide circle, stopping every couple of feet to study Wasatch. He climbed an anthill, tearing at it with his claws, sending ants boiling out of the wreckage. Then he snorted and headed off to the northwest in a fast waddle, moaning and whining, as if ordering Wasatch to follow.

Wasatch walked to the destroyed anthill and bent down to study the marks Badger had made. In the scattered sands and pebbles—outlined now with roiling red ants—the likeness of Wolf could be seen.

"Ah," Wasatch breathed. "Thank you, *Ma'ah ku.* May the sun shine on you, and may your path be broad with many fine things to eat."

New life in his veins, Wasatch dropped over the rock overhang and trotted back to where the horses grazed the thick grass below the spring. He led them to the top of the ridge, sighting along the line Badger had made after leaving Wolf's sign. Wasatch marked a point on the far rise and swung up on the Appaloosa. Sure of his direction, he continued, knowing the storm would be upon him by dark.

"To sit at the left hand of Allah could be no worse than this," Arabella whispered to herself, driving a thumbnail deep into the back of Scar Face's hand as he tried to grope her chest.

He hissed displeasure, but the hand dropped away.

At least his intentions seemed clear. What am I going to do when the time comes? Arabella drove the pain burning in her cramped body out of her mind, trying to concentrate on something besides the nagging thought of cool water—and fear.

She could see Leander, riding to one side. His hat had disappeared somewhere along the way. A bruise discolored his cheekbone but a determined glint filled his eye. Samson chained.

Clouds scudded across the west, each bone-jamming step made by Scar Face's pony racking her pained body. A new sensation had begun to disturb her. Hunger, masked somewhat by obsessive thirst, twisted her stomach.

She could see over Scar Face's shoulder. Men stopped on the high spots, always looking back toward the north before racing forward to catch up again.

An hour later they stopped, everyone changing horses.

Thankful, Arabella slipped to the ground, body giving her sensations of what it must feel like to be a side of beef.

"You all right?" Sentor called.

"For the moment," she rasped woodenly.

"Keep your head and—"

"Spare me," Arabella whispered under her breath.

Scar Face returned, leading two blowing horses. This time he bound her wrists and lifted her to the back of a horse.

"What? No sidesaddle?" she asked him, staring dully into his hard scar-lined face. "Hardly proper for a—"

He muttered to her in his language and vaulted to the back of his new mount. Gathering up the lead reins, they pelted off to the southeast again, always following the trotting horse herd.

Within minutes, she found herself scrambling to keep hold as the ground rushed past in a blur accented by clumps of that incredibly thorny mat of cactus Bram had called prickly pear. Here and there, yucca raised vicious lances toward the sky.

The wind hit them first, trying to batter her loose from her tenuous hold. Head down, she bit her lip, sensation almost gone from her dry mouth. With a conscious effort, she tried to keep from swallowing—her tongue only sticking in the back of her throat.

The first spatters of rain ripped out of the cold dusk, a godsend at first, later a curse as they lashed her, cold, wet, draining her strength further.

Avidly, she licked her lips, cool moisture a tease and blessing at the same time. She licked the water that beaded on the back of her hand, chasing it with her swollen tongue as it trickled down her face, trying to catch it in her mouth.

If only I could lift my skirt! I could wring the water out. She closed her eyes, afraid to loosen the death grip her numb fingers had on the horse's mane.

Brilliant streaks of lightning laced the clouds, thunder blasting the plains around them. The horses, too jaded to care, put their heads down and continued on their way.

They pushed on. Arabella shivered, the cold wind sucking her body heat from the rain-soaked dress. Her hips began to ache, the taste of water only aggravating her thirst. Worse, hunger tormented her stomach. Every joint in her body cried, as if they'd been pulled asunder.

Fatigue—despite the fear and discomfort—made her thoughts dull. Grimly, Arabella held to her horse.

Eternity.

A voice.

She blinked, shivering again. A change. What? Her horse had stopped. Silence, no more pounding of hooves.

The voice came again, speaking syllables she didn't know. Her reeling mind tried to fit the words into Malay, Hindi, Arabic. No, she heard some other language.

She answered in Arabic, trying to clear her thoughts. Desperately cold, she nevertheless felt fingers on her hands, prying her cramp-knotted grip loose of the horse's mane. How had she held on?

The man pulled, and she twisted out of instinct and fell in a heap, the horse tiredly shying to the side.

The man, Scar Face—it came back to her—kicked her in the side, ordering her in that incomprehensible Indian language. She lay there, fingers digging into the soggy soil. He kicked her again, harder, pain lancing through her side while his voice got louder.

"Go away," she whispered.

The next kick blasted enough pain through her to leave her gasping. She stumbled, trying to stand, and fell again. She tried to roll away as hard fingers gripped her hair, lifting her. She cried out. By brute strength he pulled her to her feet, leading her along.

Viciously, he jerked her forward, sending her sprawling face-first into a gurgling stream. Thankful, she sucked up the sandy water, feeling grit slide across her teeth, tasting mud and earth and the brackish bitterness of alkali. For long minutes, she lay there. It came back up, her stomach rebelling; she vomited into the runoff only to suck up the life-granting moisture again.

Fingers tangled in her hair, pulling her in a welter of pain to her feet. The sound issuing from her throat carried the strains of a wounded kitten. He threw her sprawling again. Uncaring, she dimly felt his hard hands binding her wrists and ankles tightly.

Despite her shivers and aches, she slept—practically before his rough hands turned her loose.

The kick came again.

Arabella winced, turned her head, feeling prickly grass and sand sliding along her cheek. She opened her eyes to a dim dawn. A light misty rain fell. Someone had dropped an old blanket on her.

Scar Face chattered above her. She worked her mouth, dirt grating on her teeth. Something tasted foul. He kicked her again and she flopped over, lacking feeling in her hands and feet.

The blanket lifted. She could barely feel his hands working on the knots that bound her. Limp, her legs fell loosely. Then her hands slipped free. The pain began, throbbing as circulation returned to her extremities. Unbidden, she cried out.

"Arabella?" Sentor called, face pale as he licked his lips. "Hang on. Be strong."

Existence drowned in pain. She barely felt Scar Face pull on her hair. Like a sack of flour, he dragged her across the ground, her whimpering bringing the attention of the other men. Some laughed, some simply watched, detachment in their eyes while pain seared her body from scalp to toes.

Scar Face dropped her at the muddy side of the trickling drainage again. He motioned, grunting an order. Numbly, she put her lips to the water, finding her thirst could make her drink over the objections of her ragged nerves. He let her have a precious half hour.

Despite the pain, she could hobble after him back to the camp. Men laughed, three playing some game, moving a small bone from hand to hand. A couple of others watched from the sidelines with interest, joking and laughing among themselves. Others tended cooking fires or mended various pieces of gear.

Her fingers worked again, but poorly. If they continued the mad ride, how could she hold on?

"Allah, why didn't I go back to Saint Louis?" She settled where Scar Face pointed, barely having the strength to stand. A wilted lump, she melted to the ground, dropping her head. Her feet and hands burned and throbbed. Arabella fought tears.

She could hear Sentor cursing in fluent French.

So, Jeremiel had been right. This wilderness proved to be no place for her. Her soul writhed. Could it be? Without James did she really amount to nothing? Had it been him all along?

She closed her eyes, remembering the times she'd sniffed at the coddled pedestalized women in Europe . . .

or the domestic chattel hiding behind their veils in the Moslem world. Oh, she'd studied among the Sufis, since they granted women the right to learn—but the rest of the Moslems made their women slaves.

A slave—no more, no less. Sab Had had jokingly offered James a small fortune for her. "Would that you'd taken it," she whispered, remembering the fine silk-hung seraglio. "Wouldn't have been a bad life. Servants, all I could eat, constant shelter. Never hungry—and Sab Had once or twice a month."

She bit her lip, eyes going to Scar Face. No—it's unthinkable!

A slave. How did it happen? Memories of the slave market in Mombasa returned to haunt her. The Somalis and their Portuguese lords treated the blacks better than Scar Face treated her. Perhaps her worst enemy might be her own imagination? True, his fingers had tried to explore her body, but he'd desisted when she scratched him. Of course they were riding on a fast-moving horse at the time.

Her stomach growled and she gagged at the sand sticking in her throat. She blinked, ignoring the sounds of the camp. The smell of a smoldery fire greeted her nose.

How will I deal with rape? What will I do? Am I strong enough? Or will my mind break? A tingle of fear tightened the bottom of her heart.

"Am I strong enough?" she repeated under her breath, her fingers going to the deadly Malay creese hidden under her skirt.

From beneath matted tumbled hair, she glared at Scar Face where he fished something out of a steaming pot at one of the fires. He blew on it, joking with Red Shirt, eyes drifting to her after each riposte. He lifted his head, mouth open to drop the long strand of meat in, chewing firmly.

*Can I stand you?* Arabella wondered. She shivered again, violently, clenching her fingers despite the pain.

James's voice echoed from her past. "Let him get close, child. Surrender. Be meek. A man loses his concentration when he lowers himself. Thinks he's won. His mind is on release. Wait, girl. After he's coupled, get him then. He'll be completely distracted."

Arabella swallowed, crunching dirt in her teeth. "Distracted," she whispered, a sickness deep inside turning her guts watery. "You can't beat me, Scar Face."

But he could.

Sentor surreptitiously got to his feet, shooting a sidelong glance at the others. He made three steps toward her before a warrior stood up, gesturing him back with an old rifle. Sentor's expression hardened. His mouth worked, but he sat down again, crouched, ready to pounce.

Arabella craned her neck, looking out into the grayness. The clouds hung low, sullen, threatening more rain. To the north, she could see two warriors on horses, staring back up the trail.

The two quiet youths stood guard on the horse herd, none of the animals looking particularly fresh after the long run. Efende stood at the edge of the herd, constantly being harassed by one of the stallions.

Back at the fire, Red Shirt had acquired a circle of men who babbled excitedly as he showed off her rifle. Another man had her pistol in hand, fingering the inlay, examining it closely.

She jumped as Scar Face growled an order from behind her. He'd approached so silently. She looked up, heart battering the bottom of her throat. He gestured.

Awkwardly, she got to her feet, feeling the weakness in

her ankles and knees. When had her boots disappeared? She couldn't remember and it preoccupied her for several blessed seconds. *What's happening, Arabella?* She struggled to keep her fear from her eyes. *You're losing your mind.*

Scar Face pointed to the grove of cottonwoods.

She lowered her head, walking delicately on her bare feet. Could it be that he'd allow her privacy to relieve herself? Frantic, she latched onto the thought, willing it to be true. When Red Shirt and a couple of others promptly left their activities and followed, her heart skipped.

A rough palm caught her in the back, sending her stumbling on tender, throbbing feet. Before she could recover, Scar Face had her by the arm. Red Shirt caught the other. Someone laughed as they dragged her toward the trees.

From the corner of her eye, she saw Leander Sentor on his feet, seeking to break free. He went down, tripped from behind. The last she saw, a man stood over him, striking down with a club of some sort.

Then she fought, struggling as they passed the gray-seamed bark of the tree trunks.

She landed in a heap on wispy grass. Last year's leaves crackled under her, the new leaves of the cottonwood rustling over her head. Fear-choked, she looked up.

Scar Face smiled.

She got her feet under her, standing.

He moved fast, ripping her skirt loose, bursting the buttons. As the fabric—already strained—tore, she dropped her hand to the carved handle of the creese, slipping it out of the scabbard. She whirled, slashing, catching Scar Face by surprise.

Off balance, he stumbled back, not quick enough to avoid the blade as it laid his cheek open and ripped the forearm he threw up to protect himself. The blade caught in the heavy leather of his sleeve as he fell backward, almost dragging it from her weak hand.

Arabella danced back, circling, trying to keep them all in sight. This time, when one yelled, she kept her attention on them all.

Another feinted, lunging.

Arabella slashed, missed, whirling as another rushed at her. Breast heaving, she waited, watching as they circled. Scar Face stood, mopping at the crimson, a crazed look in his eyes. He hurled himself, unheeding, straight at her.

He batted her wrist to one side, smashing her to the ground. One horny hand clamped at her throat, the other seeking her eyes.

With all her strength, she drove the blade into his side time after time, knowing the kind of wound the undulating steel made.

Scar Face grunted, his hold on her weakening.

Her wrist numbed as Red Shirt kicked the knife away, rage contorting his features. Scar Face, eyes quizzical, lips slack, rolled away. The air went heavy with the stink of severed intestines mixed with blood. He sat up, looking stupidly at his side where red spread in a widening stain.

Someone whispered, awed.

Arabella, arm curiously dead, scrambled out of the way, trying to get to her feet. Red Shirt hissed, death in his eyes as he grabbed her petticoats, tripping her, pulling them off her thrashing legs. Violently, he ripped her blouse, the front tearing loudly as she twisted away.

She stumbled backward, breath coming in whimpering gasps. Throwing a fast glance over her shoulder, she could see him coming, teeth gritted, as his dark eyes glared hate.

# Chapter 11

Gratefully their horses attacked the thick spring grass waving lush in the May breezes along the silty floodplain of Sand Creek. About them, the land lay broken with low, irregular ridges of sandstone and shale lined by drainages that cut through the rock in lightning patterns. Periodic rainstorms rolled coolly across the plains, dampening spirits only until the bright sun shone golden across the grasslands.

Ab couldn't explain the sense of incredible majesty that washed over him as he rode. He traveled for days on God's green carpet, his very soul exposed to the Creator. Above, the vault of heaven rose in impossible blue. At night the skies glistened almost gray with so many stars even the angels would lose count.

Jeremiel had fallen in on himself, reading his Bible, even as they rode—though he'd take time to redress Bram for his sins.

Sand Creek led them to the Arkansas and right into a band of Cheyenne.

Ab reined Sorrel up, settling the Hawken into a reassuring position on the saddle. Jake just bulled on ahead, unconcerned, waving at the rest of them to hold up.

Ab pressed Sorrel forward at a walk, nervous, waiting to see what happened. Jake held up no less than ten feet from the eight grim-eyed, dark-faced warriors. Wind teased the feathers woven into their hair, pulling at the tails of their horses. They sat, stiff in the saddle, bows and rifles in hand, gaudy in the bright warm sun. With faces like stained walnut, they watched.

"Anybody got a ceegar?" Bram asked in a cowed voice.

Jake raised his arms and muttered a string of words beyond Ab's comprehension, his hands moving in the dance that composed Plains sign talk.

"Like Samson, I face the Philistines," Jeremiel muttered, right fingers tracing the butt of the Walker Colt while the left thumped hollowly on his Bible.

"Easy, brother. Trust Jake on this one," Ab warned.

The first Indian grunted, nodding, hands flying in rapid response, guttural voice a shotgun of foreign sounds.

Ab swallowed hard, mouth gone dry as he inspected each of those weather-beaten faces. Unyielding eyes stared back. Sun-blackened, noses long over tight lips, expressions lean, they seemed fitting men for the vast untamed land. Like prairie wolves, they waited.

"We about to die?" Bram asked, hands suspiciously near his pistols.

Ab lifted a shoulder. "Most likely not. When it comes time to talk peace, Cheyennes holler it the loudest . . . and they fess up to it. That don't mean meeting whites on the trail don't make a tense situation. A lot of stupid easterners shoot at first sight figuring their scalps are about to be lifted and their women raped. Asses! Can't tell a raiding Comanche from a peaceful Cheyenne. Hot-blooded kids from Missouri and Kentucky and places like that dream of coming West to kill an Indian. Is it any wonder that folks—red and white—get a tad strained? Somebody innocent always pays for stupidity."

"Something's up," Jeremiel noted, pointing.

Jake turned his horse sideways, backing him out of the way.

"Ab," Jake called easily. "Step down and pull a couple carrots of tobacco from Molly's pack. We'll need a tin of powder and a bar of lead too."

Getting off Sorrel proved one of the hardest things Ab had ever done. A spooky feeling shivered along his spine as he realized what it meant to be afoot that close to men who could ride over him like unchained lightning. His fingers fumbled thickly as he undid the corner of the pack and got an arm in under the manty. At Jake's sug-gestion, they'd packed the stuff on top for this very sit-uation. When he'd snugged everything down, he tucked the Hawken under his arm and walked forward. Jake and the Cheyenne had seated themselves on the ground, shaking hands, smiling.

"Sit down and smile," Jake instructed. "They're out hunting buffalo for their village."

Under Jake's guidance, they sat around in a little circle on the grass. A pipe came out of a beaded bag on the headman's hip and made the rounds. Each man took his time, smoking, singing, and making merry. Jake's hands kept going like sixty while he added an occasional word. One Cheyenne did most of the speaking, the others looking on.

"What's happening now?" Ab asked easily, nodding as the Cheyenne turned to watch him, faces perfectly ex-pressionless.

"Summer gathering for trade and talk with the agent," Jake supplied. "They're about ready for the renewal of the Sacred Arrows. Traders are out from Saint Louis and Santa Fe and they're reoutfitting."

"Ask about Wasatch," Bram added, glancing back and forth, excitement in his youthful eyes.

Jake looked around, nodding at the satisfaction growing in Cheyenne faces after the powder, lead, and tobacco had been passed around. He began talking earnestly, hands and fingers in motion.

The speaker nodded, breathing out some sort of exclamation, a gleam in his eyes. He talked rapidly, motioning to the west.

"Fitzpatrick is five miles up the Arkansas at the Big Timber. He's camped with the Cheyenne, Arapaho, and Kiowa," Jake translated.

"How about Wasatch?" Ab asked, eyes having already noted no white features across from them.

"He's there too. He's been busy with some doings with the Elks." Jake went back to signing.

"Elks?" Bram asked. "He's out hunting?"

"Soldier Society," Ab told him from the corner of his mouth.

"Along with the Kitfox men and the Dog Soldiers, they're pretty powerful in Cheyenne doings."

"How'd you know that?" Bram demanded, throwing him a skeptical look.

"Something I picked up once when we had to hole up at Bent's Fort and wait out the weather. Bent's married into the Cheyenne."

More words were spoken and signed. The Cheyenne shook hands all around, vaulted to their ponies, and left most spectacularly, hooves throwing up clips of soil as they cantered away.

"Heathen damned," Jeremiel whispered. "Hard to believe I just sat across from the devil's own."

Jake shot Jeremiel a hard glance. "Yep, and they never tortured Sweet Medicine to death on any cross either, brother." He shook his head, snorting disgust as he walked to his mud-colored bay.

"Who, pray tell, is Sweet Medicine?" Jeremiel asked Ab as they legged up into the saddle, turning west toward the Big Timber. The Arkansas snaked alongside the trail, a winding, brown torrent. High with runoff, chunks of bark, sticks, and foamy flotsam whirled by in the cold current.

Ab rubbed the back of his neck, thinking. "I guess you'd call him the Cheyenne equivalent to Jesus. The Cheyenne believe he brought *Maheo's*—that is God's—will to mankind. He came out from under the earth up near the Paha Sapa, the Sioux Black Hills, in Dakota Territory. He brought the Cheyenne the word of God."

"From underground?" Jeremiel squinted skeptically. "From the devil's own den. Yea, Jesus sayeth unto him, no man cometh unto the Father but by me!" Jeremiel's voice rolled out stentoriously.

Ab lifted a muscular shoulder. "I wouldn't try and second-guess God, brother."

Jeremiel went silent. Ab watched him fret, the thoughts reflecting in his face. Finally, Jeremiel could stand it no longer. "I can't help but wonder that no missionaries continue to work with them. To bring them light." Jeremiel turned to Jake, the question in his eyes.

The lieutenant shrugged. "The Cheyenne have heard all sorts of Christian preachers. When the white man's God didn't bring them more coups in battle, they gave up for the most part. But they still keep Christian crosses in their decorations and symbols . . . just in case."

"Reckon ya cain't fault that," Bram agreed. "Mike

used to talk about a witch woman down t' Louzianna. Said she'd wiggle her fingers an' make warts grow on a feller lessen he made a cross sign with his fingers. See like this." He crossed his index fingers, pointing them suggestively at Jeremiel.

The preacher sighed. "So many fallow fields."

Jake had been listening with half an ear. "Maybe," he muttered. "But I've seen some pretty impressive demonstrations of *Maheo*'s power. Same can be said about *Wakan Tanka*, *Tam Apo*, *Ni'atha*, or any of the other names for God out here."

Jeremiel grinned. "Your faith needs attending, brother Jake. You can take second seat to Bram."

"Yahoo!" Bram exploded. "Share the burden, Jake. I'm off the hook! Reckon Jeremiel hyar kin pound on you some whilst I enjoy my sin to myself fer a while!"

Ab couldn't help but wonder about Arabella. He sighed. Well, she's most of the way back to Independence by now. Safe, thank God.

The camp in the Big Timber proved something to see. Three miles out, the grass had been grazed short. Horse smell hung strong in the air, Molly and Sorrel picking up interest as they passed the grazed areas. A huge horse herd covered the sides of the breaks to the south of the river, dots of Indian herders watchful of raiders.

The Big Timber had been named from all the cottonwoods growing thick in that portion of the Arkansas bottoms. Ab had camped in the parklike bottoms with Santa Fe–bound caravans, enjoying the good grass, the plentiful shade, and deep water in the river. Never had he seen it so crowded.

They passed the Arapaho village, then a group of Sioux, and finally a circular Cheyenne camp. People called greetings with waves and smiles. The smells of camp drifted in the warm spring air. Smoke mixed with the odors of rot, cooking meat, leather, urine, and bruised vegetation. Naked children watched with wide eyes and fingers in their mouths. Molly booted one of the camp dogs snapping around her heels into a whimpering bundle.

Last Ab saw, a woman picked it up, smacked it one last time in the head with an axe, and tied it to a tripod in anticipation of dinner.

"Whar ye headed?" a buckskinned squaw man called from the shade of a tipi. He lounged on a backrest, the bottoms of the lodge rolled up and tied to let the breeze blow through the spindly poles. Two young women sat to his right, sewing.

"Looking for Tom Fitzpatrick," Ab replied.

"Yonder 'bout a mile." The man waved, fringes swaying on his arm. "Cain't miss 'em. Got whoa-ha wagons all over like ticks in a buffler's ear."

"Thanks," Jake waved.

"Whoa-ha wagons?" Bram asked, frowning.

"Yep," Ab grunted. "Seems Injuns got a big kick out of immigrants and freighters. Some call wagons gawdams from the cussing. Whoa-has can either mean a wagon or oxen, depending on the situation. You know, from the bullwhackers hollering out, Whoa or Haw."

Fitzpatrick's outfit bivouacked under a towering cottonwood, his wagons and a couple of small tents marking the place. Some other traders out of Santa Fe, Hardscrabble, and Bent's Fort had settled in below him setting up wall tents, tipis, or hide-covered lean-tos. Trade goods lay spread out on blankets, while buckskinned men squatted in the grass fingering pelts and talking lazily in the shade of the cottonwoods.

Thomas Fitzpatrick, Indian agent for the Upper Platte and Arkansas, stood up from the crowd sprawled leisurely around his camp. Indians sat and smoked; half a deer roasted over a big fire pit. A couple of whites leaned on their rifles and watched, keen eyes thoughtful as the Cattons stepped down from their saddles.

Fitzpatrick came over, smiling and stepping over reclining Indian bodies until he faced them. He'd grown lean and thin, piercing eyes nevertheless burning through a haggard expression. Behind a hawk's beak of a nose, he squinted slightly. Weathered lines of disappointment and courage made the creases around his mouth look dour. His snow-white hair stood up like a crest, gleaming in the sun. A deep-seated worry lay heavy on him—a worry of too many troubles on his still-broad shoulders.

"So," he breathed, a soft note in his slightly accented voice. One by one he searched their faces, measuring each, weighing the man by what he saw. "I see the Catton brothers. I take it, then, the rumor is true . . . Web is gone under?"

"Mr. Fitzpatrick," Ab greeted, taking his strong right hand. The left one remained a mangled mess. The story had it that Fitz had short-seated a ball once and the barrel of his rifle exploded, taking a couple of his fingers with it and leaving him the legendary name Broken Hand.

Fitzpatrick turned to the lieutenant. "Jake! It's been a while since we've shared a fire and told any stories. I hope the colonel is fit." Fitzpatrick slapped him firmly on the back and turned to inspect the others. "Jeremiel, from your age." He took the preacher's hand before turning to Bram. "And you, youngster, I was sorry to hear about One-Eyed Mike. I rode with him years ago . . . as did your father."

"You knew about us?" Ab couldn't help but ask, face flushing.

Old Fitz nodded, mouth puckering. "Oh yes. I'd even

been considered by Web as a prospective father." A twinkle gleamed for a second. "I turned him down. Robert Campbell got you instead. Worked out for the best." He smiled softly. "I guess I suffer from the same malady as your father . . . or at least I did. I'm older now. How delightful it would be to simply sit and let the world turn.

"Enough of my prattle. I suppose you have come looking for Wasatch?" He lifted an eyebrow.

"Yes, sir," Ab told him, memories embracing the times this man had bounced him on a bony knee. Fitz never made himself a stranger to Robert Campbell's when he passed through Saint Louis. For years he'd brought Ab something from the West, an arrow, a fossil, a bit of beadwork.

Fitz tucked his broken hand into his belt, a trait he'd unconsciously picked up to hide the deformity. He looked up from under lowered eyebrows. "Wasatch left almost three days ago. Don't ask why, nobody knows. With him, no one ever knows. He just walked out of an Elk dance and sent a pipe to the Medicine Arrows—to *Mahuts*—for some reason. Sent a boy to tell me to send you to his lodge and make you comfortable."

"What's this pipe business?" Bram blurted.

Jake answered, "He's asking for blessing, for medicine power to keep him well or help him with some undertaking."

"*Another* heathen? Why me, Lord?" Jeremiel groaned.

"Thank God!" Bram sighed relief. "With Jake and Wasatch, yer gonna be so busy you'll ferget about a few stole hosses and a nip or two at a jug." His victorious smile practically cut his face in two.

"How'd he know we were coming?" Ab's eyes narrowed.

Tom Fitzpatrick shrugged his tired shoulders. "Said Wolf came and told him." Fitzpatrick continued,

"Jeremiel, I'd guess this will bother you most, but Wasatch firmly believes his wolf carries the spirit of his Cheyenne father, White Wolf. The old man died of an infected snakebite. According to the way Wasatch figures, his father's soul went into the wolf."

"Wolf?" Bram cocked his head.

Jeremiel winced, head shaking. " 'Tis a trial of faith. No doubt Wasatch's game of checkers is as wretched as Bram's."

"Bet he don't cheat!" Bram grumbled.

"So he knows he has brothers," Jake pondered.

"Oh, he's known all along. He's obviously white . . . and when White Wolf adopted him, the old man never kept it secret. In fact, of all of you boys, Web only visited Wasatch. Hold it. Now I see that look. Just listen. The Cheyenne are different from whites. They have other notions about kin and family and so forth. It didn't cause any trouble for Wasatch. He's just a little . . . odd is all."

An old familiar churning started in Ab's stomach. "Odd how, sir?"

Fitzpatrick didn't want to talk about it. Hesitant, he sighed. "It is said among the Cheyenne that Wasatch talks to the animals. He can call up game . . . tame horses within a day. Camp dogs do his bidding and wild animals come to him and tell him secrets. He's reputed for his ability to heal too. Even the old medicine men will seek his advice."

Bram jammed an elbow into Jeremiel's side, whispering. "Maybe sis ain't so bad after all."

Fitzpatrick tucked his chin, eyes shifting from face to face as he watched them, lingering a moment longer on Jeremiel's. "Boys, he doesn't have many friends among the Cheyenne. He's obviously white . . . but that wouldn't stand against him. No, what makes them nervous are his odd powers. Think of it as . . . well, makes him an uncertain quality, you see. That, and there was some trouble a while back. A man insulted Wasatch's sister—uh, that's not Arabella by the way. She's back East—"

"We've met," Jake informed.

"Good. Well, as I was saying, among the Cheyenne, they take propriety very seriously. Calling Lark thought she was eloping. Scandalous—but acceptable—behavior. The other fella, well, he thought other things and her reputation was ruined forever. Wasatch was livid. He told the man worms would live in him. That feller died about a year ago. Seems a festering wound broke open. It was full of maggots."

Jake nodded slowly. Jeremiel blinked hard as he silently questioned, "Witchcraft?" forgetting to close his mouth afterward.

Bram looked sober. "Hoodoos," he muttered. "Oh, Lordy!"

Fitzpatrick chuckled suddenly. "Boys, I shouldn't have said nothing. I can see yer all stirred up over Wasatch, but listen. I see him every time I'm out here. He ain't nutty or weird . . . just has different beliefs is all. I think you'll like him. Considering how Web decided who'd go with who, you ought to be getting used to that now. Let's see, a preacher, a businessman, a soldier . . . and Bram." He didn't call him a thief, thank God. "Now, in this country, Wasatch fits right in."

Ab decided to change the subject. "We're supposed to find some inheritance. You knew Web; did he leave any map anywhere? We were supposed to have one but none of us ever saw it. There's also something about a ring. We met Branton Bragg at Fort Laramie. He told us."

Fitzpatrick's eyes went colder than a January snowstorm. "I see he didn't kill any of you."

"No, he didn't," Jake agreed. "But he, uh . . . tried."

Fitzpatrick shook his head, turning away. "No, I can't help you. He never said anything to me about any map. And I never saw him wear a ring." He motioned. "Come, sit with me. Unpack your horses and I'll have a boy run them out to grass. Throw your packs next to the tent. My driver will watch them."

As they walked, Fitzpatrick bent to mutter something in Cheyenne to a young boy. The lad nodded, flipping ink-black braids over his shoulder, and left at a run across the clearing for the Cheyenne camp.

After a meal of hot succulent venison, Bram allowed himself a resonant belch, and sighed happily in the shade. Shucks, poor Jeremiel, he looked like a feller walking through a black night's rainstorm and the ground just dropped out from under his feet.

Fitzpatrick turned to Jake. "Has the colonel had any word on this big treaty? If we don't act quickly, it's for nothing. The Comanche won't come in. They're down south. Claim they had a medicine vision that if they came into Big Timbers they'd catch the cholera. Maybe next year they say."

Jake shrugged and stifled a yawn. "Haven't heard a thing. Father's in Kearney while I was at Laramie. All I know is that he sent quite a few letters to Thomas Hart Benton while D. D. Mitchell has been hounding Washington."

"Fools!" Fitzpatrick cried, face lining in pain and frustration. "My appointment is almost out and those idiots in Washington are politicking . . . trying to make leverage for their own careers! Don't they know what's happening out here? Every year the freighters and immigrants come through. Shoot a couple of braves. Promise anything to get their wagons past the Indians. 'Sure,' they say, 'the Great Father is sending a wagonload of gifts right behind us.' How do you think the Indians react to that? They think all whites are liars!"

Ab swallowed nervously, looking at his hands. Bram figured he'd been in caravans like that.

"New Mexico doesn't help either," Jake reminded softly. "You might put that in your report."

Fitzpatrick grunted and spit into the fire. "And they call themselves soldiers! Worthless incompetents! The Apache, Navajo, and Comanche raid with impunity. When the soldiers can get out of the garrison, they stumble about in the brush . . . shoot some jackrabbits . . . and never punish a single raider. Makes it look like Americans are worse fools than the Mexicans ever were!"

Fitzpatrick raised his hands—one whole, one broken—and looked, pleading, toward the heavens. "Once they feared our strength. Now the Comanche despise us. You know what they told me . . . admitted right out? They said they *like* to raid the Santa Fe Trail. The immigrants are easier to kill than buffalo! No, indeed, the Americans are weak, they say, nothing at all like the Texans."

"The Rangers make sure of that," Ab reminded, shifting to lie on an elbow. "A closed trail would affect business."

"Aye," Fitzpatrick agreed. "The frontier army isn't a ranger force. Can't track. Can't fight. Can't get out of the cholera-ridden forts for drunkenness. Indians steal their horses and humiliate them before the women . . . and I'm supposed to enforce policy out here?"

He raised a hand and gestured at the lodges that filled the tree-thick bottoms. His voice softened. "We'll be at war with them someday. Those white-arsed imbeciles in Washington will fool themselves into thinking there's no Indian trouble until each and every lodge you see here is at war and the trail's knee-deep in blood.

"What then? The Sioux, Cheyenne, Arapaho, Kiowa, and Comanche will control every major east-west trail crossing the plains. These are no eastern Indians ... no 'civilized' tribes. They don't have permanent villages. These people raid for a living ... born on horses. They can ride circles around the finest light cavalry we could put in the field."

"Yep," Jake grinned humorlessly, "and most of the posts out here are manned by a couple companies of infantry."

"Yer kidding?" Bram demanded, awed. "Infantry? Against folks like them Cheyenne?" A fleeting memory of the Cheyenne party they'd parlayed with haunted him. Sun flashed on gleaming horsehide as the hunters dashed away, almost one with their mounts, rifles and bows held high. Infantry? Against them?

Fitzpatrick nodded agreement. "That's right. Infantry. How am I to hold them when they become too tired of broken promises? How am I to keep them satisfied that Americans are not trying to bring them harm? How can I keep the plains from exploding when I can't put together a simple treaty session without some government official's meddling?"

Jake grunted. "Life out here is going to be getting pretty tough." He raised his eyes. "You've seen the Sioux camps around the Platte? They live by begging."

"What happened to the buffalo?" Jeremiel asked. "I thought the heathens lived off the animals."

"They do," Fitzpatrick agreed. "But keep in mind, we've been selling them things like guns and powder and cloth and lead and pots. To buy them, they have to trade—and that means buffalo hides. What do you think the American Fur Company takes in trade? So they've shot out most of the buffalo along the major trails. Of course, the immigrants have been at it too. Can't move that many people across the country without playing hell with the root grounds and critters."

"So, they could move," Jeremiel countered, thoughts far away.

"So you'd think." Fitzpatrick's steely gaze penetrated Jeremiel's shell. "But they'd be moving into Shoshone or Crow or Blackfoot or Arapaho territory, trying to live off somebody else's diminishing herds. We're only seeing the beginning, but the end isn't that many years away."

"Unless something's done," Jake pointed out. "Like the big treaty."

In the silence that followed, everyone but Bram seemed lost in his own thoughts. He couldn't get rid of the insane idea of infantry trying to chase down mounted warriors. Nevertheless, he saw her first, picking her way across the clearing. A couple of passing white traders went out of their way to doff their hats which really got his attention. How often did a white man doff his hat to an Indian woman?

Bram got easily to his feet, letting his lanky loose-limbed walk take him in her general direction. She looked better and better as he got closer. Long braids—so black they shone blue in the sun—hung from either side of her heart-shaped face. A thin straight nose separated serious brown eyes. Her complexion radiated health and youth. Wrapped in a brightly colored blanket, she walked with an athletic spring to her step.

She looked up, eyes meeting Bram's . . . and his heart stopped dead in his chest. She gasped, raising a sun-browned hand to her mouth, eyes going wide only to be replaced by puzzlement.

Oblivious, Bram missed the warrior's approach, his heart and mind preoccupied by instant all-engulfing love. The man appeared at the woman's side, wheeling her around to face him, and hissing a sibilant threat.

Unthinking, Bram hustled forward, not liking the tone as the tall warrior berated the sudden center of Bram's stricken heart.

The Indian raised a hand, as if to strike her, and Bram stepped between them, jaw thrust out, one hand on his bowie.

"Huh-uh," he grunted, narrowing his eyes as he stared into the startled Indian's.

The man—a good head taller than Bram—lowered his hand, lips thinning under the huge hook of his nose. Through narrowing eyes, he looked into Bram's face, a slight tick at one corner of his lips. A hard finger jammed into Bram's chest as the Indian growled a threat.

"Same to you, fella," Bram hissed, feeling sudden fear ambush his heart. Couldn't back out now. He waited, feeling the tension in the air, chewing his cheek for courage, meeting the growing hatred in those burning black eyes.

"Ya don't strike a woman, mister. Leastways, not one so pretty as her." Bram shoved a knobby thumb over his shoulder toward the girl, who'd backed off a step.

The Indian's tight lips bent slightly and he added something else to his threat before turning on his heel and striding away, practically bouncing on his long legs.

Bram lifted his hand to scratch the side of his head, hoping to cover the total and complete funk as his courage deflated. He wanted to let himself sink like a soggy rag onto the grass and shake. *Oh Lordy, what did I almost do to myself?* He locked his knees so they wouldn't tremble.

"Reckon I done showed him, huh?" He turned to look at the young woman, now standing with her head down.

"Hey!" Bram cried. "Why, hell, I couldn't just let him smack ya!"

"It was his right," she whispered, refusing to lift her eyes.

"His right?" Bram swallowed so fast he almost gulped. "Aw hell." His heart dropped clear down to his butt, leaving a hollow place under his throat. "Now what've I gone and done?" He pointed to where the man disappeared into the trees. "He warn't yer *husband*?"

She shook her head, stealing a glance from under lowered lashes. "No. He is a Soldier. My brother is gone. He has waited a long time for me to leave my lodge alone."

"He's yer boyfriend?" Bram guessed nervously, wondering how long he had to live this time. Damn! How come I'm *always* in trouble?

"No," she whispered. "He is my brother's enemy." She sank broad white teeth into her lip. "And now he is yours."

"Yeah," Bram grunted, nervously shifting on his feet, blushing as he stuck his thumbs in his belt. "Well . . . uh, whar's yer brother?"

"Gone," she added. "Gone to find a *Mis'tai*, a ghost, that came to him in a spirit vision."

"Yeah, well, look. I didn't mean no harm." Bram's heart pounded. Lordy, what a pretty thing! His blood danced happily in his ears.

"Thank you," she smiled shyly. "You are brave. But I am not worthy of your honor or courage."

"Shucks," Bram grinned, dimpling his cheeks. "I think I . . . uh, wall, you . . . uh, I didn't do nuthin'. You looked surprised at first. Like you knew me."

"I know someone who looks like you. It was a surprise." She shook her head, keeping her eyes lowered. "No, I am unworthy to be in your presence." She pushed past him, head down, hurrying toward Fitzpatrick's camp.

Bram, flustered, suddenly realized the love of his life was escaping. "Hey! Wait a minute! Whar ya going?"

She hesitated, looking to see if anyone watched. She raised her eyes to his, just for an instant—long enough to dazzle him. "My brother has guests. His family has come from far away. I must go and welcome them to his lodge."

"Wait!" Bram cried as she started off again. "Uh, listen. I got a brother here, too. We'll be here fer a while. Maybe so y'all could come a visitin'?" Bram's throat felt like that Council Grove hanging rope had tightened, locking his tongue in his throat. "Uh . . . if you'd want, that is," he countered, devastated by his forwardness.

She smiled. "I'd like that." She lowered her head again, looking away. "But it cannot be. I'm . . ." Then she started away again, Bram bobbing along beside her.

"Yer brother again?" he wondered. "Hell, maybe I could git my brother to talk to him when he gits here. Maybe . . ."

She turned on him then, eyes hot. "You don't understand! I'm disgraced! Shamed before my people!"

Bram kicked the dirt with his hole-toed boot. "Wall, shucks, that makes us two of a kind!" He grinned at her, seeing her desire to smile back. "Ya see, I'm a hoss thief myself!"

She opened her mouth to speak and shut her eyes, shaking her head in futility. "Please, let me go," she insisted, practically pleading.

'Yeah, sure," Bram agreed. "Uh, my name's Bram. We'll be staying here with Broken Hand if ya need me." He followed along behind her, nervous, feeling awkward and suddenly gangly.

What in hell did I do? Bram demanded of himself. Damn near got my hair lifted fer that slip of a girl, that's what! He chewed his lip, remembering the hatred in that Soldier warrior's eye. Shamed, she says? Wonder how?

Bram strolled along behind her, admiring the sway of her hips as she walked. Cuss me fer a double-dyed fool. I ain't never spoke to a girl serious before—let alone gone plumb crazy fer one!

Yet the sight of those deep brown eyes, so pained and vulnerable, haunted him. What could she have done?

The woman surprised Bram when she walked right up to Fitzpatrick's circle, standing several feet to the rear, head down.

Fitzpatrick saw her, stood, and took her hands in his. "Calling Lark," he greeted. "Thanks for coming." He gestured around the circle. "These men are Wasatch's brothers."

"Huh?" Bram exploded, a sudden clutch at his already palpitating heart.

Fitzpatrick turned, head slightly cocked. "Allow me to introduce Calling Lark Woman. I mentioned her earlier. She's Wasatch's sister."

Bram let himself drown in her deep brown eyes, feeling a spell of dizziness settling on him. The first love of his life, this enchanting angel was his . . . his . . .

"Aw, fer the love of hog slop," he muttered miserably. "Yer . . . yer my *sister*?"

# Chapter 12

*A*rabella fell, kicking the hand loose that grabbed her ankle, aware of the knot of hard-eyed men who crowded around her, blocking her escape. Red Shirt grinned victory, standing over her. His hands went to his belt, undoing it while he leered hatred at her.

So, the end had come. She could see death in his eyes as he shot a quick look to where two men tended Scar Face. He'd take her, the rape brutal. Then the rest would have her. And when they were done . . .

Something gray blocked her blurring vision, men began muttering suddenly, fright in their voices. Arabella blinked the fog from her eyes, to find herself looking at a gray fur coat: an animal! A threatening growl sounded loudly as she recognized the creature before her as a huge dog. No, indeed, a large wolf blocked her way, its head lowered, ears back, the hair along the animal's back bristling. From her angle, she could see long yellowed fangs exposed as the head swung back and forth.

*"Allahu akbar,"* she whispered under her breath. One panic blending with another. The huge creature turned its head as the men backed away, yellow eyes pinning her in place. "God is great. There is no God but Allah, and Mohammed is His Prophet."

Abruptly, the wolf lay down, long warm fur covering her bare feet, tickling the calves of her legs. Whispers and mumbled Indian speech caused her to look up, seeing the wide-eyed wonder in the warrior's eyes. They stared back and forth between her and the wolf, faces slack with awe.

Red Shirt swallowed nervously, backing away, talking in hushed tones to the wolf.

Arabella got her arms under her, crawling slowly. Heart in her throat, she slid one foot back from under the wolf's side. Instantly, the big head swirled her direction, pointed ears pricked. Yellow eyes—powerful—commanding, met hers.

She froze, her teeth chattering fear.

For long minutes, they stared, Arabella's resistance fading like shadows at sunset. Completely defeated, totally unnerved, she clenched her jaws and tried not to cry.

Wasatch slumped in the saddle, swaying wearily in time with his tired Appaloosa. Periodically the animal would stumble, Wasatch reacting out of instinct to help the horse's balance.

Blinking, he peered into the graying dawn. Which way? Wasatch lifted his eyes to the violet heavens, raising tired arms as well as his hoarse voice, chanting for Spirit help.

An owl swooped from the sky, flipping past his head, gliding out over the grasslands. Wing tips shifting as they slid above the grass, a hollow hoot echoed, showing the way. Wasatch corrected his course, noting a dark patch of cottonwoods far ahead. Even in the distance, Wasatch could make out a horse herd guarded by two circling mounts.

An hour later, the sun brimming orangely over the horizon, he caught sight of horses; a multicolored wedge, they flowed over the ground, heading his direction. He stopped the Appaloosa, stepping down to exercise his cramped legs, letting the animal stand, head hanging, the bay blowing listlessly behind.

*Tsis-tsis-ta*, Cheyenne, Wasatch recognized Buffalo Thrower riding in the lead.

Relieved, he walked forward, leading his tired horses, singing a Spirit song under his breath as he enjoyed the respite from his narrow Cheyenne saddle.

Buffalo Thrower saw him, immediately shouting to those behind, swinging wide, coming at a gallop, rifle held at the ready. He slowed as he recognized Wasatch's Appaloosa.

Wasatch raised his hands high over his head, facing into the sun, singing a prayer to the new day. He called down the blessing of *Maheo* and the powers of the four cardinal directions and *Ahk tun o' wihio* in the earth below. Even as he sang, he knew Buffalo Thrower had stopped, waiting. The others followed.

A lifting ecstasy rushed through Wasatch's tired body, pumping new life along his veins as he turned, the slight stirrings of the morning breeze like light fingers along his cheek.

"Greetings, my brothers," he called out ritually, seeing their sullen faces, noting the reservation in their eyes, the hardness in the way they looked at him.

"Your wolf came," Pawnee Stalker growled disrespectfully. "He took a woman from us." He sat tall in the saddle, his favorite red shirt ablaze in the morning light. He claimed power lived in that red shirt—power from the Pawnee he'd slain to get it.

"She brought me here," Wasatch told them quietly. Would it always be this way? Would his powers always separate him from the People—keep him at an arm's distance?

"She killed Hides To Trap Eagles. Cut his side open with a knife that looks like a snake when he tried to take her," Buffalo Thrower added, motioning as he talked, trying to explain Pawnee Stalker's rudeness.

Wasatch looked to Pawnee Stalker. "Your brother is dead?"

Pawnee Stalker's lips quivered but he said nothing, the answer burning in his eyes. He pointed behind him to where a horse bore a body wrapped in a blanket.

"White men don't like their women taken and raped. You know how they are about captives," Wasatch reminded. "To take a white women is an act of war."

"She would have had to live first," Buffalo Thrower reminded. "We have heard white women do not have enough strength to last long. They are weak . . . like the white men."

Wasatch considered that, looking out over the horse herd where Cricket and Brown Boy held the horses. "It was a good raid."

Buffalo Thrower settled in his saddle, fingering his bow. "The Pawnee didn't think we'd be stealing their horses so early before they became fat."

"This woman, where is she?" Wasatch asked, letting his eyes stray over Pawnee Stalker's angered features.

"Back there," Buffalo Thrower told him. "In the trees with Wolf scaring the dung out of her. We left the man with her too." He cocked his head. "Tell me, Wasatch, who is she? What brought you to us?"

He lifted his chin, eyes on Pawnee Stalker. "I think she is my sister."

They all straightened. Some shooting quick glances at each other. Pawnee Stalker flinched as if he'd been hit, the anger shifting into distress.

"No one had her," Buffalo Thrower said in the sudden silence. "Wolf arrived before any man could place himself inside. We did not know who she was."

In the growing tension, Wasatch added quietly, "If Hides To Trap Eagles is dead, then perhaps that is enough." He looked at Pawnee Stalker, who waited, fingers gripping a shining rifle, eyes uneasy.

"I will offer ponies to the lodge of Wasatch," Buffalo Thrower added, looking back and forth between the men.

An offer of restitution, it was good. A low mutter of praise broke out among the others. "And I, called Whistling Marmot, I would have this thing settled."

Wasatch nodded. "I will take your ponies . . . give them to the old ones."

Heads bobbed in affirmation, relief in their eyes as they watched. A weight lifted from their shoulders. Smiles even hovering on dark lips, as the men relaxed. All but Pawnee Stalker. His hand worked nervously on the magnificent rifle, a piece worth many hands of ponies. He—along with the dead Hides To Trap Eagles—had damaged the white woman, the medicine sister to Wasatch. If the affront would be carried further, it would be between these two. Unspoken, the memory of High Walker's brother—dead of Wasatch's curse—remained in their forethoughts.

Wasatch could see the unease, the threat of witchcraft in the air. To Pawnee Stalker, Wasatch replied, "I hear the voices in my head, my brother. They tell me not to pursue this. The mistakes made on both sides make the balance. I find it just, do you?"

Pawnee Stalker closed his eyes, filling his chest and holding it before nodding curtly and exhaling his relief.

Open smiles now flashed around the group. No anger or violence would come of this. Harmony would remain in the camp of the People. The Soldier Societies would not interfere. They had all acted as proper human beings, all making honor from a bad situation.

"There is property," Buffalo Thrower added. "Horses, guns. They belong to this woman you claim is a sister, and to the white man too."

Wasatch cocked his head. "You doubt, Buffalo Thrower?"

The war chief made a gesture of negation. "Her eyes are yours. Her face is yours . . . if paler." He nodded assertion. "She proved she has courage and spirit, Wasatch." A wry smile curved his lips. "She would make a warrior a fine wife. Let her know I would tie horses before your lodge."

Wasatch nodded, seeking Elk Singer leading a steeldust and sorrel forward. Cricket prodded a strawberry roan from the herd to tie it to the steeldust.

Pawnee Stalker, face a study of anguish, handed the rifle shining of so many colors to Wasatch. Such a wonder belonged to his sister? He ran his fingers down the golden inlay that dazzled, tracking the colored jewels that sent bars of sunlight flying in different colors.

Pawnee Stalker wet his lips, hesitant to lose such a prize—even for the sake of harmony among the people.

"I see Hides To Trap Eagles back there," Wasatch said as he gestured, eyes on the wrapped bundle tied to a led horse. "When we return, we shall honor his burial. Then this thing will be forgotten Let us all forget. I have spoken, my brothers."

The last trace of stiffness left Pawnee Stalker's face. He nodded shortly and reined his horse to one side. The pile of weapons and clothing had grown before Wasatch. Without another word, they rode away, the youths chirping to the horses, flicking their quirts to get the herd moving.

Sighing, his energy draining, Wasatch began packing everything on his Appaloosa before mounting the weary bay and walking him toward the trees.

Leander Sentor tried to open his eyes and still the pounding in his head. He braced his hands under him and pushed, making it to a seated position before his stomach lurched and he vomited violently.

Gagging, he blinked his eyes open, the world whirling about him. He lifted an arm to wipe his mouth and almost pitched over sideways. The pain racketing in his head blurred his thoughts. He closed his eyes again, feeling a little better but for the agony inside his burning skull. Something warm and sticky trickled down the side of his face. His stomach pumped again with less violence.

He forced his eyes open, trying to blink the blur away, wondering where he was. Empty-eyed, he looked around him in the shimmer of his wavering vision. Two fires smoldered, thin streamers of barely discernible smoke twisting into the calm air. The spring grass had been trampled flat. What had happened? Where was he?

Algeria? No, too green. France? No, too dry. Where?

On hands and knees, he crawled to the thicker grass where a trickle of water ran, and drank, washing the taste of bile from his mouth. He leaned back, letting the cool air play over his wet face. He braced himself and dabbed at the wetness, seeing bloody water on his fingers. He traced it up to a matted place on the side of his skull.

The sting as he prodded didn't dent the searing agony in his head.

"Got hit," he decided. "Knocked out . . . probably."

For seconds he stared dumbly at his hands, before the thoughts centered in his mind that the person who'd hit him might still be around, ready to do it again.

Owlishly, his wavering gaze searched the surroundings, seeing only trees, grass, the vault of an incredibly blue sky, and the smoldering fires.

Leander tried to get up, finding his balance imperfect at best. Nevertheless, he staggered to a tree and propped himself, pain flashing through his brain like an axe blade being driven through his skull. Dizziness gripped him, the world spinning violently. Panicked, he grabbed the rough bark of the tree, hugging it close, his body suddenly hot and fevered.

Far out on the plain, he could see horses, one ridden by a man. His attacker? If only he could remember.

Frantic, he stumbled on, falling heavily, a liver-deep sickness contorting him. The pain in his head flashed white, searing. Gratefully, he sank into a gray softness that blackened around him.

Wasatch circled the trees, riding up until he could see Wolf, staring eyeball-to-eyeball with the woman.

"Wolf," he called softly. "You have done well, my father."

At his words, she tore her fear-locked gaze from the big animal, staring at him with glazed eyes. Wolf stood, panting, and trotted out through the trees, headed for the last of the runoff and a well-earned drink.

Wasatch dropped from the saddle, walking forward. Her reaction took him by surprise. She backed away from him, slowly shaking her head, a slight madness in her expression.

In English he called, "Do not run. I have come."

"Leave me alone," she rasped. "Get back." Then she continued to speak in a tongue Wasatch couldn't place—wildness possessing her eyes.

She'd been poorly used, he could see. Bruises had raised on her face. Her hair, once the color of sagebrush honey, now hung in ratty strands. Smudges of dirt and soot streaked her. What clothing hadn't been ripped away and scattered about under the trees consisted of rents and rags. Her legs, part of her side, and one breast had been exposed.

She continued to crawl backward away from him, mumbling in the strange language, heedless of the leaves and grasses crackling under her.

Wasatch settled onto one knee, hands open and friendly. "I am called Wasatch. I will not harm you. Instead, I have brought back your horse. Your rifle."

She stopped her backward crawling, the insanity shifting, terror seeping away. "Wh . . . who?"

"Wasatch," he added calmly.

"Wasatch?" Wasatch C-Catton?" she stammered, blinking.

He nodded, looking closely, seeing the fright and fatigue. She had reached the edge of endurance, hanging to sanity by sheer willpower.

"Your . . . your father?" She swallowed dryly. "T-Tell me . . . tell me who?"

Wasatch let his hand dangle off the propped knee. "One father was called White Wolf. His spirit is in Wolf." Wasatch gestured the direction the animal had taken. "His is the one who kept you safe just now. My other father was a white man, Weberly Catton. Among my people, the Cheyenne, we called him the Flower Man."

"I—I'm Arabella," she managed, fighting for control.

"Raised by a buffalo man," Wasatch supplied. "His name was James." The Spirits hadn't lied to him. He'd heard his sister's call.

"Buffalo man?" she asked, head slightly cocked, chewing her lip in her confusion.

"Black skin," Wasatch told her. "Like charcoal was rubbed all over. We call them the buffalo men because their hair is like the buffalo's. Thick, curly, soft to the touch."

Her eyes closed and she sank limply to the grass. "Thank God," she whispered. "You're Tom!"

He went forward then, picking her up easily, carrying her out to the abandoned camp. He noted the splotch of blood and smelled the stink of cut guts as he passed through the trees. Wolf stood to one side near the bole of huge spreading cottonwood, head lowered, wary, sniffing at a prone man.

First he settled Arabella lightly in the shade. The man proved to be out cold, breathing erratically. He had a good-sized lump and cut on his head, which had bled freely. Lifting the eyebrows, Wasatch studied the pupils. The man whimpered in yet another language, head cocked. He could pick up a word or two. French? The language of his white father?

Efficiently, Wasatch led the horses around, unpacking and establishing a camp. Blowing the fire to life, he dragged the man next to it and went for his medicine pouch.

Arabella watched, eyes big and unsure as she tried clasping the remains of her undergarments about her body. From the bundle he'd made of her recovered possessions, Wasatch handed her a dress.

Grateful, but without a word, she slipped behind a tree to emerge minutes later, clad but barefoot. She settled weakly across the fire from him, wary, a certain spark returned to her eyes. Perhaps a dress did that for a white woman?

"Your . . . wolf. It came just in time. Those men . . ." She lowered her head, shoulders slumped in a posture of exhaustion. With grimy hands, she rubbed her face, tension drained.

"Buffalo Thrower," Wasatch said. "He took a raiding party to the Pawnee to get horses."

She gasped, looking up, half-frantic. "They're your . . . your . . ."

"My People?" He looked at her as he checked the fire and settled a tin pail full of water on the coals. "Yes. They were Cheyenne. Some were Suh'tai, others of different bands of the People."

She closed her eyes, a pained expression tightening her face. *"Allahu akbar,"* she whispered.

"You spoke that earlier. What language?"

She looked at him, a defiant gleam in her eyes. "Arabic. I'll kill them, you know. For what they did to me. Tried to do to me."

Wasatch gave her a quick evaluative glance as he took some of her white underclothing from the pile and tore it into a rag. "You might think before you declare war on them. Pawnee Stalker and Buffalo Thrower are members of the Dog Society. Powerful men. Dangerous men.

"But you might think for other reasons too. I told Pawnee Stalker it was over. You killed Hides To Trap Eagles. A death for an insult. Mistakes have been paid for."

*"Paid for!"* she cried, voice breaking. "They robbed me, beat me, would have raped me . . . and you call that paid for?"

He dipped the rag in the steaming water and slowly cleaned matted blood and caked dirt from the man's face. "You sent Hides To Trap Eagles to *Seyan*, the home of the *Tasoom* in the stars. Whites call it the Milky Way. The blackrobes use the word 'heaven.' It is—"

"I'd have sent him to *Sheol*!" she spat viciously.

"Shee . . ." He frowned, trying to form the word.

"Hell," she gritted.

Wasatch smiled, casting a wry eye on her as he reached for his small bundle of herbs. "And hell is not a just payment for beating, robbery, and trying to rape? Is even the white man's justice not satisfied by that?"

Her eyes narrowed to amber slits, but he could see her chewing on it. Indeed, his sister demonstrated spirit. Pawnee Stalker might have been surprised. She would not have died on the trail. She had too much will to live. A woman worthy of respect.

"This man." Wasatch gestured to the unconscious white as he dropped *hisse e yo* and *mah esk oe* into the broth. "He is your man?"

Her eyebrow lifted and she shook her head.

Wasatch took sweet grass from his pouch and, snaking an ember from the fire, sprinkled it over the coal, blowing smoke in the man's face, singing softly under his breath.

She told him. "No. His name is Leander Sentor. I don't know much about him except I met him on the trail and *your* friends captured him before they got me." She watched for another couple of seconds before asking, "What are you doing?"

Wasatch finished his song, blowing another faceful of sweet grass smoke into Sentor's slack features. He checked the tea then, seeing the water had boiled to the right color. "Tying his soul to his body. Without doing so, he will die."

"With smoke?" she snorted. "Barbaric savagery. Don't you know anything civilized? Bleed him!"

Wasatch laughed easily, pulling the tea from the fire to

allow it to cool. He handed her back the glorious rifle and pistol. Seeing the gnawing hunger in her eyes, he threw her a small hide sack of pemmican. First she raised a suspicious eyebrow, then attacked it greedily.

"Do not eat so fast," he instructed.

"You know," she told him through a mouthful of food, "our other brothers are on their way to find you."

He checked the water temperature and tilted Sentor's head forward, waking him enough to get him to drink.

"My sister will care for them until we arrive." Wasatch noted with satisfaction that Sentor drained the pail dry. "But tell me, why did you travel alone? Why didn't you go with them?"

She sighed, dropping to one elbow. "They thought it was too dangerous." She blinked exhaustion from her eyes, looking out over the rolling grasslands where the wind played. "Maybe they were right."

Sentor muttered a jumbled sentence. Arabella straightened, head cocked.

"What is it? What does he say?"

She shook her head. "He's speaking French. Raving. Something about his mother and father dying on barricades. He keeps mumbling about General Cavaignac and . . . the legacy of France?" She paused, thoughtful as she studied Sentor.

Wasatch pulled the Damascus-bladed bowie from his belt, slicing thin sections from a thick piece of root. He opened the man's mouth, laying them on his tongue.

"What's that?" Arabella asked, pointing to the root.

"We call it *ho tat wiseyo*. Blue medicine. It is good for headaches." He scooped up water. "Straight like that, it will burn on the tongue. He'll want a drink."

Within seconds, Sentor groaned and shifted, working his mouth. Wasatch let him drink, satisfied to see the man sink into a deep sleep.

"You should rest too," he added, seeing her struggle to keep her eyes open. She nodded, tucking her shining rifle under one arm and settling her back against a tree. Within minutes, she slept. Using a broken branch, Wasatch cleaned out a water hole to hold the last bit of the drainage flow and settled himself into a posture of repose. One last look showed him the horses still picketed and Wolf moving in a wary patrol.

"Well, I can't figure it," Cal insisted bitterly. "We been back and forth every which way. They got to be out here someplace."

Branton Bragg chewed his mustache where it drooped over his lip. "We got twenty men out here, cutting for sign. How'd they get past us?" He pulled at the white streak of his beard, eyes on the distant mountains. "Lessen they went up one of the ridges. Followed up into the mountains."

Cal Backman turned in the saddle to stare at the high Front Range. From where he sat, Pike's Peak lay to the northwest, the Spanish Peaks visible on the far southeastern horizon with the broad drainage of the Arkansas River cutting back to the west. Beyond that, the ragged skyline formed an impenetrable wall.

"We'd never find 'em in there," Cal growled. "Too many ridges to check. Too many valleys."

Branton Bragg nodded his agreement. "Yep. 'Fraid so."

Cal slammed an angry hand onto the saddle horn, the worn leather unyielding under his palm. "Jeff and me, well, we rode trail for a long time. I ain't aletting Ab Catton get away with it!" He looked back at Hank Tent's lumpy jaw and shivered. "Nope, I just ain't gonna."

Branton chuckled gruffly. "Yep, well, I ain't aiming to let Web Catton's kids git the best of me neither. That . . . and there's something I'm gonna take back for all the years and hurt he cost me." Frosty blue eyes narrowed. "Just don't you go letting me down. I don't like folks letting me down."

Cal shivered under the hard delivery. "You don't worry about me, Branton. I got my score to settle. Figger Hank there deserves better. Hell, look at him. He's gotta eat soup for the rest of his life 'cause of the way that damn mule of Catton's kicked his jaw in." He pulled his hat off, wiping the sweat off his forehead. "And I ain't gonna fergit rolling Jeff into that hole and shoveling dirt in his face down on the Blue neither."

Bragg nodded, cutting a chew from a horseshoe of tobacco. "Yeah, now, that's just real fine, Cal. I like men who're driven by more than money." He waved a beefy hand at the others lounging on their saddles, waiting for orders. "These, they ride for the cash. Can't cotton to a man that only works for money. Ain't like the old days when honor and loyalty meant something."

Cal bit back his remark, looking over the rabble. That's what they looked like, rabble. Fenton and Smart might have had some saving grace, being broke-down mountain men; only the track of the jug lay on them. Too much popskull for too long did that to a fella—left him hollow-eyed, short on nerve or guts.

The others, well, they'd have to be watched if the money ran short. Cal shifted his eyes to Branton, noting the bulge of muscle sliding under that honey-toned buckskin. Then again, only a fool would cross Branton Bragg and expect to live.

"So what do you think?" Cal asked, returning to the original topic. "Where are they?"

Branton looked up at the sun, crow's-feet lining his eyes as he squinted into the bright light. His beard worked, the white streak undulating as he chewed the quid, getting it to juice. He spat a brown streak and nodded to himself.

"Hank!" Bragg bellowed. "Take some of the boys. Go stake out the Pueblo. Cal, you take some others, head up to Hardscrabble and see if them Catton boys sneaked past us and went on into Taos."

"And you?" Cal asked, cocking his head.

Bragg's eyes turned to ice. "That ain't yer bizness, Backman. But just for this once, I'll tell you." He spat, the amber stream hitting the side of Cal's horse's head, causing the animal to jerk. Bragg waited, anticipation in his eyes, seeing Cal's anger and fear. "Yeah, like I thought. Little spit won't make you lose your head. I'll take the rest of the boys and circle around the Purgatoire. See if they cut south over Raton Pass for Las Vegas or Santy Fee. Ain't many other ways they could go, now is there?"

Cal steeled himself, screwing up his courage. "I don't want you getting that Ab Catton." He leveled a finger, using all his nerve to meet those deadly blue eyes. "All right, Branton? You talked about loyalty? Takes two. I'll stick. I'll do what you say with no questions so long as you give me your word—as a man of honor—that you'll keep Ab Catton alive for me."

Bragg's expression didn't change as he chewed slowly, thoughtfully, on his quid.

Cal's heart stopped in his chest, death looking levelly across from those cold eyes. Bragg spit again, hardly shifting in his saddle.

"Sure, Cal," Bragg whispered. Then a slow smile shifted the beard. "You know, I like you, Backman. You got guts. So long as you don't get smart, I'll keep you around. Now, git your ass up to Hardscrabble and see who's been through. Meet me back to Bent's Fort in a week, hear? Seven days, Backman. You, too, Hank. Seven days and you be at Bent's!

"In the meantime, any of you spot the Catton boys, you send a rider to me pronto! Hear? Pronto!"

Cal smiled, motioning to the men he wanted. Yeah, he'd take Smart and Fenton. Reining his horse around, he gave a wink and smile to Hank Tent as he trotted to the west and the blue-green barrier of the Rockies.

"I'm coming to get you, Ab Catton," he promised under his breath.

Jeremiel's knees ached as he stood up, dusting off his pants. Below him, the sight seemed pristine, beautiful, the rising sun just touching the tops of the endless lodges scattered about the broad valley at the Big Timber. Others lay in shadow, the cottonwoods lit in lime-green colors that dazzled the eye. Smoke wove into the air, blue-gray spirals climbing toward the blue heavens and the Holy Father.

So much peace, so much beauty, and all of it marked by the Prince of Darkness, sullied by his deceiving hand.

Jeremiel swallowed, remembering the Indian men he'd passed on the climb up the cobble terrace to pray. They'd run past him, headed for the river and their daily bath—shamelessly naked! And worse, completely heedless of the women who gathered water from the river even as they bathed!

"Lord," he prayed, "how do I touch them? How can I show them the evil of their ways?" He closed his eyes, a feeling of impotence lying heavily on his shoulders. "How can I even save my faltering brothers?"

He turned, letting his thoughts wander, anguished by his own insecurities. Bram seemed absorbed by Calling Lark Woman, the girl only a year or two older than he—and by Cheyenne standards, an adulteress!

Wasatch, the missing brother, even made a wilderness barbarian like Thomas Fitzpatrick cringe. A heathen witch doctor, a mere youth already perverted by Satan's hand no less firmly than his already damned sister.

"O Lord, my God, is there no end to this? Because I betrayed You, and myself, with lies once, do You torment me?"

Movement caught the corner of his eye. He looked over in time to see the man plodding at a dogtrot. This time the beard caught the light. Gray, grizzled, looking old. The man carried a long flintlock rifle and he looked at Jeremiel from under a badgerskin cap, the tail flapping behind the man's neck.

The fellow turned as he dropped down into a drainage, the sunlight catching the front of his hunting shirt. There, plainly visible in the clear air despite the distance, Jeremiel could make out a fleur-de-lis.

The Hoodoo man! It had to be!

Suddenly excited, Jeremiel hurried across the thin grass, cobbles shifting hollowly under his feet. How far? A hundred yards?

He was panting as he made it to the narrow cut, looking up and down the jagged cleft worn into the terrace conglomerates.

A half hour later, perplexed, Jeremiel ran a finger under his hat to scratch his head. Again he studied the bank. True, he couldn't hold a candle to Jake's tracking ability, but nowhere could he see where the man might have descended the steep sides—though his own tracks stood out well enough.

"What did you find?" Jake called from above, hunkered down on his haunches, watching.

"The Hoodoo man," Jeremiel replied, describing what he'd seen.

Jake nodded, getting to his feet. He slid down the loose walls of the arroyo, backpedaling artfully to keep his balance in the cascade of cobbles and loose sandy silt.

"Uh, I asked Fitzpatrick about that." Jake looked up and down the arroyo, thumbs hitched in his pistol belt. "Fitz described the man. You say you saw the flower on his chest?"

"Yes, quite clearly, it was . . ."

". . . a blue fleur-de-lis," Jake finished.

"You saw him!" Jeremiel cried in relief.

"Nope." Jake shook his head, eyes narrowing. "But Fitzpatrick described him." Jake tucked his chin against his chest, studying the dirt underfoot. "You heard Calling Lark refer to the Flower Man?"

"Yes." Jeremiel's guts tightened.

"The Flower Man, the fella old Fitz described with the blue fleur-de-lis?" Cool amber eyes met Jeremiel's. "That's the way Web Catton dressed when he was alive."

# Chapter 13

He's been raving about Algeria," Arabella said, face somber in the flickering light of the cottonwood and buffalo chip fire. While flames licked off the cottonwood, the dung smoldered redly, giving Wasatch's face a devilish cast. Idly, Arabella wondered what Jeremiel would think of that.

"And you only met him on the trail?" He pulled at his pipe, sucking the willow bark and tobacco smoke deeply into his lungs before blowing the smoke out to the four directions.

"I'm skeptical," Arabella told him. "Comes from living too long with James. Anything which couldn't be described as an instant coincidence made us nervous."

Wasatch grinned at her, the turn of his face carrying similarities with Bram's. "I have seen such men around Bent's Fort and Richard's Bridge. The whiskey runners act that way. You ran whiskey to these . . . uh, Arabics?"

She lowered her lashes, studying him. A sharp man this brother of hers. But then, weren't they all . . . well, maybe with the exception of Jeremiel.

"No," she told him seriously. "We didn't run whiskey. Moslems don't drink. In fact, they get most irritated at its presence among their peoples. Say it robs the mind of spirituality. Their holy book, the Koran, condemns it."

Wasatch nodded, keen eyes on her, absorbing everything she said.

He sang a soft song, scraping the ash from his pipe with a special willow stick he carried in the pipe bag. His fingers moved positively and surely as he placed the pipe in the intricate beaded sack and laced it closed around an elkhorn button.

"You act like a mullah," she whispered. "Surprising for a . . . man of your age."

"Mullah?" He cocked his head, eyes thoughtful.

"A holy man who studies Allah," she added, moving to lie on the blanket. "I'll anticipate your next question. Allah is another name for God. I'm sure there's some equivalent word in Cheyenne."

"*Heammawihio*, or sometimes we call the Great Mystery Creator *Maheo*." He leaned on his crossed legs to check Sentor. "I think he'll live. I can feel his soul tying tightly to his body."

She frowned. "You can feel it?" *Boy, Jeremiel will love this!*

His smile carried that impish quality she'd grown to expect from Bram. He lifted a shoulder in a very familiar shrug, then looked at her, betraying his perplexed thoughts. "I'm not sure I can explain it in the language of men." He gestured the futility of it. "The feeling comes here"—he motioned to his heart—"and here." Wasatch touched his forehead. "A feeling of . . . of rightness."

She pinched her lip with her teeth. "You told me earlier that a badger and an owl pointed the direction to find us out here. Is that the same?"

He looked over to where Wolf lay on his side, feet extended, toes flexing in a dream. The big animal's nose wiggled as he enjoyed whatever sights and experiences passed through his soul's eye.

"Different," Wasatch decided. "I . . . can't tell you why. The thoughts just form in my mind. It's always been that way. I know what the animals feel. Sometimes I can get an idea across to them. Sometimes I can't. It is Spirit Power. Can you tell me what makes Spirit Power? What are the ways of God?"

She straightened her legs on the blanket, rubbing her knees where they'd grown stiff. "I studied for a short time with a group of people called Sufis. They say that man is God. All is the One. Only our thoughts keep us apart."

Wasatch nodded sagaciously. "My people, the *Tsistsis-ta*, believe that the Great Creator lives up there." He pointed to the night sky. "Beyond the sun, and up the Hanging Road, which you call the Milky Way. Some have died and gone there before coming back to their bodies. Others say it is all foolishness. Me, I feel. I believe in the soul, the *tasoom*. It can travel—perhaps it is part of the Great Creator? Then we are all God. I can believe that."

She smiled. "You'd make a good Sufi. Probably a better one than I."

He waited, pensive.

"I only started the *tariqa*, the mystical way." She shrugged, curiously bothered by that part of her history. "I guess I couldn't fully commit myself. The lure of following James on his travels always enticed me more than studies." She pulled a sprig of grass from the blanket edge and twirled it. "Also, I couldn't ever convince myself to become *faqr* and give up my worldly goods."

"Your rifle is worth many horses," Wasatch agreed. "Pawnee Stalker hated to give it up."

"Red Shirt," she hissed, jaw tightening. "What I'd give to wrap my fingers around his neck and—"

"You killed Hides To Trap Eagles," Wasatch reminded. "Do your Sufis think that is not retribution enough?"

"Scar Face? His name was Hides To Trap Eagles?" She lifted her lip in disgust.

"He was a brave warrior," Wasatch added softly. "The scars he bore with pride."

"Some woman give them to him?" she asked unkindly.

Wasatch shook his head. "He trapped eagles. The way it is done, a warrior hides in a shelter on a ridgetop, usually with a dead rabbit to bait the eagle. When the eagle drops from the sky and grabs the rabbit, the hidden man grabs the eagle."

"*Allah!*" she cried, sitting up. "That's crazy!"

"A man must possess bravery . . . and power," Wasatch agreed. "The man you killed had that power. No one could catch eagles better . . . except Iron Band, but he died in the cholera last year."

"And the eagles gave him those scars?" She twirled the grass between her fingers.

"Eagles are very fierce," Wasatch said, humor in his eyes. "Especially when they're surprised by a man grabbing them out of the very air. Their spirits become one with the trapper."

Stoically, she added, "He's still better off dead than me raped."

"I think I have made peace," Wasatch sighed. "Your arrival in camp will be a momentous thing."

"What about Sentor?" She pointed with her grass spear. "He can't ride."

"He will in the morning."

"Bram?"

He looked up from where he dozed in the sun. Calling Lark still took his breath away. She settled next to him, worry in her eyes.

"Hey? That High Walker fella after you again?" He propped himself on his elbows, lifting his hat higher on his head so he could see her.

"You hear the voices back over there?" She gestured toward the trees, one slim hand brushing her braids over her shoulders.

Bram cocked his head, hearing a cacophonous mixture of whoops and shrieks. "Uh-huh? That a powwow or sumpthin'?"

"A raiding party returning," she added, anxiety behind her soft brown eyes. "The story is already going around camp. Your sister killed a warrior."

Bram jerked up straight. "My sister? *Arabella?*"

Calling Lark looked at him absently. "I don't know. A white woman Wasatch called his sister got captured by the war party on their way back from stealing Pawnee horses. One of the warriors tried to make her his woman and she stuck a snake knife in his side and killed him. Then Wolf arrived and saved her. No man will challenge Spirit Power. Wasatch showed up then and made peace between her and the people."

Bram lifted a hand. "Hold it. Made peace?"

"A man of the People, *Tsis-tsis-ta*, has been killed, don't you see? This is serious. Buffalo Thrower said that Wasatch made peace—said the insult to his sister was balanced by the death of Hides To Trap Eagles."

A cold shiver settled in Bram's stomach. "She followed

us! Damn it, she did!" Bram took Calling Lark by the shoulders, feeling her firm flesh under his fingers, ignoring what his body told him. "What do you mean exactly when you say this feller tried to make her his woman?"

"You know," she told him, making a suggestive gesture with her fingers. "He wanted to lie with her. I don't know the English word."

"Holy cow flops," Bram whispered. "Not Arabella, she wouldn't have stood for ..." He got to his feet, taking Calling Lark's hand in his. 'C'mon, we gotta go find Ab and Jake."

"At Broken Hand's, I saw them on the way to the river."

Bram's mind raced as they hurried across the camp, people generally gravitating to where the returned warriors had brought in the horses.

"Why?" Bram growled. "Why did he try and force her?"

"She was a captive," Calling Lark reminded. "What is your English word? Slave?"

"Oh, Lord," Bram whispered, "I hope we can keep Jeremiel cool."

They made their way through the trader's camp, Bram muttering, "We got trouble!"

Jake, Ab, and Fitzpatrick looked up from cups of coffee, the humor on their faces freezing.

"Arabella followed us," Bram began. "Seems as though some warriors led by a fella named Buffalo Thrower caught her. One jasper, uh ..." He turned to Calling Lark. "Who?"

"Hides To Trap Eagles. He tried to take her. Make a slave of her."

"That means rape," Bram added fervently. "Well, Arabella knifed him and he died. Then Wasatch showed up and—"

"She followed us?" Jake demanded. "Is she all right?"

"Easy, boys." Fitzpatrick placed a hand on Ab's shoulder, pulling him back down. "Let's hear all this."

Fitz turned to Calling Lark. "Wasatch made peace?"

She nodded, lips pursed. "The warriors report that he offered to honor the dead. They in turn will give horses which Wasatch will give to the widows and poor. They claim Hides To Trap Eagles and Pawnee Stalker didn't know she was Wasatch's sister and she didn't know it was wrong to kill one of the People. The two mistakes cancel."

Fitzpatrick ran a hand over his face, blowing out his cheeks as he exhaled. "Whew! Thank God Wasatch has sense."

"I don't understand," Ab grunted, a black frown on his face. "They tried to *rape* my sister?"

"Settle down," Jake added evenly. "If she's all right, and if Wasatch didn't take insult, and if no one carries it any further, no one will get hurt."

"Hurt?" Ab growled, face working. "Some Injun tried to . . . to . . ."

"And she killed him," Calling Lark reminded.

Fitzpatrick cocked his head. "And they didn't shoot her on the spot?"

"Wolf arrived." Calling Lark settled herself neatly on a blanket.

Bram refused to let loose of her hand. She didn't try to pull it away. Despite the excitement, his heart pounded for other reasons.

Jake chuckled softly. "She warned us. And now that I think about it, she never did really agree to go back. She just told us to make the arrangements . . . never said she'd obey. And do you remember when she said if the British and the others couldn't stop her, neither could we?"

Fitzpatrick ran a hand over his white shock of hair. "Sounds like she's Weberly's daughter," he sighed. "It must be a Catton legacy to always be in trouble."

Jake shook his head. "She's such a lady! And to think, she killed a man . . . a warrior?"

"Jeremiel will go nuts," Bram reminded. "He'll be shouting and raving at all them warriors, damning 'em, and tellin' 'em they'll be headed to hell right quick."

"Can't let him," Fitzpatrick said soberly. "There's a cauldron simmering here." He looked around, something hard in his keen expression. "Consider, last year the cholera went through the Kiowa and a good half of the Cheyenne, all those south of the Republican River. A lot of folks died. You get south of here along the Canadian, and there's scaffold after scaffold of dead. Now, if Jeremiel starts spouting damnation and threatening the people, it could cause a witchcraft scare. It's bad enough that Wasatch is involved. They already think he has witch powers. Jeremiel being his brother? Well . . ."

"I understand," Jake added grimly, a firm set to his jaw as he fingered his chin. "If we have to tie him up and gag him, we'll keep him quiet."

"What about my sister?" Ab demanded angrily.

"Reckon she kilt that feller," Bram reminded. "Now, big brother, no damage has been done . . . yet." Bram's face went tight. "Remember what Fitz done told us that first day? These Injuns around here is a bit worried about the future. They done got half of 'em wiped out last year from cholera. Now, how about we let Wasatch and Lark here handle it? They know the territory hereabouts."

Ab began to speak and bit it off. Bram could hear the grinding of his teeth, see the anger building red behind his flushed features, the big hands knotting and unknotting.

"Agreed, big brother?" Bram insisted. "You look me in the eye and tell me. Reckon we'll have nuff trouble hog-tyin' Jeremiel."

Ab nodded, thick shoulders drooping. He looked up to meet Bram's eyes. "Agreed." He paused, then added, "You know . . . Aw, nothing."

"Don't tell him," Lark said simply.

"Don't tell . . ." Jake looked confused. "What do you mean, don't tell him?"

She lifted a shoulder, face placid. "Jeremiel lives inside his mind. Every morning, he leaves before dawn, climbing the ridges to talk to the blackrobe God. When he is not there, he reads from the Spirit Book. He doesn't see what lives around him. He doesn't hear the birds in the trees or the calls of the children. He doesn't feel the ground he sits on. If you do not mention it, who will? Jeremiel knows no Cheyenne."

Bram let his lips curl into a smile. "You know, Lark"—he laughed—"a feller could git t' like you a heap!"

She looked at him sideways, color climbing her smooth cheeks as she smiled demurely before dropping her eyes.

Leander O. B. Sentor fought dizziness as Arabella and the Indian lifted him into the makeshift arrangement of ropes and blankets Wasatch had created. The Indian called *this* a saddle?

At least he'd awakened that morning with his memory intact, although his mind felt fuzzy and his balance would disappear all of a sudden. The world would whirl suddenly, vision blurring.

"Why don't they keep real saddles?" he asked, voice hoarse, head still throbbing despite the fiery slices of root Wasatch insisted he eat. The stuff did seem to help.

"Warriors consider them foolish," Wasatch said. "Saddles are for women and old men. A warrior worth respect needs only a horse. Besides, a saddle is extra weight for the horse to carry in war or the hunt where speed and quick movements might mean coup . . . or life." The Indian walked over to his curiously spotted horse and hopped lightly astride.

Arabella threw herself up on her steeldust and rode astride, considerable bare leg visible where her skirt hitched up. Indeed, an attractive leg too.

Ah, well, this was not Paris. That a woman could ride without a saddle didn't surprise him; nevertheless, he couldn't keep his mind off the implications of her bare flesh resting against the horse's hide. Of course, she'd be wearing underthings, but . . .

"Mr. Sentor?" Arabella asked, voice commanding. "I'm not happy about the situation . . . less so with you practically drooling."

He swallowed, nodding sheepishly after he dropped his eyes. He couldn't help sneaking another glance. Sacred infant of God. She took his heart away! He looked ahead, remembering the way the wind drifted honey-colored curls of hair about her fine cheeks, the set of her rich mouth, her classic brow. Ah, and how her complexion beamed of health and youth.

*And I murdered her guardian! But then, she needn't ever know.*

"We will not ride fast," the Indian called in accented English. "Your brain has been hurt. If you feel dizzy call quickly. We will catch you."

At that they started out, Arabella to one side under her pink parasol, the Indian to the other in case he wavered in the saddle. The movement of the horse didn't help the pounding inside his skull. Behind them, the pack animals lined out, plodding, his own meager remaining possessions tied on with Arabella's and the Indian's.

"You could return my rifle and pistol," Leander mentioned.

"I think not," Arabella told him, a cool look on her face. She studied him with a different reservation. My God, it hadn't been *his* fault!

"In this wilderness? Come, dear girl! Why, look at the fate we just escaped!" he cried. "I didn't get you into that situation! I had just returned Efende to your camp, after finding the beast loose and roaming! They came upon me before I had the slightest—"

"Tell me about Algeria," she ordered. Face expressionless as she waited.

"Algeria?" He straightened in the saddle, struggling to keep his face stoney. "Where is Algeria? I've been only to Boston and Saint Louis. I've heard of Santa Fe, is it—"

In fluent French she told him, "Immediately south of France across the Mediterranean Sea. Surely you recall. You spoke quite eloquently of it last night in your sleep."

"I babbled in my delirium," he murmured, a sinking sensation under his heart. "Delirium is just that . . . a wandering of the mind. You can't—"

"Only someone who has been to Oran could know the intricacies of the Mascara road. I agree with your ravings, incidentally; the water in the Chott Melrhir is wretched."

He fought his drifting thoughts. Despicable luck! To lose his faculties and then have to spar with her when his mind wandered like the proverbial Jew! Damnation! *How do I get out of this?*

"You are following me," she declared. "Why? Because of James?"

He swallowed hard. What do I tell her? How much of the truth? And what difference does it make now?

"I recognized him when he met you in Paris. The fact that I spotted him proved purely accidental. A stroke of luck after I met the two of you in Oran that night."

Arabella paled, throwing a quick look at Wasatch, who watched curiously. "Tell me the rest . . . in French," she ordered in that language.

Ah! She does not want this Indian to know. Then the game might not be over. Very well, in French it is. "It is most unfortunate that your James managed his shipments so well. The armies of France do not approve of those who supply rebels with arms."

"The Tuaregs, Monsieur Sentor, are not rebels. They are people fighting an invader." she told him frankly. "The term 'rebel' denotes a revolt against established authority. The armies France sent to Algeria—"

"Rebels," Sentor countered. "Their lands belong to France. All your efforts did was prolong the inevitable at the cost of more blood—French and Arab."

She laughed hotly. "A price the Tuareg—who will do the dying—are willing to pay, Monsieur Sentor."

He looked about at the empty land. "And what do you do here? Seek to bring rifles to these Indians, eh? You will arm Wasatch so he can bleed the American army when it comes to subdue him and his savage friends? Those same friends who attempted to rape you?"

"I have nothing to do with—"

"Whose side are you on, Arabella? That of civilization and the betterment of mankind? Or that of the blood-lusting savage?"

Her eyes flashed, jaw clamped tightly. "You tell me of your civilization!" she spat. "You tell me about the bloodshed the French inflicted on the Tuaregs and the rest of Algeria! For what? To keep that weak-kneed Louis Phillipe in power? What of the noble goals of the Revolution? Liberty, Fraternity, and Equality? Indeed, but only for Frenchmen ... and rich Frenchmen at that!"

"Louis Phillipe? He is gone," Leander sneered. "Deposed by the people! We rid ourselves of Guizot ... and the radical Louis Blanc. It was by the will of the people that the presidency finally ended in the *noble* hands of Louis Napoleon!" He sneered the name, knowing his feelings got the better of him.

Careful, Leander. You may be far from France, but do not let your cat out of the bag. Do not let this amber-eyed beauty trick you into admitting too much!

"A tyrant no better than the rest," Arabella jeered. "Wait, Leander, see what glories he brings France. Whatever he does, it will be at the cost of someone's blood."

"And you would prefer Cavaignac?" Leander countered. Misguide now. Be artful. Feel her out and see where her loyalty lies. "I saw what he did in Algeria and in ... in Paris." The memories of the barricades haunted him. Quickly he added, "Or perhaps you're a Royalist? You would bring back the Bourbons?"

"The time for royalty is past," she told him frankly. "But through your attacks, you have evaded the question. Who are you? Why did you follow me?"

A brilliant idea came to him. He searched for words, only to have the thoughts vanish like shadows at noon. Damn that rap on the head! He couldn't think straight!

He waved it off, trying to act casual. "When I recognized James in Paris, I immediately went to my superiors and reported. We were not sure, there are many exceptional arms companies in America. I was dispatched to follow you, to see if you would buy better rifles to exchange for Tuareg gold."

He sighed. "I couldn't figure out why you boarded the riverboat in Pittsburgh. So I followed. Then James ... died." Careful, Leander! "You did not return to the East.

A most peculiar development. Did you have some other connections? New Orleans perhaps?"

"No, I have no other connections," she added succinctly. "My family is here."

"Ah, yes." He smiled condescendingly. "You claim this savage is your brother. Much as you claimed the other ruffians were your brothers. You do have too many, Arabella. Your story suffers as a result." *But matches what I was told by Cavaignac!*

She mused for a moment before looking at him. "Tell me, Leander, which side of the barricades are you on? The people's . . . or Cavaignac's?"

"The people's," he told her powerfully, forcing himself to speak in strident tones, covering the lie with fervor.

"And your parents?" She raised an eyebrow, her words—like a knife—slicing through him. The sting of those memories returned to wrench him—a pain better left buried.

He winced. "They died on the people's side. You know of the June Days? The panic in which Cavaignac killed so many?" Seeing her nod, he added, "Then you know how my parents died . . . and why my politics are as they are." *And why they are not, most beautiful woman. The state must often split a family or two.*

His mind started to fog, vision blurring and shifting, the world whirling before his eyes. Reality dipped and swayed and he fell. Down, he continued to fall ever downward . . . only to never hit bottom.

His first cogent thought revolved around vomiting, but he bit back the urge. Hot rushes left him sweaty and disoriented. He blinked his eyes open, a haze before his vision.

"He's coming around," she said in English.

Arabella. America. He fit the pieces together, remembering. He looked up, finding himself lying in her arms, the cool plains breeze playing lightly through her hair.

"Drink," Arabella's firm voice compelled. A waterskin touched his lips and he swallowed, gingerly at first, a funny taste to the water. As his stomach stilled, he drank more, sighing as the skin pulled away.

Her lap comforted him, the feel of her arms secure around him. Ah, why had he never taken time from politics to find a wife to hold him?

"Here," she said, her voice soothing. "Eat this. You need strength and to rebuild your reserves."

Bit by bit, she fed him chunks of some sweet fatty stuff with meat in it. Wasatch walked up, his shadow looming over them. The Indian crouched.

"Try this."

Some plant, he took it in his teeth, tasting the bitterness of green leaves.

"Chew," Wasatch ordered.

Leander did, a burst of incredibly acrid bitterness causing him to immediately try and spit it out. Only Wasatch's hard hand blocked it, shoving it back in.

"Eat it all," Arabella told him seriously. "Trust him. He knows."

Leander ate, looking up into her concerned eyes, letting himself bask in the softness of her face, trying to ignore the fact that what he chewed would gag a horse.

A fierce gust of wind ripped past, bending Bram and Calling Lark in the saddles where they rode. The ominous black clouds of the thunderhead rolled down from the northwest, beyond the irregular buff-colored bluffs on the north bank of the Arkansas.

"We ain't gonna make it back in time," Bram shouted, eyes searching the undulating plains around them. "Guess we'll get wet."

"This way," she called, pointing, the fringes on her sleeves dancing. A slender brown heel tapped her pony's side and she bore off to the east, running her wiry animal.

Bram laid spurs to his roan, easily keeping the pace, leaning out over the animal's neck. The brim of his hat bent back by the wind. He let out a whoop as he booted the roan again, pulling up even with her. Buff patches of ground, mixed with light green clumps of new grass and darker green splotches of prickly pear flashed past below. Here and there, their horses jumped lithely over sunbursts of yucca and dodged occasional arms of the lanky cactus Lark called cholla.

A cold splat of rain caught Bram in the middle of the back as Lark reined to the side, her pony scrambling down an incline that opened out of the rolling flatness. The cut deepened into a narrow chasm lined with tan sandstone to either side. She pulled up, letting her horse slow as the rain began pelting down in silver drops that hit like bullets.

"There!" she called, pointing to an overhang of rock. Piled into the back corner lay a gray confusion of sticks and shriveled cactus. She bailed off, landing lightly on her feet and scurrying under the shelter.

"I'm gonna cool the horses down!" Bram called.

"You'll get wet," she answered.

"Yeah, and it's better for the horses. Be right back." He let the roan trot up the canyon, seeing how it narrowed until he barely had room to turn the animals around. Then he walked them back down the defile, seeing the trickle of water already running in the sandy bottom.

Water soaked his shirt and ran down into his pants, tracing icy fingers around his privates and down the inside of his thighs to puddle in his boots.

No problem there. Like his socks, Jeremiel himself couldn't help but approve of them boots—they was plumb holy!

To his surprise, he rounded the corner to find a small fire going under the overhang. He stepped out of the saddle, shivering. Satisfied with the way the horses were blowing, Bram crawled under the thin roof of rock, hands out to the fire.

"You could be a fish," Lark chided, shaking her head as she pulled another stick out of the gray pile in the back corner.

"Pack rat nest," Bram recognized.

She nodded. "I meant to come here before. Now I'm glad I didn't." Motioning him to bend over the fire, she added, "Take your shirt and pants off, they'll dry easier."

"Take my . . ." Bram's mouth fell open. "What . . . I . . . Uh . . ." He gulped, swallowing hard.

She looked at him, flipping a thick braid over her shoulder. "Silly man. You like to stay cold?"

"But you'll see my body!" he squeaked.

"So?" She turned back to study the pack rat's nest. "There is something wrong with it?"

"But . . . I mean only wives see a man's body!" Water dripped to sizzle in the flames and puddle under him.

She turned, head cocked, curiosity in her eyes. "I don't . . . Ah!" She chuckled wryly. "You have listened to Jeremiel. He always looks like he swallowed his food alive and its still kicking in his belly when he sees the men going bathing in the morning. The white men do not bathe?"

Bram grimaced. "Well, it ain't that eggzactly. It's more of a . . . well, ya see . . ." He felt a red rush creeping up his face. "It's just that when men and women see each other, they . . . you know . . . do husband and wife things." He picked up a pebble, rolling it around between his fingers, wincing at the thought of what he'd just admitted to the only girl he'd ever loved in all the world.

She wilted, averting her eyes and studying the fire, a crestfallen look to her.

Bram ran a hand over his face. "Hey, I'm sorry. I didn't mean it about you. I just wanted you to understand. We, uh . . . white folks, got different notions about clothes and what happens when we . . . Aw shucks, in trouble again." He flung the pebble to clatter down the rain-slashed slopes toward the brown stream running in the bottom.

"Uh, Lark, I ain't much when it comes t' talkin' with girls. Specially ones as purty as you." He swallowed, picking up her limp hand, getting no reaction from her as she stared listlessly out at the rain. "But if I could, I'd sure like to pay court to you."

To Bram, the only sound outside the chatter of the rain came from his thudding heart.

"Court?" she asked finally. "I do not know that word."

"Oh boy," Bram moaned. "Um, you know . . . when a fella likes a girl?" He lifted her chin to look into her stoic eyes. "When a . . . a fella thinks maybe the girl might like him? He does stuff. Like brings her flowers and . . . and tells her she's purty and his heart lights up when she looks at him. That's courtin'."

She took a deep breath, closing her eyes to hide the sudden confusion. Her jaw moved under his fingers while she chewed her lips. In control again, she opened her eyes and Bram enjoyed the sensation of falling into endless soft brownness, his soul swimming.

"I am shamed, Bram," she reminded, "I would not be worthy of you. A man—High Walker's brother—took me. I've been with a man who did not marry me."

"So?"

She swallowed hard. "You do not care?"

"Naw. I ain't no angel myself. I ain't never been with a woman, but shucks, I done other things I ain't all that proud of. Reckon I ain't gonna be holding no candles afore Saint Peter's Gate so I don't hold it agin ya." He gave her a reassuring grin.

She lifted his fingers away from her chin, sniffing as if her nose had started to run, while she blinked her eyes. She turned away, digging the sticks from the pack rat nest, feeding the fire. She didn't look back until the sniffing had stopped and she'd wiped her nose.

"Among the Cheyenne, no one hides his body," she added, voice muted. "At the same time, because we don't, it is important that men and women behave." She very deliberately laid the sticks in the fire. "I would have you know that, Bram. I will not misbehave again."

He grinned. "Reckon that's fine by me." The grin spread. "And since you're gonna play that way, I'll just sit here and keep my clothes on, huh?"

She giggled, pulling a big stick out, checking its heft and balance.

"What's that fer?" Bram asked, suddenly nervous he might be on the verge of experiencing some quirk of Cheyenne courting behavior.

"Dinner. You are not hungry?" She looked at him, eyes wide.

"Well, yep, I got a little growl in my gut; but what're y'all planning on eating?"

For an answer, she picked up one of the sticks from the fire, placing it at the corner of the pack rat's nest. Flames licked around the dry tinder and a long gray shape shot out one side. Lark's stick caught the rodent squarely, then she reversed it, smacking another fleeing shape. One by one they piled up.

The reflected heat from the fire dried him slowly, but Bram had to admit, pack rat wasn't half bad when a fella cooked them over the toasty coals of their own home. And it proved damn fine when a fella had a girl so pretty as Calling Lark holding his hand too.

# Chapter 14

Arabella struggled to keep her eyes open. Allah, would this journey never end? Sentor swayed in the saddle again, eyes glassy. Efende moved over—used to this new trick—and Arabella took her turn holding the sagging Frenchman on his horse.

Her arms ached; her back seemed forever bent out of shape, as if her spine would bear a permanent crook in it.

She shook her head. "I don't know. Is he really going to live through this?"

"He will." Wasatch decided. "Unless his soul decides to leave. To go away to *Seyan* and not come back."

"I never thought of myself as a nurse," she mumbled. "Why am I doing this? He followed us! Came to do us harm. Why, given half a chance, he'd have put James and me into a French prison where we'd be rotted to bones or . . . God! It's too much to think about."

She scowled and glared at the sky. "There *are* worse things than Hides To Trap Eagles and your friend, Pawnee Stalker. Sometimes I forget. I know how jailers use a woman. I've seen enough of that on three continents."

Wasatch placed his hand behind him, pushing on the small of his back, a pained expression in his eyes as he massaged. "I could let him go beyond *Seyan*. I have the right medicines in my pouch. Just mix them up and tell him to drink."

She studied Wasatch through narrowed eyes. Sentor had slipped beyond awareness. "Don't tempt me," she told him dryly.

Wasatch laughed, but the shared communication as their eyes met sent tingles down her spine.

*So, he can poison too? My, for a savage you have some remarkable skills, brother of mine. And you're so young yet?*

"I see so much peace in your eyes—and you can talk so easily of murder?"

He shrugged, searching the empty plains around them. Wolf coursed back and forth ahead of them, periodically leaping after a bounding jackrabbit.

"Death," he mused. "I have never been bothered by the dead. When I deal with *Mis'tai*, they are placid, not violent like the living."

"Sure," Arabella breathed in an arid voice, grunting as she struggled with Sentor's weight. "Wonderful thing, dying."

Wasatch tilted his chin, and his eyes followed the spirals of a buzzard as it weaved through the endless blue. "You will die one day, sister. So will I. We all know it. Humans, animals, plants." He spread his hand, gesturing across the emptiness of the land. "Look about you. See the grass and cactus? It must die to feed the buffalo and antelope and ground squirrels and mice. See the prairie dog mounds? See how barren the dirt is? They cut all the grass away, leave it bare so they can see the snake and badger. They kill the grass to live better."

"Rousseau would have loved you."

"So, why should we fear death? Without death, nothing lives. Not you, not the buffalo, not the trees."

"Why not the trees?" she demanded. "Trees don't kill things."

The lazy knowing smile didn't change. "But they do," he told her simply. "Open your eyes, sister. Here, on the plains, the cottonwoods struggle against themselves, each only getting so much water. Too many trees, and the biggest suck the water from the smallest.

"Beyond"—he pointed up at the high Rockies to the west—"I can show you where the trees grow so dense the young die in darkness under the spreading branches. There, the trees grow thin and fast, racing to keep the light. A dangerous game, for their brothers crowd close."

"So, the fastest wins."

"Maybe." Wasatch grinned humorlessly. "Or maybe the tree kills its brothers and stands alone until the first heavy snow. Then it finds the trunk has grown too thin, unable to bear the weight—so it snaps." He scratched at his ear, an inquisitive look in his eye. "So, he has killed his brothers? In the end they also have killed him."

"To what purpose?" Arabella cried. "Everything is dead!"

He shook his head. "The sky is open again. The young trees continue to race, betting speed against strength. Some die, others live. Whether a human likes it or not, it is the way. *Heammawihio* made everything that way."

"Barbaric," she growled, putting ever more strength into holding Sentor.

"Have you ever hated life, sister?" he asked softly, swinging his arms, getting the stiffness out of his shoulders where they had cramped during the time he'd held Sentor in place.

"No," she admitted, remembering the deep azure seas of the Indian Ocean, the red streamers of sand blowing across the Persian Gulf, the call of the muezzin at dawn over a sleepy city.

"How much farther?"

Sentor's consciousness continued to seep away until he slumped drunkenly against her. Efende began hedging at the sideways push.

Wasatch rode up along the other side, grabbing the limp head by the hair, bending off his mount to look into Sentor's eyes. "Not good." His other hand pulled out rawhide lashes. "I think maybe we better tie him on the horse like a dead man." Wasatch shook his head. "His head will be down. That's bad. Makes too much pressure. Something might come loose in his mind."

She rubbed the back of her neck. "Do we have any choice? We can't set up camp out here. No water."

Wasatch slid off his horse. "Help me," he directed.

Mounted again, they continued on their way south, Sentor's head and feet bouncing to the stride of his animal.

"That's right," the young trader asserted. "Was trying to force her. You know, rape her!"

Jeremiel slowed, reflexes triggered. Rape? Here? On cat feet, he moved closer to hear.

"Huh! And Catton's wolf showed up in the nick o' time, eh?" The older one shook his grizzled head, smacking his lips. "You know what kinda hell'd bust loose if news of Cheyenne rapin' a white woman got out in these parts? Why, tarnal hell is what it'd be! Bad enuff the Comanche and Kiowa is doing that down Texas way, but up here, it'd put the Cheyenne an' 'Rapaho on the war trail. That's sure."

Jeremiel stopped in his tracks, listening. White woman? His anger stirred and smoldered. Who'd dare!

"Ye'd think that Catton bunch woulda hog-tied that cussed sister o' theirs and sent her back ta Saint Looie like a pack o' plews," the young one growled, accenting it with a spit stream of tobacco juice.

"Heard tell they figger'd she'd done that," the older one said, shaking his head. "No tellin' about a woman. Cussed knot-headed at times. Got less sense 'an a fool prairie goat fawn without a mother! 'Ceptin' she cut cross-country—running smack inta ol' Buffler Th'ower's hoss-stealin' party. Why, Catton's wolf done showed up after Pawnee Stalker'd done ripped most o' her clothes clean off!"

Jeremiel's heart lay in his breast like a chunk of ice. *Arabella! She followed them!* And the heathen had tried to . . . to rape her? Laid their foul sin-greased hands on her fair . . .

And I began by offending her? My fault. I turned on her. Attacked her faith. Argued against her. What do I do now? How do I redress this evil? Someone must pay!

Reeling, he walked away, guilt ebbing into a sense of injustice which in turn led to a smoldering horror.

Anger welled in his chest as he stalked across the camp, hearing the muted boom of the drum. Dog Soldiers they were, or so he'd heard. Someone had mentioned that the Black Dogs had been out looking for food for the feast, and the dance would last for four days.

That had been yesterday and the drums had disturbed his sleep the night before, heathen sounds beating all around. Then, to make matters worse, he'd climbed the bluffs for early morning prayers—and the drums had been so loud they intruded on his contemplation.

"Behold," he whispered, Zachariah 14 running through his mind, "the day of the Lord cometh, and thy spoil shall be divided in the midst of thee!"

Now he knew what Abriel and Jake had been hiding. Oh, cunning! He'd have never known but for the slip-tongued traders. This time, the word of the Lord broke the bonds. This time, they would hear! Someone would pay!

These Cheyenne folks is just plumb fine! Bram decided, clapping his hands, doing the shuffle-stomp of the circle dance. Looking up periodically, he caught Calling Lark's eyes. His heart leapt as they shared their precious secret even here in the midst of all these people.

In the middle, the knot of Dog Soldiers danced and sang, the lilting voices of the singers mixing with the life pulse of the drum. His soul moved, happy as he'd never been before. She loved him! Yahoo! Bram clapped and beat his heels into the soft dust of the dance circle, following the lead of the man ahead of him as he turned out of the ring and into the crowd, the chatter of Cheyenne voices all around him.

Bram turned to watch, breathing deeply of the dust and the odor of sweaty humanity intermixed with sage and sweet grass from the purifying fires. Lark appeared at his side, magically snaking his hand into her own.

"You dance well," she praised into his ear.

He jerked his shoulders in a quick shrug. "Shucks, I don't know. I jest pranced and stepped."

She laughed, turning to sway with the eerie soul-searching song of the singers. The Dog Soldiers finished with a stomp as the singers gave one last reverberating thump of the drum. Men walked toward the back of the circle, antelope hoof rattles clicking, as they talked, motioning, laughing, faces and bodies painted in reds, blues, and yellows.

"Now what?" Bram asked, all eyes.

"They go into that lodge back there"—she pointed to a tall yellow-and-red-lined tipi—"and make a special medicine. I don't know what. It's Dog Soldier business, you know? They dance again sometime soon."

A commotion disrupted the crowd to the right. Bram—craning his neck to see—recognized the broad-brimmed black hat. A sudden premonition warned him. Even as the thoughts formed in his head, he could hear Jeremiel's stentorian voice boom, "Ravishers! Rape my sister, will you? You are heathens! Damned, evil heathens!"

Squeezing Lark's hand, Bram hissed, "Go! Get Jake and Ab. Now!" He pushed her away, working around as Jeremiel strode into the still-empty center of the circle, his Bible in one hand, the other pointing.

The Cheyenne went quiet, staring, awed.

"Damnation upon the nation of the Philistines!" Jeremiel thundered, passion filling his voice. "Ye be damned, having heard the word of the Lord thy God! And still you rape? Yea, though my Lord God spared backsliding Lot from the rain of brimstone and fire, so shall ye go! I foresee thee"—he pointed, eyes burning, finger darting from face to startled face—"falling, falling, into the fiery pit!

"Rape and debauchery! Ravagers in sin! Your men walk, unclothed! Defying the laws of God! Rape my sister, will you? Someone will pay!"

Bram moved out behind Jeremiel, seeing the awe in the eyes of the Cheyenne. It hit him suddenly: most of the people couldn't understand a word of what his maniacal brother was saying!

Bram looked around, searching the rapt crowd, seeing here and there a blackening face. Well, some of them spoke English. One such man, a youngster, whispered to those around him, the discontent spreading as the word traveled, increasing as others repeated Jeremiel's accusations. A sullen muttering rose among them.

"Gotta do sumpthing real fast," Bram mumbled to himself, thinking, gauging Jeremiel's broad back, wondering if he could grab him, sling him to the ground, and drag him out of the circle before they died.

"As filthy as Lot are thee!" Jeremiel boomed. "Yea, the sin that conceived Moab and Ammon is upon thee! Judgment is thy Lord God's, but I want the guilty! I want the men who did this!"

Like wildfire, anger raced through the crowd. Some of the young men started crowding forward, hands on weapons.

"Too late," Bram whispered. He moved by instinct, prancing, stepping high, head back, chin forward.

"The overthrow of Satan is upon you!" Jeremiel expounded, his finger lashing the air. "Thou hast fought against Jerusalem! A plague on all your heathen heads! Hear the words of Zachariah! 'Their flesh shall consume away while they stand upon their feet, and their eyes shall consume away in their holes, and their tongue shall consume away in their mouth.' "

Bram mimicked each movement, screwing his face up to a scowl, mocking Jeremiel's gestures. The warriors paused, faces still sullen and threatening, their attention diverted to his antic behavior.

"Babylon will fall! Wild beasts will roam through your desolate lodges, heathen!" Jeremiel slapped his Bible. Bram pranced quickly to one side to remain out of sight behind him, and slapped his belly to imitate the preacher, mouthing Jeremiel's words in silence.

A smile appeared here and there. Young girls whispered to each other behind their blankets, eyes sparkling amusement.

"Judgment will be made on Assyria!" Jeremiel added, his balled fist shaking overhead.

Bram made a fierce face, jaw jutted out, and waved his fist wildly over his head. The thunderous faces seemed less hostile. Some who hadn't heard the translations were hiding smiles behind brown hands, eyes laughing at his antics.

"Philistia! Moab! Damascus! Egypt! Tyre! So shall ye all burn as the righteous wrath of the Lord is spent upon thee! Pestilence and famine, I call down upon you!" Jeremiel speared at them with a pointed finger, shifting back and forth.

Bram danced, hopping from foot to foot, jabbing a pointed finger this way and that before accidentally poking it in his eyes, playing like it had stuck there. He struggled to pull it out, whirling and cavorting, jerking it loose with his other hand and falling on his butt in the soft dirt to the open sound of laughter.

Jeremiel stopped, perched high on the balls of his feet, suddenly baffled, unsettled by the giggles rippling the crowd.

"Dost thou laugh at apocalypse?" Jeremiel wondered.

Bram jumped to his feet, still clowning, cocking his head, trying—through several contortions—to imitate Jeremiel's disbelieving stance. More chuckles erupted.

"Then, in the name of the Lord thy God, I *condemn you, heathen!*" Jeremiel sputtered.

Bram whirled, acting the part, waving his fist, grimacing, following every move Jeremiel made, the crowd breaking into guffaws that left the preacher livid. More people began pointing, covering their mouths politely.

Jeremiel whirled on his feet, face a livid red, to see Bram pointing his finger, stamping around like a fool.

Bram stopped in midstep, seeing the insane rage in Jeremiel's face. Hastily, he swallowed, backing away, hands out in defense. "Uh, brother Jeremiel, now, I know this looks right funny t' y'all. But I reckon I do got my reasons for—"

*"Blaspheming Sennacherib!"* Jeremiel's mouth worked. "You know what these heathen did to *our* sister? And you mock *me?*"

Bram ducked the first roundhouse swing, scrambling out of the way as the Cheyenne burst out in wild laughter, the big Bible rolling out of his hands to cartwheel across the dance ground.

"Devil spawn!" Jeremiel raged. "Mock me in the work of the Lord?"

Bram rolled beyond a wild hook, darting around the circle as Jeremiel charged after him.

Scared, he just couldn't match Jeremiel mad. A big blocky hand got him by the shoulder, swinging him around. Bram gulped, going completely slack as a thick fist leapt at him. The sudden weight overbalanced Jeremiel. He sprawled onto scuttling Bram, who slipped out from under the thrashing arms and legs—only to charge full tilt into Abriel's muscle-bound body.

"Easy, little brother," Ab soothed, straightening him out.

"Ya gotta save me," Bram hissed, ducking behind Ab's bulk.

Jake had come up on the other side, lifting Jeremiel to his feet, a death grip on his arm.

"Let's go!" Jake grunted. "This is already rocky enough."

Bram shot a quick glance around, seeing happy—but

perplexed—Indian faces. "Cover me," he whispered to Ab. "Let me end this my way."

Abriel frowned skeptically for a second before lifting a beefy shoulder in a shrug. Ab took Jeremiel's other shoulder, and together, they hustled the preacher through a gap that formed in the crowd.

Bram—suddenly the center of attention again—jacked his arms up, like he was being held, and duck-walked after the rest, evoking another burst of laughter.

Outside the dance ring, he turned, bowed, and smiled at the chortling children, wiping the sweat from his face as he turned and ran after the complaining Jeremiel. He saw High Walker, standing to one side of the Dog Soldiers' lodge, his tall form stiff and unbending, his diamond-shaped face pinched with an evil scowl.

"They tried to rape Arabella!" Jeremiel thundered, pacing angrily before the lodge.

"And you ran out there, cocksure in all your righteous anger, and damn near started a war! Arabella killed the warrior who attacked her! That evens things out!" Jake gritted, pounding his fist into a callused palm.

Ab added, "Look, you gotta understand, these are Cheyenne! They think differently! You're not talking to a bunch of Christian farmers who'll be cowed when you holler hell and fire at 'em! Yell at a Cheyenne warrior—threaten him with plague—and he'll kill you on the spot. Probably by torture to drive the evil out of you and as far away from him as possible! You understand?"

Jake sighed, turning away, pinching the bridge of his nose as he squinted helplessly.

Jeremiel paced and turned, throwing a glance at Abriel. "They tried to rape Arabella," he insisted stubbornly. "I . . . Well, I just got to thinking. Have you seen the men run through camp every morning for the river?

Not a stitch of clothing on 'em! Stark buck naked! Well, it all came due. Someone had to pay. I just got mad and . . . and . . ."

"Lost your head!" Bram snorted.

"They're Satan-infested heathens! Demons of the Prince of Darkness." Jeremiel shook his head. "And to think of Arabella in their lascivious clutches . . ."

"She killed the man!" Ab insisted.

"We're all upset," Jake admitted, lifting his arms. "Think of it this way. You're a guest here. This is their village, act like it. Don't insult them."

Jeremiel froze in his tracks, glaring at Bram. "You *mocked* me! Made me the fool! Caused those . . . those *heathens* to laugh at the word of God!" He tried to say more, the words bottling in his throat.

Bram took a deep breath, blowing it out. "Yep, I did."

"He saved your life," Lark snapped.

Jeremiel spun to face Calling Lark. "What do you know of the gospel of—"

"I know Cheyenne," she insisted, handing him the dusty Bible she'd recovered, refusing to lower her eyes. "These people . . . they're warriors. Half our people died of disease. Cholera you call it. And you walk out and tell them the white man's God will make them sick again?" She snorted derision. "Good thing only me, Wasatch, and four or five others talk American. Not even Bram could save you then! You're damn lucky to be alive!" She shook her head in disgust and ducked through the flap into the tipi, rattling pots and rustling angrily through parfleches.

Jeremiel blinked, suddenly unsure. "Lucky to be alive?" Torture? To drive out evil? *My* evil?

Jake settled himself on a blanket, wearily fingering the stubble on his chin. "Yeah, lucky. Look, for all the time you spent with Sunts in the missions, you never really got to know the Indians, did you?"

The uncertainty grew, expanding to make a sick feeling in his belly. "Well, yes. We administered the gospel of the Lord whenever we—"

"You preached!" Jake interrupted. "That's all you ever do is preach!"

"Well, I—"

"Preaching is just that, brother." Jake looked up earnestly. "For once will you listen? Huh? Just listen."

"The—"

*"Listen!"* Jake bellowed, fingers strangling empty air.

Jeremiel stopped, mouth going dry. Jake's tone cut through his sudden confusion, shaking his confidence even further.

"You always preach," Jake began, trying to keep a normal tone of voice. "Try listening! These are God's children too, aren't they?"

"But the word of God . . ." Jeremiel turned to Ab, his hands spread.

"Well, practice it instead of yelling it," Abriel suggested. "Didn't they teach that in seminary?"

"I . . . Yes, they taught that," Jeremiel admitted. "Maybe I've been a fool but what more is there than salvation?"

Bram slapped his hands against his sides. "Maybe nothing, Jeremiel. On the other hand, y'all can go out and pray yerseff to death on that ridgetop yonder. Sit there till ya die of thirst praying and so on. That'll git ya to heaven in a hell of a hurry, won't it? God'll take ya, won't He? I mean, ya won't have committed suicide. And God'll know that's what ya really want is saved and ya ain't out sinnin' in the process . . . just praying." He hesitated, eyes shifting nervously as he added, "But I don't see ya doing that. Instead I see ya trying to save folks."

"That's right." Jeremiel dropped his eyes. *God, I need to get away. To think!*

"Well, if ya want to save folks, ya got to do it different," Bram insisted. "Ya got to learn who they is ... touch that part of 'em you can reach. Just tellin' 'em flat out ain't gonna make ya no hay in the meadow. Ya got to irrigate it first."

Jeremiel stood there, empty. "I ... I ..." His tongue worked dryly in his mouth. "What if I can't?"

Ab placed a firm hand on his shoulder. "I think you can. It's in you, Jeremiel. Just try making friends."

Dazed, Jeremiel nodded, eyes going oddly blurry. He ran his fingers over the leather of the heavy Bible Lark had thrust so violently into his hands, and left, eyes lowered, as he sought his familiar path to the terrace top.

The hollow boom of a drum coupled with singing that sounded like the mingled voices of coyotes drifted on the wind. Swaying in the saddle herself, Arabella caught the faint humid odor of river through the dry dusty smell of the land.

She blinked her eyes, dismayed at the sandy, gritty feeling. How long since the sun had dropped over the western horizon? Five hours? More?

Her hips burned, shooting pain tinged up her tired legs. Too damned long on Efende. Her bladder pressed angrily against her pelvis, demanding relief. Her back muscles cramped and spasmed, adding to the misery of each jerking step Efende took.

"Camp," Wasatch called from the darkness.

She gasped as Efende crested the bluffs overlooking the Arkansas. The lodges of the Cheyenne and Arapaho spread out below her like lamps, glowing yellow in the night, silhouetting the dark leaf-thick branches of the cottonwoods. Open fires flickered here and there in the blackness, and faint human silhouettes shifted before them.

"Thank God," she whispered, letting Wasatch lead Efende down the slopes. Gravel and cobbles clattered down in the darkness, her chafed bottom in sheer agony as she shifted on the horse's back.

Dully, she wondered if Sentor still lived.

So, down there, where I am going, I'll find Pawnee Stalker and the rest of those leering jackals. Every nerve in my body burns and aches, my bones feel pulled out of joint, I'm so tired I could sleep for fifteen centuries. I'm hungry, thirsty. Never in my life have I suffered such complete misery. Why did I ever leave Saint Louis?

Cooler air caressed her fevered cheeks, the scent of vegetation and water in the air. Thicker grasses rustled under Efende's feet. His ears pricked, nostrils flared at the closeness of the water.

"We're fording the river here," Wasatch called, hesitating while the horses drank greedily. "Your feet will get wet." A humming of insects filled the calm night.

"That's enough," he called to the horses, kicking his Appaloosa ahead, forcing the animal into the water.

With all her remaining strength, Arabella kicked Efende, wondering if the water would be deep enough here to drown Sentor. It wasn't. It barely reached her ankles.

Wasatch called out softly in Cheyenne, responses coming from the dark. Here, closer to the lodges, she could see better. Horses whickered greetings to them; dogs loomed out of the dark to yap and nip at the horses. Efende plodded, so tired he didn't care.

The place smelled of woodsmoke, a tint of urine and rot, and dog, and, well, Indian, she supposed. In all, the musty smells reminded her of Arab villages—but without the sweet sensual odor of coffee.

Wasatch wound through most of the camp, pulling up before a well-made lodge, his ghost form slipping to the ground.

"Wasatch?" she called, voice low. "Would you mind? Come help me. I'm afraid if I slide off, I'll just collapse. My legs are . . . well, I don't trust them."

Dark forms began ducking through the door as she felt his hands around her waist, muscular arms supporting her as she slid off.

"Thanks," she sighed, letting Efende hold her up, refusing to release her panic hold on his mane.

Wasatch began talking in Cheyenne to a woman who bent over Sentor in the dim light. Other men stood to one side. Her vision already adapted to the dark, she could see Abriel, Jake, and Bram standing uncertainly, Bram already kicking the ground with his worn-out boot.

Feeling returned to her legs.

"Arabella? That you?" Jake asked, reserved.

"It's me. Hang on a minute. As soon as my legs work again, I'll be fine." Allah! How she hated to have to admit that in front of them!

"Are you all right?" Ab asked, stilted, as if he didn't know what to say.

"I'm fine." She forced herself to be chipper. "Nothing a night or two in a soft feather bed with handservants to bring me meals wouldn't cure."

"So, sis, ya ready t' run off an' be a hoss thief?" Bram joked, stepping forward to give her a hug. He smelled of fires and Indian.

She pulled him tight. "Not if I ever have to sit on a horse again."

Wasatch had been talking quietly to the Indian woman. She helped him unload Sentor, the two of them struggling under the burden. Arabella went to help, walking awkwardly as she took up his dragging feet. Then Ab had one side and Jake the other as they maneuvered him through the door flap and into the cozy light of the lodge.

Wasatch settled Sentor in the rear of the tipi, carefully lifting one eyelid, then the other, listening to the man's labored breathing.

He looked up at Arabella. "He lives, but his soul is weak, wondering whether or not to slip off to *Seyan*."

The woman, a dark-haired beauty, reached for the metal pot simmering over the coals. She carefully lifted a horn ladle from one side, spooning a wondrously smelling broth into Sentor's mouth.

"Well," Arabella sighed, "we haven't killed him so far."

"Sentor!" Bram cried, looking close. He shook his head. "Aw, sis, and here we thought we needed t' worry about you when y'all was sportin' a gent round the countryside!"

"One of these days, Bram, I'm . . ." She broke up, laughing. "Never mind, Jake, Ab, Bram, meet your brother Wasatch." Then she left, ducking out into the darkness.

She checked Efende and the rest of the horses—seeing they were too tuckered to cause much grief—then found the bushes. When she ducked through the flap again, stepping a little more spritely, Wasatch and Jake shotgunned Cheyenne back and forth at each other. She studied her brother with a new respect.

"Reckon we'd better go find Jeremiel?" Bram asked from the side.

Arabella settled against a backrest, cleverly woven from willow strands, and looked at them. Ab and Jake looked the same. Bram, on the other hand, seemed different. A seriousness had formed about his eyes, he acted more confident. She caught a quick look shared between him and the Indian woman and a piece fit into place.

"Calling Lark," Bram said easily. "Wasatch's sister."

"I've heard a lot about you," Arabella smiled.

Lark studied her thoughtfully. "I am pleased to share my brother's lodge." Her smile encouraged.

"Yeah," Ab agreed. "He took a pretty bad drubbing. Maybe we'd better go find him."

"Jake," Arabella added, "be careful what you say when Sentor comes to. He's working for France. I'm not sure what his game is, or what his politics are."

Jake stopped, half out the door. Keen eyes met hers. "France?" he asked. Something changed in the way he looked at her, as if he were seeing her for the first time. "I'll keep that in mind." Then he slipped out into the dark.

Arabella looked to where Lark attended Sentor, stripping his fouled clothes off, seeking to make him comfortable. She considered getting up, going to help, only somewhere in midthought, she drifted off to sleep.

# Chapter 15

*J*eremiel walked, arms clasped behind him, thoughts in a roiling confusion. He bent his head back until his neck strained, and stared at the blue vault above until he became dizzy. He stood motionless, clearing his mind, stilling his confusion, as he concentrated on the breath expanding and contracting his chest.

"Where am I going, Lord? What am I doing here?" He dropped to his knees, cradling the heavy Bible to his chest, head thrown back to the sky. "I only wish to serve You, Lord, yet at every turn I find myself lost."

Jake's words echoed hollowly in his head. "All I do is preach," Jeremiel whispered miserably. "Show me the way, my Lord." He raised his Bible on high, the gesture of a supplicant. "Heal me!"

The verse came to him, haunting, soothing, "Book of James," he whispered hoarsely. " 'Confess your faults one to another and pray one for another, that ye may be healed.' But who prays for me?"

He opened the Bible, reading the fifth chapter of James, finding the final verse the most salutary.

"Let him know, that he which converteth the sinner from the error of his way shall save a soul from death, and shall hide a multitude of sins."

He searched the skies, seeing the sun slanting slowly to the west over the tablelands and buttes, silhouetting the bobbing spring grasses around him. They reached for the sky no less than he himself reached for an answer.

"What fields do I sow and reap, Lord?" He shook his head, a physical pain in his breast. "Do I not speak Your message? What manner of man am I who would serve You? I try so hard, seeking to subdue my passions; yet forever, they seem to betray me into the hands of Satan. Help me, Lord! Show me Your will!"

Eyes to the heavens, he noted the evening star, growing out of the gray haze of the lost day. Far behind him, the ironic thump of the Dog Soldiers' drum echoed as the breeze softened, surrendering its interference so the beat carried on the stilling night.

"Lord?" Jeremiel wondered, eyes still searching the darkening skies. Out among the uplands to the south, coyotes let loose with their eerie yipping cackle.

There! High up in the sky, a streak of white light cut from south to north, blazing brightly for a brief instant before it disappeared.

"Blessed is the name of the Lord God," Jeremiel whispered, awe filling him, surging through his chest in a rush of relief.

Tired, he got to his feet, dreading having to face his brothers; unsure of what the falling star meant; unsure if he understood at all what God wanted of him.

Night settled down around him, making his steps uneven as he turned back to the heathen Wasatch's lodge.

In the darkness Jeremiel stumbled, toe catching on a half-buried rock. He remembered passing this way earlier. A lot of rocks had been placed here on the flat terrace overlooking the Arkansas. Foundations for an antediluvian village? The rocks had been placed in circular shapes—now sunk into the ground with age. Who had those people been? Had they, too, been destroyed in the flood?

"Those souls You didn't damn, Lord," he whispered to the night sky, seeing the stars—ever more numerous—speckling the clear sky. "So long ago, they couldn't have heard Your word."

Again he turned his step toward the village, feeling prickly pear crunch under his heavy boots, thankful the sharp barbs would be turned.

An owl called from the soft night, its voice a whisper over the land. Something rustled through the grass to one side. Mouse? Ground squirrel?

Jeremiel resumed his steps, wondering at the shooting star. What did it mean? A foreboding memory of the shooting star in Revelation formed in his mind. "And the name of the star is called Wormwood; and the third part of the waters became wormwood; and many men died of the waters, because they were made bitter."

He stumbled again in the darkness, stubbing his toe, the Bible slipping from his grip as he sought to balance, arms flailing.

He looked about in the dark, finally dropping to his hands and knees, feeling around. There! He got hold of it, pulling the heavy book to him with his right hand. He placed the other on the grass, to push up, feeling something squirm smoothly under his fingertip.

He jerked his hand back, frightened, but not before

the cactuslike prickle stabbed his finger—and stuck, pulling against his hand, moving, twining like something alive and . . .

*"No!"* Jeremiel screamed, flinging his arm, the serpent tearing loose, vanishing into the darkness, thumping hollowly on the ground behind him. The bible tumbled from numb fingers.

"No!" he whimpered, breast convulsing, as he clutched at his left wrist, feeling the throb of the poison in his flesh. "Oh, my God, no!" Tears blurred his eyes, pain lending panic to his pounding heart. Sobbing, he bent over his bitten hand, hugging it close until his forehead touched the ground, the corner of the Bible next to his fear-sweaty cheek.

"No, dear Lord God, no!" he whimpered in fear and horror.

His body felt warm and loose, the result of too many hard days on the trail. The muscles in his chest and arms lay flaccid, worn, tired, and needing rest. Wasatch stopped at the entrance of the lodge, grateful to be home, knowing the horses had been turned over to the night guard, watered and ready to graze.

So, these were his brothers? The big man, Ab, seemed hesitant, unsure of what to say or do around him. Jake, ah yes, the son of Jason Oord, the blue shirt who rides long. Some white soldiers called him Iron Butt, but only outside of his hearing. And Bram. To him, Wasatch felt a curious empathy. Bram enjoyed living, a humor and joy buoyed his spirit.

He ducked into the dim light, seeing Lark still ministering to Sentor. The man lay naked now, his smelly clothes having been removed. Lark would wash them in the morning. The others were gone except for Arabella, who slept soundly, head tilted to one side, mouth open, legs sprawled nervelessly.

She'd been reeling in the saddle, desperately weary—but she'd hung on, forced herself to make it. And not once had she complained like the other white women he'd seen on the trails.

Moving around to his place, Wasatch settled against his familiar backrest, laying his pipe bag and knife in their respective places, before accepting a bowl of the stew.

He drank, filling his empty stomach, savoring the taste of roots mixed with big chunks of elk and buffalo. Somewhere, Lark had found onions to include—rare this early in the year. Gratefully, Wasatch emptied yet another bowl before handing it to Lark and taking his pipe out.

He sang his pipe song, physically drained, and tamped the bowl, taking an ember from the fire and puffing it alight. Ritually, he offered the sacred smoke to *Heammawihio* above, *Ahk tun o' wihio* in the ground below, and to the east, south, west, and north, in the trail of the sun. Contented, he puffed, wondering at the changes coming to his life, trying to place it all in order now that he enjoyed the peace of his lodge—even though it had become crowded with strangers.

"You made my brothers welcome," Wasatch sighed. "You did well; you honored them and fed them. Thank you. You are a good woman, a perfect sister."

She waved it off, silent gratitude in her softening eyes. "I'm glad you're back. I worried when I heard you were after a *Mis'tai*. I never know when a monster will grab you after luring you away."

He smiled. "I know the call of the monsters."

"Spirit Power makes me nervous," she averred.

Wasatch smoked in silence, unable to reassure her.

Finally he asked, "What do you think of these brothers of mine?"

"Like all whites," she told him, a lax smile on her lips, as she bustled about, tending her duties. "they have no manners in a lodge, walking between a person and the fire, cutting straight across, stepping over the fire, moving things around, sprawling here and there on the woman's side!" She threw up her hands, pointing at Arabella. "Look at that! Asleep where a young man should properly sit!"

Wasatch chuckled. "They don't know our ways. Think how we'd do in one of their cities. Remember? Like Flower Man used to tell of?"

"And another thing!" Lark added, waving a buffalo horn bowl his direction, eyes tight. "The black robe is headed for trouble here. You get him out. Soon as possible. You get him away from here or somebody's gonna get hurt."

"The black robe?" Wasatch looked at her, marking her disquiet. "That is Jeremiel?"

Lark lifted her lip. "He is fighting with the white man's evil spirit! Like all the white black robes, he's got the Evil One mixed up with the *Maiyun*! Stupid!" She shook her head in disgust. "Why don't *Heammawihio* fry them black robes with lightning? All they do is make trouble. Anyway, Bram kept the Dog Soldiers from killing him today. Played off him like a clown . . . or a Contrary touched by the *Maiyun*." She smiled, eyes drifting at the thoughts in her head.

Wasatch considered both the spoken and unspoken, reading the glow that came to her face. "This Bram is smart, then. I also hear a softness in your voice when you speak of him. Hum? Do I have to worry about stumbling over his horse in the morning when I go out to make water?"

She gave him a sober look, raising her shoulders. "I don't know. Having no manners—just like the rest of the whites—I doubt he'll tie a horse to the lodge for me to water."

"But you could teach him manners," Wasatch teased.

She lowered her eyes, sinking firm white teeth in her full lip.

"Be careful, sister." He grinned at her.

"Then you had better know High Walker and Bram have had hard words." Her eyes hardened and she made a worried gesture with her fingers. "High Walker caught me walking to Broken Hand's camp. Bram kept him from beating me. He would have. It's his right as a Dog Soldier."

Wasatch tried to put that in perspective. Bram and High Walker? Such different men. "And Pawnee Stalker is High Walker's close relative. High Walker will know how his brother Hides To Trap Eagles died at Arabella's hand." Wasatch sighed. That changed things. No telling what High Walker could stir up. Trouble in the village—especially this close to the Medicine Lodge Sun Dance—would be appalling.

"I think we must go. For the people, we must take ourselves away. This Jeremiel is trouble. Bram is trouble. Arabella is trouble. Someone may lose his head . . . forget his obligations to the People."

"What of her?" Lark lifted an eyebrow, gesturing toward Arabella. "She is a tall straight woman. She's got a nice face—hair like yours. Her hips are a little narrow. Might have trouble passing a baby, and she needs to learn to treat a man right; but are you planning on a little tusseling beneath the robes with that one? Huh?"

Wasatch scratched under his jaw, making no effort to hide his disgust at her suggestion. "No," he said flatly. "You and Bram . . . that would be all right. He is the

Flower Man's son. You are White Wolf's daughter. This one"—he indicated Arabella—"is also the Flower Man's daughter ... as I am his son. It cannot be."

Lark nodded, contrite, averting her eyes.

He frowned, thinking, then added, "And there is something else. I don't ... Um, she's not a wife for me. I like her. She has strength and courage. She'd make a warrior a fine wife ... but not for me." He looked at Lark. "You understand? We're too different."

Lark studied him for a moment before winking. "I understand." She pulled a buffalo robe over Sentor, picking up her beadwork before asking, "Tell me, what if Bram tied his horse to this lodge some night?"

Wasatch smiled at her, a warm feeling in his chest. "You would want him to? He is white. I have heard whispers in the wind. Trouble is coming with the whites. It might be hard. For him and you."

Light lines of concern traced her forehead as she ran thin thread through colored beads, stitching them to the smoked buckskin she worked. "Bram lives, brother. He makes me laugh again. I think he knows what is coming. I think he is never going back to the white country in the East. He is happy here among the mountains and plains. I would go with him. I think he is a good man. Best of all"—her eyes alight with pride—"he is a horse thief! An excellent horse thief! He will bring me much honor!" Radiant, she looked up at him, a shy smile on her lips.

"Then I will take any horses he offers for you, sister." Wasatch reached over to pat her knee affectionately. If Bram would make her a caring husband, so much the better. Her prospects among the People would always be grim—the shame of her time with High Walker's brother always a stain no aspiring warrior would overlook.

The flap pulled back, Abriel stepping inside, nervous, almost hesitant to meet Wasatch's eyes.

"Uh, we can't find Jeremiel," he admitted, anxiously shifting his weight from foot to foot.

Wasatch sighed, placing his pipe carefully next to the fire. He stood, looking around, seeing a scuffed black coat with a Walker Colt and Catton bowie knife encircled by a belt lying on top. "That is his?"

Ab nodded, giving him a suspicious look. Wasatch lifted the coarse fabric, sniffing it to get the odor, and stepped outside. He lifted his face to the stars and tightened his throat to call Wolf. Abriel, he absently noted, stepped back, hesitant.

In less than a minute, Wolf trotted up, a shape of gray sliding through the night.

"Father," Wasatch greeted in Cheyenne, dropping to his knees, holding the coat out. "My brother Jeremiel has managed to get himself lost in the night. He is a white man, so be careful if you find him. You know how foolish whites are around guns. Do you know where he is?"

Wolf sniffed the coat and snorted, sneezing once in disgust before turning and trotting into the night.

"Come on," Wasatch called, forcing his rubbery muscles to trot after the spirit wolf.

Abriel didn't keep up for long. He dropped behind on the long climb up the bluffs, blowing and puffing as he pounded along. Wasatch caught his second wind as he followed the dim shape of Wolf, who ghosted up the trail, coursing for scent.

The moon barely crested the horizon as Wolf lined out. Wasatch stretched his legs, catching the rhythm of his stride, seeing Wolf moving ahead at a lope. Within minutes, he could make out Wolf, standing, head lowered as he warily inspected a black lump in the darkness.

"Brother?" Wasatch called in English, chest heaving. "Jeremiel?"

The form on the ground whimpered, moving slowly, painfully.

"The serpent . . . has . . . has my soul. Yea, Satan has . . . taken me . . . through the curse of . . . of Wormwood!" The rest slurred into meaningless jumble.

Wolf circled, skipping lightly to one side, a low growl of warning coming from his big chest.

Wasatch squinted, seeing the rattler moving to one side, lethargic, slow with its loose skin. *Shinshin'o'wuts* always became dangerous when he shed his skin.

"Snakebite," Wasatch realized. He bent, getting an arm under Jeremiel's, lifting him to his feet, feeling the feverish heat in the man.

Wolf circling, they met Abriel and Jake halfway back. It would be a long night.

"I'll not be doctored by—by Satan!" Jeremiel insisted, head flopping back and forth, skin sallow and sweaty.

"If you're not, you're likely to be dead," Jake insisted.

Arabella watched from the side, lips pursed, reservation in her weary eyes.

"Boiled coneflower," Jake said, watching Wasatch's movements, seeing what he ground into paste.

"We call it *shinshin'o'wuts tse'i'yo*, rattlesnake medicine. It is good for drawing out the poison."

Lark handed him a bowl with a round rock in the bottom.

"Sit on him," Wasatch ordered. Bram, Ab, and Jake pinned Jeremiel, who screamed and thrashed as Wasatch punctured the wounds and bled the arm. Jeremiel wailed hideously and went limp, weeping in his fever. Next, Wasatch spread the mixture on Jeremiel's hand and arm, now swollen and mottled.

Arabella winced, looking away.

". . . not be . . . doctored by . . . Satan," Jeremiel mewed. "Not by . . . Satan." His voice faded. "No. Not . . . by . . ."

Wasatch handed Jake leaves. "And this?"

"We call it pursh," Jake said, looking pensively at the common weed.

"To us it is *to wani yukh ts*, to-make-cool medicine. I will grind it up and give it to Jeremiel to relieve his fever and let him sleep."

Bram settled by the fire, watching as Wasatch concocted his brew. Leander Sentor groaned and rolled over.

Arabella sighed, dully watching the man, regretting her earlier callousness. Chalk it up to exhaustion and physical discomfort.

"What 'now?" Abriel asked. "We're all together. What about Web's treasure? Wasatch, did he ever leave a map with you?"

Wasatch looked up, shaking his head, rich brown braids catching the light of the fire. "No. He left nothing with me—only the knife."

"Any other ideas?" Ab looked around before watching Wasatch lift the bowl to Jeremiel's lips. Fevered, the preacher drank, throat working methodically.

"Let me see the knives," Jake suggested, curiosity and interest competing behind his animated amber eyes. One by one, the known legacy of Web Catton passed hand by hand to rest on the hides before him.

Each identical, Jake looked them up and down, studying the wavering lines in the Damascus blades, concentration etching deeply into his forehead.

Arabella went back to sleep.

When she awoke, hours later, he still studied them, curiously inspecting the fleur-de-lis decoration woven about the leather handle. She sighed, took a breath, and rolled over again.

Ab stirred, hearing the soft padding of feet. He blinked sleepy eyes, seeing Wasatch's tame wolf nose past the flap. The big animal looked around, yellow eyes meeting his, before walking to Wasatch and dragging the youth up from a sound sleep.

Ab listened and watched in disbelief as man and wolf squeaked and growled to each other. Finally, Wolf spun and left—stepping high over the sleepers as if he didn't want to touch them—to leap gracefully out the door. Wasatch got to his feet, dressing quickly, heedless of a white man's modesty, before ducking out the door.

Ab could see Jake and Bram, heads up, looking back and forth, groggy-eyed and confused. Jake shrugged and rolled back over.

Ab lay there, thinking, trying to decide what it had all been about. Cuss it all, it looked like Wasatch and Wolf had carried on a succinct conversation.

Of course, Fitzpatrick said the boy thought the wolf carried the spirit of his foster father. And last night, with Jeremiel lost, he could have sworn the wolf understood every word Wasatch had told it. But . . . *naw! Just couldn't be!*

Ab lay there listening to the sounds of the waking camp. Women cackled, laughing and joking, calling back and forth. Dogs squealed under kicks, kids shouted and shrieked happily while horses whinnied greetings to rising masters.

Blessed mercy, an Indian camp made a heck of a racket.

A half hour later, he jumped to his feet, rolled his blanket and stepped over bodies to the flap. Ab wandered back to the bushes before returning to stand before the lodge, stretching, yawning, enjoying the cool feel of the morning, and wishing he had a cup of hot coffee. The eastern horizon brightened, sending golden bars of light into the tops of the trees. Cottonwood leaves rattled overhead. Occasional bits of white fuzz had already begun to form on the high seedpods.

Wasatch came walking toward him, talking and motioning to a bandy-legged Cheyenne warrior. Wolf trotted to one side, disdainfully ignoring the slinking Indian curs who slipped out of his way, tails wagging between their legs.

"Brother Abriel," he greeted. "This man is Buffalo Thrower—a great war chief. He has stolen many horses and taken many coups. He has just given us twenty horses. In all of our names. I have given those horses to others who need them more than we."

Ab shook the man's hand, meeting hard competent eyes.

"Tell him I'm honored," Ab replied respectfully. "Uh, what's up? What do you mean?"

"Brother, this man led the party which captured Arabella," Wasatch explained seriously, emphasizing his words. "He did not know she was my sister. My sister did not know it is forbidden to kill a warrior of the people. I have told this man that honor was satisfied. No one need pay more. There is grief on both sides. I have said that. I believe that. Can you speak for my brothers that no more evil will come of this thing?"

Ab wet his lips, meeting those searching amber eyes. "You know the people here," Ab hedged, seeing a tightness come to Wasatch's eyes. "Yeah, hell, I'll back you up, Wasatch. I'm calling it finished."

The younger man nodded, a quick smile ghosting at the corners of his mouth. He straightened. "I have given gifts to the family of Hides To Trap Eagles, honored his wives and father, and said prayers under the scaffold where his body is. I have asked the spirits to lead him quickly to *Seyan*.

"But it is not all good. His cousin High Walker is making bad talk. He says my sister, Calling Lark, is a bad woman. He says our sister, Arabella, did wrong to kill Hides To Trap Eagles when she was a captive, that a white woman is not of the people and deserves to be a slave, and a slave deserves to lie with a man who captures her."

Ab tensed as Wasatch continued.

"Pawnee Stalker is wavering, unable to decide what to do. High Walker tells everyone what Jeremiel said at the Dog Soldier dance. He says Bram insulted him and is a coward without coup."

"He's a liar!" Bram erupted hotly, stepping through the flap. "High Walker tried to hurt Lark. Reckon I couldn't let him. Ifn he wants, I'll face him. Anyway he wants to go."

"Settle down, little brother," Ab soothed. "Let's not let it get that far."

Buffalo Thrower said something, gesturing as he talked, speaking earnestly to Wasatch, who translated.

"He says there is bad blood between me and High Walker. High Walker accuses me of being a witch, of killing his brother with worms after he shamed my sister. Now the poison might get out from between us and cause a sickness here, in the camp of the People. Now would be a very bad time since it is just before the Medicine Lodge—the renewal of the arrows and the world. It would not be a good thing."

"Probably not," Ab agreed. "What's right? Some ritual combat or something?"

Wasatch stiffened, a ghastly look coming to his features. "Never say that! That would be terrible. No, brother Abriel, this is a matter of the *Tsis-tsis-ta*. I will go and tell the Forty-four—the council who rule—what is being said by High Walker." He added something to Buffalo Thrower in Cheyenne. The warrior nodded—giving Bram and Ab a quick word, shook their hands again—and turned to walk away.

"I have told him there will be peace. But first you must know, there is more," Wasatch said, looking back and forth between Ab and Bram. He gestured to where Wolf sat, tongue lolling as he panted, yellow eyes knowing and intelligent in his scarred and battered face.

"Wolf came to me this morning to tell me of a medicine dream. He sees a big white man—a man bearded with a white streak on his chin—riding across our tracks. He will be here soon, this man. With him comes an evil violence."

"Bragg," Ab breathed. "Well, we knew it wouldn't last forever. But where do we go?"

Wasatch pointed to the west. "There and to the north. Wolf has seen it in his dream."

"What about High Walker?" Bram insisted. "We can't just up and turn tail on him! He'll figger I'm runnin' out . . ."

Wasatch placed a familiar hand on Bram's shoulder. "We are not whites, brother." He smiled. "I will go tell the Forty-four that we are leaving to keep the peace. Among the Cheyenne, there is great honor in being the one to avoid conflict among the People. High Walker will become the center of scorn and ridicule. The council may exile him for this. He has"—Wasatch looked suddenly sad—"harmed his soul and the People by his selfishness."

"And Jeremiel?" Ab wondered.

Wasatch spread his arms. "We will take him. In a week he will have the use of his arm. It will be stiff, but he will not lose it. I feel his soul fighting. It is good."

"Yep, and then thar's Sentor," Bram added. "No telling how Arabella will do 'thout her boyfriend."

"He can't travel," Ab said. "I don't know about that knock to the head. Surprised being packed like a sack of flour didn't pop his skull wide open as it is."

"He is tough," Wasatch added soberly. "I think, from what Arabella told me, he would not like to wake up in a Cheyenne lodge."

"How 'bout leaving him with Fitzpatrick?" Ab asked. "He's got a wagon and white men and all to look after him."

"Kind of a burden to drop on Fitz," Bram grunted.

"He'll croak or cure," Ab countered.

"Yeah," Bram grinned. "And Arabella'll throw a fit when you leave her boyfriend ahind!"

"You look upset, Wasatch," Ab commented. "What is it?"

The young man lifted his eyes to where the sun was strengthening. "I will miss the Medicine Lodge this year. I would offer myself again as I have in the past. I have to dance two more times before I can begin to learn the songs and the ceremonies."

"Yep, well, we'd all do things a sight different, little brother, if other men didn't stick their noses into the middle of things."

Bram watched the lodge go down, Lark binding the poles quickly and efficiently to a gray gelding. Arabella helped fold up the cover to rest on the lodgepoles. When he tried to help, Bram got a quick lecture on not interfering with women's work—especially since the Cheyenne would consider him a laughingstock.

On a second pony, Wasatch and Jake rigged another travois, lashing the groaning Jeremiel onto the poles.

Bram took a quick look at the swollen arm—then

wished he hadn't as his stomach turned. "What if we have to amputate that?" He gestured toward the mottled flesh. Yellow smears streaked the skin, dripping down on the cattail mat Jeremiel rested on.

"Wasatch says it'll heal," Jake added. "If it doesn't, I've cut men's arms off before."

"You've . . ."

"Comes as part of being Jason Oord's boy," Jake added grimly, going to check on his horses.

Bram counted the packs, seeing they were all together, hearing Arabella where she talked to Sentor, trying to keep her voice down.

"It's all right. Tom Fitzpatrick is a man of considerable reputation in this part of the world."

"I want to go!" Sentor insisted, trying to sit up, the color draining out of his face.

"Stay here! You'll die on the trail." In a lower voice she hissed, "I'm not running guns to the Indians here. And if I was it'd be no business of France's!"

Running guns? Bram grinned suddenly, eyes on Arabella's Benjamin Bigelow where it leaned against a cottonwood. So that's where she got that fancy repeating rifle-shotgun! Son of a gun! His sister? A gunrunner?

"So I ain't the only shifty one in the Catton outfit," he mumbled happily under his breath.

"I'll come after you! I swear," Sentor continued, fingers wrapping around her wrist.

"Why?" Arabella demanded hotly. "James is dead! My future lies here now."

Sentor shrugged, working his lips. "Perhaps I need to. Honor. Duty."

Bram slid behind a pack, sticking his nose over the top so he could see. Arabella went pale. She shook her head. "You needn't worry. I'll never return to France.

Your duty is ended. Go back, Leander. And I . . . well, thank you for trying to save me on the trail."

He lowered his eyes, rubbing his beard-shadowed jaw. "Perhaps we could spend time getting to know each other?"

"You'll have a considerable quest," she added tartly. "I have no desire for a man to start with—let alone for a French spy!"

*Spy!* Bram's mouth watered at the implications. *His* sister? Fooling around with a *spy*? And to think he'd always figgered hoss thievin' was exciting!

A hand dropped on his shoulder, sending his heart leaping up into his throat. Bram was pulled inexorably back until the pack hid him from Arabella.

"What are you doing?" Lark hissed hot reproach.

Bram grinned. "Keepin' track of my sister! Ain't that what brothers is made fer?"

Lark stole a peep around the pack. "She doesn't care for him. It isn't in her eyes—not yet. She only dreams of what he could be."

"How you know that?" Bram demanded skeptically. "Why, she's just—"

Lark clamped a hand on his mouth, stifling his outburst. "You make so much noise stealing horses? No wonder the white man almost hanged you!"

A half hour later, they had the horses loaded, the party filing out of camp, splashing across the muddy Arkansas. Bram set himself on the north bank, looking back, letting his eyes trace the high bluffs over the river. Memories drifted up from deep in his head. A lot had happened there in that Cheyenne camp. He'd saved Jeremiel from dying horribly, come to love a woman, danced and made friends with a different people, and come to be a man on his own.

Lark wheeled her pony to pull up next to him. "You are leaving thoughts behind?"

"Reckon," Bram agreed. "You know. For the first time, I was happy there. Funny, ain't it? All them years ridin' the grub trail with old One-Eyed Mike, and I come into that camp the first day and found you. My whole life changed, jest like that."

She nodded, looking back over the Cheyenne camp, seeing things in her own mind.

"Poor Sentor." Bram shook his head. "He sure hated bein' dumped inta the back of ol' Fitz's wagon."

"He will come," Lark told him. "I saw it in his eyes. It is not all Arabella. He is torn inside. Some other thing fills him, drives him."

"Hell, half his head is caved in!" Bram snorted. "That's tore enuff, ain't it?"

Lark narrowed her eyes. "No, he is torn over something else. Something I do not understand, and Arabella is making his decision very hard."

"Yo!" Jake called, his voice already distant. "You two coming or not?"

Lark laughed, pulling her pony around, trotting off down the trail.

Bram hesitated for one last look, fastening the sight in his mind to remember forever.

He saw the figure standing at the edge of the trees, back in the shadow where he couldn't be seen easily. Even across the distance, Bram could make out the flaring cheekbones, the long nose that dipped over those thin angry lips. High Walker! Even over the distance, he could feel the hatred.

"Reckon you and I will come face-to-face one of these days," Bram decided. "And it'll be Katy-bar-the-door when we do!"

# Chapter 16

The next morning they passed the ruins of Bent's Fort—mostly intact but for the exploded powder magazine. Jeremiel—seeing it through a haze—noted the toppling adobe walls washing back into the same earth from which they had once sprung.

Grimly, he clung to his Bible, miraculously returned to him by Arabella—of all people.

Against the horror backdrop of his delirium, the suffering of his waking hours seemed merciful. Awake, his physical discomfort vanquished the satanic phantoms of imagination in a cadence of pain.

Wasatch, however, couldn't be banished as a phantom. Each time they stopped, his malevolent witch-brother appeared, bending over Jeremiel's traveling sickbed and muttering some heathen incantation. Then he'd do something devilish with bits of plant that crackled in his fingers and change the poultice.

Despite frantic protests, brother Wasatch poured potions down his resisting throat—often with the help of Abriel, whose muscle-corded arms bent Jeremiel to the heathen's will.

"But I resist, my Lord," Jeremiel mumbled as his travois clattered and banged, jarring his vision. "Satan has cast his hand upon me, but I see through his lies. Thy kingdom come, Thy will be done. Amen."

His world continued to bounce and grind along, the travois poles grating over gravel, grass, and cobbles. When he didn't sleep—or the pain didn't totally absorb him—he could see where he'd been. Oftentimes Bram and Lark would ride behind him, talking animatedly. Jeremiel frowned, foggy with the swelling ache in his arm, fever ravaging his body in hot and cold streaks. I ought to object to Bram and that woman, he decided, but the thoughts shifted and he couldn't quite put his finger on why.

"Hold up!" Jake called, voice drifting through the perpetual torture that had become existence. Jeremiel croaked relief as his world stopped shaking and shuddering.

Above his head, he heard the horse break wind. A man never truly understood how often a horse did that until he lived day after day behind one.

"Here," Wasatch's soft voice commanded. Satan's emissary had returned, blocking the sun. "Drink this."

Jeremiel reacted to the cup placed against his lips, drinking the sour fluid. Blessed Lord God, what could that stuff be?

"I'm taking the pack off your arm. Let's see your hand."

Jeremiel gritted his teeth, making himself recite the

Lord's Prayer as Wasatch drained his hand yet again. Lances of agony flashed fire in his mind, scattering the Lord's holy words like so many minnows in a disturbed pond.

"How bad?" Jeremiel asked, gasping.

"Your hand is stronger today. Bend your arm."

So easily said. Jeremiel blinked his eyes a couple of times. "Give me strength, Lord." Moving his arm, making the elbow bend, he swallowed the cry that bubbled on his lips, sweat popping out on his forehead.

"Very good," Wasatch praised. "We do that again, tonight. Fever is breaking. Your body is growing strong against the poison." Wasatch pulled something green and foul-smelling from his satanic bag. "Chew this. You must chew it for the rest of the afternoon, even when it gets pasty. Chew it until I tell you to stop."

Jeremiel lifted his lip. "I have the faith of the Lord to keep me fit. I don't need your . . ."

Wasatch hunkered down to peer into Jeremiel's eyes. Almost casually, he said, "Jake has told me about the times he has amputated the arms of soldiers. Sometimes frost killed the end of a limb and it rotted by spring. Another time a bullet shattered a man's elbow. Jake has never cut off a man's arm for snakebite, but he did cut off a horseherder's leg once. He says that time the poison got so high up the thigh, he had to cut clear up to here."

Jeremiel flinched as Wasatch ran the edge of his hand across his thigh just below the crotch. He shivered, blinking, seeing in Wasatch's amber eyes what would have been honesty in his own.

"With Abriel's help," Wasatch added soberly, "I can get the root into your mouth. To keep you from spitting it out, we would have to gag you. You will not get all the medicine that way but you will get some."

Jeremiel scowled at the thick section of root Wasatch

held up. What do I do now, O Lord? They'll force me if I don't ... and maybe, just maybe, it would be all right? Just this once?

*Yea, though I walk through the valley of the shadow of death* ... Jeremiel opened his mouth, biting down on the vile-tasting root.

As they rode, the Rockies drifted slowly out of the western horizon. High in the incredible blue sky, the sun burned hot, a searing white orb. Arabella dug her *kafia* from the parfleche Wasatch had given her. Where the burnoose had disappeared to was anyone's guess, but she'd saved her pink parasol.

Heat waves rolled across the bottoms, shimmering over a straggling herd of buffalo winding down the bluffs to drink. Around them, the land bloomed, flowers in a riot of color spreading in fragrant carpets. Lush grass filled the Arkansas floodplain to the delight of the horses. Even ornery Molly acted placid.

Jake noted a party of Taos traders on the opposite side of the river and forded, needing a shoe for his bay. He returned with a dangling canvas bag of clinking shoes and a grim expression.

"Traders say a party of hard cases passed through a couple of days ago. Said they was closemouthed and hunting."

"Bragg with them?" Ab asked, jaw set hard, cheeks rippling muscle to accent his bent nose.

"Nope. I asked about that beard of his. Nobody with a beard like that ... nobody that big either. You know anything about a man with a mashed face?"

Ab nodded. "Hank Tent. They're Branton's boys. He likes to hire his help rough." His eyes drifted to where Arabella listened.

"I can handle myself," she defended, feeling foolish,

knowing Ab had to be thinking about Buffalo Thrower—and what Pawnee Stalker had almost accomplished. All right, she'd failed once. Never again!

"Best we make tracks, then," Jake grunted, bending over his saddle. "Sooner we're out of here, the less chance Branton has of finding us."

Make tracks they did, crossing Chico Creek in the last dusky light of day. Lark and Bram set about establishing the camp, chatting happily, laughing, sharing glances and smiles. Wasatch attended to the horses while Ab and Jake trimmed the bay's hoof and tacked a new shoe on with no little inventive language as the bay proved fractious and their tools insufficient.

"Arabella?" Jeremiel called hoarsely from where they'd laid him next to the fire.

Eyes strained from squinting in the flickers of firelight, she looked up from reading her Koran and walked over. "Need something? Water?"

He shook his head, clearing his throat. A little color had come back to his cheeks and his eyes didn't seem sunk quite so deeply in his head.

"No," he added quietly. "No, I just wanted to apologize for that day on the trail, and to thank you for returning my Bible to me." He fingered the thick book, looking up sincerely.

She smiled, adding, "I wouldn't know what to do without my Koran. I just thought, well, religious books are special. That one means a lot to you. This"—she tapped the Koran—"means a lot to me. It was a gift from someone very special."

He licked his lips, dropping his eyes. "The Bible belonged to William Sunts, the man who raised me. Before that, it was his father's clear back to England. It's old. Printed over a hundred and fifty years ago."

She settled on a fallen cottonwood log, squashing a

mosquito that landed on her arm. "This Koran," she told him, "was given to me by a sheikh, a Moslem holy man . . . a teacher. His name was Ahmad ibn Idris, one of the most respected Sufi sheikhs in Mecca."

"Why not Jesus Christ? I . . . I don't understand." His eyes softened. "I don't mean to restart an old argument, but why?"

She lifted her shoulder. "The religions aren't that different. According to the Koran, Jesus brought an important message. Here, wait, let me see. Yes. Let me read you from the Imrans.

" 'Say, we believe in God and what is revealed to us; in that which was revealed to Abraham and Ishmael, to Isaac and Jacob and the tribes; and that which God gave Moses and Jesus and the prophets. We discriminate against none of them. To Him we have surrendered ourselves.'

"And then if I skip down"—she flipped a couple of pages—"I can even find a quotation which speaks to the salvation of non-Moslems. Here: 'Yet they are not all alike'—Mohammed refers to Christians and Jews here. 'There are among the People of the Bible some upright men who all night long recite the Revelations of God and worship Him; who believe in God and the last day; who enjoin justice and forbid evil and vie with each other in good works. These are the righteous men: whatever good they do, its reward will not be denied them. God knows righteousness.'"

"Let me see." Jeremiel reached for the Koran.

"It's written in Arabic, I'm afraid." She handed it over anyway and Jeremiel stared, face darkening.

"Chicken tracks could be read as easily." He looked at her critically as he handed it back. "They still make Jesus a prophet like Moses. He wasn't, you know, he was the son of God."

"The Koran agrees." She thumbed back a couple of pages, reading, "This revelation and this wise admonition We recite to you. Jesus is like Adam in the sight of God. He created him of dust and said, 'Be' and he was." Then she read him the story of the Divine Conception.

Jeremiel listened. "I learned that Mohammed placed himself above Christ?"

She shook her head. "Islam thinks they have the complete revelations of God, that you can't follow the straight path of God with only the Torah, the New Testament, and the Ten Commandments. You've got to have all of them as well as the Koran."

"Then what is this Sufi? In all my studies in seminary, I never heard that word, or if I did I've forgotten." He scowled, pulling at his beard with his good hand, the Bible resting over his heart like a protective shield.

Arabella sighed, telling him, "Yes, well, not even all of Islam can make up their minds about Sufis. Through the ages, the Sufis have been tormented and burned and beaten ... and even crucified. The difference is that a woman, like the saint Rabi'a, can become a holy teacher. And the Sufis believe that they can bridge the chasm separating man from God and ..."

Jeremiel gasped, face going pale.

"Now you know why most orthodox Moslems—the Sunna—like to hang Sufis by their toes even though Sufis still follow the *shari'a*, the Divine law established by the Koran."

Jeremiel looked at her, shaking his head, eyes wide. "Once I worried about the Tempter in the Wilderness. Now I know not what to believe. Does heresy wear so many faces? Can you say the words of John 14:6 are meaningless? 'Jesus saith unto him, I am the way, the truth, and the life: no man cometh unto the Father, but by me.' "

Arabella nodded. "I know I'm not a very good Moslem." She ran her finger along the edge of the Koran, lost in thought. "But to me, Allah, God, *is*. That's all that's really important—not the name you tag on him. The Bible and the Koran both speak of righteousness and the Sufi teach contemplation and prayer."

He narrowed an eye, a brow going up. "And how is it you aren't a very good Moslem?" His face betrayed a sudden hope. She could see it in his eyes as he grasped that straw, desperate to find a lever with which to pry her from Islam.

She chuckled. "I don't pray to Mecca five times a day to start with. But I keep my fasts, give to the poor when I can, and utter the *Shahadah*—if under my breath. But, I fall down on diet and piety and humility and I can't accept a lot of the restrictions the Koran places on women—"

"I am the way," Jeremiel added firmly. "That is the truth of the New Testament. Perhaps . . . perhaps you just haven't had proper male guidance to provide a proper perspec—"

Arabella stiffened. "I don't think you heard a word I said." She got up, shaking her head. "Can't you just think about it? That maybe people have to find their own way to God?"

"But I . . . Wait!"

She slapped at a mosquito that hummed near her ear as she walked over to settle herself where Wasatch hovered at the edges of the campfire cleaning his musket.

"I don't know what to do with him," she muttered, sitting next to him. "I've never seen a man so stubborn."

"Yep," Bram agreed, "but, sis, he's lost a little steam. He ain't the thunder jaw he started out as."

"We'll see who he is when the fever passes," Arabella added tartly.

\* \* \*

"Looks pretty dismal," Ab noted as they passed yet another deserted field. "I heard tell that most of the folks down here took off for California last year. Part of the gold stampede. Still, I'd never have guessed the whole Arkansas was this deserted."

"It's been sliding," Jake reminded, squinting into the hot sun. "Remember when Bent sent John Hatcher down the Purgatoire in the spring of '47? Wanted him to grow corn? That was the handwriting on the wall. Utes burned him out, stole all his stock, and smashed his wagons. Told him to get out—and not to come back."

Ab took a deep breath and nodded. "I know. I rode east with Barclay that year. Saw Tharp's grave on Walnut Creek where he and DeLisle held off that bunch of Indians. Course, with the shooting of old Chief Cinemo that year, who could blame them? That was that young bastard herder with Fowler's train did that. I liked old Cinemo. Called him Tobacco back then. Took him five days to die from that bullet . . . and all the while he pleaded with his warriors to keep the peace."

"Yeah, well, in the words of the old-timers, brother, the buzzards have come home to roost. Trouble's coming. Too many peaceful Indians are getting shot. It'll blow up someday soon."

Ab turned to look. "You think Fitzpatrick won't be able to keep the lid on?"

Jake hawked and spit into the dust at the trail side. "For a while. Time being, he's the only man in this part of the country keeping heads cool. That's why that big peace treaty's so important. Maybe, if we could get something in writing, the politicians might see a reason to enforce an equitable peace out here—and let my fath . . . uh, Colonel Oord and me put together a Ranger force like the Texans use."

Ab gave him a wicked grin. "You could always use Germans like the army did at Fort Mann a couple of years back. Gilpin put them boys in there, didn't he?"

"And came so close to a war you wouldn't believe it!"

"Huh?" Bram asked. "A war?"

Jake squinted. "Damn fools let a whole war party of Pawnee inside the post. Fed 'em all the whiskey they'd drink, and when the Pawnee got rowdy, killed and wounded half of them."

"Can't figure why the Pawnee didn't get even," Ab grumbled.

" 'Cause Jason Oord bought them off," Jake told him flatly. "That's not common knowledge, brother, so keep your hat on it. There's been a loose coalition of folks out here trying to keep things calm. Colonel Oord, Fitzpatrick, McKinney, Robert Campbell, and to some extent, Benton."

"Figures." Ab rubbed his neck.

"Uh-huh. An Indian war would be a strategic debacle." Jake scanned the green hills to the north. "There's no way the Frontier Army could do a thing. All them folks who fought in Mexico aren't ready for a wilderness campaign. Infantry? Out here for God's sake?" Jake screwed his face up unpleasantly. "Worse, all them dandy citizens in New York and Boston and Charleston would have to be taxed for pay, equipment, animals, wagons, and all the rest. Think they'll stand for that?"

"Nope," Ab clipped.

"You wait," Jake admonished. "When white graves come every other mile, then you'll get action—and it'll be the people out here who'll make it work."

"Maybe." Ab noted another vacant dugout. "You know, Barclay himself abandoned the Arkansas. Moved down to the Mora to build a fort. Seems like settlement is losing ground all over out here except California and Kansas."

Molly brayed from behind as Sorrel kicked at her. Ab turned to look in time to see her extend her head again, teeth bared to nip at Sorrel's flank. She saw him— stopping as if nothing had happened—smacking her lips, eyelids lowering, ears back.

"I oughta blow your scheming brain right out of that cussed bent skull of yours, Molly!" Ab growled.

Despite the lead, Molly shook her head, rattling the halter and slapping the heavy rope against Sorrel's hip to irritate the horse even more.

"You know, you could always find somebody you didn't like and give them that fool mule," Jake offered, grinning from under his broad-brimmed hat.

"She's all yours, brother. Free of charge!"

Jake looked at him, face stony, as they followed the dusty trail into the open valley of Fountain Creek.

"What buildings are them?" Bram called, pointing to a cluster of wooden cabins. The doors hung open like gaping mouths. Weeds had sprouted along the walls and made a green fuzz in the corrals where only manure-beaten dirt should have been.

"Mormon Town," Jake called. "Whole party of them came here back in '46 led by that rascal John Richard." He pronounced the Frenchman's name as "Reeshaw."

"Now," Ab cautioned, raising a restraining hand, "I'm not sure you can call Reeshaw a rascal. He's just a trader doing what a trader has to do. I've been in his shoes. I know what it's—"

"You been running whiskey to the Indians?" Jake asked, expression mild. "Selling guns to the Comanche and Kiowa? Providing military intelligence to the Mormons?"

"Now, hold on a minute!" Ab protested, knotting a

fist. "The Mormons was real good to Reeshaw. Kept him alive during some of the slow years in the trade. And you can't say he's giving military secrets away. That's unfair!"

"Uh-huh," Jake grunted.

Ab smoldered silently as they rode up to Fort Pueblo. At least here tracks could be seen. Recently a horse had left a pile of green road apples before the big gate, flies now circling greedily. Boot imprints remained in the dust. Brown star-shaped spatters remained where a man had spit tobacco.

"Must be somebody here," Jake called, stepping down.

Arabella slipped off her horse, slapping dust from her dress as she hid in the shade of her parasol.

Wasatch immediately went to see Jeremiel, who sat up now on the travois looking around.

"How's he doing?" Ab asked, walking back.

"Move your arm." Wasatch gestured with his own, watching Jeremiel imitate the movements, to straighten, bend, and turn it. "Now, clasp your hand."

Jeremiel did so, eyes betraying a slight tinge of pain. "Feels numb."

"Amazing." Jake looked astonished. "I don't know of a single military doctor who would have bet on his having the use of his arm again."

"The Lord cares for His own," Jeremiel asserted, avoiding Wasatch's eyes. "Faith in my Lord has vanquished the serpent. Yea, let it be a lesson to you, sinners. As is the Truth in—"

"Think I'll see who's in the fort," Ab interrupted, backing away, knowing Jeremiel had a good head of steam.

"Hell," Bram snorted. "Wasatch? What'd ya go and do to us anyway? Ain't you got no medicine to slow his mouth none?"

Wasatch chuckled lightly, checking to make sure the travois poles didn't chafe the horse.

"Yep," Ab mumbled under his breath, "he ain't sick no more."

"Reckon I'm back to guarding my sinning again," Bram said with a sigh, turning to Lark and shaking his head.

Jeremiel's humor sounded genuine. "Gotcha, little brother! Wouldn't want you getting bored!"

Ab started for the big gate where it hung open a crack. Perhaps a hundred feet long, adobe walls stood ten feet high to either side of the thick picket-post gate. Bastions provided flanking fire to cover the walls, and loopholes had been cut here and there.

"Anybody here?" Ab called, noting the ditches hadn't been used; the corrals had suffered neglect, a yellow spot bright where a bored horse had chewed one of the poles.

And Hank Tent moved to fill the narrow opening in the gate, a ghastly smile twisting his broken face.

"Hewow Catton," he slurred. "I bin waithing for hyou."

Ab suffered a tingling sensation as Tent's rifle centered on his belly. Too close to miss—too far away to slap aside.

"Careful, Tent," Ab warned, his throbbing heart cramming into the bottom of his throat. "Remember last time you messed with me?"

"Yourh mhule dies nexsht," he promised, lumpy face contorting. A keenness glinted behind those hard eyes, a heady anticipation of death. Tent laughed, twisted smile showing missing teeth.

Ab caught the instant flinch, pitching himself violently down and to the side, a blast of speckling powder and smoke batting him in the ear-splitting report of the rifle.

One hand clawed the Dragoon Colt from his belt as Tent, howling like some incredible animal, charged down on him, rifle held by the muzzle, clublike.

Ab twisted to one side, pistol bucking in his hand as the rifle butt hissed past his skull into his shoulder. Feeling in his arm and hand disappeared in the meaty thunk of the rifle butt against flesh.

Gunfire crackled behind them.

Ab kicked out, planting a boot in Tent's lower stomach. Tent doubled over, eyes going wide before he charged. Ab met him halfway. Right hand useless, he swung an uppercut into Tent with his left, the punch landing below the heart. Tent staggered, falling, dragging Ab to the ground with him.

Fingers clawed for Ab's eyes as he jacked a frantic knee into Tent's crotch. With his left hand, he beat curled fingers from his eyes, elbowing hard enough to leave Tent grunting, and got a grip on the man's throat, feeling muscle and trachea slide beneath his fear-strong fingers.

Saliva trickled out the corner of Tent's ruined mouth, eyes glazing as he stared into Abriel's. In a last desperate measure, he thrashed his feet and legs, arms flailing impotently.

Adrenaline pumping, Ab kept his grip, feeling the very life in Hank Tent draining from under his cramping fingers. The memory engraved itself. Never would he forget the skin puckering around his iron fingertips, the way the tendons jumped and corded on the back of his tanned hand, or the glassing in Hank Tent's eyes.

Panting, scared, Ab forced himself to let go and shove the limp body off. Rolling out to one side, he tried to sit up, looking down at the sticky wetness on his chest, horrified at the way the blood matted, shiny in the sun, soaking his clothes.

"My God," he whispered to himself, heart stopped in his surging chest. "I'm dead!"

Disbelieving, he waited for the pain, curious at why he hadn't felt the bullet's impact. With trembling fingers he probed, seeking to find the wound, the welling origin of the blood.

Then Jake bent over him, a smoking pistol in hand. Viciously, he ripped Ab's shirt open, searching, eyes frightened. Confused, he looked over at Tent, a wash of relief spreading over anxious features.

"I think you're dying of Tent's blood," Jake admitted, sheepishly, looking to one side.

Ab frowned, stupidly looking over to where the corpse lay, a spread of red seeping into the ground. "Guess I didn't . . . didn't miss." Feeling started to creep into his right arm as the fear-flush faded.

Weakly, Ab got to his feet, picking the Colt out of the dust and walking to sit on a bench carved from a hollowed-out cottonwood. Mouth dry, he began reloading the empty cylinder, propping the pistol between his knees, using his left hand. Except he'd begun to shake—and it got worse, racking his whole body.

Barely cognizant, he felt Wasatch kneel by him, a warm hand on his shoulder. "Eat this." Wasatch placed something next to his lips. Ab bit, chewing, the pulpy taste running over his tongue, soothing his throat and calming him.

He glanced up to see Wasatch striding away, seeking to comfort pale-faced Arabella, blue smoke twining from her fancy rifle as she leaned for support against Efende, one hand interlaced in the thick mane. He followed her pinched stare to where a man lay pitched forward on his face, the back of his weirdly canted head glistening blood.

Bram and Lark moved about checking corpses, rifling

pockets. There stood Jeremiel, the big Walker Colt hanging in his good hand, the hammer back as he looked down at a sprawled form.

Ab gritted his teeth, pulling the loading level down, and stood up, energy thrilling his nerves as Wasatch's medicine reached his stunned body and mind.

He went to Arabella first, seeing she chewed a piece of Wasatch's root. "You all right?"

She nodded, the fine muscles of her face quivering as her delicate fingers knotted and twisted in Efende's mane. "I . . . Yes. F-Fine." She took a deep breath. "He lifted his gun. I shot."

"You did fine," he soothed, seeing her jerk a quick nod, confusion and horror in her eyes. Otherwise, only Jeremiel seemed upset. Lark's face carried a wolfish gleam as she and Bram engaged in an animated discussion about mutilating the dead.

He walked over. "How about you? All right?" Ab placed a hand on Jeremiel's shoulder.

"O Lord God, Thou hast smitten all mine enemies, Thou hast broken the teeth of the ungodly." He lifted the big Walker in his hand, staring at it with a fixed horror. Then he raised his eyes to Ab's, disbelief writ large there. "I killed a man, brother Ab. It happened so quickly. He came around the corner of the fort—lifted his rifle to shoot . . . The pistol, it was just in my hand. I don't remember . . . The pistol went off . . . and he dropped like . . ."

"Done right good too," Bram added, walking up, a sober look about him. "Plumb shot his right eye out."

"That's where I was looking," Jeremiel mumbled. "I was looking into his eyes."

Jeremiel carefully lowered the hammer on the big Walker to an empty cylinder. He looked dully at Ab. "Every man's work shall be made manifest: for the day shall declare it, because it shall be revealed by fire; and the fire shall try every man's work of what sort it is." A look of revulsion filled his eyes. "A man of peace? Who prays for me?"

# Chapter 17

Leander O. B. Sentor sat up to eat his evening meal, vertigo giving him a bit of a turn until his blood readjusted. Fitzpatrick was off carrying on what he called palaver with one of the Arapaho chiefs.

The continual dizziness had begun to ebb. For the first time in days, his vision didn't blur and he could think straight. The headache abated slowly and his memories were coming back. Quite a wallop on the head that Cheyenne warrior had given him. He didn't even remember the rifle barrel coming down.

"Well, General, you may have gotten lucky this time," Leander whispered under his breath. So, Arabella didn't want him on her trail? They had left riding west. That way he, too, would go, praying all the while the rain would hold off so the travois trail wouldn't wash out.

The image of Arabella's face floated in his mind. He

could picture the healthy glow of her skin, imagine the soft touch of her full lips against his. Ah, he could drown forever in those odd amber eyes. If only his duty weren't so implacable.

"I am mocked by God," he decided, knowing someday he would have to turn down this fascinating woman for France. The dread of that day lay heavy on him. Still, there might be a chance if she could perhaps see the enormity of what lay at stake for France, and for all the world.

"Howdy!" One of the herders called out, standing up from the fire, pulling his battered hat back on his head.

Leander turned to see riders coming up the trail. White men dressed in skins and homespun, long rifles lay crossways on their saddles. The first of them proved to be a bear of a man. The others—in Leander's eyes—wouldn't do to send across the Pont Louis for a loaf of bread.

"Howdy yerself," the big man boomed, drawing up his horse, wicked blue eyes searching out every aspect of the camp, pinning Leander and the white bandage wrapped around his head. Their eyes met for a brief bone-chilling moment.

The fellow wore a tan buckskin shirt with long fringes. His wide dark brown hat didn't hide the weather-beaten squint around those deadly eyes or the odd white streak in his beard. The fellow dropped lightly to the ground, relieving a seventeen-hand horse and moving easily despite his huge body.

"Whose camp?" the big man called, the others stepping off their horses, surly, wary, muttering under their breath at the immense spread of Indian lodges disappearing into the trees. Already, curious children and women had gathered to see who these newcomers might be, their whispers barely audible behind blankets.

"Tom Fitzpatrick's," the herder announced.

The big man froze in his tracks, an animal quality in the way he crouched. The others in his party looked back and forth, beards moving as they whispered to themselves, wary, eyes flicking this way and that.

"So, whar's Fitz at?"

"Big shindig over to the Arapaho camp." The herder had become uncertain, beginning to shift from side to side. "Uh, who're you?"

The big man laughed, motioning his men to remount, stepping into the saddle himself. "Tell Fitz his old compadre, Branton Bragg, rode through. Sorry he wasn't around to talk a little about the old times," the big man called, saluting as he kicked his horse into a trot. The ragtag behind shot sullen and hostile glances at the herder as they rode out. From the grim set of their lips, they seemed just as happy for distance from the gawking Indians too.

At the name, Leander stiffened, supper forgotten although the hot food radiated heat through the tin plate into his leg. So the giant was Branton Bragg? That was the man he'd come all this way to . . .

Setting the plate to one side, Leander gathered up his things.

"What're you doing?" the herder asked.

Leander smiled. "Mind bringing my horse over?"

"Uh, no. But you shouldn't oughta be goin' gallivantin' around with that head neither!"

"Sorry, friend. But business calls."

The herder shook his head. "Any bizniss with that Bragg snake ain't bizniss worthy of a Christian man!"

Within minutes, Leander had saddled his rested horse, strapped his blanket and meager remaining belongings to the cantle, and trotted out to the west, the tracks left by Bragg clearly defined in the slanting sun.

He made no more than five miles before his head began to pound, strength flagging; a sick feeling had settled in his stomach. Most of the blurring cleared every time he took a deep breath.

At the point of turning back, a man stepped his horse out from behind a screen of cottonwoods, long rifle centering on Leander's heart.

"Whar up, pilgrim?" Thin, he wore grease-shiny leather clothing that hung on him. Only the rifle seemed well maintained. The face proved familiar.

"You're one of Bragg's men," Leander greeted easily, recognizing him as one of the more nervous back at Fitzpatrick's camp.

"Yep. An who're you?"

"Leander O. B. Sentor."

The voice from behind came cool, deadly, "And why're you on our trail?"

Leander turned to see yet another of Bragg's thugs, a big Colt pistol in hand and aimed at Leander's back. The man had evidently circled, cutting off retreat.

"Why, just riding," Leander lied.

"Then you better just let us relieve you of any excess weight. Wouldn't want you strainin' that hoss. Looks like a fine animal," the hind man decided.

"Willy, get his rifle and pistol. Mister, you go to fooling around, and you'll be needing more than that white bandage on your head," Thin and Greasy ordered.

"I . . . uh, wouldn't think of it," Leander agreed easily, handing his weapons over as Willy rode up to get them.

"Where's yer cash?" Thin-and-Greasy asked. "Case you didn't recognize it, this hyar's a robb'ry."

Leander took a deep breath. "I don't think your Mr. Bragg would approve."

The hollow clicking of the Colt's pistol shivered his

soul. In the silence, Leander could hear the sound of birds, the buzzing of insects in the grasses.

"Mister, you can get off yer horse and hand yer stuff over. That's it."

Leander's heart strangled in his chest. The damn fools were going to kill him!

"Kill me and Bragg will have your hides," Leander bluffed. "I've come a long way—at *his* invitation—to speak to him. My boss and yours would take a very dim view of my death. It could be, well, painful for both of you gentlemen."

Thin-and-Greasy frowned, his brow lining. "And why should we believe you, mister. Men say funny things when they're about t' be shot."

"Because you follow the Cattons." He added it easily, seeing shock on Thin's face.

"Move!" came the gruff order from behind him.

They pushed on to the west, making good time as the sun sank low, finally dropping behind the ragged horizon. Leander's skull left him feeling it would split in twain, pain lancing like Welsh double-jacks split the very bone.

A fire winked in the blackness.

"Hold up here," the man behind ordered. Willy rode forward.

Voices called back and forth as Willy reappeared. "Come on in."

Leander rode forward, almost weaving. He caught himself as he stepped out of the saddle, one leg almost buckling. Gods, perhaps Arabella had been right. Perhaps he'd been sicker than he thought. Worse, for the moment, he might need his wits more than he'd ever needed them before. His throat had gone dry.

"Well, now, that white bandage makes a right fine target in the dark," Bragg's voice caught him unaware. The big man loomed out of the blackness, a big pistol in hand.

Leander walked over to the fire, sinking down gratefully, head spinning. "And who are ya now?" Bragg asked, pistol keeping Leander centered, a chunk of antelope speared on a sharp stick in the other. Bragg took a bite, ripping the meat loose with straight white teeth.

"Leander O. B. Sentor, at your service, sir."

Someone laughed to the side, silencing as Bragg shifted slitted eyes his direction.

"A gentleman," Bragg sighed, his very manner changing. He laughed. "You know, I've been out here so long, I forgot what polite company's like. Well, the boys wouldn't have brought you in unless they thought you was . . . uh, were dogging my tracks." He motioned with the meat. "You want to explain? Some of these handsome gentlemen don't cotton to Mr. Fitzpatrick. He frowns on the whiskey trade, on the gun trade, and ransoming Mexican captives from the Comanche, and just about anything lucrative in these parts anymore."

Leander nodded. "I see." A wry smile twisted his lips. "I can more than assure you, sir. I am *not* in the employ of Mr. Fitzpatrick . . . or the American government for that matter."

"Then who are you?" Bragg inclined his chin, chill blue eyes pinning Leander. Unconsciously, he squirmed where he crouched.

He looked around. Wolfish bearded faces gleamed in the firelight. "If you would, could we step away from the fire for a moment? I would speak to you in confidence."

Bragg chewed on the meat, thinking, the white streak of his beard garish in the firelight. "Get up." He motioned with his head.

Leander bit his lip, keeping his balance by force of will. Firming his step, he walked out into the darkness.

"That's far enough," Bragg's voice came cold as the breeze off a glacier. A loud click sounded as a pistol hammer cocked under a thick thumb. "Now, talk."

Leander turned, making out the bulk of Bragg's thick body.

"You're a difficult man to find. I missed you at Fort Laramie."

"Had other business than whatever you're into. And I ain't buying, Mr. Sentor. Hate to waste the company of a gentleman—but like I said, I got other business."

Leander's heart leapt. "Pull that trigger, Branton, and you'll destroy whatever you hoped to accomplish with General Cavaignac."

Bragg stood stock-still, Leander's heart thumping against his chest.

Finally the big man, laughed, the hammer clicking as he lowered it. "So, you're here at last! About high time. I thought he'd lost interest." Bragg snorted. "Could be a fatal mistake for a man trying to do what he is. Come on, have something to eat. We'll talk about it."

"How did they find us?" Bram asked as they settled around the fire. "I just don't understand."

Arabella listened absently, continuing to relive the moment when she'd pulled the trigger, the bullet going high, hitting the man in the throat just under the jaw.

The shot had been instinctive, just like James had taught her through the years. All that practice and she'd functioned perfectly. Perhaps it came from bird hunting. The unconscious lift of the shotgun from low to high, settling the end of the barrel on the target, squeezing the trigger.

By her hand, a man lay dead—buried deep in the earth. His body had gone cool by now. Dirt lay packed all around him, heavy on his sightless eyes, in his motionless mouth, intruded into the bullet hole that had broken his neck.

She closed her eyes and swallowed hard.

Wolf had appeared just before they made camp, walking in as if he hadn't been gone for several days. Now he studied her from across the camp, ears pricked, yellow eyes evaluating. Unconsciously, she rubbed her hand, touching the pad of the trigger finger.

"There aren't that many places to go out here," Jake said, voice listless. "Travel is restricted to water. If we didn't go down the Front Range, we would have had to go down Sand Creek. I should have thought of that. If they checked Ceran Saint Vrain's, they knew we were still headed south. We got lucky and saw them first on Cherry Creek. After Uncle Branton cut for sign, he must have figured we got by him somehow. He sent one group with Tent down the Front Range following the Platte and then Cherry Creek to the Boiling Springs and from there south on Fountain Creek while he cut across, maybe paralleling our trail to Sand Creek. Somewhere, he would have seen some of our—"

"Why'd Tent try and take us?" Bram's face mirrored confusion.

"Pride cometh before the fall," Jeremiel suggested absently from where he reclined on the travois, eyes on his work as he finished cleaning the Walker and drove the barrel key in.

In the ensuing silence he continued, "Jeremiah tells us, 'For my people is foolish, they have not known me; they are sottish children, and they have not understanding; they are wise to do evil, but to do good they have no knowledge.' "

"Might be," Ab agreed. He fingered his thick-bearded chin, a grimness to his lips. "Revenge can give men funny ideas every so often."

Jake squatted on a blanket, having spent the last half hour trying to put the five knives together this way and that. None of the wavy patterns in the metal formed any kind of map.

Bram noted it, adding, "Now me, I'da lost patience with that ten minutes ago and cut my thumb off when I got mad." He smiled, winking at Lark where she dished up various assorted bowls of stew.

Arabella took the bowl Lark offered, retrieving her spoon, dabbling, appetite gone. The man she'd killed would never eat again. Why should she? How fragile life proved. That little bit of lead she'd loaded had killed so quickly, so efficiently.

"And he tried to kill you," Jake whispered in her ear as he stood to get more firewood.

"Halloooo the camp!" a voice called from the black ness. Quick as scat, bowls spilling among elbows and flying feet, each of them lay hidden behind packs, rifles up and ready. Only Wolf remained unaffected. He yawned, looking out into the darkness.

"Hello yourself!" Ab called, looking around for Wasatch.

Arabella chewed her lip, the cool stock of the Benjamin Bigelow combination gun resting against her cheek. Wasatch had taken off earlier to scout around. Where could he be? Fingers of worry traced through her. Awed, she realized she could kill again this night. Grimly she let her finger trace the curve of the trigger. If Bragg hurt Wasatch, she'd . . .

"This hyar be Dick Wootton. I reckon I'm a friendly sort," the voice called back.

"We been shot at once today," Jake answered. "If you're friendly, come on in, Dick. This here's Jake Oord."

"Ab Catton here. I remember you from when I was hauling freight down the trail to Santa Fe for the army!"

After a short pause Wootton called from the darkness. "Catton? You mean Web Catton? He's the onliest one I ever knew. Aw, hell, if yer of a mind go ahead and shoot me. Ain't nuthin' doing round hyar no more anyhoo, and a feller's better off dead than bored!" The voice grunted disgust.

Arabella wondered at that, remembering the man she'd killed. All broken and sprawled, his head had rolled as they laid him in a hole for Jeremiel to say words over.

A medium-built man wearing skins and trade cloth, long rifle in arm, entered the light of the fire. He looked slightly dissipated, cheeks carrying beard, quick eyes darting around.

"Wootton all right. Looking a little older, a little more run-down around the moccasins," Ab's voice came softly as he stood and took the man's hand.

"Same to ya!" the bearded trader snapped back. "Reckon if you'd been stuck hyar, bored, ye'd look a mite shaggy too!" His gaze stopped at Arabella, calculating. She tensed, reading his thoughts.

Dick Wootton squinted at all the muzzles pointed at him, shied away from Jeremiel's suspicious stare, and sat down next to the fire. Weather-gnarled fingers pulled a pipe from his possibles.

"You boys are just a tad jumpy." His voice rasped dry as he grabbed a stick from the fire and pulled at his pipe to get it going. "Purty women too! That'd make any man jumpy."

"Get that way when you been shot at," Ab told him uneasily, shooting wary looks to the darkness.

Wasatch called softly and appeared out of the night. "He comes alone," he said casually before he drifted out into the piñon again.

At that, Wootton pulled his pipe from his mouth and snorted, "Cuss me, I'm gettin' old! How'n hob's name did I miss that coon out there? He's that Cheyenne, Wasatch. Now, that was Catton's boy. I heard aboot that oncst. So you must be all the rest of his kids that was strung aboot hyar and thar." His eyes gleamed as he mused over Arabella.

Introductions were made while Wootton shook hands and passed his pipe around. "Huh! I'm sure a sight of glad t' have someone t' palaver with. That valley's all gone t' hell. Most of the folks round the Pueblo, Hardscrabble, and Greenhorn done took off t' Californy. Gonna dig gold! Huh! That's poor bull ifn I ever heared it!"

"Noticed the abandoned farms," Jake agreed.

"Used to be quite a settlement hereabouts." Wootton shook his head. "That Californy gold an' the Mormons over to Salt Lake city done took most of the trade up round to the north. Bad doings, but you watch. This hyar Colorado land'll come back with a ring-tailed roar. I got me a feelin' in my bones."

"You knew Web Catton?" Jake asked.

Wootton grinned. "I should smile I did. He trapped most of this hyar country from the time it was first growed. Why, he seed this land when that thar Pike's Peak war a hole in the ground!"

"You sure he's dead?" Ab couldn't help but ask.

"Hoodoo," Bram whispered.

Wootton frowned. He pulled at his pipe, bulbous nose and square features frowning. "I'd reckon. I hear that Branton Bragg feller's bin around fer a year er two. It'd take him that long to snuffle out old Web's trail. Catton, he knew Bragg was after his hide. Knew he was agittin' a little closer every year. Shoulda shot that coon! Why, only a damn fool—"

"He couldn't," Ab said, voice low. "He gave his word to my mother."

Wootton spit into the fire. "Poor doin's that! Shoulda shot him anyway. Huh! Life's done gone plumb boring round hyar. Reckon the onliest folks happy 'bout that is old Broken Hand Fitzpatrick. He done changed oncst he got that Injun agent job. Been after us fer runnin' Taos lightning to the Injuns fer years now. Thought for a while that ole Reeshaw was gonna shoot his arse."

Jake looked at Ab and shrugged—some secret communication passing between them.

"Buncha new graves down to the Pueblo. They was dug maybe t'day?" Wootton's eyes shifted from face to face. "Uh-huh, you boys done did git shot at. Anybody I'd know?"

The hard look came back to Ab's face. "I don't know. Hank Tent and two other fellers whose names we didn't quite pick up in all the festivities. They friends of yours?"

Arabella tensed at the stiffness in Ab's voice. Surreptitiously, she rotated the cylinder, making sure it wouldn't bind if she needed it.

*Oh, James. This country has changed me. I'm hard now, tougher. I'm not sure you'd like who I've become.*

Dick's face had a sudden granite look. He pulled on his pipe, a slight squint in his eyes. "Son, I reckon I make friends with whosoever I wants. This child ain't no lily white, I'll grant ye, but I ain't never had me no truck with Branton Bragg neither! Now, that uncle of yourn got all you boys a right bit het up and I ain't gonna deny he's pisen mean, but I don't cotton t' his likes and ye've no call t' go agittin' rude with the company!"

Ab bit his lip and nodded, lowering his eyes. "It's been a tough day, Mr. Wootton. I already thought I was dead once."

Wootton took the apology in stride and smiled, adding, "Happens out hyar with regular frequency, don't it? That's the nice thing 'bout this hyar country. A body don't git bored none with everyday livin'." He grunted and laughed to himself. "Till the neighborhood hauls freight fer Calyforny. Bah!"

Bram grinned, setting his pistol to one side, fishing for his half-spilled bowl of stew.

"Nope, aside fer the comp'ny, I come t' tell ye I run into a Cheyenne hunting party day afore yestiddy. They was all excited-like 'cause some buck got hisself throwed out of camp. Seems he tried to do some dirt to a bunch of white brothers what was camped with 'em in the Big Timber. You boys know of any other Catton brothers out hyar asides from yerselves?" Wootton's eyebrows arched.

The long pause brought Bram up straight, the whites of his eyes gleaming as he looked at Lark.

"High Walker," Jake muttered. "If he's been exiled, he'll have nothing to stop him from coming after us."

"Yep," Wootton agreed, staring out from under his faded felt hat. "I sort of thought that. Web Catton saved my life a time or two. Just thought maybe I'd pay me back the debt. Now, a man can't never tell. One of these days, I may be needin' a little help myself. Reckon I'll keep you boys in mind."

Jake chuckled. But Bram was the one who granted, "Mr. Wootton, I reckon you and One-Eyed Mike was cut from the same mold. Yep, I reckon I'll keep ya on my list of fellers to steal hosses with!"

"And maybe he could teach you a thing or two about checkers," Jeremiel groused.

Wootton continued, "Now, I noticed that you boys got that stew abubbling. How aboot I makes you a deal. You throw some of that in a bowl and I'll mosey on out t' my hoss and bring in a jug." Wootton's eyes went the circle, seeing Bram's eyes light up.

Arabella lifted her lip, keeping her own council, but her eyes met Jeremiel's across the fire. The first belief they'd yet shared. Lark began muttering something incomprehensible in Cheyenne.

"Satan comes, his feet are even now whispering in the sands!" Jeremiel's voice began that deep-toned, preaching rumble.

I reckon we'll pass on the jug, Dick," Ab replied evenly. "But go right ahead and fill yourself on the stew."

Hope died in Bram's eyes. Instead he bent to the checkerboard Jeremiel had set up, grumbling under his breath.

The next morning, being Sunday, Jeremiel woke them all as the sun rose red over the somber lavender of the horizon.

"For this morning," Jeremiel began, looking at each of them, "I would offer a sermon. Perhaps . . . after yesterday, we could use a period of spiritual reflection."

"Uh, reckon I'll see you folks around," Wootton whispered as Jeremiel caught his stride. He nodded politely to Lark, gave Arabella a hesitant look, and quietly sneaked into the piñon.

Unconsciously, Arabella's eyes shifted to the southeast. Out there, somewhere, High Walker followed. Memories of Hides To Trap Eagles and Pawnee Stalker shivered through her mind.

"Amen," she whispered.

Thick, gray, and endless, the clouds rolled over the Rockies, alternating drizzle with streamers of rain. The creeks ran swift and brown. The rivers—already bankfull with high-country runoff—swirled in muddy torrents, whole pines and firs vomiting from the mouths of narrow canyons.

Bram had taken the lead, figuring he could lay a trail beyond Bragg's ability to follow. In misery, they crisscrossed ridges, keeping to the red-brown sandstone of the hogbacks. After a solid week of rain, the horses lamed easy, hooves going soft. Saddles chafed, the leather thoroughly soaked. No dry clothing or blankets remained to any of them. Expressions glum, the only constant came from shivering or cursing as someone tried to get fire started with soggy wood or brush.

"Leave the lodge," Wasatch directed Lark, hearing groans of protest. Only the tipi had provided relief and shelter.

Wasatch pointed at the hogbacks Bram intended to drag them over. "It is extra work for the horses. As well, the poles leave a trail even a *wihio* white man can follow. For all this climbing and trail hiding, why make it easy for Bragg?"

"You got a point there," Ab agreed. Nevertheless, expressions were gray as the lodge came down the last time.

Lark carefully set the lodgepoles against a Ponderosa, using the travois crosspieces to make a platform on two of the sturdy lower limbs. In a group effort they lifted the heavy damp buffalo hide up out of harm's way.

"How you gonna get it back?" Bram wondered, scratching behind his ear.

"We know where it is," Wasatch said simply. "It will be here when we come back."

Lark looked at him, unsure. That's when he heard Wolf. He bent down, hugging the animal, listening.

"Go, Father. You will know how to find us."

Wolf turned, trotting away to the north, bushy tail switching as he went.

"What's that all about?" Ab questioned, skepticism in his eyes.

Wasatch smiled. "My father chose not to go to *Seyan* when he died. He decided he needed to know more of the life of men and animals. When he feels he has learned what he needs to know, then he will take his *tasoom* out of Wolf and go beyond the Milky Way, to *Seyan*, and hunt in the company of *Heammawihio*. Until then—like now—he takes off to seek, to learn."

"Blessed Lord," Jeremiel whispered where he rode his black, the big Bible carefully protected by the gutta-percha cover.

As Bram led them out, Wasatch dropped in to ride beside Jeremiel, ignoring the rain as the preacher slouched in the saddle.

High above, thunder boomed and rolled. Wasatch turned his head to listen, letting his senses loose as he swayed in the Appaloosa's saddle.

"Branton Bragg has found our trail," Wasatch said, feeling the rightness of the words as they came to him. Thunder crashed and banged again, spewing its message from the heavens. Wasatch squinted, waiting for words to form in his mind, only they wouldn't.

Jeremiel gave him a curious look, face pinched.

"This time I do not hear the words."

"Satan, begone," Jeremiel mumbled, his thumb rubbing the pink scar of the snakebite.

"You think I hear the voice of the Evil White God." Wasatch pulled his blanket up to shed a little of the increased rain that pattered from where Thunderbird brewed this latest storm.

"Once, I would have told you Satan spoke through your lips, brother." Jeremiel blinked up at the clouds. "Now? Who knows? I can't make sense of anything. I don't know if this is reality, or a test."

Wasatch said nothing.

"I saw you talk to the wolf. Jake tells me you told the wolf to find me after the serpent struck its poison into me. I . . . It's hard for me to say but thank you."

Wasatch gave him a sideways look. "This Evil White God doesn't deserve to be believed in."

Jeremiel shook his head. "No, he brings death and sickness. It is his purpose to destroy the world, enslave the souls of men. Chaos and disharmony are his aims."

Wasatch thought about that. "The blackrobes claim their God is the most powerful God. Is this really true?"

"I can read you from Revelation, 'I am Alpha and Omega, the beginning and the ending, saith the Lord, which is, and which was, and which is to come, the Almighty.' "

"Then, if your God is so powerful, He is stronger than this Evil One? That's what you have just told me."

"Indeed, such is the power of the Lord God that He shall cast Satan into a pit. He shall—"

"Why does He allow this Evil One to make sickness and pain? If this God is powerful, why does He not stop all the things wrong in this world? Why does He allow young white men to shoot the elders of my tribe? Why does He allow babies to die of hunger and starvation?"

Jeremiel opened his mouth to respond, a pained look on his face, but Wasatch added, "Think, brother. This Evil One you fight, he can only exist because your God lets him. Satan, as you call him—if he is less powerful than God—must be doing something for God, just as the *Maiyun* are our links to *Heammawihio*, the Great Creator, the Great Mystery."

"Satan doing God's will?" Jeremiel asked, blinking, looking down at his hands despite the trickle of water that ran down from the brim on his hat as his head tilted. "No. Injustice, you see . . . Well, take the Book of Job when God proclaims—"

"He never answers the question!" Arabella called back. "Read it. Job asked, 'God, why did You do all these terrible things to me.' And God never answers. He just goes on about everything He knows and how Job is a poor mortal . . . so if God wants to inflict every sort of misery on him, it's not his business to ask."

"That's not the way it is!" Jeremiel insisted, eyes narrowing. "Who is Job, a man . . . born of woman, to question God?"

"If a child asks his father, does he not deserve an answer, brother Jeremiel?" Wasatch wondered.

Trying to turn the tables, Jeremiel countered. "And how do you, Cheyenne, in your damnation explain the misery that befalls you?"

Wasatch smiled, lifting a shoulder. "Bad things happen, because *Heammawihio* made the world that way."

"Why?" Jeremiel insisted. "For what reason? I see the hand of Satan!"

Wasatch shifted his blanket, looking up at the gray sky. "Consider the marmot."

Jeremiel frowned, giving a grudging nod. "All right, a marmot."

Wasatch continued to search the rain-soaked land around him. "What if *Heammawihio* had made the earth and the skies perfect? If there were no hunger and the sun always shone? What if Coyote never hunted him? If Eagle didn't drift in the sky? What if *Ho'imaha* never brought winter down from the north? What would a marmot do?" He cocked his head, awaiting an answer.

"I don't know that much about marmots," Jeremiel countered. He chuckled lightly, mockingly. "Theology, brother Wasatch, isn't your strongest—"

"Like your God, you, too, do not answer," Wasatch

continued, ignoring the barb. Then he supplied; "A marmot would find a warm rock and roll out on his belly and lie there, forever."

"I don't understand—" Jeremiel began.

Wasatch smiled inoffensively and added, "Then perhaps you should spend more time studying God, brother. And less time studying the words in your medicine book."

# Chapter 18

Cold spring rains continued to pelt them relentlessly, falling endlessly from a leaden sky. They slept in soaked bedrolls. Boots squished when they walked. Skin became swollen and chafed.

Bram had laid a merry trail, winding up through rocky ridges, across the hardpan, through stands of pine and fir where tracks remained hidden in the duff. Wasatch ranged far and wide, amber eyes scanning the rolling horizon seeking any sign of Branton Bragg or High Walker, periodically bringing in deer or antelope, the fresh-killed carcasses hanging over his saddle.

They crossed the divide from Fountain Creek and worked down to the South Platte, picking it up where it courses through the upthrust folds of the timbered Front Range. They forded it, swimming in the icy waters, and worked up the broken country amidst hogbacks of bright red sandstone.

Arabella studied the thick groves of Ponderosa and wild plum they approached as night fell. "I've had it. Build me a fire—a big one!"

She reeked of horse and mud and mildew. Where the men had only their coats and pants and shirts, each layer of her dress and petticoats held their own weight in water.

"Ah," she whispered, "but for one blistering hot sirocco to blow through and dry me out." As she stepped out of the saddle, she wrung the water from her hem in a solid stream.

No one objected. Bram plied his axe stripping layers of wet wood to get to the dry core of a deadfall.

"Reckon if it rains anymore, I'm gonna turn into a dadblasted fish!" Bram growled, hovering over dry bits of kindling as he struggled to light the fire he'd laid. Within minutes, he had a cheery crackle, feeding it bits of kindling until he had a roaring blaze.

Arabella thankfully bent over the flame, heedless as her voluminous skirts began steaming. A look of rapture filled her finely chiseled features, full lips curved into a thankful smile.

"You sure learned to hide tracks, boy," Jake admitted from where he smoked his boots over the coals, watching the steam rising out of them.

"One-Eyed Mike larned me that," Bram said, face going slack. "Reckon it was a tad rougher in Arkansas country. Different ground there. A hoof leaves a print, bruises the plants, and sinks inta the dirt. Hyar, now, why this be right fine country fer hiding a trail. Lots o' rocks, lots of hard ground where a feller kin lead a hoss and scuff it over so's it looks like critter doin's."

"High Walker will follow though," Wasatch added from where he huddled under his old four-point trade blanket.

"He will know," Lark agreed, letting Bram take her hand.

Jake felt of the leather to make sure he hadn't cooked it brittle and set about dealing with his socks, trying to toast them. Satisfied, he pulled them onto his feet, a dreamy smile on his lips. He then bent his head to fiddling with the knives as he did every night.

Bram followed Lark into the dusk, coming to stand beside her where she looked out over the Saint Vrain River bottom, now hidden in the dark trees below.

"Long tough ride." Bram swallowed hard and put his arms around her shoulders.

"I am proud of you, Bram," she told him simply. "If anyone can fool High Walker, it will be you."

He grinned. "Yeah, well, I done my best." The smile slipped off his lips as he looked at her, losing himself in her eyes.

After long moments, he bent down, softly brushing his lips on hers. "When this is over, will you come with me? Marry me?"

She nodded, smiling. "Among my people, it is proper for you to leave a horse tied at my lodge. I will water it and feed it, brush it and care for it to show my willingness. Then you must deal with Wasatch, tell him what you will give for me."

Bram chuckled. "Now, that oughta be interesting. Yep, reckon I'll do'er." Hand in hand they walked back toward the flickers of light that marked camp.

Jake had Bram's knife in his hand, tinkering, when the pommel came loose. Carefully, Jake unscrewed it. "Ab? Come look."

"Now, that's the neatest job of fastening I've ever seen. Threads were cut on there by a master blacksmith." Ab settled on his haunches, rubbing his chin as he studied the knife thoughtfully.

"Hey!" Bram growled, arriving from the dark with Lark on his arm. "Put that back together!"

Jake did, but he looked uneasy, as if something floated around inside his head and just wouldn't come out.

"I had horse guard last night," Smitty protested, hands on hips.

Branton Bragg stood, eyes slitted. "Git! You heard me."

Smitty swallowed hard, turning to the others for support. Heads dropped, faces suddenly hidden by hat brims. He looked back at Bragg, a stiffness in his face. "Naw, this ain't worth it. I didn't sign on ta be treated like no dawg. I'm ridin' out. And ya kin keep my back pay." He walked away.

Leander silently breathed a sigh. Smitty had been trouble since Bragg caught him drinking three nights before. Better to have the man gone and on his—

Leander jerked at the sudden shot, startled upright, heart pounding. He entertained a slight consciousness of Smitty, stiffened, freezing in place—and then the man keeled limply into the dirt, his body making a sodden thump on the damp ground.

Getting half to his feet, Leander froze as Bragg turned, the smoking pistol sweeping the rest of the camp. "Anyone else turning yellow on me?" Bragg asked softly, eyes gleaming a weird blue. "I pay good. I don't pay for quitters."

Leander's mouth went dry as he watched the men shuffling, shaking their heads, looking down at the ground before their feet.

Leander got to his feet, lost in thought as he walked to the corpse. Branton Bragg didn't have a normal mind. A sickness lay deep in that weather-beaten head—a corruption, dark and terrible. Only the day before, the man had beaten a packhorse half to death, to the point they'd had to leave the staggering animal behind. Just now, he'd shot Smitty down. Leander checked, seeing the bullet hole, perfectly placed high between the shoulder blades. Smitty had been dead before he hit the ground.

"Something wrong, Sentor?" Bragg asked softly.

Leander turned on heel and knee. "No, Branton. Your shot was perfect. He never felt a thing."

His heart quivered as Bragg's devil-blue eyes measured him, the eerie glow shaking the root of Leander's nerve. *He wouldn't! He wouldn't shoot me. I'm his only link to Cavaignac. If his claims about Catton are true he'd cut his own throat by killing me. He's not that stupid even if he's crazy!*

Bragg's lip lifted under the beard, raising the odd white streak. "Hah! You're a brave man, Sentor." The smile widened, exposing large white teeth. "I think I could come to like you . . . as well as your business."

At that, he holstered the pistol and walked away.

Leander forced himself up, willing himself to walk to the edge of the fire. Once there, he took a deep breath, settling his heart. He had to lock his knees to keep them from trembling. Better to face Tuaregs than Branton Bragg.

"Him crazy man, like whiskey-headed all time," the Indian, High Walker, grunted, spooking Leander as his voice came from behind him in the darkness.

Leander ground his teeth, turning, studying the dark shadow that became a man. "Indeed. He is." He thought of that, remembering High Walker when he rode into sight behind them three days before, whistling, pointing up a rocky ridge.

When they'd ridden back, High Walker had calmly pointed out the trail so carefully hidden by the Cattons.

From that moment on, he'd taken the lead, saying nothing to any of them, but pointing the way.

Even now Bragg watched him, fingering his beard, that deadly squint betraying a cunning mind at work. To any of Bragg's questions, High Walker just grinned and shrugged, claiming he didn't "sabe" English.

"So, why do you stay?" Leander wondered. Doesn't speak English? Like a fox, he doesn't!

High Walker's grin carried a touch of the macabre. "I crazy too." His gimlet eyes gleamed in the faint light, the long nose hooking down over broken teeth exposed by the leer.

Leander stilled his impulse to run. "Maybe we all are," he decided, stepping away from the satanic face, haunted by the deep-shadowed grin. Uncertainty filled him as he fought to keep Arabella's face from his mind.

*Mon général*, how much do I owe you and my country? Only he knew—as if etched deeply onto his very heart. He remembered the blood-spattered bodies of his parents, the emptiness in his mother's blank eyes, how the flies settled on her face, crawling into her drying mouth. He remembered the hot summer sun beating down, and the stench of blood and less savory body fluids as they drained down through the barricades.

"Never again, my France. Never again," Leander whispered, turning to find his rain-soaked blankets. "Even if I have to buy your destiny from a madman."

The following morning, Leander endured yet another of the heavy June rains that poured out of the high Rockies. Never had he been so wet and cold. He crouched under a borrowed slicker and wished for his hat, lost so long ago by the Cheyenne.

High Walker led them down a steep incline—the horses hesitant for footing—and onto a flat overlooking a broad drainage below. From the vantage point, Leander could see bends of the river, brown and swirling, through gaps in the trees.

"Camp here," High Walker called. "See. They go there. Make climb there." He pointed across the drizzle-spattered canyon to the slope on the other side. Even through the mist, Leander could make out a line of horses disappearing into the trees.

"Got 'em!" Bragg crowed, knotting a fist.

"Bad place," High Walker warned. "We go. I know way around. Fast way. Ketch them good, huh?" And without another word, he kicked his horse to one side, following the faint tracks toward the lush bottoms below.

"I'm sorry, Arabella," Leander whispered under his breath. "If I can save you, I will." The honor of France had demanded sacrifices of greater consequence than a single woman and her brothers—even if she was so unearthly beautiful.

It blackened above them. The heavens opened in a regular gully-scouring downpour. Crouching under soaked hats, each hunched in the saddle, slickers cascading rivulets of water. The horses dropped their ears and heads, plodding on, slipping on occasion, hooves slopping in the fetlock-deep slimy mud. Above, lightning flashed and cracked, pounding them.

The cloud passed slowly to the east, then the sun broke through, bending a huge double rainbow around the sky over their heads, vivid against the deep black of the rain clouds.

"Praise the Lord," Jeremiel whispered, wiping water off his carefully covered Bible.

"What river is that?" Arabella asked, looking out over the cottonwood-choked bottoms. The land contrasted in the bright light, a deep red soil blazing against the water-sparkling green vegetation. The valley looked like an

Eden, the river spilling out of a slash in the rocky wall of the mountains to the west.

"Big Thompson," Jake called.

Ab muttered something, finger pointing to the eleven horsemen who lined out and walked their horses out of the screen of trees. Less than two hundred yards away they could finally make out that white streak on the blond beard on Branton Bragg's face.

"Hell," Bram grunted, one of his pistols in hand. "Reckon thar's High Walker, too."

"Leander!" Arabella gasped, face going white as she pulled her Benjamin Bigelow from its scabbard, checking the charges, wincing at the water that had beaded on the cylinder.

"Hope our powder ain't wet," Ab added fervently, wiping off his Dragoon Colt.

"And now Israel went against the Philistines to battle. And the Philistines arrayed themselves against Israel." Jeremiel's jaw muscles twitched as he slid the big Walker Colt from its holster. "Lord, make me not into your instrument of vengeance. I fear blood enough rests upon my unworthy soul."

"Guess we face them," Jake growled. "Looks like we don't have any choice, and I'm not running."

There, on the right hand of Uncle Branton, rode Cal Backman, a smile quickening his lips as he caught sight of Abriel.

Ab checked the cap on his Hawken. "Hold up here," he decided. Then, in a loud clear voice, he called out, "No matter what, if they start shooting, the first target is Branton Bragg!"

Bragg raised a hand and his riders fell in behind him. He had his rifle out as he pulled up, no more than ten yards away. Ab noticed Cal's hand slowly bringing his rifle to bear, hatred in his eyes.

"Branton, if Cal shoots, you're a dead man." His tone conversational, he could hear a hammer click from behind where Bram had aimed one of his pistols.

Horses stamped. A meadowlark trilled out in the suddenly quiet afternoon.

"How pleasant to see you, Mr. Sentor," Arabella called. "I'm pleased to see our efforts to save your life have borne such wonderful fruit."

Sentor whitened, stiffening in the saddle, a grimness to the set of his mouth.

"If Cal don't lower that rifle, Bragg, I'm shooting you." By its very toneless nature, Ab's voice left no doubts.

"Cal!" Bragg's voice cracked suddenly. "You drop down that rifle, or I'll kill ya meself!"

Eyes burning hatred, Backman lowered the gun. "Later!" he added, lips twitching under his black beard.

"Uh-huh, and I buried Hank Tent at the Pueblo. You remember that, Cal. Killed him with my bare hands. His riders are resting easy with him too." Ab resettled the Hawken on the saddle for emphasis.

Cal's face twisted with hatred, going red, the veins in his neck standing out.

Turning to Branton, Ab's rifle centered on his belly, he asked, "So, what's it going to be, Uncle? Do we all die here?"

"I want my pistols back," Branton said, voice even.

"Nope. You was gonna kill us with them, remember? Never had me a gun a man shot at me with before." Ab smiled. "Don't ever want to be shot at with this pistol again either, Uncle."

Branton made a gasping chuckling sound as the weird light grew suddenly and burned behind his eyes. His beard worked as his facial muscles contracted. "All the Catton boys . . . and you must be Arabella," he said absently. "See, Leander? You can see it in them. I told you. Each one is worth his weight in gold! The ransom of the French empire! Pack their heads in salt and send them to Cavaignac . . . to France! The reward's mine! Just wait until I get the ring!" As suddenly his eyes cleared, madness ebbing.

Leander called softly from the side, voice uncertain. "I need the proof, Monsieur Bragg. These people could be anyone. I need the ring." Expression pained, he looked at cool-faced Arabella, misery in his eyes. To her he added, "I'm sorry, *mademoiselle*." Bowing at the waist, he inclined his head.

"Now there you go with that ring again! I don't have it, so you're wasting your time, Branton," Ab growled.

He nodded. "You'd say that if you had it. You'd know then. You'd know who . . . and what you are . . . and how important the ring is." Bragg squinted. "But we can forget that for now. I want the rest of the map. Give me that and you might ride out of here alive!"

Jeremiel pushed forward, Walker easy in his hand. "Speak, man who is my uncle! Tell me in your own words that you would brand yourself with the mark of Cain!" His voice rang loud in the calm air.

"And you're the preacher," Bragg grunted, eyes flat. "Another pompous Bible thumper."

"Perdition awaits you, flesh of my flesh! Seek not the counsel of thy family, sinner. Your soul will flay in the fires of hell!"

Bragg's voice came low, sibilant. "I bring my own kind of hell, preacher." His weird blue eyes bored into Jeremiel's and went crazy again. "Where's the map? Hand it over and you can all ride out of here. Dally with me . . . and I shall see your bodies run red with blood!"

Jake interrupted. "We don't have any map, Branton. I read the will; all we got were the knives . . . no map." He added, "Don't forget, Uncle. One false move and you get the first volley. You'll fall with the rest of us!"

Voice deep and sure, Bragg fixed them with a death-cold stare. "I'll take the knives. Hand them over."

Ab reminded, "I think you're forgetting what we said, Bragg. Lift one finger, say the wrong word, and you're dead in the saddle. Your men can't kill us all before we get you. Looks to me like a Mexican standoff, Uncle. You push it and we all die."

Branton's lip curled under the beard, eyes deadly, gleaming a shade of blue that froze Bram's bones. "Perhaps. What if I . . . I just ride forward?" His voice became a piercing, knowing whisper. "Will you shoot first?" He walked his horse, step by step, ever closer.

Arabella couldn't swallow. A cold sweat began to bead on her lip as her finger twitched on the trigger. If she shot, death would be all around. Tension rippled the air. Horrified, she watched Bragg's huge horse take another step.

An eerie sound startled them all. Wasatch's voice, haunted with flutelike melodies, trilled up and down the scale as he sang in Cheyenne.

High Walker, the first to understand, began muttering under his breath, tension filling his body for the first time. Eyes darting, he looked away.

One more step and Bragg would be too close. Ab lifted his Hawken, sighting carefully on Bragg's full chest. A half second before the horse reached the dead-line he'd drawn in his head, it stopped, ears pricked toward Wasatch.

Bragg kicked the animal as Wasatch's song grew louder, hanging in the air with some strange tranquil power. Branton's men were glancing at each other with uncertain eyes. They began swallowing nervously as their horses turned toward Wasatch, ignoring the reins, ears pricked. One or two backed up, the others hesitating a second before following despite the urgings of their riders.

Bragg's animal quivered as the man's spurs dug into its side.

Wasatch sang louder.

Bragg's big horse backed up a step, then another. Slowly the rest of the line backed away while riders exploded in angry shouts, kicking and quirting their mounts.

Leander's face betrayed amazement, then cleared as he looked in wonder at Wasatch, and let his animal back away.

High Walker purposely backed his animal, fear bright in his eyes as he stared slit-eyed at Wasatch, who sang with all his soul, his arms raised to the westering sun.

Bragg's face turned a livid red, his white-streaked beard quivering as he raised his rifle and pounded it over the animal's head. The horse staggered, shook its head, and backed another step.

A trickle of red ran down from the poll, creeping across the animal's forehead. Bragg's eyes turned completely crazy as he savagely beat the horse. The animal faltered, weaving crazily on its feet, then sagged slowly to its knees. Bragg stepped off, still beating it over the head, the hollow thunking of the heavy-barreled rifle brutally loud in the air as he swung it like an axe.

"Stop it!" Bram cried out, anguished. *"He's killing the horse!"*

Wasatch's song came to a high-pitched end as Bragg's dun quivered, snorted, and collapsed into a heap, eyes staring, tongue lolling out of its mouth. It shuddered and died with a spasmodic kick.

Bragg turned those oddly lit blue eyes on Abriel. The look stopped the heart in his chest. If he'd had the power to breathe, he'd have shot Bragg dead without a second thought. It would have been reflex, the kind used to swat a mosquito, or shoot a buzzing rattlesnake that just struck a boot.

"What did you do to my horse?" Bragg's voice came as if through a hollow tube. "What did you do to him? Why did he . . . did he do that?"

Wasatch spoke, voice carrying an unearthly calm. "The horses were told to go away from trouble. I sang them their deaths . . . and they backed away. You, Branton Bragg, have no harmony with this world. Your mind is an empty blackness. There is no medicine to cure you. There is no purpose in your life which pleases the Spirits or the Powers. Like a skunk with the foaming-mouth disease, you are hideous to all below and above."

Bragg's eyes centered on Wasatch. To Ab's amazement his brother's face went white and he thought for a second the boy would be physically ill.

"I'll kill you, Injun. I'll cut you into pieces to feed the coyotes. I'll beat you to death the same way I beat that horse. Only I'll do it slowly, easily, stroke by stroke, until the blood running down your head blinds you, until you choke on it, until it runs and pools under your butt like a lake!"

Wasatch recoiled, practically weaving in the saddle, features deathly gray.

"I think that's enough," Jake said softly, rifle on Bragg. Ab looked to see the other riders backing away on their own this time, faces white, eyes looking nervously to each other.

Leander watched from the side, noting everything, eyes darting to Arabella, mouth a thin line in his pinched face.

High Walker's diamond-shaped face had turned grim. He worked his lips in silent song, fingering the medicine bundle hanging on his chest, making symbols in the air with quick fingers.

"Get out of here, Branton!" Ab rasped, voice betraying his fear.

"I'll be back," Bragg promised, fist raised. "I'll get you . . . and the ring. You have the rest of the map. All the important parts. I need them to fill in the gaps. I'll get you then, each and every one. Indeed, the legacy of France will be brought to an end. I shall free the people and joyously will they dance upon the blood of kings as they shower me with gold!"

Leander flinched as if he'd been struck, a wretched look in his eyes. Shaking his head slowly, he looked his anguish at Arabella. She sat, stony-faced, refusing to acknowledge his presence.

Bragg backed a step or two and—in an incredible show of strength—lifted a man from the saddle with one hand and vaulted into place. A second rode forward, hauled the unfortunate up behind him, and turned to ride away.

As they cantered off, Bram sighed from way down deep in his gut. "That man's plumb outa his mind! In my days on the trail, I met some loco characters. I thought the spookiest was Jim Kirker, but I got to hand it to Bragg when it comes to a man that shivers me down to my toe bones!"

Jeremiel's voice sounded a low moan. "I have seen the embodiment of Satan before my eyes. I have seen the fires of perdition burning as they looked into my face and chilled my soul."

"That man's a foul abomination!" Jake said, spitting into the deep grass, eyes going to the body of the horse that lay bleeding on the ground. Blood pooled on the torn flanks where Bragg had spurred it. From the scars it hadn't been the first time.

"His soul is twisted," Wasatch added, voice quavering.

"Did you really sing those horses back?" Bram asked, the first to recover his usual spirit.

"No," Wasatch said, voice growing calm. "I sang the danger to them. They themselves chose to back away from it. Horses do not love blood and death. They simply did not understand until I told them."

Jeremiel began, "That is blasphem—" and stopped, face going slack as if remembering. Voice gravelly, he added, "Your power stood us in good stead, my brother. The Lord God works in mysterious ways."

"They'll be back." Ab remembered the promise in Bragg's eyes. "Something is behind all this. He wants us too desperately for it to be an old family feud. Something real powerful is driving him. He was almost ready to run right over the rifles to get us. Almost ready to accept his own death for it."

"More talk about a ring and that damn map!" Jake snorted. "And what's this business about France and kings? Anybody know about that?"

"Kings? Gold for a legacy of France?" Arabella squinted, frowning after Leander Sentor as he rode away.

They lined out on the trail, splashing across the roiling river, and made for open country. The horses traveled smartly, miles dropping behind their hard hooves. From the ridgetops, they could look to the back-trail and see the line of horsemen filing along their tracks.

"Blast him to hell and back!" Bram declared. "I never seen a man treat a hoss that way! Man like him don't deserve to breathe the same air with real men!"

"You thinking on lecturing him about manners?" Jake asked dryly.

Bram pursed his lips, frowned, and scratched his peach-fuzz cheeks. "Reckon a feller like that shouldn't oughta own hosses. Seems t' me he oughta walk fer a while 'til he larns respect fer his critters."

"If there were justice on earth, he would," Jeremiel's deep voice boomed, "—and will!"

Arabella caught Wasatch and Bram trading glances. Collusion, if she'd ever seen it.

At that moment Wolf came loping across the grass, falling in place behind Wasatch's horse. The Appaloosa he rode never even flicked an ear although Molly showed the whites of her eyes, crow-hopped a tad on the lead rope, and let out a shrill whistle. The others moved away too, leaving Wasatch somewhat to the side.

Worry displacing fatigue, they pushed on until late that night. Jake wanted to make the most mileage balanced against wearing the horses down.

Lark pointed to a high pinnacle of outcropping sandstone—a natural fort that allowed vantage in all directions and a field of fire downslope from the protection of the rocks.

Camp that night proved somber, Wasatch and Wolf disappearing into the darkness. Jake again began working on the knives. Arabella helped Lark put the meal together, a frown etching her delicate brow. Periodically, she shook her head, as if in disbelief.

"Fooled me," she mumbled under her breath. "I would have sworn he had more to him than that."

Lark studied her, eyes shifting uneasily to where Wasatch had returned to crouch next to Bram. Wolf was sitting nearby, watching with keen yellow eyes.

Far behind, out on the flats, a pinpoint of light flickered—the fire where Bragg had laid up for the night.

Jeremiel settled himself next to Arabella as the fire crackled. "Seeing stars overhead again is a blessing," he said, absently fingering his Bible.

"Like Bram, I thought I'd turn into a fish," she agreed,

chin propped on her knee as she poked a stick into the fire. Her thoughts kept returning to Sentor and to the strange look he'd given her. And she'd helped save his life?

"I . . . What do you think Wasatch did back there?" Jeremiel asked, eyes absently searching the flames for an answer.

She shrugged. "Sang the horses back. Like he says."

"But it can't be. Such things don't happen. A man can sing until he's blue in the face. No matter how I believe, I can't sing to the dumb beasts."

"Maybe they're not dumb beasts?" Arabella sighed. "Oh, I don't know, Jeremiel. Myself, I don't believe it either. Not on any intellectual level anyway." She pursed her lips. "At the same time, I've seen some remarkable things. Men and women dancing on coals so hot you can't stand nearby—and not a blister on their feet afterward." She shook her head. "When it comes to God, and men of faith, I'll believe anything."

Jeremiel opened his Bible, letting his fingers trace the fragile paper. For long moments he sat there, turning page after page. "Why is it so hard for me?"

Arabella chuckled. "In your Bible, there, how often do you find men of faith having an easy time of it?"

"But what do I do?" Jeremiel cried uneasily. "Where is the truth? Nothing makes sense anymore. Singing horses back? Impossible!"

She moved to ease her cramped muscles. "Wasatch tells me he's felt the power of *Heammawihio* during their Sun Dance. Says it filled him and the world. He danced for four days without food and water. Tore skewers out of his very flesh."

"The Lord my God would never demand that of any man. Had Wasatch not turned Satan back today, I would claim such doings those of Satan." Jeremiel knotted a fist over the text.

Arabella laid a hand on his shoulder. "Just believe, brother." She waved a hand. "God is all around you. Feel Him with your soul and act for your own salvation." A bitterness lay on her lips.

He nodded. "I . . . I suppose so. Only, so much is so different here. Wasatch, you, so different, yet you aren't evil. No matter how I try to convince myself, I can't see Satan in Wasatch. His actions are for good—not evil."

She placed her hand on his shoulder. "Truth never comes easily. Your Bible should tell you that."

"I suppose," he agreed, still looking lost.

She smiled at him. "Tell you what. You're not going to find ultimate reality tonight. How about teaching me how to play checkers. Bram's disappeared so I'll see if I can't provide a tougher challenge."

"You'd . . ." Jeremiel swallowed, suddenly looking away and blinking. "Yes . . . sure, sure, I'd like that."


The muted thunder of hooves brought Abriel out of a troubled sleep. Galvanized, he grabbed his Hawken, rolling out of his blankets, heart battering ribs as he blinked into the darkness, the horses coming closer.

"C'mon!" Bram hollered. "Get up."

"What the . . ."

"Don't shoot. It's us. Bram and Wasatch and Wolf. Get up, we gotta get outa here!" A mounted shadow detached itself from the night, Bram's roan carrying him from the herd of horses to stand at the edge of camp. "Get packed. We done stole all Bragg's hosses!"

"You *what*?" Jake demanded, staggering to his feet, a pistol hanging from his hand.

"We stole Bragg's hosses!" Bram insisted. "How many times do I gotta tell ya! Get packed, they'll be follering

along—specially that High Walker—and I figger they'll
be a tad bit mad when they ketch us!"

Ab looked around, bewildered, seeing Lark already
bringing in their own horses, throwing packs on the animals, Molly braying her displeasure.

"Oh, you didn't!" Ab gasped, seizing the implications.
"You didn't ride down there alone? Put your neck in
Bragg's noose?" He stamped back and forth. "Of all the
stupid, no account—"

"Hell!" Bram exploded. "I didn't go alone. Wasatch
went with me! Him and Wolf. Who do you think's helping hold these hyar hosses?"

From where he saddled his bay, Jake threw in, "Forget
hiding the trail. Let's rustle. We'll plain outrun 'em!"

Ab realized Lark had Sorrel by the halter, leading him
up. Not to be lost in the dust, Ab wheeled and grabbed
his saddle. As he pulled the cinch tight, and tied the bedroll Jeremiel handed him to the cantle, he muttered,
"Crazy damn kids. Coulda got themselves killed!"

But a glow of pride lay warm under his heart.

# Chapter 19

Knowing better, Ab watched Jake and Jeremiel take out their worry on Wasatch and Bram as they headed north. Lark, in the meantime, literally glowed with pride as her eyes gazed on Bram. He noticed, blushing bright red, grinning back.

From a high point, they caught one last glance of Bragg's men fanning out, searching for their horses as dawn broke over the rugged emptiness. They turned north, passing below the Horsetooth, moving into the hills after swimming the Cache la Poudre.

Weary, saddle-chafed, they camped late that night in a wide, flat-bottomed canyon bounded on both sides by hogbacks. Bram had put together a middling fire over which roasted a quarter of antelope shot earlier in the day.

"You're still down at the mouth," Abriel observed, studying his sister's haggard look.

She shook her head, listening to the sounds of the night. "I just can't figure Sentor out. Why Bragg? What does he see in that man? Sure, Leander is a French agent, but what does it all mean? What ring? How can France have anything to do with Web Catton, an old fur trapper?"

Ab lifted a shoulder. "Got me. But to my mind, your Mr. Sentor didn't look any too happy back there at the Big Thompson."

"Must be the company," Bram muttered through a grin.

"He got what he deserved," she decided, a look of irritation about her. "I—I just thought better of him." She bit her lip, looking away into the darkness. "Thought that despite our differences, he would have been a . . . a gentleman."

Jake kept throwing hard looks at Bram and Wasatch, mind only half on his inevitable fiddling with the knives. From a pack, Wasatch pulled out a small piece of tanned hide.

"What's that for?" Bram asked, stirring the coals with a length of mountain mahogany. He laced his fingers into Lark's, shifting ever closer to her until he could touch shoulders, a happy look on his face.

Arabella watched him thoughtfully before turning to speculate on Jeremiel where he prayed just beyond camp.

"I will draw a record of our raid, brother Bram." Wasatch explained carefully. With colors taken from a pouch, he began smearing a dark blue over a corner of the leather. "Here, we are sneaking on the camp of Uncle Bragg." He quickly drew in the figures, showing him and Bram working around a group of men sleeping on the ground. One, a guard, stared out into the night, eyes drawn big to indicate he'd been staring at the fire and couldn't see.

"Here we have taken up the pickets." Wasatch drew him and Bram gentling the horses, pulling the ropes from the ground.

"This is when the horses made noise and Branton's men came awake." He drew men jumping to their feet, pulling up guns. "And," Wasatch continued, "here is Wolf, running through their camp and distracting them from us." The form of Wolf emerged on the leather, bounding through the confused men, some of whom were screaming and falling over themselves.

Wasatch drew a scene on the final portion of the hide. "Here we are stealing all the horses away to the south—fooling them—with Bram leading the way." He paused from his artwork and looked up, devilment behind his eyes. "If I had more leather, I would draw big brother Abriel hollering at us."

"Uh-huh," Ab grunted. "I still ain't been talked out of whacking on your bottom for a while!" At that, Wolf opened his eyes and studied Abriel from pools of yellow. "Oh, stop that!" he snapped. The yellow eyes obediently went closed again as Wolf dropped his nose on his paws.

Ab opened his mouth to say something more, biting it off to mumble under his breath, perplexed eyes on Wolf.

Jake had only been mildly interested, running his finger over his bowie. He frowned, chewing his lip as he watched Wasatch carefully roll the soft leather into a cylinder and begin lacing it tight with leather thongs until it became a long, firmly bound tube.

"By God!" Jake whispered. "That's it!" His eyes had a sudden gleam and he picked Bram's knife from the lot, fingers straining as he twisted the pommel loose.

"Huh!" Bram exploded, pulling away from Lark. "What are you doing to my knife! Cut that out! Dang it all, leave it alone!"

Jeremiel, drawn by the excitement, came to see.

"No!" Ab cried, putting a restraining hand on Bram's shoulder as he started to dive for Jake. "I think I get the idea. It's worth a try."

Bram settled back, expression pained as he watched Jake's nimble fingers unscrew the pommel. Jeremiel and Wasatch leaned to see, the latter throwing more wood on the fire.

"Of course," Arabella whispered. "After all the smuggling we did, why didn't I think of it?"

Jake held up the knife, brow furrowed as he studied the silver wire binding the leather handle. Slowly, carefully, face a mask of concentration, he began unwinding the fleur-de-lis pattern.

Bram groaned, clapping hands over his eyes so he couldn't see. Then he opened the fingers to slits, unable to resist.

Jake had to unwind the wires almost to the guard to free the leather from the tang. Even Bram——recovered and resigned enough to watch——leaned forward as Jake's hands smoothed the leather on the ground before the fire.

Ab could hear Jeremiel's intake of breath. Jake began to chuckle. Bram cursed quietly. There, neatly inked, lay a map consisting of several meandering lines that had to be rivers. The pointed, zigzag line might be a mountain range. But which one?

Jake attacked his knife next, grunting as he fought the pommel.

"Here." Ab reached for it, huge muscles bulging as he gritted his teeth and twisted. Skin slipping on the worn brass of the pommel, it squeaked and broke free.

"I know how they're wound, let me undo it." Jake held out a hand, tense. "I don't think you want the pattern ruined when we put it back together."

Ab nodded and handed it to him while he went to work on Jeremiel's. When he had each one loose, Jake undid them, laying another piece of the map on the ground.

"Don't make sense," Bram grunted. "I don't know that much about the country here, but that don't look like no mountains I ever seen!"

"Not only that, what kind of words are these?" Jeremiel wondered, leaning forward to see.

"French," Arabella began. "Uh, let me—"

"That piece fits there." Ab pointed, cutting her off.

Teeth sunk in his lip, Jake's quick mind put the map pieces together this way and that.

"If you'd let me—" Arabella tried again, pulling at Abriel's blocking shoulder.

"Try putting them in order," Ab cried. "Mine on top, then Jeremiel's, yours, Jake, Bram's, and finally Wasatch's."

Deftly, the map reordered under Jake's fingers and it all became clear.

"Yahoo!" Jake hooted victoriously. "Look! Here's the Platte! That's Fort Laramie. These are the Black Hills and this is the Yellowstone River. If only we could read the French!"

"If you would let me take a—" Arabella gave ground to Ab's thick shoulder, forced back as pushing male bodies bent over the map.

"Notice how the Big Horns are drawn in such detail?" Ab asked. "Compare them to the other mountain ranges. Not only that"—he squinted, leaning close—"but there's a fleur-de-lis drawn on the west side of the range. Notice, too, how well the Big Horn River is drawn here, kind of like the scale is off. There's just a black hole on that ridgetop overlooking the river."

"Seems like that's a cliff from the way it's shaded," Bram pointed out.

"Huh!" Jake grunted. "Why'd he hide it right on the ridgetop? Seems like that would be right out in the open!"

"Here's another fleur-de-lis down here," Jeremiel added, pointing to the bottom map. "Which one do we need? The detail here is excellent too."

"Bigger fleur-de-lis around Sante Fe," Jake observed, fingering his chin. "The biggest one is the treasure? How do we know?"

"Look!" Bram pointed. "Here's a bunch of big arrows. They all point that way. Like they was passes over the mountains or such."

"That's it," Ab breathed. "South! Santa Fe! He never took all the gold north. It's there. Makes perfect sense! Why tote it all to hell and gone when—"

"Wait." Jake raised a hand. "Look, there's a fleur-de-lis on each map. Some have faded a little, but each one is marked like that. Maybe it's spread all over the country? A bit here, a bit—"

"If only I could read French," Jeremiel sighed. "Look, each fleur-de-lis has something written beside it. Faded, true, but legible. Why did I never study French?"

From behind them, Arabella shouted at the top of her lungs, "Do you dolts think it might not be a coincidence that I was raised by a man who spoke French? That I spent time in France? Do you incredibly *clever* men think that perhaps, if you'd let me take a look, I could read what my father wrote there? Or would you like to spend the rest of the night guessing just for the intellectual exercise?"

They turned, looking back to where she stood. Arms crossed, she wore an angry scowl, one eyebrow cocked expressively.

Ab looked at Jake, grinning sheepishly. "I don't know. Think we ought to let her see?"

Arabella made a strangled sound as she pushed past them, Lark laughing in the background. She leaned over the patchwork map, bending close to read. When she sat up, her lips held a catlike smile. "Of course! Web, you old rascal!"

"What is it?" they all said at once.

Her face ethereal in the yellow cast of the fire, Arabella laughed. "Most of the fleur-de-lis are misleading." She looked around, pulling her long hair back over her shoulder. "The key to the map, boys, is this: 'To my firstborn goes the legacy.'"

Jake's face soured. "Well, of course! That's always the case."

"There's the will," Ab interjected. "Says that everyone gets an equal share of the—"

*"Allahu akbar!"* Arabella hissed, eyes searching the sky overhead, pleading as she clenched delicate female fists above her head. "Give me strength. They have brains like granite!" She turned to Abriel. "'To the firstborn goes the legacy!' It's on your map, Abriel! Don't you see?"

"The Big Horns," Jake whispered, nodding. "Of course, Arabella. We'd have gone south instead. Anyone would have. Why is the big fleur-de-lis there? What's it say?"

She bent over, squinting again. "Uh, he's written this in a smuggling code James used to use. It's not like reading straight French. The fleur-de-lis there indicates the spot where he stole Armijo's gold." She shifted. "Um, he killed his first white bear on this spot. Over here, he . . . Faded there, but I think it says he bought his first wife from the Shoshone there."

"So." Bram grinned. "Lessen we'da had Arabella with

us, we'da never figgered whar ta look. We needed her all along!"

Acidly, she noted, "Imagine that!" An eyebrow lifted to the dismay of Jeremiel, Abriel, and Jake. "A fact I do hope you *clever* gentlemen will remember in the future."

Jake spent most of the rest of the night putting the knives back together. "Most interesting," Jeremiel ruminated, looking at the fleur-de-lis pattern on the hilt. "Everything has a fleur-de-lis on it. Knife handle, map reference point, and so forth."

"And the Hoodoo man!" Bram reminded from the side.

From his bedroll, Wasatch said quietly, "When Web came to visit, he always had that flower beaded on his vest. To me, it was just a flower."

"It's also a symbol of France." Ab fingered his knobby chin. "Remember Bragg's constant preoccupation with France? This whole country was French once. You don't suppose this has something to do with the Louisiana Purchase, do you?"

From where she lay in her blankets, Arabella called, "And there's Leander Sentor."

"Yeah, yer French spy!" Bram chuckled. "You're all right, sis. From runnin' guns to hobnobbing with spies!"

She shot bolt upright. "How do you know I . . ." She gritted her teeth, fist threatening. "*No!* You little no good thieving . . . You listened! May Allah pour scalding water in both your nostrils, you little . . ."

Big-eyed, Bram muttered, "Whoops!" and vanished into the night as Arabella stumbled to her feet.

Jeremiel chuckled, trying to hide behind his hat. He didn't even wilt at Arabella's black glare as she stomped around the fire mumbling threats under her breath.

Jake finished screwing the pommel back onto Bram's

knife. "That, brother Ab, might explain a great deal," he added, ignoring Bram's flight and Arabella's distress.

"But how? There wasn't much more than a transfer of money to Napoleon and we took over. No money ever went out West. There were no scandals associated with it. Everything was aboveboard except for the Spanish reaction. They felt cheated."

"Web took Armijo's gold," Jeremiel reminded. "But he was the Mexican governor at the time."

"He also served Spain once upon a time." Jake leaned back, pulling at his pipe, watching the smoke rise into the night sky. "Back before the revolution in 1821."

Ab yawned. "Get some sleep, I'll take the first watch." Long into the night, he paced back and forth, thinking. France? Gold? How did Web fit into that? What interest could France or General Cavaignac have in Web Catton? Nothing made sense.

A gliding shadow moved in the night. He crouched low, the Dragoon Colt reassuring in his hand. The shape glided closer. Ab drew a quick breath as he realized it was Wolf.

"Lonesome, old friend?" he asked. "Guess I'm glad you're along to take care of Wasatch and the rest of us."

Wolf stood there, looking around before sniffing the wind and padding off into the darkness. Whether it was really White Wolf's soul in that animal or not, it felt good to know his nose was out there in the night sniffing around for trouble.

Only Molly's cussedness kept the thief from getting all the mounts. She made a ruckus, squealing in the dark. They came awake to the pounding of hooves. The next morning the tracks were plain to see. Bragg's horses had vanished with the cadence of hooves.

"Cheyenne," Jake decided, looking at the moccasin stitching imprinted in the dust.

"High Walker!" Wasatch nodded to himself. "I know his track."

"Didn't hear a thing. It is as if he were a spirit of smoke for all the noise he made." Jeremiel looked around, his face a study of confusion and frustration, since he'd been on watch.

"He also waited for Wolf to go hunt," Bram pointed out. Since the horse raid, he'd been real fond of that big canine.

Jake took them west to the Medicine Bow, then through the Shirley Basin and into Bates Hole. From there they followed the Platte past the Red Buttes and along the river.

Ab spit a stream of tobacco into the dust of the Oregon trail as they passed Bessemer Bend. Three fools in a light spring wagon had just made the crossing.

"Headed for Californy and all the gold we can scoop up!" one yelled across. "Gonna be the first to make it this year!" And they were off.

"Gold fever!" Jake shook his head. "Can't imagine anyone idiot enough to drop what he's doing and chase halfway across the world to look for gold!" His face twisted with distaste.

"What about us?" Bram asked, mouth in the usual crooked grin, eyes challenging.

"That's different!" Jake muttered, looking suddenly sheepish.

"Uh-huh," Ab grunted. "Reckon we'd best move on down to Reeshaw's."

"He's a cussed whiskey runner!" Jake continued, still sore over the theft of the horses.

"He's a trader first, second, and last," Ab defended. "And he's married to two Sioux women, and if there's anything going on out here, he knows it. Not only that, but if the folks in Washington wanted to enforce the Intercourse Act and stop the whiskey trade, they'd do it. You know everyone wants the Injuns stripped of all the fur they can get. Whiskey is the cheapest way to do it. That's all."

Jean Richard's was the biggest settlement in that part of the territories. Only Fort Laramie and Fort Bridger were any larger. Reeshaw's post and bridge remained a regulation little city just up from the Mormon ferry. Richard was how he spelled it; but he was as French as they came and pronounced it *Reeshaw.*

Composed of several log buildings, the post included stables, blacksmith shop, icehouse, rooming quarters, meat smokehouse, and a lavish well-stocked store. Behind the main post lodges and dugouts dotted the grassy plain.

The Cattons swung down easily, beating the dust from their clothes, stomping about, conscious of the crowd of gold seekers already pouring West.

Inside, Reeshaw, coming out from behind the counter, gave Ab a wide smile. A short stocky man with black hair and a neatly trimmed beard, he grabbed Ab up in a bear hug, swirling him around, almost knocking over a stack of food tins.

"Well, if it is not Abriel Campbell!" he bellowed in a booming voice. "You are well, eh, my friend? You look fit, if a little travel-worn."

"So, how's business?" Ab asked, having hauled freight to him only the fall before.

"Outstanding! And I thought the gold seekers last year brought me riches beyond belief! Ah, if only now the Mormons would find gold in Deseret. Then some be found at South Pass. Then some be found in the Salt

Lake. Then some be found on the Green River. Then I buy the White House and become president!"

Ab laughed with him until Reeshaw's warm eyes went cool as he recognized Jake. "Ah, you travel with interesting people," he whispered into Ab's ear. "The son of Colonel Oord!" Then he caught sight of Arabella. "And what is this? A lady! You are traveling most interestingly indeed, old friend!" He looked at Ab cock-eyed. "No! Not you! You do not go after California gold? Eh?"

Ab shook his head. "You ever heard of Web Catton?" he asked.

"But *oui*, he ees a good friend! He come here often. Many a time. He hunt for me all winter. He help cut ice from the reever when she is frozen. For that man, I give my life should he ask!"

Ab cleared his throat. "Yep, well, you see, Web Catton was my father. Same for Jake there and all the rest of us. We only just found out. Seems we were raised by just about everyone but the man who sired us."

It didn't set Reeshaw back. He nodded quickly, dark eyes knowing. Scratching the side of his big nose, he said soberly, "I knew he had family, Abriel. He tell me this one time. He tell me about Branton Bragg too. I am to understand that Web is dead? That, perhaps, Bragg may have keelt him?"

Ab shrugged. "Looks that way."

"I am sorry. Tell me, what do you wish of Jean Reeshaw? Ask, it is given freely to all of you. Come . . . you too, Jake. My house is yours. Be at home here." He spread his arms and pulled them all into a big tight hug. "I even have quarters for the ladees!"

In the three days they stayed to recuperate and reoutfit, Ab traded for tobacco, powder, lead, a couple more blankets. Then he had the horses reshod, stocked up on horseshoes, nails, and trade goods like beads, mirrors, and iron arrowheads.

On Sunday, Jeremiel got to preach to a following of gold hunters in the shade of the huge spreading cottonwood before the post. Listening, Ab frowned. His brother didn't have the old vigor. Perhaps he still felt fatigued from the long trail?

Jake almost caused a brawl trying to get Reeshaw to take any payment for the supplies as they mounted the fourth morning.

"*Non!*" Reeshaw cried, motioning with his muscular arms. "All these years, Web Catton come and work here for the winter. All these years he does not take pay from me. When Web Catton comes through, I outfit him. When he needs a place, my house is his. It will be so with his children, too."

After waving a farewell, the horses thundered and clomped hollowly over Reeshaw's wooden bridge.

Still shaking his head as they climbed through the sand dunes north of the river, Jake looked back at the settlement snuggled there in the floodplain. Black Mountain rose sharp and stark to the south. "You know, for all the years I've heard bad about him, he sure treated us decent."

Ab let Sorrel take his head, feeling the wind buffeting his face. "Yep, well, keep in mind, brother, a different world spawned him. He's Sioux down in the bottom of his bones. His wife's people adopted his heart. Sure, he trades them whiskey now because he always has. Reckon he's headed on a collision course with the army too. He ain't gonna change, Jake. The old ways are good enough for him and he won't see any reason to do different until they bury him."

Jeremiel's booming voice added, "The Mormons sure think highly of him. Not only that, but people on the trail almost talk about him like he's a saint. When Israel departed from Horeb, they 'went through all that great and terrible wilderness, which ye saw by the way of the mountain of the Amorites, as the Lord our God commanded us,' . . . and Reeshaw did deliver those in want for the sake of a pittance in trade."

Ab laughed. "Yep, and that's how he got all them redwood tree coffins. Some bunch come through taking them back to the States, and Reeshaw, he saw they couldn't pay toll for his bridge so he dickered away all them coffins for the horses, food, and the outfit they'd need to make it on to the States. Now, what's he gonna do with all them coffins?"

"Make a great bonfire!" Bram interjected. "Did you see all the stuff in that storeroom of his? Why, he could furnish the whole town of Little Rock with chairs, dressers, and doings!"

"Yep," Ab agreed, "he'd trade anything to get a wagon across that bridge of his. Not only that, but I've heard tell of him riding a hundred miles to help folks that broke down or got caught in an early—or late, for that matter—snowstorm up around South Pass."

"So," Jake said wearily, "perhaps he's not so bad as the colonel thinks. I heard he wanted to put a ball into Fitzpatrick for dumping out his whiskey one time."

"He didn't, though," Ab reminded. "Doubt he ever will, too. That's talk. How would you feel if someone ruint yer whole season's trade of a fine day?"

"Reckon I'd be a heap mad." Bram said.

"And I reckon Reeshaw will find tougher and tougher times as things change out here. But for one, I'm sure glad he considers us good friends."

They missed the trail that ran north to Salt Creek. Somehow, Jake got turned around—went too far west—

and ended up in all the broken country at the foot of the Big Horns. Wasatch took over then and chose an unerring trail roundabout through the ridges and upthrust slabs of sandstone and shale, finding his way with surety.

Arabella looked around, measuring the forbidding buttes. "How do you know where you're at?" she wondered, patting her steeldust. Efende tossed his head.

"Here"—he grinned to Arabella—"I played as a boy." His face turned warm with memories as he leaned forward, braids dangling. "From the Big Horns, I went southwest, across the trails to the place of red earth and where for miles it is flat. I crossed that land short of water, for it was a dry summer, and I crossed the Green River—which the Crows call Seedskadee—and went far up into the mountains called Wasatch by the Utes. There, I made medicine and found my Spirit Power.

"The Utes caught me then and chased me for days through the timber until one day I found myself cornered in a hole in the rocks." He paused, thinking. "As the Utes closed to kill me, I heard the sound of the white bear and looked back behind me.

"He was very big and very old, his fur white on the tips, shining in the light of the sun. I called to him and sang of my medicine and I heard his voice in my head. I had run from the Utes for four days and nights without food and without water and very little sleep. Together, Bear and I fell upon the Utes and with my own bow did I strike coup on four and kill two of them. Those scalps I took home to my people as proof of my deeds."

"Heathen deeds!" Jeremiel whispered where he rode behind them. "To take a man's hair is a sin in the eyes of the Lord God!"

"Seems to me you done read sumpthing about spoils a time or two," Bram chimed in, eyes challenging.

"Whar's it say a feller cain't take his spoil offen a dead man?"

"But the flesh of man?" Jeremiel's eyes showed his shock. "If it's not mentioned, it ought to be!"

"Cain't tell me where it's writ in the Book, eh?" Bram's eyes twinkled. "Hot damn, reckon I kin take me a scalp er two 'thout my soul going to all them hot places, Jeremiel! Funny Bible you got. Seems cutting a dead feller up ain't near the sin stealin' his hoss is!"

Wolf picked that moment to come trotting in from the thickening sagebrush. He beelined for Wasatch, growling, nuzzling, and rubbing against his leg.

Wasatch pulled up and stepped down, nipping at the scarred muzzle with his mouth, whimpering and growling in return.

Jeremiel looked away, face a somber, anguished mask.

Bram leaned forward, eyes eager. "What's he say?"

"Others come," Wasatch said, straightening. "Wolf has crossed the trail of the Pawnee. They are here, somewhere, looking for horses."

Arabella watched him mount and take the lead again, following the winding drainages.

"Some country," she added, letting her eyes roam the sagebrush flats, feeling the arid sprawl of the land around her. Overhead, the sky had become an endless blue vault. The dry breath of the land filled her nostrils, pungent, enticing.

"You could lose an army in here," Jake agreed. He shook his head. "But Pawnee? This far west?"

She let her eyes scour the terrain. "Parts of Africa look like this. I've waited for an ambush there, too. What of these Pawnee? Do I shoot first with them? Are they like Berbers?"

Jake lifted a shoulder. "I don't know Berbers. The Pawnee are supposed to be at peace with the whites. Out here? Who knows? If they decide to take us, no one would ever find the bodies."

Arabella nodded, eyes slitted as she looked over the rocky ridges. Lonely sandstone sentinels thrust up against the sky—each capable of hiding a rifleman. The feeling of eyes left her nervous, long fingers stroking her rifle butt.

"They are out there," Wasatch whispered. "Wolf smells them, hears them."

"How many?" Ab called from where he led Molly.

Wasatch shrugged. "I do not know. Wolf does not count."

"He does everything else," Ab muttered under his breath, searching the heights around them.

Jeremiel helped with the camp chores that night, remembering Reeshaw's post with regret. They'd let him preach there for the first time in how long? He paused from where he pounded in the picket pin, looking out over the darkening hills so somber and peaceful now in the twilight.

He checked the knot and patted his black. Taking his Bible, he walked past where Lark tamped coals around a roasting quarter of antelope and settled himself at the edge of the camp, falling to his knees.

He took off his hat and clutched the book to his chest. "Lord? Hear me." He wet his lips. "I ride through a desert land—yet nowhere is so barren as that which is in my breast." He lowered his head, thinking, trying to find the words he needed. "At Reeshaw's, Lord. I faced them. I looked out over Your flock . . . and I had nothing to say. No spirit moved me as it had in the past."

Far out beyond the ridges, a coyote yipped and whimpered to be followed by a cacophonous chorus of mates.

From even farther away came the soul-seeking cry of the buffalo wolf.

"O Lord," he whispered, hugging the Bible in a death grip. "Why do You no longer fill me with Your grace? I have sinned, Lord. Taken the life of my fellow man. Walked in the shadow of the ungodly. Save me, Lord. Show me the way. For Thee, I will walk the Damascus road as did Paul. In all Your mercy, show me the way to truth so I can spread Your message. Amen."

Head bowed, he waited for the feeling of peace which used to fill him—experiencing nothing.

"Jeremiel?" Abriel called. "You waiting to stop a Pawnee bullet or what? Get in here where we can keep an eye on you!"

With a sigh, Jeremiel got to his feet—empty on the inside—and walked back to the fire, now nothing more than coals so no silhouette would give a Pawnee a target.

Abriel jerked awake, blinking sleep from gritty eyes. The Colt came reassuring and cool to his hand as he rolled out from under warm blankets and checked the load in his Hawken. Dawn grayed the east.

Jake and Bram were staring out from where they lay behind rocks.

"Anything?" Ab asked, seeing Arabella stirring. Lark poked a sleepy face out of her covers and stretched her arms over her head, a big yawn splitting her face.

"Yep, Pawnee," Jake said with clipped certainty.

Ab wormed his way out past the horses and sniffed the rich cool air of morning. The odor of sagebrush, rabbitbrush, new grass, and greasewood made a pungent aroma. He saw a quick movement in the morning shadows.

"They know we know they're there," Bram said, not bothering to keep his voice down. Wasatch and Jeremiel were both awake, keeping low, moving out to the perimeter.

By the time it grew light enough to fill the shadows, Jake surprised everyone when he called out in something Ab and Wasatch recognized as Pawnee.

"What in tarnation?" Bram's voice echoed in the rocks.

"Asked them to send in one warrior to parley," Jake translated.

"Where did you larn Pawnee talk?" Bram insisted warily.

"I grew up with the military. The colonel has certain talents he uses to get information. I was a good son, I learn fast." Jake gave Bram a big grin. "You're not the only one in this family with talent, you know. At least what I learned won't get my neck pulled out of joint."

"Just scalped," Lark added from the side where she packed a cooking pot. "You don't talk that way in Cheyenne camp, brother Jake."

"Unlike your Bram, here, I learned sense," Jake added, turning his attention back to the tall sage below them.

An old familiar tightness began to form in Ab's belly. He tried to shake off the spooky sensation of knowing the Pawnee were out there. Like all the other Indians in 1850, they were friendly—or claimed to be. Again, that wore thin in some situations. A person never knew when they'd last been taken by a white man, or if one of their warriors had been shot by an idiot immigrant.

A voice called out, rising and falling in guttural.

Jake answered and stood up easily.

Ab had to admit, his brother had more guts and gumption in that instance than he did. He winced, half expecting the crack of a rifle. Then Ab saw a man stand up not fifty yards out in front of his position.

Dressed in a calico shirt, the Pawnee had a trade blanket around his shoulders, his hair roached in that shaved Pawnee style that left the sides of his head bald. His trousers were made of canvas that looked suspiciously like wagon top. The rifle in his hands gleamed, shiny with brass tacks, as he walked slowly forward. Everywhere Ab's eyes went, Pawnee warriors kept popping out of the rocks and sagebrush.

Jake met the man halfway. They shook hands, embraced, and patted each other on the back. In the usual plains ritual, both sat down and smoked. Ab tried to swallow while Jake's hands flew and he carried on a jocular dialogue.

What seemed to be years later, they parted, Jake smiling. Ab slowly recovered his ability to breathe as he unstuck his tongue from the roof of his mouth. "What's he say?"

"Says they're out looking for Sioux scalps." Jake squatted in the dirt, fingers idly tracing the soft sandy dust. "Says they got hit real bad down by Fort Laramie. The Brulé kicked 'em but good and chased 'em out here. Wanted to know if we was friends with the Sioux. I told them we was friends with anybody until they tried to steal our horses."

"Reckon me and Wasatch could lift a couple of theirs." Bram asserted. He had all his pistols on the saddle in front of him, easy to reach.

"Reckon we won't." Jake snorted. "They're in a plain hostile mood. I made sure Two Coups—that's the Pawnee war chief out there—saw my pistol. They got a downright dread of Colt guns. Still, it's a standoff. We're invited to come feast with them tonight. I told him no."

"Why?" Jeremiel asked. "Surely they wouldn't violate a truce when we were breaking bread with them. For a man to—"

"Surely they would." Jake's eyes went flat. "Keep in

mind, brother, these here are Pawnee. Every people out here has a different way of doing things. The hearth isn't sacred to Pawnee—but they know we think that way."

"So they'd try and kill us?" Arabella asked, her combination gun ready, the hammers for the rifle and shotgun cocked. The gold inlay gleamed dully in the brightening light.

Wasatch shook his head, smiling at her. "No. They will only kill me and Lark. The rest of you they will rob, take your horses, and humiliate. They are at peace with the whites. They are at war with the Cheyenne."

"Some peace!" Bram grunted.

"Different ways, different notions," Jake reminded.

"So, what are we going to do?" Ab demanded, turning on his heels. "Being set afoot out here just don't fill my bill of goods. Not with High Walker and Bragg behind us."

"I told them we were going to ride out of here." Jake yawned and straightened. "I told them that our brother Wasatch had been living with the Cheyenne and that if they attacked him, we'd clean house and they would have broken the peace. Further, I told them my father, Colonel Oord, would remove Fort Kearny from their lands, and their names would live in disgrace before Morning Star and Buffalo for breaking a treaty."

"So we just ride out of here?" Bram laughed, slapping his knee. "Just like that? Hop on the horses and ride past all them Injuns hiding in the rocks with their rifles pointed at us?" His voice went up an octave. "Do that? After we can't even sit down to dinner with them?"

"That's right, Bram. I guess you'll just have to trust me on this one." Jake's voice had a melodious note to it and he looked smug.

Bram turned to Jeremiel. "Reckon we're gonna find

out real soon ifn yer preachin' done saved me, brother Jeremiel. Reckon heaven or hell ain't that far away!"

The nervous shiver running down Ab's back agreed as he scanned the dark somber Pawnee faces watching from the sage as they began throwing saddles and packs onto the animals. Ab swallowed convulsively as he lifted himself into the saddle, back almost itching, awaiting the impact of a Pawnee bullet.

Jake continued to smile, nodding his head this way and that, Colt pistol easy in his hand. A lump the size of a melon grew in Ab's throat. Somehow he, too, smiled into the black eyes of the Pawnee warrior who started to reach for his bridle as he rode past. He was still smiling as he settled the Colt on the Pawnee's head and pulled the hammer back.

# *Chapter 20*

*T*hat true? What Bragg said about sending them
Cattons back to France? Their heads all
packed in salt?"

Leander shifted from where he squatted, looking out
over the Platte, to study Cal Backman. "Yes, I suppose it
is. The general would want them—if they are who
Branton believes them to be."

Backman stroked his long black beard, squinting out
over the shimmering heat waves rising from tan and buff
buttes and ridges. "Huh! And there's a heap of money in
that?"

"Where power is concerned, there is always money to
be had." Leander waited, tapping a twist of dried sagebrush against the hard dirt. A funny land, this. So
empty. Unlike Algeria, this West seemed vacant, endless.
Even in the deep desert, Algeria bore the traces of man.

Here, he could see nothing but a black herd of buffalo in the distance moving down toward the river.

A land of rolling ridges, each sandstone-topped, each as desolate as the next rising toward the far horizon where green-blue mountains dominated. Its soul called to him nevertheless. In the dry wind caressing his cheek, he could feel the fingers of a seductress. Tendrils of desire reached to him, creeping from the very rocks, wrapping themselves around him, comforting him in such a frightening way. Here lay the siren of his dreams, here lay freedom.

Uneasy, Leander rubbed the back of his sun-burned neck. Freedom. The cause that had led him to the barricades, following the promises of his general. Where he had rushed headlong in France, seeking to find it, this vast empty waste reeked of it. Freedom, true freedom, lay all around him. Faced now with the reality, he shivered, uncertain if he dared to embrace the seductress.

"Money," Cal added thoughtfully, breaking the silence.

"Isn't that why you follow Abriel Catton?" Leander tried to shake his uncertainty, bring his mind back to his duty. "You are on Branton Bragg's payroll."

Cal sniffed, flaring his nostrils, shaking his head slowly. "Naw. Ab Catton kilt a friend of mine. Poor ol' Jeff. Grew up with him. Hell, he never had nothing. Neither did I. His maw raised me. Found me in a empty wood crate on the docks next to the river in Natchez Under the Hill."

"Orphan?" Leander wondered.

"One way or 'nuther," Cal agreed. "Anyhoo, Jeff's maw, she scrambled. Kept us kids fed doin' whatever she could. Sometimes she'd sell herself to boatmen. Sometimes she'd pinch whatever she could off the drunks. Wash clothes, or do day jobs when she's on her uppers."

Cal squinted. "Then she got sick once. Woman trouble. Bleeding, an' all, and it wouldn't stop. Man won't pay fer a woman bleeding like that. An' she lost weight and looked pretty bad. Me and Jeff, we took to the streets. Just kids, you know? Found a drunk, beat him over the head with a chunk of lumber and rifled his pockets. Made 'nuff to get Jeff's maw a couple doses of laudanum. Seemed to help but she never really was right after that. When she died, Jeff and me, well, we just floated."

"And Catton killed him?" Leander prodded. *Why do I worry? On Cavaignac's payroll, I killed James L'Ouverture.*

"Yeah. Thought we had that coon. Thought he was dead to rights in his blankets. Only he skunked us. Got wind 'cause of that damned mule of his. Mule ruint Hank's face and Catton, he split Jeff's head with his rifle butt." Cal shook his head. "Damn fine ambush we laid fer him, too. Shoulda just shot him in his bedroll from a distance. Shouldn'ta took a chance."

Leander cocked his head. "But it's still the money keeping you on his trail, isn't it? I mean, he just defended himself. When you—"

"Naw," Cal grunted, spitting a stream of tobacco at the pebbles under his feet. "Naw, it's honor, that's what. Jeff never had it good is all. Man don't deserve ta be laid down by some rich bastard who never scrambled to make do." Cal's face pinched, as if he struggled with some deep concept. "And it's—it's just honor. You know, a payback 'cause he was my friend. 'Cause I grew up with him. That's justice, ain't it?"

Leander looked out over the land again, feeling the draw of the emptiness. "I don't know," he added, voice almost a whisper. "Loyalty is a slippery concept sometimes."

"Yeah," Cal mumbled, jerking his head in a short nod.

"Loyalty. That's what it is. I owe Jeff loyalty . . . fer what his maw did."

Leander changed his position, the painful memory of his parents stabbing at him. With a conscious effort, he forced it back, concentrating on Backman's words. "So, you'll kill Catton because he defended his life and in so doing, killed Jeff? All that because you owed his mother?"

Cal tilted his head, skeptical eyes on Leander. "That's right, Frenchy. Ain't that the way it is in France? Honor's all that sets man over beast. Loyalty, like ya said."

Leander lost himself in that, frowning.

" 'Sides," Backman added lightly, "afore we pack 'em in salt, there's that girl with 'em. You see her? Some looker, huh?" Cal smacked his lips. "Yeah, I ain't never had me a woman like that. Can't wait to rip them petticoats off her. Why, I can imagine what she's like underneath—all soft and fresh. Bet she's never been had afore. Why, she's needin' luvin, I'll—"

Leander stiffened, jaw tensing. "What of honor? Don't men in this country treat women with respect?"

Cal made a smoothing motion with his hand. "Sure they do, Frenchy, but all we're sending back is the head, ain't it? We ain't sending the rest of her back to France." His gesture widened to include the country. "Out here, we're free. With all this space, who's gonna know the difference, huh? Ain't no law here, Frenchy. Ain't nobody to find the body."

*I killed James . . . and she saved my life! What perverse debt do I owe her? Honor? Why did this have to happen? She must never know about James . . . Never!*

Leander's pulse raced as he forced himself to remain still. "All for the glory of France," he whispered under his breath. Unbidden, the memory of his dead parents shoved into his mind. He beat it back, feeling the guilt and pain under his heart.

He stood, walking back to where they rested the horses. Amazing how High Walker had stolen them back. More amazing that young Wasatch had managed to work magic that day. The men—tough though they might be—still hesitated at the mention of the fact. Bragg stamped and cursed every time he recalled his humiliation—the others avoiding his violent stare.

Settling under the lone cottonwood that provided shade, Leander leaned against the bark, closing his eyes, hearing the buzzing of insects, the low voices of men, and the swishing of horse tails.

*Only her head is going to France ... Ain't no law. Freedom.* A horror he'd managed to subdue ate at the edges of his thoughts. Arabella? In the hands of these ruffians? For a brief instant he pictured his head in her lap again, saw the concern in her eyes.

Leander threw himself sideways, cushioning his head on his arm. The power he sought here would reshape France. The symbol Cavaignac needed was waiting out there, somewhere behind those forbidding arid buttes. And France would remake civilization.

Human destiny always called for sacrifice.

Leander's eyes jerked open and he sat up, running grimy hands over his sun-browned face. He looked at his hands, seeing the calluses, the trail dirt ground into the fine lines and under the nails. He'd kept his hands so fine until Algeria.

*Like my soul now.* He shook his head. "No," he whispered. "I have already sacrificed too much." A hollowness lay within him. Born the day he'd recognized his parents' bodies. "Arabella, the future can only be built upon a foundation of blood. If I can sacrifice my parents in the name of my country ... I can lose you, too."

He swallowed, wishing he could be rid of her memory. Yet, every time he closed his eyes, he found himself sick with dizziness, head in her lap as she stroked his face, Wasatch singing in the background.

The Pawnee stared up at Ab over the sights of the pistol and—to Ab's reckoning—saw his death because he smiled faintly and nodded before letting go of the halter and stepping back. Eloquent in those black eyes was the promise to meet again—as if a challenge had been made. Sorrel threw his head, trotting past, Molly shying to one side, fighting the lead as she bared teeth at the Pawnee.

Two Coups didn't waste any time. Ab looked back to see a kid bring up the horses, warriors headed for the animals at a trot. Mounted, they lined out behind them in jig time.

"Is that part of the deal?" Ab asked, thumb pointing over his shoulder as he rode up beside Jake.

He looked casually and nodded. "Yep. They'll be after us until either they steal our horses, or we kill each other, or we lose them somewhere."

"Thought there was peace between the Pawnee and the whites." Jeremiel reminded.

"There is," Jake told him. "What's peace got to do with stealing horses? That just means they won't kill us or seriously hurt us. Taking a few horses—maybe humiliating us and making fun of our condition—that's not really warfare. Different people have different beliefs out here, brother." His brow furrowed and he barked out, "Wasatch!"

He came riding up, measuring amber eyes intent on Jake.

"What's the quickest way out of here? Take us straight north on the fastest line possible. We want to make time without killing the horses."

Wasatch grinned and led the way up over loose shaley slopes, topping out on windswept ridges where wheat-grasses and phlox poked through the rock before winding through scattered ponderosa and limber pine, then dropping down into rough, rocky canyons—only to climb out and do it all over again. And the day wore on. Leading sweating horses, they stumbled up the steep places on foot to save the animals, panting in the hot dry air, mouths sticky and foul-tasting, limbs quivering.

But climbing on foot drained Arabella. She staggered along, jaw clenched, a fire of determination in her eyes, unwilling to slow them down, pushing forward by force of will alone.

By late afternoon they descended the rocky ridges to the South Fork of the Powder River. As they waded across, the water looked like liquid mud.

"Seen potters in Saint Louis use stuff that looked like that," Ab muttered with disgust. But the horses drank greedily.

Exhausted, Arabella stared at him, dull-eyed, her blouse sweat-darkened, shoulders slumped.

Bram pulled his mare up, water dripping in rivulets down its flank and looked back to where the Pawnee were scrambling down to the river.

Wasatch eased up next to him and gazed off toward the rounded heights of the Big Horns. A grim smile on his dark face, he watched Jake's dun claw its way up the crumbly bank. Wasatch pointed a lean hand out to the west. "What if we took the straight route? I know a quicker way."

Jake bent in the saddle, stretching his back muscles. "I was figuring on going all the way around to the north, then dropping south along the Pryors."

Wasatch's eyes were on the Pawnee where they had

stopped to water their horses. "Let them follow us," he said in challenge.

They camped that night at a little spring that seeped out of the side of a sandstone ridge. Wasatch had them on the trail before the sun even thought of breaking over the eastern horizon.

"I'm going to die," Arabella mumbled wearily as she clung to the saddle. During a break, Wasatch gave her a scaly-looking green plant to chew; she seemed to perk up.

The trail led across a land tipped on end. The horses buck-jumped up unstable slopes, kicking loose rocks and cascading dirt to top out on deflated rocky ridgetops. They passed stone circles so old they had sunk into the ground, with patchy wheatgrass and steppe bluegrass growing around them. Lichens mottled the rock in reddish colors.

"These"—Wasatch pointed—"the ancient ones placed to hold down their lodge covers."

"Who'd camp up here?" Jake demanded, looking around for water or cover from the incessant wind.

"Ancient ones. The ones from the times before Sweet Medicine." Wasatch lifted a shoulder, reining his sweating Appaloosa, and led them over the edge, dropping into the endless steep arroyos, zigzagging through the dissected land only to climb out again. Leading the animals straight up slopes, they would stop at the crest—lungs burning, the backs of throats raw—and look back to see the Pawnee forever dogging their tracks.

Sweat streaking her dusty hot face, Arabella leaned on Efende's saddle and asked, "Wouldn't it be easier if I just went back and shot them all?"

Bram and Wasatch had their heads together, nodding as they talked. Ab frowned, remembering the last time they'd talked that way.

The sun slid behind the bulk of the Big Horns. They wound out of the chopped uplands and splashed into the cold clear water of the Middle Fork of the Powder. By the time the tired horses had drunk their fill, night had fallen stove-kettle black. Wasatch led them across rippling inky water as the horses slipped on mossy cobbles and the river ran around and into their dusty boots.

"Hold up!" Bram ordered in the blackness. Ab could hear splashing as he pushed his horse next to one of the pack animals, checking the cinches.

"Wait here," Wasatch ordered.

"This have a purpose?" Jeremiel asked. "This water is freezing my feet."

"Arabella?" Lark called. "Come, we change you out of white man clothes."

Horses moved and splashed in the darkness.

"What's up, Bram?" Ab insisted.

"Shhh! Gotta plan to shake them Pawnee."

"We push too hard and Arabella's gonna fold. Hell! *I'm* gonna fold!" Ab complained.

"Rather walk back to Saint Looie?" Bram asked conversationally. A shadow, he thrust an arm under the manty and pulled out some cloth. Then—barely visible in the darkness—he slopped up onshore and put a small fire together with an ingenious array of branches that would drop in as their supports burned through. Wasatch bound a cloth around some loose brush that hung down in the water and bobbed unevenly in the current.

"We ready?" Lark whispered from the blackness as horses splashed closer.

"This way!" Bram's voice hissed. "We got to stay close to the bank."

Ab could barely see him in the light of the quarter-full

moon as he worked upstream, his horse clinging to the shadows next to the bank.

"Reckon thar'll be some tough spots up ahead, what with spring runoff and all. Hang onto yer hoss no matter what and don't make ary a squeek!"

"Wonderful," Arabella mumbled softly.

"You just lead," Ab grumbled, feeling how cold his feet were getting in that icy water. How far was it up the Powder before that same water wasn't more than melting snow?

He couldn't help but smile when he looked back. It sure seemed that a man's figure hunched and moved at the fire where Wasatch's cloth and stick arrangement bobbled with the current. Before they rounded the bend, Ab could see another blaze spring up on the opposite side where the Pawnee were unloading for the night.

"Where'd you learn that?" Jake envied.

"Works like a charm on posses," Bram snickered.

Hours later, wet, shivering, cold, and miserable, Bram led them up onshore. Ab himself had been dunked a time or two and the feeling had gone from his feet. To get his boots off proved a chore—even with Bram helping. He sighed and drained the water out of them.

The horses, too, were stumbling with exhaustion. Arabella shivered in a wet deerskin dress that outlined every curve of her figure. Ab looked away in embarrassment. Arabella—oblivious—huddled over the fire, shivering so hard her teeth chattered.

Bram, however, couldn't keep his eyes off Lark as her wet clothing clung to the fullness of her figure.

"Uh, little brother?" Jake asked, haggard. "You mind not drooling in camp?"

"He see what be his someday," Lark joked. "Make him offer more horses, eh?" she said saucily at Jake, who went white and retreated to the darkness. Wasatch laughed, and winked.

Jeremiel missed it all, exhausted, huddled under his blanket, checking to make sure his Bible had made it. He gasped in horror at the wet pages.

Ab vaguely remembered unloading the pack animals and loosening the cinches on the horses.

"All right, folks," Bram added, chipper. "Cash in yer hardware."

He and Lark, talking happily, pulled the balls from the pistols and rifles, scraping caked powder from the bores and drying them over the tiny fire. Jeremiel, blanket draped like a tent, continued drying his Bible page by page. His eyes had gone uncharacteristically soft as he fingered the wet pages.

"Sure hope God's got a sense of humor," Bram cackled with a challenging grin.

Jeremiel leveled a finger at Bram and drew a deep breath, held it for a moment, changing his mind and letting it out slowly, too tired to push it. "Oh, I suppose in His wisdom, He, too, knows the Pawnee and their perfidy."

Bram shook his head, a wicked smile on his lips. "Hope He don't know 'em too well! Ifn He does, the old boy's likely to drown!"

Jeremiel bowed his head. "Why do I even try?"

As cold as he was, Ab didn't remember falling asleep. Within what seemed seconds, Bram's hand on his shoulder brought him awake.

"Lend a hand, brother." And Bram strode off into the darkness.

Almost wavering on his feet, Abriel began packing the weary horses again.

"Just leave me for the Pawnee," Arabella pleaded.

"They'll be meaner than Hides To Trap Eagles and

Pawnee Stalker," Wasatch told her directly. "Not only that, there are many more of them. Sometimes they also sacrifice women prisoners to Morning Star."

"I'm up," Arabella growled, struggling to her feet, greedily devouring the half-cooked remnants of the last antelope roast.

And before he knew it, Ab found himself back in the river, Bram picking the course through shallower water this time. He still got wet as the horses slipped in the blackness, dunking them in the bone-chilling water. When morning lightened the eastern sky, Bram found a tributary heading south and forced his way in under low-hanging brush where the horses dropped their heads and each rider had to pull the scratchy stuff over bent backs while step by step they battled up the narrow winding stream.

"See why we put you in Indian dress?" Lark called to Arabella. "That white man stuff would be all through here in shreds."

"Does this have a purpose?" Ab demanded after a jagged snag ripped his cheek open, taking half his beard with it.

"You see any tracks of ours?" Bram called back.

He looked down at the rocky bottom of the creek bed and shot a quick look at the brush around them. Thunderation! Nobody would punch a horse through that with all that wonderful flat ground around.

"Nope." Ab winced as a particularly sharp branch gouged his back.

"Then neither will anyone else, big brother." Bram's voice had a cheery note of victory in it.

Having lost his hat twenty times to branches, bleeding from a hundred scratches, Ab joyously watched Bram work his way out on an outcrop of trackless quartzite. From there, he headed up, the horses moving slowly, weary step after weary step. By afternoon, Bram led them out onto a high sandstone ridge and there—for the first time—his strategy fell flat like a drunk on the board-walk.

"I'll say this, the view is spectacular," Jake gasped, letting his eyes sweep the panorama.

From where he sat, the wind pulling stoutly at his worn torn body, a bright red-orange sandstone wall fell off below into a dizzying depth. Against the violent red, a broad north-south valley glistened emerald in the sun-light. The slopes of the Big Horns rose in an easy grade to the west, the rocky climb dotted with pine and scrub brush. Even haggard-eyed Arabella—hair in stringy wisps around her soot-smudged scratched face—sat up straighter, dazzled by the sight.

Ab swallowed, eyes gritty, every muscle feeling loose and pulled out of socket. Looking to the north, the only break he could see was the cut where the Middle Fork ran through the tall red wall.

"What now? The Pawnee will be headed right for that gap in the rock!" He wiped at the clotted blood on his scratched face and sighed.

"This way," Wasatch called. "There's a trail."

Looking to the south, the wall got taller, if anything.

"What kind of trail?" Jeremiel asked, an image of doubting Thomas.

Wasatch's grin carried a note of devilment. "The kind which will tell us just how good our horses are."

That should have been a hint. Only Ab missed it—being too bone-weary. He missed the next hint when Wasatch decided he should tail-hitch Sorrel and lead Molly down on foot. After all, any idiot knows a mule can go places a horse can't. A double-damned idiot, on the other hand, knows a horse will let himself follow a mule through places impossible for him to cross—so long as you don't tell him. By the time Ab realized what Wasatch had him into, there was no turning back.

When he and Molly kicked them up, that trip down didn't bother the herd of mule deer any. They just bounded and jumped and sailed right to the bottom of that steep trail in a cloud of red dust.

Molly wanted to throw a ruckus. Ab could tell by the way her eyes glared into his and her nose flared. From the hold of her head, the stiffness in her neck, and the "I'll get you for this" promise in her pool-like brown eyes, she considered doing it on the trail and killing them all. At least for a second she did. She scraped the packs on one side against gritty red sandstone while she walked pigeon-toed on the other to keep her hooves on the trail.

He winced, knowing his mule.

An eagle might have liked that trail; Ab didn't. He spit a stream of tobacco off past his left foot and it took it five seconds to splat on the rocks down there. Halfway down and he looked and called back over his shoulder, "I'll be a three-footed fool if there ain't a dead elk lying broken in the rocks down there!"

"You ain't an elk, are ya?" Bram called from above.

"Well, no. But I—"

"Then don't worry about it none!"

Ab tried to swallow his heart back where it belonged. "Brothers," he muttered, considering how elk do in rough stuff—and that scared double-dyed hob right out of him.

Molly started to slide down on top of him and he pushed her back onto the trail somehow or another. That was about the time he realized he didn't have any use for heights. After that, every time she started to fall, she'd use the leverage of her neck against his weight.

"Molly, if you throw me offa here, so help me God, I'll kill you . . . if I live through it!"

Ab threatened, shouted, cussed, and all she did was look at him with the promise that if she ever got to the bottom, she'd kick his teeth in.

The worst part came when the trail pinched off. Ab looked over a three-foot drop into the soft dirt where the slope colluvium fanned out. Molly propped herself there, legs braced, Sorrel ready to run over her and blowing like a freight train. The horse's eyes rolled as he trembled, ears swiveled this way and that.

Ab let loose of the lead rope and patted her nose. She tried to bite him. "Well, girl, this is it. You gotta do it or die trying." At that, he jumped out, hit the loose stuff running, and slid down that red mess, boots kicking. Gravel, dust, and dirt aflying, arms pumping like an Irish washerwoman's, he fought to keep from pitching on his face.

Molly came blasting by him, legs braced as she slid on her hocks, ears forward, eyes wide, and Sorrel right on her rear. Ab got stopped, scrambling for a hold as Molly found footing and raced to the flatlands. Fortunately, Sorrel's lead rope came loose when Molly finally blew up.

Ab, gasping relief, settled himself onto a large rock—well out of the way—while she took out her frustration. When Molly cut loose, she didn't fool around. She had the pack saddle almost completely unloaded before the britchen broke. Ab's cast-iron fry pan exploded on a rock. Blankets sailed through the air. He watched ten pounds of powder arc into the dust. Then came the hammer and axe, which didn't hit her—thank God! Then after the breast collar snapped, she managed to get the pack saddle rotated around her middle and stopped in disgust, kicking out behind her with violent fury.

In a final statement on the nature of affairs, she

brayed as foully as she could into the summer afternoon and stood, ears twitching this way and that, eyes slitted as she watched Abriel.

Wasatch was sliding his Appaloosa down the trail as he looked up at that sheer rock wall and shook his head.

Molly turned to stare and kicked one last time to vent her disbelief.

"Yep," Ab sighed. "I don't believe it either."

Last but not least came Arabella, walking down where Wasatch had led Efende and the rest of the pack animals, singing in his eerie way to calm them.

Jake shook his head. "How in the name of God did we ever get down that?"

"Now where?" Ab asked, rubbing his face, wondering why it felt like a mask.

Wasatch pointed.

"I was afraid of that," Arabella sighed. "Always up."

Following Wasatch, they led the horses up the backbone of the Big Horns. One after another they climbed the hogbacks, dropping down the other side—but nothing like the Red Wall.

"Spirit Road," Wasatch told them, indicating a huge pile of rocks. One by one, as they led the horses up, Wasatch would toss another rock onto the cairns they passed.

"Must be hundreds of them," Jake gaped, looking up the long line of rocks. Here and there, a wooden pole stuck out the top, a faded hide twisting in the breeze.

"Marks the Spirit trail up the river you call Middle Powder," Wasatch explained.

"Cheyenne?" Jake asked.

"No, old, very old. Feel the Power here. Old Spirits walk this. Bad things happen to people who don't throw a rock on to praise the Spirits."

Ab shrugged, finding a fist-sized rock, carting it over

to add to one of the piles. To his surprise, so did Jeremiel.

That night Wasatch led them to a camp in a thick stand of trees where a little spring ran out of the rock. Molly and the rest of the horses simply blew when the packs were lifted off and hung their heads in exhausted sleep.

"Wolf and I will watch," Wasatch said, blinking from sleep-ridden eyes.

He didn't get any argument.

They broke camp late the next morning, heading for the high timber, working along elk and sheep trails.

"Look at that!" Arabella gasped, pointing. "What kind of creature is it?"

"Big Horn," Jake called. "A mountain sheep."

One good ram had a double curl of thick horn on his head.

To the east, the plains stretched out in a green-brown vastness that went on forever. Just ridge after ridge and tableland that reached to the blue haze of the horizon, only the Pumpkin Buttes stood out, dark mounds in the distance.

"No wonder it's a Spirit road," Arabella breathed.

"Amen," Jeremiel agreed, eyes lost on the hazy distance.

Wasatch led them across the headwaters of the Middle Fork and followed the divide to the heights. He cut across a low pass before heading north, keeping to the high country where the good grass replaced flesh the animals had lost on the long trip. Patches of snow melted in the shade and on the north slopes. The water tasted good and cold, bracing in the sharp clear air.

Arabella began to feel alive again, reveling in the incredible swell and bounty of the land. Her strength returned as they dined nightly on elk, buffalo, deer, and grouse. Wasatch shot one of the elk with his bow and arrow, having called it to him with an eerie song. As she feasted there on the heights, Arabella couldn't stop looking out over a huge brown basin to the west hemmed on all sides by majestic jagged mountains.

"The Absarokas," Jake mumbled through a mouthful of meat, pointing with his bowie. "They're more than a hundred miles away. Up there are the Pryors. That river down there is the Big Horn. Where it runs through the mountains is where we have to look for Web's treasure."

The Big Horns flattened off on top, stands of trees intermixing with large open meadows of thick grass that supported large herds of buffalo, elk, mountain sheep, and deer.

"I've seen a lot of this world," she confided to Jake. "But never have I seen the like of this!" She filled her lungs with the fresh air. "I could remain here for the rest of my life. I feel like I've come home."

Jake had ridden ahead looking for game when he saw him. The fellow stood on a limestone point, the wind whipping his hair and beard and tugging at the long fringes on his hunting coat. One hand held a long plains rifle by the muzzle, the butt resting on rock.

Jake pulled up his bay and stared. The man stood, leg braced, gray-haired, and grizzled. His buckskins looked old and grease-stained. A fur cap made from a badger's hide covered his head.

Jake squinted, trying to make out the details, heart suddenly jumping. He stood so far away Jake couldn't make out any of the details except the device on his chest—a blue fleur-de-lis on a white beaded background.

Jake swallowed and waved, but the man gave no indication he saw. Turning toward him, Jake shot a look over his shoulder to see how far behind the others were.

When he looked back, the man was gone. As if fingers had snapped and an apparition vanished.

Desperately, he spurred the bay ahead and cantered up to the point. Nothing! Eyes searching, he stepped down and inspected the barren rock for a track—knowing it wouldn't take an impression. The wavy grass wasn't even crumpled. Standing, he looked around, seeing no place a man on foot could have run to in that time. The nearest trees stood a quarter mile away across the broad, flat, bowl-shaped meadow.

Jake hunkered down, frowning, and pulled his plug from his pocket, letting his trained eye absorb the spot, trying to figure any avenue of escape. His chew juicing, he spat his disgust as the rest rode up.

"What you got?" Ab asked, leaning across the pommel of his saddle, legs out straight to stretch.

Jake stood, running a toe over the gray ripply rock and looked up, squinting. "I *saw* a man standing here. He was dressed like a mountain man with a long rifle. And Ab, he had a fleur-de-lis beaded on the front of his hunting shirt."

"Web Catton?" Ab asked, eyes measuring.

"The same man I saw below Fort Laramie?" Jeremiel ventured, head cocked. "Does a spirit walk the land?"

Jake sighed. "No tracks. Nothing. He couldn't have run that far before I got here." He pointed to the far trees.

"Hoodoo!" Bram muttered uneasily, eyes wide and shifting.

"Hoodoo!" Jake mocked. "Tarnation, boy, I don't believe in Hoodoos! Spirits? Come, Bram, this is a modern enlightened age."

Bram shot a quick look at Wolf where he'd settled himself, bushy tail around his big feet. The yellow eyes were half-lidded.

"It's been a long tiring ride," Arabella offered. "I've wondered if I didn't see a man like that myself a couple of times."

"I *saw* him," Jake insisted.

"*Tasoom* do not always go to *Seyan*," Wasatch replied.

Jake cocked his head, noticed a stink bug walking long-legged across the rock, and knocked him over with a stream of tobacco juice. He gave Jeremiel a glare for good measure and climbed lithely into the saddle. Wasatch's eyes were impassive, as usual. Ab looked skeptically at him and the last he heard as he reined the bay away was Bram muttering "Hoodoo." under his breath.

# *Chapter 21*

*I* know, it was solid rock. Prints wouldn't just jump right out like they would in sand or dust or some kinds of clay. Still, there should have been tracks out there in the grass ... unless he sank into solid limestone. So where did he go?" Jake lifted his hands helplessly.

Bram flattened a fly, listening, remembering the old stories he'd heard in Arkansas. What was that runaway slave woman's name? Aunt Mam? Sure nuff, remember how big her eyes got when she got to yarnin' about Hoodoos? Uh-huh, well, maybe Jake didn't believe. Didn't mean Bram had to be anyone's fool about it.

"Now, I won't say it couldn't have been my father's ghost," Ab said, hovering over the fire. "Course, I got one brother who believes in a world with no ghosts or spirits, and everything is subject to Newton's laws of science. I got another who believes his stepfather's spirit inhabits a wolf. I got still another from Arkansas ... and Lord alone knows what they believe down there! Hoo-doos, for goodness' sake! Then there's Jeremiel, who sees Satan in anything that doesn't wear a cross and hallalooyha the word of God. And from them I'm sup-posed to make sense of what Jake saw?"

Arabella laughed at him, a twinkle in her eye.

Bram hunkered down so he could lean against Lark where she sewed a new set of sun-hardened soles on Wasatch's moccasins. A deep-seated pleasure warmed the bottom of his heart.

"All right," Jake cried, ticking off his fingers. "There's three possibilities. One, Web Catton ain't dead and he was standing there. We already talked about the prob-lems with that. Two, Web Catton's dead and somebody is trying to look like him. So, why would anyone do that in the first place ... and where did he go? Three, I saw Web Catton's ghost, spirit, haunt, Hoodoo, *Tasoom*, or whatever you want to call it."

"You look tired," Arabella added, her cultured voice softening as she patted his knee reassuringly.

"I didn't sleep well," Jake admitted sheepishly. Then he raised his hands in exasperation. "Come on, we've lost the Pawnee, lost Bragg, let's make tracks."

Bram considered as he helped Lark pack up their pos-sibles. Yes sirree, he'd just get to the bottom of this Cat-ton's treasure business and marry her. He enjoyed watching Lark, seeing the swell of her hips against the soft buckskin dress, the way her breasts moved under the soft material. When their eyes met, he could see secret promise in those gentle brown depths. The little things touched him, like the way her thick raven hair trickled across the smooth curve of her cheek.

"You have a warmth in your eye," she told him, her

smile letting him get a glimpse of straight white teeth behind ruby lips.

"Thinking of you," he answered. "Wishing you wasn't sleeping on the other side of camp."

She lowered her eyes, a cascade of thick black hair hiding her blush. "I wish I wasn't either."

"When we find Catton's gold," Bram promised. "We could, well, we got us a preacher. Reckon I don't figger Wasatch'll throw much of a fit ifn I just promise him a hoss or two. After all, that cussed High Walker done stoled his back."

Bram stuck his lip out, crossing his eyes slightly as he looked over to where Wasatch talked to Wolf. "Just a cussed minute, here! He ain't agonna raise no ruckus nohow! He's my little brother, fer Gawd's sake! He mouth off ta me, I'll just up and whup him!"

Lark stifled a series of giggles and covered her mouth with her hand. She reached up quickly, making sure no one noticed, and brushed her lips against his.

"That is for later, Bram."

"You can bet on it," he said with a grin, and helped her onto her horse.

"Trouble here," High Walker muttered. "Much bad trouble."

"How's that?" Bragg asked. He stepped down from the saddle, holding the reins as High Walker returned from scouting a wide circle.

"Pawnee lost 'em." High Walker made a grandiose gesture with his hand. "Go way round. Look for tracks and find nothing. They passel mad and go east. That way." He pointed.

"After the Cattons?" Branton asked skeptically, eyes slitting as his mouth worked.

"No. They take a different trail. Go hunt Sioux.

Mebbe hunt 'Rapaho or *Tsis-tsis-ta*. Cattons got away."
High Walker crossed his arms over his chest, broadly
flaring cheekbones making his mouth look small in his
sun-blackened face.

"Hell!" Bragg cursed, stepping away from the horse,
pounding a fist into a giant palm. He looked around,
eyes studying the cottonwoods along the banks of the
Middle Powder. "Which way would they have gone?"

Leander stepped out of the saddle, leading his horse
forward, grateful for the feel of the earth under his tired
legs. A nice spot this, cool water, shady trees, plenty of
grass and wondrous scenery. Ah, if only he could stop—
put France on the warming shelf for a day or two—and
drowse in the sun. Perhaps then he could settle his nagging doubts, redefine his duty to Cavaignac and his
country.

"High Walker, what would you think?" Leander asked,
turning to the Indian, aware Bragg glared at him, uneasy
at the feel of those weird blue eyes on his back. The
memory of Smitty never completely stilled when Bragg
stood behind him. Why did France's destiny have to ride
in the hands of a crazy man? Damn this whole business!

The Indian raised a muscular arm, pointing to the
west. "I think there. They go up Spirit Trail."

"Spirit Trail?" Leander mused. "Like a—a place
Wasatch would head for naturally?"

"Hey!" High Walker smiled happily. "You one smart
pilgrim for a white man." He slapped his thighs, a wide
grin exposing broken yellow teeth. "You betcha!"

"What're you after, Sentor?" Bragg asked. His big
hands worked reflexively, grasping in the air, tendons
standing out on the backs.

"Well, just this." Leander bent down and sketched in
the dirt where the Pawnee had camped and trampled it
soft. "Tell me if I'm wrong, High Walker. They cut off

the trail headed for the Yellowstone back above Reeshaw's Bridge. Now, there's nothing here but these mountains, correct? No major trail a white man would know about anyway. This is off the beaten track to any but an Indian or a trapper. Web Catton trapped. He'd know these mountains like a prostitute knows a mattress. And I'm betting Wasatch does too. How about it, High Walker?"

"He lived here many years." High Walker gave a curt nod. "He'd know'd 'em plumb well."

"And then there's a Spirit trail here." Leander studied the map he'd drawn. "So, I agree with High Walker. I think they'd have gone up the Spirit Trail." He looked curiously at the Indian. "How many passes cross the Big Horns? How many choices of trails do they have?"

"Don't need 'em." Bragg pulled at his beard. "The top's flat like a big park."

"So we could cut for trail across the top?" Leander lifted an inquiring eyebrow. "At least we'd know."

"Get me to Catton," Backman grunted from where he watched.

"Might lose another day," Bragg hedged. "They get Web's legacy too far ahead of us, and I might never get that ring." He shot a quick look at Leander. ". . . Or France's gold, eh?"

"Produce the proof, Branton, and I'm sure General Cavaignac will be *most* grateful." He smiled. "In fact, I would imagine a suitable estate could be yours in France. If you would prefer a return to the life of a gentleman."

*Who am I kidding? This man? A gentleman? How long before the peasants rose and butchered him in his sleep?*

Bragg's smile sent a shiver down Sentor's back. This business of dealing with savages had begun to wear thin on him. "For the glory of France," he whispered under his breath as he turned away, mounting up as High Walker took the lead.

They lined out, trotting westward, deeper into the broken country around the Powder. Gray hills rose to either side, weathered quartzite cobbles spilling down the terraces. Farther back, upthrust ridges rose, aqua-tinted under a mantle of sagebrush, the gullies splashed in bright greens as serviceberry leafed out. The wind rustled in the stately cottonwoods overhead as the land rose even higher to either side.

By that afternoon they passed through a gap where the Powder had cut through a high red-rock wall, the grandeur of it taking Leander's breath. Lush grass flattened beneath his horse's hooves, mashed into rich red soil.

"Eden on earth!" he breathed.

"Spirit Road!" High Walker called, pointing to a long incline of sagebrush that rose to the west like a tabletop set at an angle. The Middle Fork of the Powder cut through a narrow defile immediately north. To the right, their arrival spooked a herd of grazing buffalo that thundered up the valley, red dust curling behind flying hooves.

Like riding a ramp to the sky, Leander thought as they walked their weary mounts ever upward. He turned to look behind, seeing the red deepen as the setting sun bored into the rock. Far to the east, the land began to unfold as they climbed. Nothing had prepared him for this. The glory of the distance locked his eyes to the ever-growing vista.

"*Hoooookaaaiiieee!*" High Walker called, shaking his old flintlock musket over his head as he danced his horse around. "Tracks! Catton tracks!" the Cheyenne yipped. "I find the way. Wasatch travels Spirit Road!"

"Last time that bastard did anything spirit, it scared the hell outa me," Rupe grunted.

"I got me a bad feeling 'bout this," Ames agreed, talking low. "If I thought I could get outa this hyar outfit, I'd cut an' run like sixty. Ain't nuthing up that damn mountain but death."

A premonition? Leander lost the rest of their grumbling as they fell behind. He looked around him. Indeed, spirits were sagging. At least for all but Cal Backman, who grinned to himself as he bent over his saddle to study the tracks High Walker pointed out.

"Spirit Road!" High Walker chanted, pointing to a long line of cairns that traced their way up the mountain no more than thirty paces apart, each almost as tall as a man on horseback.

"How many rocks in each of them?" Leander wondered. "How incredibly old?" The pole standards sticking out reeked of the roosts of ghosts.

Bragg laughed as he watched High Walker carefully stop and place a cobble on each of the piles.

Leander shivered, fighting the urge to do so himself. "Ignorant superstition," he decided, forbidding himself the urge.

They passed that night in the Cattons' old camp.

"Two days ahead," High Walker decided, feeling the ashes of the fire. "They lose time losing Pawnee . . . ha!" His grin lit fires of revenge behind those pebble-black eyes. "I get Wasatch and his bitch-woman sister. That's right, huh, Bragg?"

"Yeah," Branton agreed heavily. "That's right, High Walker. She's all yours."

Leander looked down at his coffee cup. The images of the Indian woman remained hazy in his head. He'd been fevered then, vision blurring, but he remembered being in the lodge. Her hands had been cool, gentle. Very much like Arabella's. And what was an Indian woman to the whole of France? To the future? For that matter, what was Arabella—or himself?

The scorn of Arabella's remark that day on the Big Thompson returned to haunt him. Taking a deep breath, he stood, tossing off the last of his coffee—rationed to a cup a day a man—and walked into the dark, looking up at the stars, awed by the clarity of the air. Like smoke they grayed the sky overhead.

He jumped when Bragg appeared behind him, having approached on soundless feet—incredible for so large a man.

"You worried about something, Sentor?" The raspy voice grated on his very soul. The whole situation proved as insane as the look in Bragg's eye. The destiny of France? Here? He rubbed his eyes.

"Of course," he added truthfully. "We're getting close. Why shouldn't I worry? What if it's all a hoax? What if France's future isn't locked away up here in these mountains? What do I tell my general?"

Bragg shifted, rock grinding loud under his foot. "It's there," he whispered passionately. "When I killed Web, I got a letter out of his pack. He's the one." He shook his head. "Huh! You know, my Laura, she always hid it, used it against me. I remember her saying, 'If only you knew.'" He hitched up his britches. "Well, I know now. I know who Web Catton really was. And it don't make a damn bit of difference. I'd kill him again if I could."

"But the ring wasn't on his body?"

"Naw. I went back after I read the letter just to be sure. Snow was too deep to get in that canyon. Come spring, I went and checked again. Never found his bones but I went over him good that day I shot him. Wasn't no ring on his finger. Wasn't in his possibles or any pocket or hangin' on his neck. No, it's with Armijo's gold. And if it ain't, there'll be something else with it. Some proof.

I just figgered he might have sent it to them bastard kids of his. They don't have it. I could tell."

Out of impulse, he asked, "What of Arabella?"

Bragg looked at him. "What of her?"

"I . . . I know Cal wants her."

"So?"

"So, I would prefer that she not be harmed." He crossed his arms, feeling those eyes he couldn't see boring into him. His throat went dry at the hunching of those thick shoulders. The memory of Smitty, Bragg beating his horse to death, the insane rage that took him, all lent fear to Leander's trembling knees. Yet, honor demanded.

"Huh!" Bragg grunted. "Maybe you'd pay for her?"

Leander tilted his head. "I know you offered Cavaignac all their heads . . . and I . . . well, it's my duty to see he gets them. At the same time, the thought of her suffering—"

"You ain't going soft on me, eh, Frenchy?" Bragg's sibilant hiss loosened his guts.

"No, of course not. It's just that letting men like Backman abuse her first does no honor to France. A gentleman—"

"Bah!" Bragg exploded, waving his hands in the dark. "What do I care of France's honor? Eh? Honor? I want my gold, and my estate outside Paris. After that, honor take the hindmost. Power and money are all you'll find in life, Sentor. And with them, you can buy your honor. With enough of both, people even create your honor for you."

"You've become a cynic, Monseiur Bragg. This savage land has polluted you with its egalitarian ethic."

Bragg laughed—a gut-rumbling sound—as he spread his arms to the night. "Ah, and who was it who cried *Liberté, Egalité, Fraternité*?" He paused. "No, my young friend. Your general and I will see eye-to-eye. Power makes honor. And when I find the Cattons, I shall send them all. As 'the Twelve Who Ruled' sent Marie Antoinette, hum? So shall I send Cavaignac the lovely Arabella."

Leander bowed slightly at the waist. "Very well, that was the deal, wasn't it? At least promise me she will die quickly."

Bragg laughed again. "I'll leave that detail to you. Just don't mess up her head." And with that, he turned, walking away into the darkness.

Leander looked once more at the stars, feeling the cool night breeze on his suddenly hot cheek. "I promised you, my general," he whispered numbly, a sinking sensation in his breast.


"Fascinating," Arabella decided as she stepped down from Efende. "Which people are these?"

"Think they're Sheepeaters. Not many left," Jake told her.

Arabella looked around the shabby camp. "Oh, and why is that?"

"Got me. I don't know much about them," Jake added. "Just heard they lived up here."

Indians had been in the lodges just before they rode up. That much could be seen with a casual inspection. The fires were still smoking and household items had been left as if they'd been dropped. From the looks of things, the evacuation had been quick—and thorough.

The sensation proved eerie—like walking into a town where everyone had vanished.

"More Hoodoos?" Ab asked with irritation as he looked over the little hide shelters and smoking fire pits. Half-tanned mountain sheep hides, bowls made from ram horns, bone fragments, and a scatter of stone flakes lay about. The horn bowls still had soup in some of them. A rudely butchered quarter of elk hung from a fir behind the camp. Scraps of trash, hafted stone tools along with a grinding slab and mano, were set to one side.

Arabella bent to look into one of the small conical huts, seeing hide bedding, woven baskets containing flowers and roots, and bone tools lying about the living floor. Buffalo paunches hung from tripods near the rock-filled fires that heated boiling stones, warm liquid standing while flies buzzed over the whole.

Wasatch rode close. "These are the people who eat sheep. They are a band of Shoshone who live only in the high mountains. They are very rare and very shy. They do not raid or steal. They only stay in the high places and talk to the stars."

"Talk to the stars?" Jeremiel asked. "Yea, but that Satan makes the weak in spirit his unholy prey!"

Bram looked at the primitive tools and the scanty shelters. Jake kept his gaze roaming the surrounding trees, knowing they were under observation.

"Looks like pretty poor doings," Bram muttered, getting off his horse. Ab had shucked his pistol, keeping an eye out for anyone sneaking close enough to let fly with an arrow.

"What are you doing?" Jake asked, ever more nervous as Bram began digging in the packs. Molly tried to step on his foot but Bram proved mule-wary and avoided her.

"Leaving them some tobacco and some of these hyar beads. Hell, they ain't even got a pot to . . ."

"Well, hurry up!" Ab snapped. "I feel like a target here!"

Bram left a bolt of cloth, a couple sticks of tobacco, some beads, and a couple of mirrors. Last he dropped his little cast-iron kettle near the fire. "Reckon that'll help some. Heck, can't have folks cookin' in skin bags all the time." Making a snap decision, he emptied the paunch of stew Lark had fixed the night before into the kettle and put it on the fire to keep warm.

Arabella legged up on Efende and they rode out, looking behind, half expecting to see people appear in the silent doorways. No sound followed them as they rode into a canopy of trees.

"Hell of a place to be ambushed," Ab decided, looking at the shadows to each side. "They could wait up in the trees. We'd be right underneath them and never know what hit us."

"Not the Sheepeaters," Wasatch disagreed. "They met the mountain men years ago. They consider the whites to be magical savages. Fierce men with thunder weapons and animalistic natures to be avoided like demons. Sheepeaters are peaceful, preferring to be left alone to talk with the stars."

"They think *that*? About *us*? And *they* talk with the stars?" Jeremiel glanced quickly at Wasatch before returning his eyes to the forest around them. "How do they do this?"

Wasatch bit his lip, a deep frown on his tanned face. "You know, I'm not sure. I've seen where they build special places high on the mountain. You know, like the tipi rings—but these are for medicine. They look like the wheels off a wagon, with spokes and a hub of rock in the center where the medicine man sings. When the season is right, they sing and pray, dancing along the spokes, talking to the stars."

"A world of heathens," Jeremiel sighed, bending his head to look up at the patches of sky visible between the trees. "Such a beautiful land . . . and all without the loving hand of God."

Wasatch cocked his head, making a gesture with his hand. "I know little about the Sheepeaters, brother

Jeremiel but it is said among some of the holy men of my people that the Sheepeaters believe one day they will be taken up by God, the Great Mystery Above, and taken into the stars."

In the silence Jeremiel refused to break, Wasatch continued, "Tell me is that not a loving hand?"

Jeremiel looked at him, eyes curiously unsettled. "To be frank, brother Wasatch, I no longer know." Sadly, he bent his head forward contemplating his hands, swaying with each step of his black gelding.

Next morning, a skin bag full of steaks hung from a tree outside of camp. The morning after, a beautiful robe made from finely dressed mountain sheep skin with the fur on gleamed golden in the sun where it had been neatly folded over a branch in the night.

"Reckon you made an impression," Ab grunted to Bram, who wrapped that decorated robe around his shoulders like a king.

"He hath given to the poor: his righteousness remaineth for ever," Jeremiel quoted, a smile on his lips. "Can my humble teachings have affected your soul, brother Bram?"

"Reckon not, brother Jeremiel," Bram said with a big grin. "I didn't do nuthin' fer my soul, just some poor folks."

"And what's Wolf been doing?" Jake wondered. "All these strange ghost Injuns sneaking around and he lies by the fire asleep all night."

Wasatch laughed, looking over to where the big animal watched Arabella take her turn fingering the fine hide. "He knows their hearts, brother. Were they evil, he would have told me."

Almost shyly, Bram draped the robe over Lark's shoulders, blushing slightly at her joy at the gift.

The dim trail they followed led up to the highest

point overlooking the Pryors and the broken canyon land below. From there they wound down, the wind almost winter cold as the Big Horn Basin opened before them.

"Down there," Jake pointed. "We're almost there!"

The moon rose full that night. Jeremiel walked out from the sheltered copse of trees where they camped, climbing up the ridge to look out over the moonlit splendor of the basin below.

He dropped to his knees, lost in prayer as the moon silvered the land around him. "Lord," he whispered. "I have witnessed charity in the hearts of the savages. I have stood in awe at the majesty of Your works. What is become of me? What is become of the word I carry to the hearts of the benighted? Here, in this wilderness, I find good mixed with evil. Every question leads a man to a different answer. How many sides do you have, Lord? Are You this *Heammawihio*? Are You this Great Mystery Above? Are You Allah?

"Your commandments tell the Children of Israel to have no other gods before You. Yet we of Christ's blood believe the Father, the Son, and the Holy Ghost to be one. How many ways can man divide the Trinity and still have the same God? How many ways can You, who are Almighty, divide Yourself among the peoples? Have You truly divided Yourself among the house of man, giving each a different teaching? If so, Lord, give me a sign that I might know. The path is crooked here, winding and beset with many pitfalls. How can I, a man of faith, follow?"

He looked up at the thick stars, eyes on the black heavens above.

"Jeremiel?" Arabella called softly.

He turned his head, seeing her where she stood.

"Excuse me." She bowed her head. "I didn't want to interrupt, but maybe you're trying too hard."

He stood, walking over to her, head down, hands clasped behind his back. "I no longer know what to believe. All the ordered concepts, all the truths seem made of sand—and it's raining as if to wash it all away."

She settled herself on a rock, wrapping a blanket tightly around her shoulders against the high-altitude chill. "If I may, could I suggest that you spend more time reading the Gospels, and less time bogging yourself down with the Epistles?"

"I don't understand." He settled next to her, propping his chin on his palms.

She smiled at him, putting her arm around his shoulders. The gesture soothed him, and with a start, he realized he'd never been physically touched by another human being. He blinked, curious at the sensation her caring evoked. Had he truly been so lonely?

"I mean read what Jesus said," she explained. "What message did he bring to mankind? Think about it. If he stood here before you right now, what would he say? How would that man who died on the cross answer you? Isn't the heart of your problem—no, the entire *Christian* problem—Paul? Isn't he the one who dilutes the word of Christ, making up the stupid little rules?" She snorted. "As I read the book, he can't even get straight what happened to him on the Damascus road!"

Jeremiel shivered slightly, a giddy feeling in his gut. "I . . . I don't know. Maybe. I need to think on it. To consider and read."

She hugged him close, adding, "I'm always here if you need someone to talk to, Jeremiel."

She stood, walking back down the hill, head bowed as if lost in thought.

"Wait!" he called, getting to his feet.

She turned, and, with the moonlight on the blanket, he could very well believe he looked at the Virgin herself.

"I . . ." He stumbled, making a desperate gesture with his hands. "Why are you doing this? Why do you want to help me?"

She tilted her head, lifting her shoulders. "You're my brother, Jeremiel. And I . . . well, I guess I know what you're going through. How difficult it is to make peace with God. It's a crooked path like you admitted in your prayer."

They looked at each other in silence while the coyotes yipped and wailed in the distance. An owl hooted plaintively in the night.

"Thank you," Jeremiel said simply. "No one has ever offered to help me before."

She nodded, and he could see her smile in the moonlight. A curious pang filled him as he watched her pick her way back to camp.

"Forever alone," he whispered, and a tear traced down his face.

The sun stood high in a cotton-patch cloudy sky as they crested a summit leading down a high windswept ridge. Wasatch lifted a hand.

"There is Power here. Lead the horses—we will go on foot."

"Huh?" Ab asked, "What sort of Power?"

"More Hoodoos!" Bram muttered.

"Feel it?" Wasatch asked, voice low. Wolf sniffed the wind nervously and the horses stamped.

Ab nodded, climbing down, "All right, on foot."

Jake and Jeremiel both began grumbling, but Ab could see what Wasatch was talking about when he skirted a yawning fissure in the ground and led Sorrel and Molly to the top of the ridge.

A huge stone circle of angular white rocks had been aligned on the ground. What appeared to be spokes radiated out from the middle and slim wooden poles were braced in piles of rock. Each one had a bit of hide with drawn figures flapping in the breeze. Various colors of clay had been placed about inside the ring of rocks.

"Don't step on it," Wasatch cried as Jake was about to walk across the center of the ring. "Walk around!"

Jake's face screwed up funny—but he did as he was told.

"What is it?" Jeremiel asked.

Wasatch had a hand on Wolf's uneasy head as he looked up at the sky. "It is a place where the Sheepeaters talk with the stars. There is much power here."

*"Allahu akbar!"* Arabella called softly. Lark kept her eyes down, watching her feet as she walked past the big stone circle.

Jeremiel hugged his Bible to his chest, lips moving as he mumbled a prayer.

A feeling of unease prickling his back, Ab went around and into the wind to stare over the edge. The view stopped him in his tracks, the whole Big Horn Basin spreading before him. The Pryors crouched below to one side as he looked down.

"I understand why the Sheepeaters chose this place," Ab said, voice hushed in reverence. He felt as if he could reach his fingers up to scrape the sky, although other higher peaks rose in pointed knobs to the east.

"There!" Jake cried, pointing with a straight arm, his very body tensing. "There's where the Big Horn runs through the mountains. See! That cut is the canyon. We're almost there."

Ab looked and it was as if the map in his knife handle had been drawn from the very spot. "Looks like a trail goes down over there." Ab pointed to a ridge that sprawled out leaving a not-too-impossible slope that might lead down to the west and the lowlands where he could make out the ridge they wanted. He couldn't see any big black dot on it, though.

Mounting up, Ab looked back to see Wasatch place the leather he'd drawn the horse raid on next to one of the wooden standards that flapped in the breeze.

Jeremiel watched, a curious smile on his lips. He rode silently for the rest of the day, oblivious, thought lines etching his brow.

They didn't make it down that day—or the next. The trip became a constant battle through tangled timber where deadfalls piled high in the elk trails. Time after time, Ab resorted to the axe to clear the way. The pack animals—Molly in particular—took great delight in trying to scrape the packs off their backs. They broke cinches, breast collars, and britchen bands so that for all intents and purposes, Ab and Bram sewed and spliced their way to the bottom.

Finally, they rode out on a broad juniper and pine-covered flat that stuck out from the side of the mountain. The thin soil sprouted occasional wheat-grass and needle-and-thread grass, while the view remained spectacular. On the west, the flat shelf of the mountain was cut by steep-walled drainages slicing through the limestone cap, dropping incredible depths before feeding the Big Horn River below. One by one they traced out the ridges, noting the irregularities against the one traced on Ab's map.

At noon the next day, Bram came cantering across the flats waving his hat. "I found our ridge!" he whooped, sliding his mare to a stop.

Sure enough, on the western side, it dropped off straight down in sheer, steep walls about a thousand feet to the river. Abriel threw a rock as far out as he could and counted twenty before it clacked into the slump-off way down there. The walls proved straight up and down, lined in different colors and pocked by caves in the limestone.

"Blessed Allah!" Arabella cried, a hand to her heart, her face flushed. "I could see eagles, hawks, and such, sailing far below me."

"So, we made it," Ab said, knowing his father had probably stood at this very point. He watched Bram wing a rock as far as he could, eyes glowing as he watched it drop out of sight, and turned, plucking Lark from the ground and whirling her around, feet flying.

"Now, where do we find the treasure?" Jake asked.

Ab shrugged, grateful for the warm sun on his back. "I guess the best thing is to spread out and look for it. Heck, this thing is as flat as a camp cook's flapjacks! Shouldn't be too hard to find."

But it was. They combed the ridge, up one side and down the other, no closer to finding it that night.

"Do not ride over that." High Walker pointed to the circular rock alignment on the ground. To Leander it appeared an effigy of a carriage wheel.

"Bah!" Bragg growled, leading his men over the peculiar shrine. Leander, suddenly leery, suffered a tension deep within him. Impulsively, he slipped from the saddle, following High Walker's example.

He winced when Cal Backman rode around the circle, knocking the skinny poles out of the neat rock cairns. On the last one, he took the pole up, whirling it around his head to send it flying over the edge of the precipice.

High Walker's features tightened into a sour frown. Nervously he looked around, a mumbled song on his lips. Though he'd omitted the habit for years, Leander crossed himself.

Bragg took up one of the poles, finding a roll of fresh-looking leather on the end. He snorted as he studied the colored page, spit on it, and dropped it to the ground.

"They been here." Bragg placed both hands on the saddle horn and leaned forward. "Tracks head down thataway. Let's get to it."

The feeling of presentiment didn't lessen as Leander turned his back on the pagan shrine. Some feeling of power lay behind him. Now as he rode down the ever-steepening ridge, he could see the tension in High Walker, accented by the way the Indian moved, his black eyes thoughtfully on his white companions.

Not even the sight of axework on the trail lightened the heavy feeling weighing on Leander's mind. Again and again, he suffered the memories of his parents' bodies. And once, late in the day, his imagination caught him by surprise, placing Arabella's face on his mother's corpse.

Next morning, Bram and Wasatch split off and began searching the caves in the cuts under the assumption that the black dot with the fleur-de-lis only indicated they had the right ridge.

Arabella and Lark set about mending tack and making a hearty stew for dinner after filling a pot with water from a nearby seep.

In the meantime, Jeremiel, Jake, and Ab lined out, walking back and forth within sight of each other across the flat ridgetop, looking in the trees, checking the occasional rock that lay on the hard surface.

"Tarnation!" Ab grunted, seeing the thin wash of red dirt over the solid limestone. A feller couldn't even dig in that stuff! How in hob do trees grow on it!"

Ab didn't react to the first gunshot, figuring a deer had jumped up in front of someone and had just ended up in the stew. Then he heard the shouts, and a whole volley of gunfire.

# Chapter 22

They broke out of the trees at a trot, Leander with his rifle at the ready.

"Remember, now, we don't kill 'em until we know where Web's cache is!" Bragg roared. "I want 'em alive at first!"

Leander noticed several of the riders peeling off for the trees. Where would Arabella be? He caught a glimpse of the preacher, Jeremiel. The man's pistol bucked in his hand as Kirby Smith jerked in the saddle, going limp, falling face-first into the dirt.

Leander could see no more, the trees hiding the scene. Nevertheless, the Cattons had been on foot. Hunting. So, the end of the quest lay here. One way or another.

Leander's horse thundered around a juniper and he caught a glimpse of picketed horses, recognizing Arabella's Efende and Wasatch's peculiarly spotted animal.

Pulling up, Leander jumped to the ground, charging into the circle that made the camp. Empty!

He turned on his heels, searching for a sign of Arabella. Foulest luck! She must have been out with the men. He cursed and started back for his horse, hearing the crackle of gunfire.

A shot startled him, coming from behind a screen of juniper. Leander sprinted forward, prickly needles crunching underfoot. Another shot—so close—brought him up short. Carefully he walked around the tree, catching a glimpse of buckskin.

A bullet whistled past his ear, clipping green sprigs from the juniper. Leander stepped around, seeing two of Bragg's thugs running forward. To his surprise, it turned out to be Arabella in the hide dress. She calmly lifted her rifle, firing, the bullet catching the closest man.

Before Leander could react, the second jumped for her, expression a contortion of rage. Smoothly, she swung the rifle, a second discharge erupting in the man's face.

The fellow pitched to the ground at her feet, his face a mask of gore. The first assailant groaned and rolled over, a hand clasping his left breast, bright blood leaking between his fingers.

Arabella turned, raising the rifle. Only quick action saved him as he knocked the barrel aside, its discharge ringing his ear, powder burning into his sleeve, leaving it smoking as he grabbed her close.

A series of Arabic curses filled the air as Arabella kicked and battered at him.

"Hush!" Leander growled in her ear. "Quiet! I've got to get you out of here before—"

"Figgered you'd go for the woman, Sentor!" Bragg boomed as he rode into the little clearing. Behind him, a horse bore a flopping load. Leander swallowed hard, recognizing Jake's body.

Bragg looked about the clearing, seeing the wounded man, his face a ghastly gray now, the blood an unstoppable stream.

"Cut the arteries," Bragg mentioned casually, looking at the other man. "Hell! Blew his whole face off! You do that, Leander?" The eerie blue glint animated his eyes.

Leander closed his eyes, shaking his head, grip still tight on Arabella. With his right hand, he pried the Benjamin Bigelow from her grip. His heart dropped in his chest as he looked into her angry eyes.

"I would have saved you," he added softly. "Now it's too late." In a lower voice he added, "Play along, maybe I can turn you free yet."

"Don't bother," she snapped, lip trembling in disgust. The hatred in her eyes stung him.

Bragg laughed again, motioning. "That their camp there?"

Leander nodded. With a tight grip on her arm, he steered her back toward the camp.

*"Get him!"* Ab heard Bragg yell, and saw him point a finger at him as the riders swirled past in the red dust. Guns cracked and Ab's leg went suddenly limp as he heard the spat of a bullet. Wobbling unsteadily, he ran, diving between three junipers that had grown in a little knot as bullets clipped branches over his head.

Two riders lined out on Bragg's orders. Frantic, Ab ducked down as a ball thocked into the thick wood next to his ear, another plowing up prickly juniper needles by his foot.

He centered his Hawken on a rider's back and triggered it. The world went away in smoke and concussion, the rider stiffening, going slack, and falling from the saddle like a sack of grain.

The second man had wheeled his horse and came at the run. Ab pulled the Dragoon Colt and snapped a shot. The rider ducked down and raced for a little hump of rock. So, that would be the end. The rider would sit there, out of effective pistol range, and riddle Ab's hideaway with the rifle he carried.

Except it didn't work that way. The horse kind of jumped up in the air and opened its mouth—only when it came down, it slipped soundlessly right into the rock . . . *and disappeared!*

Ab bit his tongue to make sure he hadn't passed out from that bullet wound. No kicking feet, nothing! The horse didn't stand up and no rider came hobbling out of a horse wreck. That little hump of rock had swallowed them slick as could be!

Ab shivered from fear, or the wound in his leg—he didn't know which, but it felt like the heebie-jeebies.

"Hoodoos ain't real," he gritted, pulling himself up, propping his weak limb with the Hawken. Bone wasn't broken. Periodic shots racketed in the distance.

"Damn you, Bragg," Ab gritted. "I'm coming, and this time, hoss, it's you or me!" Grimly, he started forward, leaning on his Hawken.

"Found Ames, Mr. Bragg," Simms was saying.

Leander was oblivious as he watched the preacher, head bloody, dropped in a bound heap next to unconscious Jake. "Reckon he's dead. Been shot plumb center. Cain't find hide ner hair of Carter. Whichever Catton boy that was, old Rupe's working out his trail. We found a couple of drops of blood. Looks like he got winged."

"Then he can't be far. Take some of the boys and make a circle on foot. Don't take any chances, just get him here alive. If you do that with a couple of holes in him, that's fine. I just want him to talk for a while." Bragg hesitated and turned. "And watch out for Backman! Keep an eye on him, hear?"

Arabella's lips tightened, she sat straight where her bound arms and legs cramped her. Leander lifted his chin, aware of the daggers she glared at him.

Bragg watched the man leave and smiled queerly at Leander. "Seems the Cattons are saving me money. Cutting the final payoff, eh?" He turned, taking a spilled kettle, splashing the remaining hot water into Jake's face.

"Wake up," Bragg commanded. "You're shamming, seeing if you can buy time. I won't have that!"

Jake's eyes opened, defiant. "What would you know, Uncle? I thought you had all the answers!"

The ringing slapping of flesh caused Leander to flinch. At the grunt the captive made, he looked away.

"Now, Jake, how long have you and your brothers been here?" Bragg's voice was tight, the weird glow behind the eyes.

"Got here yesterday," Jake muttered, his voice sounding strange.

"And have you found the ring and the gold?" Bragg pressed.

Silence. Then more of the slapping sounds. Leander walked to the edge of the camp, seeing Wasatch's wolf slinking through the trees. The slapping continued for a long time before Jake said through a thick voice, "Go ahead, Bragg. Kill me. See what you learn then."

More water splashed. Leander heard Jeremiel groan.

"Ah, preacher," Bragg gloated.

Leander looked back, seeing Bragg squatting before the fire, watching Jeremiel's expression clear. Absently, Leander added a couple chunks of juniper to the fire from where they had been piled to the side.

Through a hole in the trees, he could see High Walker pushing a woman, Calling Lark, before him. So, both the women would be sport for the men? Leander started to look at Arabella and turned away, unable to face her, shame filling him.

He stood, clasping his hands behind him, heart riding in his chest like lead. "Come, Branton," he added wearily. "Get this over with. The sooner we get answers, the sooner we are on our way to Paris."

He saw why Jake talked funny. His mouth had been pulped to a bloody mess, lips smashed and swollen. Bragg dropped the water bucket while Jeremiel shook his head. To his credit, Jeremiel glared hatred, no fear there.

And I'd be shivering in my boots, Leander decided. He turned to look at the three men laid out on the other side of the fire, bloody bandages around their chests. The Cattons didn't go easily, it seemed.

Bragg leaned over Jake and pulled that wood-handled bowie knife from his belt.

"You tell me, Jeremiel." Bragg's beard wagged as he smiled. "Tell me what I wish to know. If you don't, preacher, I shall cut an ear from your brother. Then the other. And a finger. And . . ."

"What you do is Satan's—"

"*Do you understand?*" Bragg's voice thundered; the bowie dropped to quiver over Jake's ear.

Leander's fingers tightened on the knife at his belt. He closed his eyes. If only his duty didn't demand . . .

The thought of his parents' bodies kept haunting him. *I didn't know,* he pleaded to himself. *How could anyone know they would have been there. Yes, we disagreed about politics, but they were wrong! Cavaignac . . .*

He looked up as High Walker, grinning, pushed Calling Lark forward, his rifle gripped in victory before him. Leander hadn't paid attention to the dappled gray mule.

She caught the rifle with both hind feet and smashed it into the Cheyenne's chest, cartwheeling him in the air and dropping him in a heap while she brayed her dissatisfaction to the world at large.

In the sudden turmoil, Leander caught the movement from the corner of his eye. A black square against the sky, it arced from behind the packs, smacking into the fire in a puff of ash. Acting by instinct, Leander grabbed Lark, throwing her down, piling on top of her and Arabella as men jumped to their feet.

The ground jumped. The concussion blew two men over backward and catapulted Branton Bragg right over the top of Jake and into the junipers.

Ears ringing, Leander moved stiffly. With the bowie in one hand, he slashed at Arabella's bonds, jerking her to her feet.

"Go!" he shouted, pushing Lark after her, pointing with his knife. He turned toward Jake and Jeremiel, only to see Abriel, hobbling with gritted teeth, knife in hand. For a split second they stared at each other, waiting, then Leander bent, cutting the preacher loose.

He'd forgotten Molly and the rest of the horses. Panicked by the blast, they ripped the picket loose and bolted through the middle of the men who staggered up. Wasatch's Appaloosa hit Bragg as he got to his feet and knocked him spinning as he hollered orders.

Leander watched the Cattons stumbling into the trees as one of the junipers, which had caught a flying chunk of burning wood, erupted in a gout of flame. In the confusion and smoke, he ran, catching up the reins of his spooked red, vaulting onto the animal's back, leaning down to get his rifle. At that, he turned, spurring his animal, heading back up the trail.

Then he saw Arabella, running with all she had. He

bent from the saddle, grabbing her from behind, swinging her, kicking and screaming, into the saddle.

Out of time! Holding the Hawken one-handed, Abriel shot the black-bearded man through the chest as he came running. Jake, he just threw over his shoulder and—urging Jeremiel ahead—took out like all hell was busted loose behind him. Possibly the case as he looked back to see swirling smoke, ash, and dust, a crater where the fire pit had been. A juniper exploded in flame and a man screamed.

"Most amazing," he muttered hoarsely, "what five pounds of FFg gunpowder does to a fire pit!"

Ab's leg almost buckled, blood tracing hot down his pants to squish between the toes in his boots. From the corner of his eye, he caught a glimpse of Wolf flying through the air, jaws snagging a man who crashed out of the trees after them, pistol raised. Wolf must have ripped his arm out of the socket when his weight hit, dragging him down, the pistol discharging into the ground.

They would have been run down again if not for Wolf. He appeared, leading the way, looking back over his shoulder, urging them on. Ab's pep seemed to drain out all at once. Things were getting a little hazy. All of a sudden, he was on the ground, looking stupidly at that red dirt.

"Ab, get up!" Jeremiel pulled at him.

"Can't!" he gasped. "No gumption left. Get out of here. Go on. Save yerselves."

Jeremiel's strong arms locked around him. Together, his brothers got him up.

"God! Look at the blood! He's hit!" Jake cried. "He's leaving a blood trail they can't miss. Give him to me."

Ab vaguely noted the world turning and he was over Jake's shoulder. Body bouncing like a sack of potatoes, he slipped in and out of focus, sometimes seeing the world all shimmery and other times feeling a sharp stab of pain running up and down his leg.

A bullet made a *thussshhh* past his ear and Jeremiel jerked the Colt from his belt. Ab barely heard it bang loudly from one side.

"Jake!" Bram cried from somewhere.

Another pair of arms grabbed him. He experienced a sensation of falling that proved beyond his power to prevent. A gunshot cut the haze and everything filled with gray. His final conscious thoughts made him feel like he was underwater, looking through the waves at the world.

"He's awake." Wasatch leaned over, a hand placed to check for fever.

"Anything to drink?" Ab croaked, and Wasatch placed a skin to his lips.

"Go easy on that, Ab. It's all we got." Wasatch checked the compress on his leg, eliciting a groan.

"Everybody all right?" Ab asked, trying to sit up.

A spat-wing noise was followed by chips of roof rock clattering around.

"We're all here," Wasatch assured. "Everyone but Arabella. She's . . . Well, we don't know. You got a bit of fever and the wound's inflamed. I think you'll make it."

"What happened?"

"We're holed up in one of those caves in the side canyons." Wasatch leaned back on his haunches. "Bragg's men are out and about. Cal Backman is out there, hopping mad, shouting insults at you. When they put their heads up too high, we chase 'em back down with a bullet. Jeremiel says that's quite a rescue you pulled off."

"Yeah," Ab rasped. "Don't know what Sentor's angle is. He cut Arabella and Jeremiel free while I got Jake. Wolf showed up at just the right time, too."

Wasatch hugged his knees, amber eyes thoughtful. "Bragg says if we'll tell him where the gold and the ring are, we can go free. We've been talking; it might be worth it. We only have so much powder and shot left. You have all the water."

"He can't have it," Ab decided. "I found it. I know where it is. Wasatch, I'll die before I let that man have it."

"You sure, Ab? Might be our ticket out of here." His voice was soft. It didn't condemn, but it simply accepted.

"Heck, yes!" Abriel frowned. "The man killed our father! He's hounded us from one end of the country to the other. He's hired men to kill us and caused us nothing but grief. I'm getting a little mad, Wasatch. Why should we let him run over the top of us like this? Who in hob's kingdom does he think he is anyway?"

"Our uncle!" Jake's voice echoed from the mouth of the cave.

"How's Jake doing?" Ab asked, inclining his head.

"I'm fine, thanks to you." A cocky note filled his voice. "Wish we had a spring and that powder you blew up. We're short of rifles."

Spat-wing! A couple of chunks of roof made a clacking as they hit the floor.

"Any other way out of here?" Ab asked.

Wasatch laughed. "I don't know. Things have been busy here. If Wolf was here, he could check that hole out. It's kind of small for a man, and on the other side it's real black and dark."

Ab craned his neck and looked. Sure enough, a black gap could be seen between the roof and the mound of fill dirt that rose from the floor of the cave almost to the ceiling.

Bram crouched over and darted back. "I been trying to get Jake to let me take a look. Shucks, back in Arkansas we hid in lots of caves. That was limestone country back in the Ozarks."

"So, go!" Ab stuck a thumb toward the hole. "Just be careful!"

Jake's voice drifted back. "We thought maybe we'd get a chance to get out of here. If that was the case, we didn't need anybody back in that hole. If we go, we have to go fast and together."

"And does that look like a real live and kicking option, brother Jake?" Ab asked, slightly sarcastic.

Jake kept that cheerful sound. "Reckon not, brother Abriel."

"You sound like you're enjoying yourself!"

"I am!" he chortled. "Why, here I am, burning more powder than any other officer in the army. It's a desperate situation. I'm surrounded, outgunned, and outnumbered. This is the time for a shining young West Point graduate to snatch victory from the hands of defeat."

Ab rolled his eyes and looked at Bram. "Go see where that hole goes. And Bram"—Ab took his hands—"be real careful. There's lots of holes that drop out from under you in these hills. I've seen 'em swallow a man and horse into blackness."

"You betcha you be careful!" Lark called sharply, shaking a finger at him. "We got business you and me!"

Bram gave her that endless grin. "I'll be careful. I promise."

Smack-wing-clatter! Another bullet left a gray streak on the roof.

"Gonna marry you," Lark added as Bram was swallowed by the hole.

Time began to drag. The shadows on the other side of the canyon lengthened until the far wall turned gray and the light faded into night. A whole string of bats came boiling out of the hole Bram had disappeared into.

Jeremiel shook his head and closed his eyes to offer a prayer.

Jake—a bloody cloth wrapped around his head—faded back to the rear along with Wasatch. The fire had burned down and Wasatch didn't replenish it from the pack rat junk that lay about. Firelight would have given Bragg's boys a silhouette to shoot at.

In blackness they waited. Another shot smacked into the roof. In Jake's hands, Ab's rifle erupted fire and sparks, and while he rolled away, bullets pattered into the dirt where he'd been.

An hour, maybe three, passed before a scraping came from behind and Bram's voice called out from the inky back of the cave.

"Come on. There's a way. Reckon it'll be kinda rough on Ab. Floor's real uneven and there's a couple of holes that drop clear down to hell."

"You found a way out?" Jeremiel's voice echoed hope.

"It's a way." Bram's voice carried reservation and a little hesitation.

Outside, a man screamed, shots rattled. Wasatch's voice betrayed relief. "Wolf is there. They will live in terror of the darkness."

"Blessed be that animal!" Jeremiel muttered in his deep preacher voice. "I'd begun to fear that he might have fallen prey to their guns."

"We're gonna fear the darkness too," Bram warned. "It ain't an easy climb outa hyar!"

Jake hesitated. "I . . . I don't like black holes. I used to dream about . . . about being buried alive when I was a kid. I'd wake up screaming in the night. I don't want nothing to do with any pits in the darkness. I'll die here, thanks."

"Pray tell, brother," Jeremiel asked quietly, "did you dream of Branton Bragg cutting pieces from your body?

For us, verily do I believe salvation will require that we pass through hell. Yea, the strong of heart will bypass the evil of Satan." Conviction had returned to Jeremiel's voice. "Come, brother Wasatch. Follow Bram's lead and help Abriel. Jake and I shall follow and make sure Ab doesn't fall or lose his wits in the blackness."

"Cuss you, I'll be fine. Just git me to my feet!" Ab turned to Lark, muttering, "The nerve of them. You'd think I was some kind of skinny kid or something."

As Lark helped him up, he came close to fainting like a blushing bride.

After he got his wits, the pain came. Abriel remembered sweat dripping down his face and how wringing wet his shirt became. He fought the urge to lie down and let darkness wash over and through him. It would have been so easy to give up there in the eternal night.

Jake's voice pierced Ab's mind, laced with the fear he tried so hard to cover up. Jake was the one who helped Ab over the place Bram had found where the floor dropped into bottomless emptiness. Their feet traced a little ledge and he could feel Jake's muscles trembling and how clammy his hands were as he helped Ab's swaying body pass that section by leaning out over the eternal blackness to keep him from falling.

Ab could remember Wasatch singing a medicine song and translating it into English while Jeremiel muttered "Amen." Their words began to sound hollow in his head and the fight became centered on keeping mind and body together.

The way out turned out to be a man-sized shaft that rose to starlight above. The tricky part was that the cavern dropped off into a huge gaping hole—the end of the line.

Bram dropped a stone down and it rattled and clattered and banged for minutes.

"Folks," Bram began, "we don't want to slip." And there wasn't any Bram humor in it.

"Go on up," Jake said. "I'm the strongest after Ab. I'll take the bottom."

"You know what it means if he slips?" Jeremiel's voice boomed back in the blackness.

"Get up there!" Jake's voice came tight, strangled.

"Sure hope Arabella's all right," Bram mumbled. "Come on, Lark, I'll be right behind you. Feet shuffled in the blackness.

Then the starlight disappeared.

Ab couldn't help much when his turn came. Body numb, he could feel blood leaking down his leg again. His brothers pulled him up that narrow chimneylike hole. Jake—last in line—braced himself over black eternity and grunted as he heaved Ab up.

Abriel tried. He braced his body when he could, but his mind kept wandering and he'd lose his hold and slip. Jeremiel fought to hold him from above, a hand knotted in Ab's shirt while Bram in turn held him. Everybody braced to keep Ab from falling down on top of Jake.

He'd never forget Jake during that climb. Ab could hear him swallowing his fear down there underneath his sweaty, bloody body—and he knew that drop widened forever in his mind. The blackness began reaching up, wrapping itself around his straining legs where he braced and slipped on the rounded sides of that shaft.

Abriel gasped, trying to find air to breathe in the plugged shaft. When he exhaled, he could feel it bounce hot off the wall before his face. They were trapped in a stinking blackness buried in rock—entombed in the earth.

He tried to force his body to help—to get all that thick muscle to work for him, to lessen the strain on Jake, who literally lifted Ab's two hundred pounds straight up. Jake's boots sought any purchase, his back and knees wedged against Ab and gravity. Through his haze, Abriel could feel his brother's muscles trembling.

"Blast!" Bram's voice came down, throttled by the bodies above. "If we only had a rope!"

Abriel caught himself when Jake slipped and fell. Lights flashed in his brain as he wedged himself there in the darkness and heard Jake's whimpering cry from below. Gasping, he couldn't speak.

"Jake?" Jeremiel's voice boomed fear. *"Jake?"*

"I'm all right!" It came softly, muffled by Ab's sweaty flesh. "I caught myself. Hands won't ever be the same, but I'm stopped. Let me get my breath."

The muscles in Abriel's back started to spasm. He bit his lip until the blood ran, pain forcing him to keep his back stiff against the wall. Jeremiel's fingers wound through his shirt in a different grip and Ab felt sweat drip off Jeremiel's nose and onto his cheek. He was muttering a soft prayer.

Thankfully, he heard the scuffing sound and Jake's hands shoved while Ab scrambled. Dirt rattled down the sides of the walls and trickled onto his hot shaking body. It got in his eyes and he blinked tears and tasted earth, the smell of blood and sweat and fear clogging his nose.

"Near the top," Jeremiel assured, breath coming in gasps.

Ab could feel his fingers slipping and he kept having to stop and get a new hold. Below, Jake could be heard panting like a foundered horse. Ab fought the sudden urge to vomit in that narrow coffin space.

. . . And Jeremiel was out and the stars were bright over Ab's upturned face and four sets of hands lifted him up and onto the ground. Back firmly on the prickly grass, he felt the cool breeze on his cheek. Jake came next, kicking weakly, from the earth to lie heaving for breath beside him.

The wetness on Abriel's face was tears. The taste of blood in his mouth mixed with the gritty dirt that had fallen down. His leg ached, a numb pathway of agony.

He reached out weakly and took Jake's hand. "Guess I owe you one, brother."

"Paid in full from this afternoon," he got in between gasps. "Can't tell you how scared I was when Bragg had that knife to my head."

"About as scared as I was in that hole!" Ab squeezed his hand and saw him flinch. Then he noticed how the skin had been ripped from the palms stopping that fall.

"Wasatch," Ab called softly, "see to Jake." Then everything went hazy again and he shimmered off to empty restful bliss.

Bram moved on cat feet, hands out for balance. The guard nodded, lifting his head periodically to stare at the fire.

Fool! The action left him night blind on top of being half-asleep. Swallowing hard, Bram looked over the packs, most of them completely rifled now. Bram hunched behind the one he needed. He nodded to Wasatch where his brother padded on moccasined feet. With careful fingers, he picked up the articles he needed—wary eyes on the guard—and stashed them away.

One of the wounded men moaned and Bram ducked behind the bulk of the pack. The guard straightened, eyes uneasy as he looked at the tossing form under the blanket. Nevertheless, within minutes he was nodding again.

Wasatch hunched, settling beside the man, knifepoint pricking the man's neck as Wasatch whispered in his ear.

The guard stiffened, nodding slowly as the keen edge tickled the front of his throat.

Satisfied, Bram moved to one side, seeing the gleam of metal in the firelight.

Where were the rest of Bragg's . . . ah, of course, watching the cave mouth where all the Catton family remained trapped. Bram grinned into the night, looking around—seeing no Arabella tied up anywhere. He picked up one gun at a time, treading lightly. He lifted the several powder flasks and bullet pouches. Last, he got Jeremiel's Bible and he lifted the pack over his shoulder, catching up the final horse tied at the picket and leading it into the dark before throwing the pack over its back. Behind him came Wasatch, knife still held to the passive guard's quivering throat.

"Where's Arabella?" Wasatch hissed. *"Tell me!"*

The guard whimpered, knees sagging in fear. "D-Don't know. G-Got a-away." He swallowed, skin sliding under the blade. "I swear!" Tears had begun to trickle down his face in the moonlight.

"Tie him," Bram hissed. "He ain't lying."

They left the guard hog-tied, winding their way back into the night.

Jake picked a spot with an incredible view where he could see the trail below and control any attempt by Bragg's men to climb it. Wasatch managed to come up with game out of thin air.

Ab's leg had started to mend and itch and Wasatch had somehow killed the infection with all the various concoctions he'd been plastering on it. Stubbornly, Ab had climbed on crutches for two days, which helped as well as hurt.

"Oh, we're a sight!" Bram chuckled.

The remains of Jake's shirt bandaged his head. His

mouth scabbed over and bruised where Bragg had pounded on him. His hands were wound up in more of the stuff. Jeremiel's head was bound up where they'd laid his scalp open, making him tractable enough to throw on a horse. Wasatch had a bullet graze along his arm and Bram, somehow, looked as ragamuffin as always.

"Think they'll find the gold?" Jeremiel asked, settling himself on his belly to look out over that flat they'd fled.

"Nope," Ab said, shaking his head. "That hole can't be seen for more than ten feet in any direction. We would have walked right past it that day and it'd still be hidden if that fool hadn't ridden his horse into it."

Jeremiel took a deep breath. "I've been somewhat of a trial for everyone. I mean, well, with all the moralizing and preaching and all."

Ab squinted, pulled what little was left of his chew from a torn pocket, and carefully sliced it in half. "Well, now, don't go riding yourself—"

"Thanks, but I know how I've been." Jeremiel pulled his Walker Colt from his belt and checked the loads. "Arabella suggested I read the gospel for what my Lord meant. He didn't mean bombast and narrow-minded dogma. I've seen right and good come from the actions of Wasatch—I never gave him a chance. My sister is Moslem—and she pardoned me, showed me charity—a most Christian thing."

"Now, don't go—"

"But I must." Jeremiel smiled, running fingers down his pistol. "I've been asking God for the answer to my problems when I needed to look within myself. You see, I'd always been alone, Ab. Never had anyone care for me until I met all of you. Do you have any idea what it's like to suddenly have a caring family? If you've been alone all your life, untouched by loving hands. It can be a frightening thing."

"And you thought your preaching proved your worth," Ab supplied.

"Yes." Jeremiel lowered his head. "I couldn't think of any other way."

Ab nodded. "I think we all understand that. And brother?"

"Yes."

"You'll never be alone again."

Silence stretched.

Jeremiel swallowed loudly. "Arabella's down there somewhere. I owe her."

Ab spit out a stream of tobacco. "My leg's feeling a sight better. I don't know what it is that Wasatch has been putting in them poultices, but it sure seems to do the trick. Reckon it won't be long before I'm ready to wander down there and kick old Branton's butt good and hard."

Jeremiel smiled wickedly. "And when you go, brother Abriel, I shall stand beside thee to smite the heathen." His long fingers clicked the cylinder over to the empty chamber and like lightning, that big wicked-looking Colt slid into its holster.

# *Chapter 23*

*A*rabella nipped at her lip while she waited, nervous, aware of the far-off echoes of gun-fire. Absently, she slid another stick into the crackling blaze. "So what now? Am I supposed to believe the dying protestations of love you made at Big Timber? Fall into your arms like the Sabine women?" She raised an eyebrow.

"No," Leander sighed. "I just couldn't let Cal Backman do as he wanted. I don't know what to do with you now."

She crossed her arms over her chest, leaning forward at the waist. "But you'll sit back and watch my brothers die?"

He leaned on his rifle and looked into the night. "I don't know what's right anymore, but my duty demands. Believe me, if there were another way, I'd—"

She was on her feet. "*Another way?* Another way to

*what*, Leander? Why does a French intelligence officer care about Web Catton's gold anyway? France has no . . ." She stopped, thinking. "Or have you gone off on your own? Become an adventurer? A freebooter? Does the promise of gold lure you more than national honor?"

He turned to look at her, asking weakly, "Honor?" He barked a sharp laugh, throwing his hand up helplessly. "Tell me, Arabella, what's honor? How do you pin it down? During the past weeks I've heard so many people talk of honor . . . and always, it's different. No, I'm trying to do my duty for my general and for my country."

"Cavaignac?" she asked, an eyebrow lifted. "He's your general? Such a delightful man! We saw his handiwork in Algeria!"

"Damn!" he cried, face working as he continued. "How can a country—any country—continue to grow with mob rule? How can we bring civilization to the Arabs when they ride out of the south Sahara and rape, plunder, and pillage? Order is essential for civilization! Essential!"

"And my family?" she demanded, wincing at the echoes of another rifle shot. "My brothers may be dead or dying out there! Now! Here! On this very mountain! What in the name of Allah does that have to do with order?"

He raised his arms, calming her. "Because if Bragg's claims are correct, you—you're a threat to France. All of you."

Her mouth dropped open. Speechless, she stared at him for a full thirty seconds before slowly shaking her head. "I don't believe I'm hearing this."

Leander took a breath and began, "In 1793, the Twelve Who Ruled decreed life and death in Paris. They—"

"And a freighter . . . a horse thief . . . an Indian . . .

and a preacher *are threats to France?*" Arabella cried in disbelief. *"You've lost your mind!"*

"There was a child," Leander continued. "The youngest son of—"

"You're in *America!*" she insisted, cutting him off. "All right, James and I smuggled guns to the Arabs. I admit it. That was the business we were in. Besides which, as L'Ouverture's son, he had no love of France to begin with. Any chance we could find to cut an imperial throat, the better off the people were for our efforts. So take it out on me and let my brothers—"

"I didn't come here for James!" Leander told her in a huff. "I just happened to spot him in Paris and recognized him. I had no idea you were involved in the present affair."

At the sound of another shot, Arabella turned. "I'm going to help my brothers," she informed him shortly. "You can come or stay as is your whim."

"No. You will not interfere," he added, dropping his voice. "I won't allow it." He stepped to block her.

"Won't allow it?" She looked up at him, fire in her eye. Flinging out a pointing finger, she hissed, "Wasatch is out there! Duty? Honor? *He saved your damned life!*"

He flinched, closing his eyes. "I . . . I would. Only it's impossible. My duty stands before me." He seemed to wilt, crumbling inside.

Confused, Arabella cocked her head. "Duty? You keep talking about that. I have a duty, too, to my family."

"Families don't matter!" he cried. "What's a family? What are you or I against the needs of an entire country? An entire civilization? Don't you understand? People don't matter when entire societies are at stake!" His fingers tightened around the muzzle of his rifle until the knuckles whitened.

"The hell they don't," she spat, trying to duck past him.

He caught her arm and spun her around. "That's right, the hell they don't! Let me tell you something. General Cavaignac took me as a fumbling boy and raised me out of the dirt. That's right, I was a street urchin—the son of a cabinetmaker of all things. Cavaignac saw beyond that, saw to my training and gave me a command in Algeria." His eyes blazed into hers. "Some of the men I was responsible for died from the very weapons your beloved James smuggled them! You understand that?"

He swallowed his rage, seeing the defiance in her eyes. "Anyway, you talk of duty. The general gave me that chance, turned me into a gentleman, a man of promise. That same dream should belong to anyone in France. We can't afford symbols now."

"Where were your parents during all this?" She stepped back from him, wary.

"Supporting Thiers and his radicals. Then when the violence broke out in 1848, they joined the rioters when the National Workshops were dissolved. They helped build the barricades during the June days."

She pursed her lips, arms crossed. "Sounds like you were on opposite sides. Your Cavaignac brought in troops to quell that rebellion."

He stiffened, face tightening. "Yes, he did. I was one of them."

Eyes narrowing, she watched the pain in his face. "Care to talk about it?"

He shook his head, dropping his chin. "No, the need for words is . . ." He shot a quick look at her and swallowed dryly. "I . . . I ordered one of the barricades removed. My men went forward. The rioters resisted. Rocks were thrown. One of my men got his head bashed in. I ordered them to open fire. We finished them off with bayonets. And then, when I'd seen to the wounded and walked up to supervise the removal, there they . . . they . . ." He blinked hard and looked away.

"My God," Arabella whispered. "You didn't know? Couldn't you see them?"

He shook his head. "Bonfires were everywhere. Some of the buildings were burning. The smoke was thick—the wind against us."

He dropped to sit on a long-dead juniper trunk. "So, I have my duty. If the state is orderly, parents do not end up dead at the hands of their sons. Revolution breeds horrors, Arabella. France can't afford any more." He looked up, pleading. "You see? My duty to my country sent me to kill my own parents to restore that order. The general did the right thing, bringing peace to Paris. I know. I was there. But they . . . my parents can't have died for nothing! It's my job to see it never happens again!"

She paused, thoughtful in the silence, shaking loose from his grip. "A most interesting justification. Twisted, but I can see how it makes sense to you." A piece of firewood burned through and tumbled out of the hearth. Carefully she toed it back in. "You don't have to accept the responsibility that way. Instead, an ideal—blameless—takes the guilt. Shining Cavaignac becomes the embodiment of that ideal. Serve the ideal and you never need face yourself."

"Stop it!" he cried, jumping to his feet, face panicked, grabbing her arms, bending her backward to stare into her eyes. "You don't understand! Sacrifices have to be made!"

She looked into his eyes, daring, taunting. "Then sacrifice me," she challenged.

Leander's breathing came heavily. "I can't." As if against his will, he bent down to kiss her on the lips.

Ab saw the Indian as he hobbled back toward camp. He wore loosely wrapped mountain sheep skins. His complexion had been burned black from sun, wind, and blazing snowfields. Glinting black eyes didn't waver when they met Abriel's. Instead, he nodded and beckoned in a swinging motion, then, without looking back, left at a trot.

For a brief instant, Ab hesitated before he hopped, hobbled, and hitched after him at his best speed. The Indian realized Ab did his best, waiting for him but never letting him get close.

Ab reassuringly patted his Colt, ducking the thick limbs of fir and spruce, wincing his way over the deadfall. He looked uneasily through the black timber, knowing how easily he could be ambushed.

The Indian appeared again, standing on the other side of a small clearing of trees. He gestured down a narrow path and jogged away, uphill out in the open, oblivious to Ab's panting, awkward advance.

Ab stopped at the narrow elk trail and looked into the thick black tangle of fir trees. The Sheepeater was still headed up, not even looking back. A trap?

Catching his breath, Ab pulled his Colt and sighed. Carefully, a step at a time, he entered the shadowy path, stiff-legging over the deadfall, eyes searching everywhere, even up into the trees. Nothing. Only the twittering of the birds and shafts of bright yellow sunlight poked through the green and gray world.

"They could pepper my hide with a pincushion of arrows before I could even find a target." Ab's mouth had gone dry.

One of the little gray squirrels almost got shot off a branch when he bounced out, chattering and chirruping.

Ab swallowed his heart back where it belonged. Cautiously he walked on.

The timber opened into a little enclosed meadow. Some saplings had been placed across the path and there—in that natural corral—were Molly, Sorrel, and the rest of the horses.

Ab chuckled to himself and nodded. Old Bram did them right well when he left that kettle for the Sheepeaters. They had reckoned the horses gone for good since Molly'd left. That, or Bragg's boys had rounded them up.

Ab felt like he had the world by the tail as he rode into camp.

"Where did you come across them?" Bram demanded, running to his deep-chested roan.

"Sheepeaters penned 'em up in a little meadow over yonder. Reckon when we pull outa here, we'll leave 'em anything we got left," Ab replied, stepping off Sorrel and wincing as his leg jammed into the ground. Quickly, he checked them over, finding a couple of scratches here and there. Molly even seemed glad to have him cussing at her again.

"Horses look real rested," Jake observed.

"So do we," Jeremiel added.

"Arabella's down there somewhere," Wasatch reminded. "Wolf is with her. I feel it."

"You boys figure you'd like to ride out of hyar on our own saddles?" Bram asked.

"I got me some talking to do to that Bragg." Jake's expression went black. "If he's hurt Arabella . . ."

Ab raised a hand. "Hold up. We go riding down there looking for trouble and somebody's gonna get shot. I don't mind but . . . well, I ain't interested in burying any of you. I say, find Arabella. Get in, get whatever's in that hole . . . and get out."

"What about Bragg?" Jeremiel asked.

Ab shrugged. "I don't know. On the one hand, he needs hanging. On the other"—he met their eyes one by one—"do we really want to live with the knowledge that we killed our own uncle? Boys, I'm thinking on down the road a piece. That's something that weighs on a man. I say pull the skids out from under him . . . and leave him be."

"He'll come after us," Jake pointed out. "He's convinced that having us dead will profit him."

"You want to be the one to shoot him?" Ab asked. "I can't stop you, Jake. I won't. But I ain't gonna have nothing to do with killing him."

Jake threw up his arms. "Oh, tarnal grief, all right. Let's get our outfit and get out of here!"

"And you're staying here." Bram insisted, pointing a knobby finger at Lark. "We don't come back and you make tracks back to the Cheyenne. Got that?"

"I go with—"

"No," he insisted stubbornly, taking her in his arms, looking down into her face. "If I have to fight, I can't take time to worry. I . . . aw, hell, I couldn't stand it if you caught a bullet down there. Wait for me. I'll be back. Promise?"

She nodded, not liking it one bit.

So they rode, five battered angry men, each with his own thoughts as they led the horses down the bad places and rode bareback out onto that limestone-covered flat. In the bright moonlight, Ab found the gaping black hole, locating it from the coyote-chewed body of the man he'd shot.

Ab pointed. "Be careful. When that fella rode his horse in there, I dropped a rock. Sounded like a hundred fifty feet at least."

Jake thoughtfully fingered the weathered fleur-de-lis that had been carved into the soft limestone.

Bram had his arm over the edge. "I don't like this. I feel Hoodoos down there. Wait. Uh, got a spike here. It's rusty and that's a rope on it."

"Who's gonna lean over that and pull them spikes?" Jake asked, face going pale as he looked into that black emptiness.

"I'll do it," Ab said. "I saw how them spikes was put in in the daytime. I know what to do. But dang me if I know how Web Catton pounded 'em in."

Wasatch had a short length of rawhide rope he'd put together, and with that tied around Ab's ankles and everybody else sitting on his feet he leaned over that black emptiness and felt the cool air rising out of that hole.

His mouth went dry as he thought about the rider down there in the blackness—maybe still sitting on that horse. *His dead eyes might be looking right up into mine.* His heart had started to beat and he could smell a slight whiff of death blowing into his nostrils.

The first spike to meet his fingers felt cold, damp, and clammy as he got a fist knotted around it and took up the rope that hung down. A heavy weight jerked loose and almost dragged him in as the spike came out.

The vigorous energy that comes with fear helped Abriel pull the heavy rope out of the hole. Wasatch took it, muscles knotting under the strain.

Ab wiggled to a new purchase on his belly and reached for the second spike. Like ducking into an abyss, he could feel the cold fingers of the dead caressing his cheek. The dank odor from below caught in his throat.

Did the blackness move? Even as he fumbled at the spike, did something rotten twine through the blackness reaching for him?

A fluttering passed his ear, cool air pattering his neck.

Ab jumped, crying out.

"Bat," Bram gasped hoarsely.

Leaning over the blackness, he could hear the gravel they knocked loose clattering hollowly down there in the dark. In his imagination it fell onto that dead man.

The next bundle proved even heavier; but he was ready this time. Then he crawled to the next, and the next, and then they were all out, sitting there like black lumps, coils of rope piled beside them.

"That's it, boys. That's what our father left us." Ab rubbed his forehead, feeling how warm it was. "Never gonna lean over that hole again."

Bram did an excellent job of lashing the bundles onto Molly and another pack animal. The knots wouldn't hold long, but the idea was to get saddles back in jig time.

The old camp lay quiet and abandoned when they came sneaking in through the trees. Then Wolf appeared, creeping out of the shadows, and whimpered into Wasatch's hands.

"This way!" And Wasatch led them off to the west. There, along the edge of the canyon rim, a small fire burned.

Ab dug elbows into the prickly duff under the junipers and inched forward, Jake to one side, Jeremiel to the other. Bragg had chosen a better position for defense—but it also proved a dead end. To their backs lay that horrible sheer wall that fell away a thousand feet to the torturous rapids of the Big Horn.

Jake got to his feet and motioned. The guard—looking owlishly down the end of Jeremiel's revolver—was taken totally by surprise. Bram began picking up rifles, pistols, and knives, sailing them out into the night and over the edge of that drop before any of Bragg's men even came awake.

"Don't make a noise," Jake warned. "We could start shooting anytime. Now, you wouldn't want that, would you?"

Branton Bragg rose to his feet. "So, you returned?" He moved carefully forward and kicked a log into the fire. "I thought you would have run."

"Where's Arabella?" Wasatch demanded, eyes narrowed to slits. In the firelight, he and Wolf looked so very much alike.

"You hurt her any," Bram threatened, "and none of you will leave this mountain alive. I promise—"

"Not here," Bragg grumbled. "Think she cut and run with that Sentor. Now I gotta bone ta pick with that one."

"You're twisted in the head," Jake told him. "I don't know why our mother ever stood up for you. Web would have done mankind a favor if he'd shot you long ago."

Bragg stiffened. "You don't mention her name, bastard child! She was too good for the likes of you." And his eyes turned ugly, careless. He started for Jake, fingers reaching.

Fear triggered Ab's responses. Hardly realizing what he'd done, the Hawken came up. A thing alive, the barrel smashed into Bragg's jaw with a loud snap. The big man's head whipped back under the blow and he dropped, poleaxed.

"He'll kill you for that," Cal Backman muttered from the side, eyes glittering hate.

"You shut up!" Ab barked, scared by what he'd done, remembering Jeff, who he'd killed so long ago back down the trail.

"Bram, see to the saddles!" Jake ordered.

Ab bent down quickly and felt Branton Bragg's head.

His jaw seemed unbroken and his breathing was all right. He sighed as he straightened.

Wasatch and Bram had the saddles packed and were pulling handfuls of tack from around the fire.

"I owe you a lot of grief, Ab Catton." Backman's voice turned deadly. "You'd better hope Branton kills you first 'cause he just wants you dead. I want you to suffer first."

"Shut up," Ab growled again, feeling himself heating up. A ring of faces stared up at them. The wounded ones didn't look any too good.

"That's about it," Bram called, terse.

Ab snagged up his coffeepot from the fire and backed away. "Listen, boys. Don't try and follow us." He cocked his head. "We've been chased, shot at, hurt, and plain pushed up against the wall. If any of you do that to us again we'll kill you just like it was a war. Understand?"

Heads nodded slightly but Ab caught the bitterness in Cal Backman's eyes. Then he slipped into the darkness, hobble-running for Sorrel.

"I ain't sure we shoulda throwed all them guns over the edge. Reckon that leaves 'em in the bind." Bram shook his head.

"They brought trouble on us," Jake said softly.

"Amen." Jeremiel's voice had a defiant ring. "Let them place their faith in the Lord God! Yea, He shall stand in judgment of their souls and fates. In Him lies salvation!"

"And where's Arabella?" Bram demanded, looking around nervously. "We can't leave 'til we find her!"

"Let's get Web's loot out of here. Leave it in our camp. We can come back, spread out, see if we can find her."

The sun silhouetted the Big Horns in bars of white light against the blue vault of the sky as they climbed back up the steep trail, leading the horses through the rough spots, taking their time. Below, Ab could see the animals they'd let loose on the flats. Bragg's men were chasing them down one by one. But try as he might, he could see nothing of his sister. No fire, no animal, nothing.

"Where is she?" Jake asked, face lined. "I'd give all of what's in those packs to get her back."

Wasatch called, "Wolf says don't worry."

"Sure," Jake snapped. "Wolf says!"

"Relax," Ab called. "Growling at ourselves won't help to find her."

Tired, dispirited, they made the final bend, to see their camp.

"I'll be jiggered!" Ab cried.

"Arabella!" Bram spurred his roan forward, leaping off to hug her. Jake unloaded next, tearing her away, almost crushing her in his embrace. Wasatch sat on his Appaloosa, leaned forward, a curious smile on his face. He looked down at Wolf and shook his head expressively.

Wolf sat, eyes drooping half-lidded as he yawned.

"What happened?" Jake demanded.

Arabella shook her head, motioning with her hands. "It's a long story. You won't belive who Bragg thinks we are. Anyhow, Web seems to be—"

"Uh," Ab interrupted, seeing Leander Sentor to one side, looking on hesitantly. "I don't want to be a spoiler, but we got what we came for. Let's make tracks before Bragg can organize."

Within minutes, Lark and Bram had things packed, Arabella was mounted on Efende again, her shining rifle back in its place in the rifle boot.

After a hard day's ride—and a brutal ascent up the trail—they unloaded the weary animals. Fatigue reflected from everyone's eyes. Molly took her customary roll and stood up, nodding on her feet. Dinner went down in subdued silence, with Bram and Jeremiel dropping off to sleep. Wasatch prowled the dark for a while, then entered the light of the fire and rolled up in his blanket, Wolf making a big ball of fur at his feet.

"Think they'll follow?" Jake asked, baggy eyes thoughtful where he gazed at Arabella's bedroll.

Ab shrugged absently. "Cal Backman will. I think Branton Bragg will, too. The others, who knows? I only counted six men there last night and three were looking real bad. They won't be able to move the wounded."

"Bragg'll leave them to die," Jake sniffed. "So, where does it end? What's the purpose of all this?"

"If it would bring us any peace, I'd vote to give him the gold. But there's something more at stake that drives him." Ab chuckled ironically. "I don't know if you've noticed but he ain't exactly normal in the head."

"Yep." Jake's voice was dry. "So what are you going to do with your share? That's a lot of money."

Ab shrugged. "I could use a few new wagons. I'm a freighter at heart. Reckon I'll invest it. How about yourself?"

Jake stifled a yawn. "I don't know. I'm a soldier, Ab. I've got certain responsibilities. I owe Jason Oord." He waved his irritation. "Oh, what the heck, I'm doing what I want to do. The West is this country's future, and I'm part of making it grow. Maybe I can help it grow with a few less problems than it's headed for."

"So, maybe Web Catton did all right by splitting us up. Maybe he knew what we would be and passed us out among the right kinds of people." He leaned down in his blanket and looked up at the evening sky.

"Maybe," Jake agreed.

When Ab looked over, Jake slept.

Abriel reached over to the lightest of the bundles. Absently his fingers undid the heavy lashings around the thick stained canvas.

It awed him. His father's fingers had tied those nice

neat knots. The musty canvas reluctantly came apart and he spread the contents by the fire: separately wrapped bundles.

The largest came to his fingers first and he carefully undid the bindings. As the cloth fell away, the firelight flickered and gleamed on precious stones. Abriel lifted a heavy crown free.

The metal was gold, no doubt of that. His breath caught in his throat. Ab frowned, trying to remember any telling of Armijo having a crown. Squinting at the pattern the jewels made in the metal, he sucked in his breath. Dancing in dazzling rays of reflected color was a large fleur-de-lis!

*So that's where old Catton had gotten his family trademark.*

Thoughtfully he rewrapped the crown and took up a square package, laying each of the folds of cloth apart, producing a wooden box full of letters. Some appeared very old, written in French and something else he guessed was Latin. He found a couple in English and started to unfold the most recent-looking. He stopped— eyes on where his brothers slept so soundly—and shook his head. It could wait.

Last came a small packet. Ab undid the laces, not in the least surprised when the ring fell out. Made of gold—jeweled like the crown—it proved to be a seal ring with an ornate inscription in Latin. He read: *"Louis Reg. In Nom. Domini."* Trying it on, it only fit his little finger.

Bragg's words stuck in his mind that the ring was his as the oldest. An inheritance? That French puzzle was getting worse. What did any of this stuff have to do with French Louisiana? Ab repacked it all and retied the canvas around the bundle like he'd found it. A quick check showed the bulky heavy bundles were filled with neat stacks of gold bars—each marked in Spanish words—

with numbers to indicate the weight. There, at least, he assumed lay Armijo's stolen gold. That much made sense, thank God.

So where had Web Catton stolen the crown, the letters and the ring? Body dead tired, leg aching and itching where the bullet wound had been abused through the tough days, his mind wouldn't let him rest.

Sighing in resignation, Ab pulled out his old battered and banged coffeepot and emptied a waterskin into it with some of the remaining coffee grounds. When it boiled, he poured a cup and wandered out into the darkness beyond the fire.

He stood on a point; the west wind blew its cool fingers over his hot skin. The basin shimmered in the moonlight and the far-off Absarokas made a dark line against the stars. Maybe Bragg thought the French would pay handsomely to get that crown back. It had to be some sort of national treasure.

So, had Web Catton been a pirate among the other nefarious occupations he'd embraced? Where else would he have come across a French Crown? Maybe he stole it during the Napoleonic Wars? He would have been a young man then. Perplexed, Ab sipped his coffee. Just who had his father been before he came to Saint Louis? Freebooter? Pirate? Mercenary? Rogue?

By the time Ab was born in 1826, Web had been in Saint Louis long enough to have killed Laura's father and married her. Napoleon was whipped at Waterloo clear back in 1815. Web Catton, a French soldier? Just how old had he been when Bragg caught up to him?

No closer to an answer, Ab returned to camp and kicked Jeremiel awake before finding his blanket.

The basin below lay in still shadow as they loaded the packs onto the horses. Briefly, Ab recited his discoveries and speculations from the night before. "Any ideas?"

Arabella started forward, eyes on where Leander O. B. Sentor rolled his bedroll.

Bram whooped as he climbed into his mare's saddle. "My paw, a pirate! Just think twarn't old One-Eyed Mike what made me a hoss thief! It come nachural in my blood!"

"Sin is born in any man's blood, wretch!" Jeremiel thundered. " 'Thy first father hath sinned, and thy teachers have transgressed against me,' so spoke the Lord God of Jacob! Beware, sinner, for thy soul will roast in perdition!"

Bram closed his eyes and scrunched up his face. "Liked him better when he was a little worried 'bout Wasatch an' his wolf. Ever since he wrassled Satan an' his serpent, life's bin gittin' harder for us easygoing hoss thieves!"

"We'd better be making tracks," Jake called from the precipice. "Bragg's boys are starting up the trail."

"It's a hard day's ride just to get this high," Ab reminded.

"Bram, you take the lead, let's keep these tracks in the high and far between." Jake vaulted into the saddle.

"Wait!" Arabella called, brooking no interruption this time. She shot a quick look over her shoulder to where Leander lashed his possessions to his horse. "Quiet!" she hissed, searching their eyes. "We're not out of this yet!"

"Huh?" Bram wondered. "I don't—"

*"Trust me!"* Her eyes flashed with the gravity of it. "Will you do that? At least until we know Bragg can't catch up? Not a word about France! Not a word about crowns, or rings. Understand? The only thing in those packs is Armijo's gold! *Promise!*"

She saw Sentor lead his horse closer, a dull look in his eyes, as if his thoughts preoccupied him.

Ab looked around, seeing the reservation. "You got it.

Keep mum, boys. We don't know what we're into here."
Ab gave Arabella a wink, seeing her flush of relief.

They found a Sheepeater camp the next day—empty
of any soul—and left half of what remained of their
flour, tobacco, and beads. No one said anything when
Bram left Uncle Branton's walnut-handled bowie knife
there on the ground. Seems he'd taken a liking to it
when he was winging the rifles over the edge that night.

Once again, Wolf saved them. Wasatch had been
weaving a winding track through the trees, taking rough
routes where they rode on rock—leaving no easy-to-
follow trail—drifting through herds of buffalo and using
every trick he knew coupled with Bram's suggestions.

Wolf came loping up just as they were about to break
from the trees and head down a ridge that would finally
take them out into the Powder River Basin to the east.
From there, it would be a couple of days' hard travel
across the flats, turning south at the Gourd Buttes—
sometimes called the Pumpkin Buttes. There, Wasatch
expected to follow the track right on south to the Platte
and then down to Fort Laramie.

Only problem was Wolf stopped them cold, snarling
and driving Bram's horse back into the timber.

"What's with this critter, Wasatch?" Bram demanded,
struggling to keep his roan under control. "He got
hydraphobee or something?"

Wasatch quickly dismounted and ran to Wolf, who
muttered, whined, and nuzzled at his hands. "No, Bragg
comes."

So they dismounted, snuffled up the horses, and
waited. Bragg following behind High Walker, his men
strung out behind, rode into the big wide meadow.

"That boy don't never larn!" Bram hissed incredu-
lously.

"I know of another trail." Wasatch frowned, running

his tongue over his lower lip. "High Walker, too, may know of it, otherwise we must go south along the mountains and around the Peak of Clouds."

As Ab led Sorrel back, he noted Arabella, her eye on Leander, one hand on her rifle, no trust in her eyes. What had happened between them during those long days she'd been in his company?

Ab chewed on that as they backtracked. She didn't seem to hate him, just distrust him.

Bram had been riding behind, keeping an eye on the backtrail, but he was unusually silent that night while they made camp. He drew Ab off to one side.

"Ab." He looked nervously at the scuffed pine needles between his boots. "I saw him this afternoon. The Hoodoo man." It sounded like he was confessing to murder.

"No place he could of skipped off to?" Ab asked.

"Nope."

"Well, let's not mention it to the rest. They're jumpy enough." Ab patted his shoulder and went back to camp.

The next morning, filing down another one of those elk trails, Molly was having second thoughts, as if memories of the trail down the Red Wall were building in her cunning mule brain.

Below, the Powder River Basin stretched gray, green, red, and brown in successive layers. Far out against the horizon, a grass fire sent a column of smoke high into the blue sky while clouds were building over the Big Horns.

"You sure there ain't no surprises on this trail like there was on the Red Wall?" Bram asked suddenly, his mind evidently working like Molly's. Ab couldn't decide if that was a complimentary thought or not.

"There is only one real bad place—and we're almost there," Wasatch called back cheerfully.

"Me," Ab grunted sourly, "I've had my fill of elk trails,

black timber, deadfalls, scraped-up packs, mending harness and rigging at the fire at night, and generally putting up with slick footing and trails that disappeared into tangles of blowdown."

"Forest is great for hunting on foot but it's a regular pain to put a pack animal through," Jake agreed, stretching, wiping sweat from his brow.

They broke out on the side of a huge rock wall that towered high above. What looked to be a mountain sheep trail ran across the top of the talus just under the wall.

"You gotta be kidding!" Jeremiel muttered. "The angels of the Lord would hesitate to tread here with their winged feet!"

Wasatch looked a little glum. "I remembered it to be in better shape than this."

"Well, we can always go back up," Ab grumbled. That's when he looked back around the edge of the ridge they'd just crossed. Branton Bragg, High Walker, and three of his men including Cal Backman had just cleared the trees above them.

# Chapter 24

*G*o!" Ab hissed, waving, looking back to where High Walker trotted on foot ahead of the horsemen. "We either make it, or fort up and shoot it out."

"They don't got guns!" Bram cried, looking irritated.

A bullet clipped a branch over his head. Bram yipped and pushed his roan through the trees hot on Lark's wake.

"Guess you wasn't as efficient as you thought, Bram," Jake couldn't resist calling out.

Wasatch dropped from the saddle and led his Appaloosa out along the crumbly trail. Ab unlimbered his Hawken and stepped off Sorrel on the off side. Not that it took much, that stirrup was dragging dirt anyway. He kicked the animal on down the path—knowing he'd follow the rest—and took up a position in the rocks.

Arabella saw her chance, ducking off Efende, one eye on Sentor where he took a pack animal's lead from

Lark, talking softly to soothe the animals. Shoot him? They'd be safer. Unwilling, she turned and hurried into the trees, her Benjamin Bigelow in hand.

She made the other side of the thick stand of fir in time to see Ab shoot. As the smoke cleared, he was limping along after the others. A bullet cracked a rock beside him and he hopped along a little faster.

In a group of boulders, Arabella settled down to wait. Bragg's horse was bucking and kicking, evidently from Ab's shot. The others had gone to ground. When a man popped up, sprinting for cover, Arabella shot, kicking up dirt just in front of him. Arabella turned the cylinder, taking aim where the man dropped.

"Who the hell . . . *Arabella*! Get outta there!" Ab roared, an underlying tension in his voice.

She ignored him. Way up there, Branton Bragg scuttled along, headed for the wall of rock. Backman circled around below, trying to flank the position she'd taken. She took a shot, forcing Backman to dive for cover. And as his head came up—expecting the interval to reload a muzzle gun—Arabella shot again. Dust spatted from the rock before him. He dove again—and didn't come up.

Then she turned her attention on Bragg, two shots pinning him in place.

*"Arabella!"* Ab bellowed.

Over her shoulder, she could see Jake pushing Molly past the slide. Two shots left. Jumping to her feet, she ran, seeing Ab shoot and reload. A bullet made a *thooosh* past her ear.

She scrambled across the loose slippery stuff and into the trees as a bullet cut a branch over her head.

She looked at apoplectic Ab, and grinned. "Guess he forgot he was shooting downhill. Didn't hold low enough. Otherwise, he'd a got me."

"Just what the hell do you . . ." Ab ducked as a bullet slapped a tree trunk beside him.

"Saving our lives," she returned coolly, indicating the rifle. "The caliber is small, but I pinned them down with it."

Ab grumbled under his breath, lifting his Hawken, sighting and firing, before beginning the reloading chore.

"This way!" Jake called.

"Hurry!" Arabella waved Ab back, lifting her rifle to snap a shot at a running man. He flopped on the slope, belly down in low brush. Taking Ab's hand, they fled, she bearing as much of his weight as she could to save his leg.

What they saw as they cleared the trees reeked of a nightmare. The thin strip of trees they'd passed grew up between two walls of rock, reaching only as high as the cliff twenty yards above. The trees came to an abrupt end just below in a drop of sixty to seventy feet. Ahead, a ledge crossed a hundred feet of cliff face. Out on that narrow ledge, Wasatch sang one of his medicine songs while he led Molly across that thread of trail.

"That's the tough part," Jake said grimly.

Ab nodded, biting his lip. If one of the horses spooked, he'd take Wasatch with him to his death on the rocks below.

Arabella's breath caught in her throat as Molly jerked her head and pranced with her back feet.

Another bullet snapped through the trees and they ducked. "Jake, help me cover the backside," Ab ordered, heading back through the trees.

Arabella dropped to a crouch, breaking her rifle down to free the cylinder. As rifle fire cracked behind her, she poured powder, seated the balls and pressed them home, almost fumbling in the rush. With shaking fingers, she pinched caps on the nipples, reassembling the complicated gun.

How long? A minute and a half? She took a quick look, seeing Lark and Sentor starting across with the pack animals. Heart beating, she crept back through the trees.

Jake's Mississippi rifle barked as Ab reloaded. And there they stayed, anxiety building at the thought of Wasatch back there singing those horses across that little rocky ledge. She settled herself and shot at Bragg where he tried to flank them. The shot drove him back into the cover of some big rocks.

*What happened to Backman?*

"I'm gonna tan her butt!" Ab shouted to Jake as he heard her shot.

"I suggest you keep your thoughts directed at our survival, brother," she retorted, lifting the rifle as High Walker limped from one tree to another. Too late. She bit her lip, waiting.

A bullet spat dirt and needles. "Looks like they're getting the range," Ab growled.

"Jake? Abriel?" Jeremiel called. "The horses are across, Bram is feeling his way over now. Come on!"

"Feeling?" Ab asked. "Go on, Arabella! Jake and I'll take the rear guard."

She hesitated, drove a bullet into High Walker's tree, and turned, running for all she was worth, scrambling out over the height. She swallowed, forced her heart back into her breast where it belonged, and closed her eyes, feeling her way, thankful she'd taken Lark's other dress. Long skirts on *that* trail would have been a death sentence.

The last thing she cogently remembered outside of fear was the anguished look in Sentor's eyes. Well, maybe he really did care?

\* \* \*

Ab took one last shot at Bragg's hole and wondered where in the name of hob Cal Backman had gotten to. Reloading, he trotted out and saw what "feeling" meant. Jake shuffled along halfway across, back to the wall, eyes closed as he sidestepped, fingers feeling along the narrow ledge.

On the other side, Arabella stepped off the trail, trembling, Sentor catching her in his arms.

Jeremiel appeared by his side. "Go first, I've been across once already. If you get nervous on heights, it's best to keep your eyes closed."

Ab moved out on that sheer face of rock and began working his way across as fast as he could. The way the rock bulged out over his head, it seemed perched, ready to fall. He looked down and would have toppled had Jeremiel not put a restraining hand on his shoulder.

"How do I get into these messes?" Ab groaned. "How did Wasatch get them horses across this?"

"Faith, brother Abriel." Jeremiel's voice sounded strained.

Ab looked up again to see that big chunk of rock hanging there by what seemed to be a thread. The whole thing pointed down like some sort of big needle, dangling over the trail. He gasped relief as he passed under it.

"Ab Catton!" the voice cried out, and he looked over at the trees.

Cal Backman stepped out from the bottom of the fir stand.

"Oh, this is good, Catton!" He slapped his knee. "First I'll kill your brother, then I'll kill you!"

Ab tried to bring the Hawken up and almost fell off the ledge. Impossible! He couldn't hold that much iron over the edge without overbalancing. He tried to turn but Jeremiel's hand clamped on his arm, restraining.

Backman's rifle came up.

*I can't do a damn thing!* Panic tightened on Ab's heart.

The Walker Colt's report almost did for Abriel what Backman's rifle was supposed to. The smoke rose from around Jeremiel's belt. Ab looked over to see the snout of the big Colt poking past his side. It thundered again as he watched. Ab twisted his neck to see Cal's rifle drop, a funny look on his face as he took a flying dive for the trees, dirt spattering around him.

"Go, brother Ab," Jeremiel whispered wearily, "I'm sorry I missed. It's the angle I had to hold from, and it's so far."

Ab didn't wait to see if Cal would try again. Instead, he closed his eyes and continued feeling his way along fast as he could.

"I'll get you yet, Catton!" Cal shouted from the safety of the trees.

Jake grabbed him and pulled him around a corner in the rocks. Wasatch was lining the horses out on a nice, beaten-down, *flat* trail.

"What about Bragg?" Ab asked. "Soon as we're out of sight, he'll come around the same way we did!"

"You want to sit here and wait for him?" Jake asked, raising an eyebrow. "On the other hand, it will be a little scary crossing that trail. Would you want to be first?"

He had a point there. They didn't make fifty feet before a holler rolled out. Bragg stood at the band of trees.

"Catton!" he called.

"What do you want, Bragg?" Jake thundered back.

"You can't get away from me! Leave the ring and you can go in peace!"

"I ought to pick up my rifle and shoot his butt full of

holes once and for all." Jake screwed up his face, resisting temptation.

"Why?" Ab shouted, cupping his lips. "You tell me why that cotton-pickin' ring is so important!"

Bragg hesitated, irritation in his posture. His other men were lining out behind him.

"The ring is the seal of France!" he shouted.

"What the . . ."

"Look!" Wasatch thrust his finger up over his head.

Ab followed it to the figure who clambered over the rocks. Even over the distance, he could make out the buckskin clothes, the beaded white hunting shirt, and the long gray hair that blew in the breeze.

"There's your ghost," he whispered to Jake. "We're all seeing him now."

Bragg craned his neck to see, looking up and finally making out the figure of a man who leapt from rock to rock like a mountain goat.

Branton's head shook in disbelief. *"He's dead!"* The words carried in the suddenly still air. "I tell you, *I killed him!"*

Bram's voice seemed to thunder but he spoke softly. "Hoodoo!" At the word, Bragg staggered.

The bullet almost parted Ab's hair, to be followed a split-second later by a shot. They scrambled for cover.

"Cal!" Bragg roared. "Put that rifle down! *Now!"*

Backman lowered his gun, face red with anger as Ab stood up again. Glancing for the Hoodoo man—seeing nothing to indicate a man had stood on the point.

"Look out!" Ab bellowed, waving Bragg back. An angular gray boulder tottered from the point, falling out, cracking hollowly against the rock wall. Smaller rocks cascaded with it and a second large rock tumbled loose.

That dagger of faulted rock that had scared everyone so quivered as it was buffeted by the debris from above.

Like something alive it shivered, creeping down the cliff face, picking up speed to thunder into that little ledge where Cal Backman would have killed him. The ledge sheered away and the ground shook as rock roared and boomed into the depths below.

Through the dust Ab could see Branton Bragg and his boys running like goats back the way they came, the firs shaking and bending.

Ab looked back up the cliff, empty now, as if no one had ever started that rock fall. Bram's voice sounded hollow, almost a whisper. "Betcha ifn we was to be up thar, he'da disappeared again and thar wouldn't even be a single track!"

Surreptitiously, Arabella settled herself in the rear of the camp circle. Her fingers wove around the grip of her Liege pistol, loosening it in the holster.

Ab read the letter out loud:

Dear children:
This box contains all the papers that came with me from France. I don't think there will be any more because the men who knew about it are all dead now. What you see before you are the final documents of my father's reign. You see, they smuggled me out of prison as a very small boy. I went out in a maid's basket of clothes. I was the heir to the throne and, of course, they couldn't have that. Now, looking back at who and what I have become—I can see why. Reckon I'd have made a poor king, maybe as poor a ruler as my father and mother before me. The crown was my father's, of course, and the Sun King's before that and so forth all the way back to Saint Louis IX.

There are some—even today—who would call you back to France if they could. There are others who would stop at nothing to make sure the line stops here. Don't trust a soul with such knowledge. It's your secret—keep it that way. Oh, I suppose you can tell your boys about it one of these days, but that's up to you. It's a new country and a new life here.

I assume that Abriel made it this far. He's the oldest and so the crown and ring go to him for safekeeping. After that, it will be placed in the care of his eldest and so forth; unless he has no children to take it, in which case it is passed to Jeremiel's oldest and so forth.

The other gold here is all that I stole from Governor Armijo. That greasy Spaniard had the nerve to sentence me to hard labor in a Mexican prison. They almost killed me down there so I got even when Kearny rode through in '46. It would make quite a story to tell you how I got the gold out and up to the Trap there in the Big Horns.

I guess there's not much more to add. The blood of kings runs in your veins—be worthy of it. The idea that the "Lost Dauphine" is a fur hunter, soldier of fortune, mercenary, and whatnot has always brought me a little humor in times of stress. I suppose it will serve you the same. I wonder how Napoleon would have reacted to know White Wolf was raising France's youngest. Think on that, my heirs! I reckon that's it for old Web Catton. You're adults now, France is a dream. If you've made it this far, I'm already proud of you and I did the best I could.

Weberly Catton
King of the Rockies

The only sound came from the crackling fire and Wolf scratching after his fleas. Ab cocked his head and picked up the seal ring and crown.

"I'll be jiggered!" Bram mumbled. "King Abriel! Put that crown on."

He did. It barely fit. Ab looked uncomfortable and took it off.

Jake said softly, "The man that was first fashioned for is considered to be a saint. Our native city is named for him."

Ab held the ring up to the firelight. "Ring feels funny on my finger too, like the ghosts of too many men are hanging on it." He placed the ring and the crown on the stained worn cloth that had nurtured them and looked around.

Jake picked up the crown and studied it carefully. "Louis the XVI and his queen, Marie Antoinette, were beheaded on the guillotine before the masses of the revolution."

"I don't know." Ab shook his head obstinately back and forth. "How much of this can we believe?"

Jeremiel was going through the papers in the box. "Would he have also stolen these?" he asked, holding one of the fine parchments up to the light. "Papers are not the sort of thing a brigand would take."

Wasatch leaned back, arms crossed, eyes half-closed. "You assume your father would lie to you. A lie must have a reason behind it. The man I knew as Web Catton had no reason to lie about such a thing as his past. Who is Napoleon? Did he know White Wolf? Would he be surprised to know he was my father too?"

Jake laughed. "It's a little involved. I'll tell you later."

"Thunderation!" Bram whistled, awed. "Reckon I'm the highest and mightiest hoss thief they is! Who'da thought them boys in Council Grove was gonna stretch a *royal* neck?"

Jeremiel's voice held that note of authority. "Brethren, before us lies not only a problem of veracity but a problem of perception. As the letter stated, there are those who would use what Web Catton believed against us should the story get out."

"Quite so," Leander agreed, Jake's pistol in one hand, his rifle balanced in the other. "Gentlemen, if you'll step back where I can keep an eye on you."

"Tarnation," Bram whispered. "Fergot he's a damn spy!"

Arabella's voice remained firm as she settled her Liege pistol on Leander. "No, Leander," she said calmly. "You may shoot me, if you wish. The choice is yours. But you will not leave here with our inheritance."

Sentor swallowed, a thin film of sweat forming on his lip. "I'm sorry, Arabella. France . . . my general . . . needs this crown, this ring. With them, we can build a whole new orderly society." He turned, eyes on Abriel. "If you'll come, we could use you. The backing of the lawful king of France would—"

As if from the very dark, Branton Bragg's thick arm reached around Arabella, neatly plucking the pistol from her fingers. He threw her effortlessly across the fire into a heap. Even Wolf jumped, startled.

"Not so fast, Sentor," Bragg growled, a lump still on his jaw where Ab's rifle had hit him. "We had us a deal." He looked at Abriel. "Oh, it's all quite true, Catton. I had old Web's letter checked. This here's the legacy of France. My ticket home at long last. I'm gonna be a noble, *you hear*?" Bragg laughed, a weird reedy sound. "Me, a noble—and on Catton blood!"

"No," Leander added thoughtfully. "We will leave them alive, Bragg. Heads in salt are meaningless. The crown, the ring, the documents, they are the heart of the matter."

Bragg spun on his heels. "Huh-uh! That ain't the deal.

What if they show up someday? Claim they're heir to the throne?"

"Who'd believe them?" Leander cried. "A bunch of rowdy American frontiersmen? With what proof? The proof—*the only proof*—lies here before us!"

Bragg's eyes slitted. "You got no choice. Cavaignac said he wanted the ring, and the heads." Bragg turned, lifting the Liege pistol. "Who first? Ab? You're the oldest." The pistol lined on Abriel's head.

Bragg's eyes shifted to Leander, frosting blue. "No," he whispered. "Arabella first." The white streak in his beard twisted and the color drained from Leander's face. " 'Cause she tempted you," Bragg decided. "Took you from your duty."

"No," Sentor told him, a quiver in his lips as he shook his head.

"Don't move, Jake! Ab! First one moves a finger, and I shoot her. That's it. Easy, boys." Bragg laughed, his thumb pulling the hammer back. Arabella's jaw quivered as she watched, horrified, as the pistol bore centered on her chest.

Leander closed his eyes, swallowing hard. "Very well, Bragg. We'll take the heads back. First, however, you'll want payment. My saddlebags are behind you there." He smiled weakly, looking at Arabella. "I'm sorry. I know you tried to help all those days when we talked about Paris, and duty, and honor. I truly needed someone to talk to. The ghosts will rest easier."

Bragg laughed wickedly. "You're a good man, Leander. I'll tell the general how much your honor means to France." He bent over, picking up Leander's packs.

"I do hope you will," Sentor added seriously. As Bragg straightened and pulled the saddlebag open, Leander shifted. The first shot from his rifle caught Bragg full in the chest.

Branton dropped the saddlebag, trying to pull the Liege pistol up as Leander deftly emptied all five rounds from Jake's pistol into Bragg's chest.

In dead silence, they waited. Bragg froze in his tracks, body stiff, face contorted as he slowly rose on his toes.

Leander carefully stepped out of the way as the big man fell, thumping heavily into the dirt, a wheezing gasp gurgling from his blood-choked lungs.

Leander sank to his haunches beside the big man, handing the pistol back to Jake butt-first. Muscles jumping in his cheek, Leander stood, blinking, to give Arabella a weak smile.

" 'One among thy brethren shalt thou set king over thee: thou mayest not set a stranger over thee, which is not thy brother,' " Jeremiel mused. "Thunderation! I'm spawned of a line of Papists!"

Bram's voice was reserved. "We ain't sure Catton's dead. Who was that up on the rocks? For a Hoodoo, he sure let loose a landslide!"

Ab's stomach churned. "Oh? Did you see him push that rock over?"

Bram opened his mouth and shut it, perplexed.

Jake refolded the letters and placed them in the wooden box. "One way or another, it doesn't make much difference to us. If it's really Web Catton, and he wants to disappear, I say let him. Respect his reasons for whatever they may be. As far as France and crowns are concerned, he had a chance to go back many years ago. I'm not interested for myself. Anyone want to go and make a claim for the French throne?"

Leander looked around the circle, a question in his arched eyebrow.

Heads shook around the fire with the exception of Wasatch and Wolf, who just stared back blankly.

"Then it's settled," Jake said slowly. "I would suggest,

however, that we hide these things again." He motioned at the crown and ring.

"Could be a little difficult to think up a good story about how we got them," Ab agreed dryly.

So the crown of France and the royal seal were left in the protection of the earth again—this time, under the rimrock of the Gourd Buttes.

Leander shrugged. "I don't want to know. I'll wait out of sight."

Arabella tilted her head. "Want company?" She looked up at the slope. "I'm not sure I'm up to the climb."

He smiled. "Yes," he added gently. "I—I'd like that."

Jake came back from scouting the distant riders, face sour. "Would it surprise you to hear that we're being followed by that bloodhound Injun, High Walker?"

Ab asked, "Don't he ever give up?"

"Looking for God's wrath!" Jeremiel laughed—his fingers rested lightly on the butt of his pistol.

"Come on!" Ab turned Sorrel around and started trotting back down the trail.

Backman and High Walker were out in the flats, coming up on a slight rise. They had no warning until the Cattons broke over the ridgetop and rode down on them. Ab raised a hand and Backman motioned for his riders to stop.

They faced each other. "Looks like your little army keeps shrinking," Jake greeted.

Backman's eyes glared hot and black. "You ain't won yet, Abriel."

"Oh, yes I have, Cal. I don't have the ring anymore. Bragg's dead."

"I'll get even someday." Cal spit into the saltbush. "Not only that, but you got a lot packs back there. I seen

Bragg's map, Ab. You give me half of Armijo's gold, and we call it even, huh?"

"Let's get it over, right here and now, Cal," Ab said, voice deadly calm. He could see Wasatch and High Walker eyeing each other. High Walker's eyes kept shifting uneasily to Wolf.

"Someone else will have to kill High Walker," Wasatch spoke suddenly. "He is of the People. I will not spill their blood."

"Then the sinner shall feel the wrath of the Lord thy God!" Jeremiel laughed wickedly. The big Colt appeared magically in his hand, centered on High Walker's chest.

"Nope," Bram added in a husky voice. "Shooting starts, and I'm blowing High Walker apart."

Arabella leveled her Benjamin Bigelow. "I have seven shots, Mr. Backman—And then there's the shotgun. I hear you wanted to ravish me. Although I'm a lady, sir, I'm predisposed to placing every shot into your body."

Backman's men were easing their horses back, leaving him out alone in front of the rest of them.

"Looks like it's falling apart, Cal." Ab managed easily, his Hawken shifting to cover the men. "Don't you think enough of your boys have died? Branton's dead. Leander, here, is with us now. We cut you up pretty bad when you had us outnumbered. Now, do you want to push this, or leave us alone?"

"You talked of honor once," Leander added quietly, studying Cal, his rifle easy in his hands. "I have found a man must determine his own honor. You set on Abriel— tried to murder him in his bed. I consider that without honor. The debt you feel you owe your friend Jeff, how- ever, is something else. Then do you swear on that honor to leave us alone? I'd say it breaks out evenly in the end."

Cal opened his mouth to speak, then bit it off. "Ride

off, damn you! Leave! You're free this time, but I'll find you all again. Another time and I'll make it all even." He'd raised his fist.

"All right." Ab backed Sorrel carefully, making sure his rifle kept them covered.

High Walker kept shifting his hate-filled eyes from Bram to Wasatch to Lark, but those boys backing Cal Backman would have been just as happy if they'd been carried magically to Santa Fe.

"Tell Web Catton I'll kill him!" Backman shouted after them. "I know that was him up on the rocks. I'll get him too!"

Ab looked around as he topped the ridge.

"Hoodoo," Bram muttered, head shaking.

"Any guesses as to what Cal'll do now?" Jake asked.

"Yea, the sinner knows not the transgression of his ways." Jeremiel had a lean look in his eyes, fingertips still dancing over that Colt. "He'll come after us again until we shall be forced to dispatch his black soul to the pit." He winked at Bram. "Or else I'll have to preach him to death!"

They put a lot of miles under the pounding hooves, headed southeast toward the Platte. Jake led them across the Dry Fork of the Cheyenne River, his thoughts on making camp.

The Pawnee came out of the ground like magic.

Hard hands reached for Sorrel's halter.

"Don't shoot!" Jake called. "I'll handle this."

Ab had his pistol out, looking down the barrel into implacable black eyes. He looked up and smiled at Ab—again!

Jake's voice rang out and Two Coups rode up, grinning happily. Ab and the brave faced each other while Jake and Two Coups gestured back and forth, hands waving, and Wasatch offered the last of his tobacco for the smoke.

Then, suddenly as it began, Two Coups shouted something and the brave let go of Sorrel's bridle. The Pawnee backed up a step or two and talked among themselves. Two Coups gestured and—in a cloud of dust—they galloped off down the backtrail.

"Now, what was all that?" Bram demanded, color coming slowly back into his face as he reached over to hold Lark's hand.

Jake started grinning. "Oh, nothing much. I just told them there was a party behind us that wasn't so tough. I told them they were bad men, that a renegade Cheyenne was with them and he had long black hair."

Jeremiel shook his head. "Could be a sin, brother. Sending the heathen to do the Lord's work."

Ab's heart was still settling into his chest after the scare of facing that brave. He heaved a sigh, and couldn't help but notice how Jake was grinning.

"Relax, preacher, these are Pawnee, they ain't at war with the whites." At that Jake slapped his horse into a trot and headed out across the rolling land, bound for the Platte.

"Riders!" Bram called the next afternoon.

They pulled up to see the Pawnee coming at a jog trot. Everyone could see High Walker's scalp dangling from Two Coup's coup stick. Ab noticed Backman's horse and a couple others that belonged to that party. The Pawnee arrived grinning as they rode up to within a couple hundred yards and began dogging the trail.

Jake had a sour look on his face. Bram's grin spread. Wasatch threw an unconcerned look over his shoulder.

"Well," Jeremiel sighed, "it would appear we're going to have to see just how good our horses are again."

"You got that right," Jake groaned.

Leander laughed, seeing the consternation on Arabella's face.

"Well, foller me!" Bram called.

"Quite a wedding," Leander decided, watching Bram and Lark walking away, arm in arm.

Arabella laughed. "Did you see Bram grin when Jeremiel got to the sinning part?"

"I wonder how he and Lark will make out?"

She shrugged. "Bram's been bitten by the frontier. He wasn't meant for white laws anyway."

They walked out from under the cottonwoods. She looked up. "How about yourself? What are you going to do now?"

Sentor bit his lip, chuckling softly. "You know, I can never thank you. I meant it the night I killed Bragg. All those long talks we had up there on that mountain, well, they put things in perspective. I suppose it turned into a confession of sorts. My soul is clean." *Almost. You will never know I killed James. That guilt I must bear in silence—forever. My last service to my general and to France.*

He kicked at a stick, hearing the bellowing voice of Mr. Skye—the local Fort Laramie guide—roaring drunk in the background while his Crow wife berated him. "I still apologize for kissing you that night." He looked at her from the corner of his eye. "Tell me, you had that curvy knife against my side. Why didn't you use it?"

She dropped her head, tawny curls falling about her face. A slim shoulder lifted. "I'd ... well, never been kissed before. If you'd tried to go further ..." She lifted the shoulder again.

"Anyway, to get back to what I was telling you, I'm staying here." He turned, looking down into her eyes. "It's the country, you see. I have sought freedom all my life. That ideal got twisted under Cavaignac. I loved my parents. They taught me to revere the concept of being free." He waved beyond the limits of Fort Laramie. "The land here calls me. The people call me. Something creeps out of the very soil to stir my passions. I . . . Well, I'm home."

She nodded up at him. "I'm glad, Leander." Then she sighed. "I fear I am, too."

"Tell me." He paused uncertainly. "What would an ex-spy have to do to kiss a woman like you again?"

She narrowed an amber eye, an impish grin coming to her lips. "Oh, I don't know. Do you think you're clever enough to find out?"

Leander spread his hands. "Time will tell."


"Quite a journey." Jake smiled wistfully, looking across the amber liquor in his glass.

Jason Oord nodded, his stiff mustache ends twitching. "Odd for Two Coups to be so far to the west. The Sioux chased him quite a ways." The cold eyes warmed. "I'm proud of you, Jake. I did the best I could for you."

He nodded, a tightness in his chest. "I know. Between you and me, I couldn't have had a better father."

The old man smiled. "Thank you. But tell me. Just how did you lose Two Coups the second time?"

Jake sipped his cognac and chuckled. "Well, would you believe Bram and Wasatch sneaked out of camp one night and—along with that wolf—stole all their horses?"

Oord cocked his head. "Stole the horses?"

Jake waved it away. "Well, it wasn't like we were at war."


The night sounds of Saint Louis lay muffled in the thick mantle of fog. Water dripped sporadically from the eaves, plopping onto damp wood.

Ab tossed, dreaming of the crown, and the ring, and the letters. Web Catton ghosted through his mind—an elusive phantom, ever watching. In his dreams, the power of the crown sent tendrils of longing over the miles to draw upon his soul and bend it around the haunting echoes of voices calling to their king.

He woke up to stare into the darkness, the images ripe in his mind. Ab filled his lungs with longing breath.

"France," he whispered into the damp night.